ZIA SUMMER

Also by Rudolfo Anaya

BLESS ME, ULTIMA
BENDÍCIME, ÚLTIMA
ALBURQUERQUE
THE ANAYA READER

ZIA SUMMER

RUDOLFO ANAYA

WARNER BOOKS

A Time Warner Company

Warner Books, Inc., 1271 Avenue of the Americas, New York, NY 10020

Ⓦ A Time Warner Company

Printed in the United States of America
First Printing: June 1995
10 9 8 7 6 5 4 3 2 1

Library of Congress Cataloging-in-Publication Data

Anaya, Rudolfo A.
    Zia summer / Rudolfo Anaya.
       p.   cm.
    ISBN 0-446-51843-3
    I. Title.
PS3551.N27Z35   1995
813'.54—dc20

94-44282
CIP

Book design by Giorgetta Bell McRee

Dedicated to the old people who walk on the Path of the Sun and who remind us that clarity of the soul is possible, even in these violent times. I also thank my mother, Ana Rosinski, Rachel Lawless, Patricia my love, and the spirit of Ultima, women who have encouraged me along the path of illumination that comes with Lords and Ladies of the Morning Light.

ZIA SUMMER

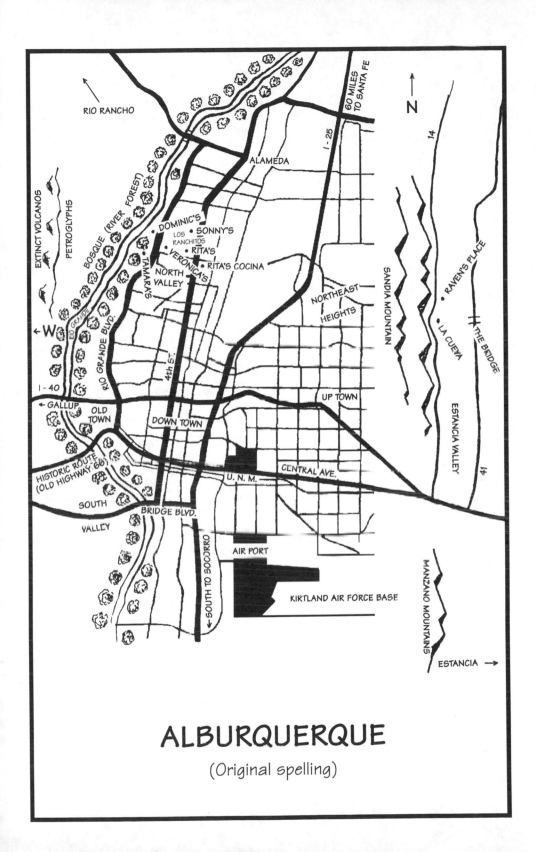

ALBURQUERQUE

(Original spelling)

1

Sonny awakened to the sound of a chain saw and felt it slicing through his leg. He kicked out wildly as the searing chain ripped through flesh and bone. A cry of pain tore from his throat, and as he jumped back to escape his tormentor, the nightmare faded.

"Chin-gaaa-o," he groaned, reaching down to massage his numb leg.

Outside, the buzz of a chain saw tore through the morning silence. He sat up, remembering that don Eliseo had been talking all spring about cutting down the big cottonwood that grew in his front yard.

Sonny shook the cobwebs of sleep and rubbed his leg. It was okay, just a bad dream, but who was the woman? Lord, she was good-looking. A dark gown hugged her curves, revealing long legs, lots of cleavage, lips glowing ripe as cactus fruit, green eyes like hot jade, a seductive, alluring voice. But as he reached out, she raised a chain saw and whacked at him. Sonny had felt the slash and blood oozing from his leg.

It was his left leg, the foot he had broken while bulldogging two years ago. He looked down and expected to see blood, the scene in the nightmare had been so vivid.

Outside, the gas saw sputtered, then died. He had promised don Eliseo he would help cut down the old tree, but he had been too busy. Too lazy, he admonished himself, to help my neighbor. What's a vecino for?

The woman in the dream had meant to kill him; her lunge was forceful, aimed right between his legs. A spurned woman from his past? No, he wasn't that kind of guy. He always parted on good terms with women. And it had been years since he had rented the Texas chain-saw murder video. So why the hell a nightmare full of chain-saw gore and violence?

He didn't like it. A dream like that meant no good. His mother believed dreams predicted the future. There was the grim flash of death in the woman's eyes as she swung the saw at him.

"Too much party time," he mumbled as he looked out his window into the bright blue skies of a clear Río Grande morning. Soon the solstice would officially mark summer, but already the heat had been relentless. The clear light hung over the valley, scintillating on the cottonwood leaves.

"Marry me," Rita had whispered last night, "I'm tired of letting you have it for free. It's time you settled down."

"With you?"

"Yes. You're not getting any younger!" she reminded him.

"I'm only thirty," he laughed. "Too young to settle down."

They had gone to her place after dancing, and as they made love, she whispered, "Eres un cabrón, but I love you."

She was great in bed, but it was more than that, he had to admit. Her love was the most satisfying he had found since his divorce. It was more than just sex; he worried he might really be falling for her.

Was it Rita who appeared in the nightmare? No, of course not, it was another woman, someone threatening. Pues, getting married could be threatening, he thought. If he married Rita, he would have to give up the lady friends he had cultivated the past two years.

Sonny prized his freedom. It was the ability to call his own shots that had attracted him to take up with Manuel Lopez a few years ago and learn how to be a private investigator. Or perhaps it was the fact that Sonny's great-grandfather, El Bisabuelo, was Elfego Baca, the most famous lawman New Mexico ever produced. True, more people knew about Pat Garrett, the sheriff who killed Billy the Kid in old Fort Sumner on the night of July 14, 1881, but that was only because history wasn't fair.

Of the two sheriffs, Elfego Baca had been more interesting, more complex. Sonny felt a special kinship to his Bisabuelo.

Or, and this he didn't like to admit even to himself, perhaps he had become a private investigator because in his daydreams he saw himself as a hero. In his fantasies he was always doing something heroic, putting down the evildoer or rescuing women from perilous situations. His mind was always active, always creating stories, and he made himself the hero of each story.

Whatever the reasons, he endured the lousy take-home pay because that way he could be his own boss. He came and went as he pleased, took just enough cases to make a living, and had not given a thought to the future until Rita came along.

She wants me to marry her and help her run Rita's Cocina, he thought to himself. "I'm not a taco pusher! Sure, I like her cooking. . . ."

Rita's image appeared before him. "That's not all you like," she said. "You like to make love to me."

She was brown, a soft, sexy tan, like the earth of the valley after rain. Her long, jet-black hair fell in cascades over her round

3

shoulders. She put her hands on her hips and swung them slowly.

"Yes, but I like to make love to all the women," he answered with a gleam.

"You think you're a big stud. Mr. Macho Man"—she glared back—"but I'm going to tame you!"

"I'm not a horse!" he shouted.

"You're a coyote from the hills," she said as her image dissolved.

Sonny swung his legs free of the sheet. "Chingao," he repeated as he jumped up, stumbled to the window, and pulled up the blinds.

He sniffed the air. The calm, hot morning was heavy with the aroma of green leaves, alive with the twittering of sparrows outside the window, the darting flight of the swallows from the river. He smelled coffee brewing, tortillas cooking on a comal, beans boiling, and simmering green chile: the aromas of home and peace. Why, in the midst of tranquillity, a horrible dream?

Across the narrow dirt street don Eliseo was directing operations as his grandson, who had restarted the saw, pushed it into the tough, gray bark of the old alamo. The giant cottonwood was over ten feet in circumference; its dark, gnarled branches rose high into the sky. It had been witness to the last hundred years of history in the village of Los Ranchitos in the North Valley of Alburquerque. Its spreading branches had shaded don Eliseo's family for many generations.

But over the years this old valley cottonwood had succumbed to disease, and now it was June and there were still no leaves showing in its age-worn branches.

"Trees get cancer, just like people," don Eliseo said, "or their livers and hearts grow weak. Just like people." So he mixed well-cured cow manure and bonemeal in water from the acequia, and each day he poured some of the healing solution into the holes around the drip line of the giant tree.

Sometimes Sonny would see the old man with his ear pressed

against the tree, like a doctor listening to the heartbeat of a patient.

He stuck his head out the window and shouted, "Hey! Don't you know it's Sunday? A day of rest!"

Don Eliseo turned and waved. "Buenos días te de Dios, Sonny. It's not Sunday, it's Friday. Come and have some coffee."

Don Eliseo kept chairs and a small barbecue grill under the tree. He made coffee early in the morning, and in the summer he cooked breakfast and supper there.

"Be right over," Sonny called. "Soon as I shower."

The tough bark of the tree had kicked the chain off the bar of the saw, and don Eliseo's grandson was now taking the saw apart to fix it. No way was the young man going to make a dent in the tree, Sonny thought.

He groaned and stumbled toward his small kitchen, then paused in front of his hallway mirror. He smiled at his image and bared his teeth. He had a handsome set of teeth, even, made hard and white by the calcium-rich South Valley water. Good Mexican teeth, his mother said. He had been in his share of fights in South Valley bars after he graduated from high school, but he never lost a tooth, and his aquiline nose hadn't been broken. His eyes were dark chestnut in the light. Women liked his long eyelashes.

"You're tan all over," a gringa once exclaimed in surprise.

"What did you expect?" he answered.

The Nuevo Mexicanos had been in the Río Grande for centuries, so Indian blood flowed in their veins.

And lots of other genes, Sonny thought. Not only the history of Spain but the history of the Nile was his inheritance. In the summer when he tanned dark from swimming, some of his friends said he looked Arabic. Maybe he had a drop of Jewish blood, too, the legacy of the crypto Jews who came to New Mexico with the Oñate expedition centuries before. The Marranos, the Catholics called them. He probably also carried French-Canadian trapper blood, German merchant blood, Navajo,

Apache, you name it, the Río Grande was the center of a trading route. Here a grand mestizo mixture took place. The Nile of the desert Southwest. All bloods ran as one in the coyotes of Nuevo Mexico.

The gabachitas loved his color, the Chicanas didn't find it unusual. He touched the dimple on his square chin. His mother said he had the square, no-nonsense chin of the Bacas. She was a Jaramillo from La Joya, Diana Jaramillo, a proud woman.

"You are a handsome devil," he said, smiling at himself. He also got the dark, curly hair from his father's side of the family. His father, Apolonio Baca, Polito everybody called him, was from the Baca family of Socorro County, the grandson of Elfego Baca.

The Chicanos of New Mexico knew the stories of Elfego Baca's escapades, and the story most remembered was when he stood up to a bunch of abusive Texas cowboys in the little village of Middle San Francisco Plaza, or Frisco, in southwestern New Mexico in 1884.

That was Elfego's first gunfight, high up in the Tularosa Mountains. He put on a badge when nobody else would, and in a scene straight out of *High Noon,* he arrested Charlie McCarty. When Charlie's friends came to threaten Baca, he shot William Hurn and forced the wild gang of cowboys to back down.

El Bisabuelo had carried a .45-caliber single-action Colt, the same pistol that had been passed down to Sonny's father and which now belonged to Sonny. He had a license to carry the pistol, and since he'd started working as a private investigator, he kept it in an old leather holster in the glove compartment of his truck. Unlike el Bisabuelo, Sonny had never had the occasion to use it.

In the bathroom Sonny glanced into the mirror again. Women told him he was handsome. Six feet, trim and muscular, he kept himself in shape by running as often as he could on the dirt trails along the acequia. Once a week he did weights at the gym. But thirty was nagging at him. He pounded his stomach, still flat, but he knew when he ate too much junk food, it grew round and soft. Also when he partied too much or drank too much beer.

"Got to watch the beer," he thought as he headed for the shower. Maybe it was time to settle down.

He showered and shaved, then slipped into an old black T-shirt, a pair of jeans, and a comfortable pair of work boots. Three years ago he had taken up rodeoing on weekends to kill time while the divorce was settled. The boots were a prize he won for steer wrestling. That was the sport that challenged him. He relished the excitement of slipping off the horse, grabbing the horns of the steer, and wrestling it to the ground. He liked to test his strength and agility.

One Sunday afternoon on the Bernalillo County sheriff's rodeo grounds, an ornery steer with a twisted horn had broken Sonny's hold, then turned and gored him. The horn ripped into Sonny's left ankle, broke bones and severed tendons. It had taken almost a year for the wound to heal. Sonny still limped slightly, and even now when he pulled on his boots, he favored the foot.

When a storm system came over the valley, or on cold winter days, he felt the pain hidden deep in the bones of his left foot, a weather thermometer he tried not to notice. Aching bones were for old people, he scoffed, but there it was, reminding him he could not run as fast as he could when he was scoring touchdowns at Rio Grande High.

"But I can still dance up a storm," he said to himself.

And he loved women, which is why his marriage to Angela never worked. He blamed himself for the divorce. He knew he had turned to Angie after his first true love left him. He had sought to repeat the lost passion in Angie and discovered not all women are alike.

He had partied a lot after he broke up with Angie. From the South Valley bars where he drank with his old high school friends to the North Valley, from the few bars up in West Central to the fancy places up in the Northeast Heights. It was all the same: young singles, and some married, looking for action. Looking for themselves.

After Angie, bulldogging had obsessed him. There was something about bringing down the animal that satisfied him. He thought that if he had been born in Spain or Mexico, he would have been a matador, facing the bull on foot with only a cape.

But this was Nuevo México, land of no-bullshit vaqueros, and so he learned to slide off his horse, drop down to grab the steer's horns and twist the head until the six hundred pounds came down. He loved the sweet smell of horse sweat, saddle leather, his own smell after an afternoon's ride. The arena, the cowboys, and the horse shit were *real*.

"A lot of bulldoggers have had the steer come down on them," he thought aloud. "Many a cowboy walks with a limp."

Maybe that was another reason why his first marriage hadn't worked, he thought. He liked the extra challenges too much. He spent all his free time doing something physical, tuning his body, keeping it in shape, and drinking with the boys. Maybe that's why teaching didn't satisfy him. He had gotten his degree from UNM and taught a few years at Valley High, but he found the classroom too confining. So he had quit to learn what he could about being a private investigator from Manuel Lopez.

He had gotten into a few tight scrapes, but he had never felt the sting of mortality until the steer gored him. Then something new and strange crept into his thoughts. The pain at night reminded him that he was vulnerable.

Before that, he played baseball in the summer and basketball in the winter. He took up skiing, tried hang gliding off the Sandia Crest, volunteered to help kids through the Police Athletic League, and finally realized he was into too many things because the marriage just wasn't working.

He wandered into the kitchen and flipped through the day-old newspaper. The spring was so dry that bears looking for food were wandering down from the Sandias into the Northeast Heights. They poached garbage in backyard trash cans.

He glanced out the kitchen window. He had heard noises last night, strange noises. Bears didn't come this far into the valley, they were usually caught up in the Heights and taken back up in the mountains. Maybe hungry raccoons from the river.

The hot weather was upsetting the balance of things. The anti-WIPP groups were threatening action if the Department of Energy went ahead with the proposed Waste Isolation Pilot Plant test: transporting waste material laced with plutonium from Los Alamos Labs down to the WIPP site near Carlsbad. The editorial supported the test.

A picture of the mayor adorned the city section. Marisa Martinez, the incumbent, was still ahead of Frank Dominic, his cousin Gloria's husband, in the mayoral polls, but the race was heating up.

He flipped to the sports page. José Valencia was pitching tonight. The Dukes were leading the league. He had promised to take don Eliseo and his friends to a game before the summer was over.

He thought again of the images of the nightmare. He would have to tell Rita about it. Somebody had tried to kill him in his dream. That wasn't good. Rita would know what it meant; she could interpret dreams. A woman wants to kill you, which means to get power over you, she would say. She went for your pingo. You better watch out, Sonny Baca.

"Coffee," Sonny heard his stomach growl, "I need some of don Eliseo's coffee."

He was just about to step outside when the phone rang.

"Sonny, I need you to come quickly!" a woman's voice said.

Sonny recognized his tía Delfina's voice. She never called.

"Qué pasa?" he asked.

"Gloria's dead. Somebody murdered her."

"Gloria—" He felt a tremor in his gut. No, it can't be. "Tía—" he began again, but she cut in.

"She's dead, Sonny, Frank just called me. They found her this morning. She was murdered last night. I want you to take me there."

"Murdered?" Sonny shook his head. What the hell was going on? "Did you call—"

"Yes, I called your mother. There's nothing she can do. I have to see my daughter. I want you to take me there."

"Yes, yes," he replied, still not believing the words he was hearing, but feeling the shock spreading through his body. His cousin Gloria dead? It wasn't possible.

"I'll be waiting," his aunt said, and the phone went dead.

2

"Gloria," Sonny whispered, and slowly dropped the phone on its cradle. No, she couldn't be dead. He saw her face, her smile, then a shudder went through him. "God, no," he cried. He didn't want to believe what he had just heard.

He flipped on the police band on his CB. The police radio was buzzing with the sketchy details. Gloria Dominic's body had just been discovered.

"No," he kept repeating, his mind still not accepting the message. It was a mistake.

He flipped on the small black-and-white television on his kitchen table. Images of Frank Dominic's elegant home on North Río Grande appeared, police blockades, news reporters. Bedlam.

He slumped down on a chair. The last time he had seen Gloria was at the mayoral announcement party that Frank had thrown in April. He had danced with her, and for a moment re-captured the time he had spent with her when he was in high school. During high school he had often turned to Gloria with his problems.

His father had died when Sonny entered high school, and he never felt he could talk to his mother, so cousin Gloria became his confidante. When he needed to talk, he would call her. He was always welcome at her apartment.

He was as involved in his sexuality as everybody else at school, but he didn't seem to be able to go all the way. Everybody in school was getting laid, the girls were as aggressive as the boys, and Sonny had offers, but he was holding back and he didn't know why. By his senior year he still hadn't made it with a girl.

"Being raised Catholic, I guess," he confided in Gloria.

"Sin and guilt," she replied, going to the core of his concern.

"Yeah. The way I was brought up. It just ain't right. I want to— Hell, I don't even know if I can."

"You have time." She touched him, held him to her.

He believed her, allowed himself to be held, felt the warmth and security she provided, and something else. A startling flow of need to really hold her, make love to her.

He drew away. He was eighteen, she was twenty-eight, they were cousins, friends, that was all. It was the first time he had felt the way a man would feel for a woman he wanted to make love to. She was beautiful. She could have any man she wanted.

"And you?" he asked, studying the serene beauty of her oval face, the arched eyebrows, the light green eyes.

"You're the handsomest guy I know," she replied. "You could have any of the girls. Maybe you need someone special."

The last week of school she invited him to her apartment. "Your graduation party," she said. He had spent many an evening with her, talking, sharing ideas of life. That night she taught him about love. She gave herself to him; she was the someone special he had been looking for.

Then she left for Los Angeles. She left a note, explaining a job offer had come up. She wrote Sonny a couple of times, telling him things she was doing, but she never gave an address. She had landed a job, she was modeling, and she was making money, a lot of money, and she was meeting men who made film offers. Finally it dawned on Sonny that she had become a call girl.

He had fallen in love with her; he wanted to go to her, help her. In his thoughts he rushed to her, took her away from the movie moguls who lusted only after her body, brought her back to New Mexico, where she belonged, where they could be happy. Daydreams that didn't stop even after he married Angie.

He knew he had married more or less on the rebound from Gloria. He tried to find in Angie the joy of passion Gloria had given him, but it wasn't there.

Gloria returned three years later, and she and Sonny ran into each other. They met at Epi's Bar and talked about old times. The men in the bar paid attention to the nice-looking, well-dressed woman, and she flirted with them, acknowledging their stares with smiles. Sonny felt self-conscious.

She had changed. The love they had shared was gone. Gloria guarded herself closely. During the years in LA, she had encircled herself with a protective shell not even Sonny could penetrate.

Then she starting dating Frank Dominic, the most influential man in the city. Within months they were married.

Why? Sonny had wondered at her wedding as he sat in the back of a packed St. Mary's Church. It wasn't love. It had to do with Dominic's political aspirations. Of course Dominic was drawn to Gloria's beauty, but there was more. Gloria fitted his plans. Dominic was a man driven to be not only the mayor of the city, he also wanted to be the new duke of Alburquerque. He yearned to be connected to royalty, anything that had to do with the Spanish blue blood of the first conquistadores. The names of de Vargas and Oñate were heroic in his mind, they were the Españoles who led the colonization of New Mexico, northern New Spain.

Gloria had grown up in poverty. The family had once owned valuable land in Old Town, though it had been lost long ago. But their father's family tree went way back. The Dominguez family had been in the Río Grande valley since the first conquest of New Mexico, and they had returned with de Vargas after the 1680 Indian Pueblo revolt to resettle in the Alburquerque area.

Sonny's mother had told him the story. "The Dominguez family used to be ricos. They went from here in Atrisco to la Plaza Vieja. They owned a lot of land, and when the railroad came, they sold some, but lost most of it to crooked lawyers. Their family name is mentioned in the old records. You know my sister Delfina is so proud she married into such a family."

Yes, tía Delfina was a proud woman, like Gloria, and that's what Dominic wanted. A young and proud and beautiful woman at his side, one with a bloodline, one that was related to the original duke of Alburquerque's mystique. Spanish blue blood. Royalty! That was the trump Dominic would play as he furthered his ambitions.

Now Gloria was dead.

"Damn!" Sonny cursed and dialed Frank Dominic's number.

A voice answered. Al Romero, Dominic's attorney. "I need to talk to Frank," said Sonny, explaining who he was. There was a wait, then Dominic's voice.

"Yeah?"

"I just heard about Gloria."

"She's dead," Dominic replied. "Murdered."

"I have to see her."

There was a pause. Dominic was talking to someone else in the room, perhaps Romero or the field officer in charge of the investigation. "No. It's impossible."

"I'm bringing Delfina," Sonny said.

"No!" Dominic objected, but Sonny just hung up the phone. He grabbed a shirt on his way out.

"Hey, Sonny!" don Eliseo called from across the street as Sonny stepped out. "Come and help these pendejos!"

"No puedo, don Eliseo," Sonny called back, "just got an emergency call."

"Qué pasa?"

"I'll explain later!" Sonny waved as he jumped into his truck. The old man shook his head and made the sign of the cross. "Cuidao," he called as the old Ford roared to life.

Sonny gunned it down the dirt road to Fourth Street, south across the downtown area into the Barelas barrio. His tía lived in a small house on Pacific. She was waiting at the front door, dressed in black, already in mourning, standing stiff and straight. She wouldn't call Turco, her renegade son, even to take her to her daughter's death. In time of trouble she had turned to her nephew.

Sonny jumped out and opened the door for her. "I'm sorry—"

Tía Delfina looked at him, her eyes dry, coffee-brown and penetrating, but dry. She took her seat.

"We should only be sorry," she replied, "if we never know the murderer of my daughter." She stiffened and stared ahead.

Sonny looked at her. His tía was a handsome woman, the source of Gloria's beauty. The high Mexican cheekbones, the oval face, the dark eyes with carefully arched eyebrows. But Gloria's green eyes had come from her father, as did the full lips, the arrogant pout.

His tía was distant, not warm like his mother; they were not like sisters at all. Today she was even colder and more distant, but who could blame her for being withdrawn?

"I never liked Frank," she whispered as Sonny started the truck and headed out of the barrio, past the Barelas Center and through Old Town.

She waited, and when he said nothing, she said, "I never trusted him."

He held the steering wheel tightly as they drove past Old

Town and north on Río Grande. The traffic on the wide boulevard moved to the slow tempo of the hot June day.

Sonny knew a lot of people couldn't stomach Frank Dominic. He was a power-hungry manipulator who let nothing get in his way, but surely he wasn't a murderer. Maybe somebody was trying to make him drop out of the mayor's race by murdering Gloria? Alburquerque was on a drug route; it wasn't Chicago or LA, but there were those who, for the right price, would hire out to do anything. But who would want to stop Dominic that badly? He wasn't ahead in the polls, just days before the election.

Gloria's sweet fragrance filled his truck, and he saw her image. He turned to glance at his tía Delfina. She used the same perfume. Yes, Gloria's perfume. He knew Gloria provided for her mother, saw to it that her mother, who did not want to leave the barrio, had everything she needed. She even brought her her own favorite perfume.

"Do me a favor," Frank had said to Sonny at the mayoral party. "Dance with Gloria. I've got the press here, all these people—"

He had turned to greet his guests, and Sonny hated him for his smugness. As if he alone had any claim to Gloria.

But he was glad to dance with her, glad to hold her again and dance as they had so many times in the past. And she was in good spirits. The protective shell had evaporated, at least for the night.

"Just like old times," she said with a smile as they swirled to the waltz, a dance she had taught him, leading him just slightly until she felt the urge in him to take over, then letting him take the lead, content to feel his body guiding hers.

Frank didn't know that Gloria had taught Sonny to dance when he was in high school. Evenings when he visited her, they ordered pizza and drank wine in her apartment; sometimes they smoked pot. She loved to take off her shoes and dance. She was a romantic at heart, one who had been hurt early in life. With Sonny she felt safe.

He couldn't have saved her from her desperate past, but as the glamorous wife of a powerful man, Gloria seemed to Sonny far beyond that now. Even after she'd survived incredible abuse, evil had come for her at last.

Damn! Sonny thought. Hadn't she been through enough in her life? If he hadn't been able to help her in life, he knew he now must find who had caused her death.

3

A cop waved for Sonny to slow down as he approached the Dominic home. The street was blocked off, but Sonny explained that the woman beside him was the victim's mother, and the officer at the detour talked into his walkie-talkie, then waited for what seemed to Sonny a long time. The truck grew hot, and finally the officer said okay, he could park near the cordoned area and report to the officer at the door. He waved them through.

One of the television reporters stopped him as he parked and helped his aunt out of the truck. "Francine Hunter, News Four, Mr. Baca. I covered the bust in the Sandias. The dentist and the marijuana farm," she reminded him. "I interviewed you."

He nodded.

"Why are you here? You a relative?"

"No comment," Sonny answered.

"Who's the woman?" She nodded at tía Delfina and pushed the mike under his chin.

"Family. Now give me a break." He took his aunt's arm and pushed past the reporter.

He had to stop at the front door. Howard Powdrell from the city's forensic lab was dusting the door. Howard and Sonny were compadres. Four years ago, Sonny had been working with the South Valley Neighborhood Youth Center as a summer counselor when the kids ran in shouting that a little girl had just fallen in the irrigation ditch that ran behind the center. Sonny had arrived in time to pull her out of the water and apply CPR. The little girl, Howard's daughter, had not suffered complications, and Howard and Sonny had become close friends, compadres.

"Howie."

Howard took his hand. "Hey, man, I'm sorry, really sorry."

"Gloria's mother . . ."

"My condolences," Howard said, and tía Delfina nodded. She stood quietly, gathering her strength, Sonny knew, for the difficult task of viewing her daughter's body.

Sonny sniffed the air. The fragrance of flowers and burned candle wax drifted into the foyer. "What happened?"

Howard shook his head. "Terrible," he muttered, looked at Delfina and tried to fill in the awkward silence. "Front door wasn't locked," he said.

Sonny noticed the key ring with keys hanging on the inside doorknob. The gold key ring was embossed with the initials FD inside the coat of arms of the old duke of Alburquerque.

"Where's Frank?" Sonny asked.

"Inside," Howard replied.

"Can we go in?"

"I'm done," Howard nodded, "but let me clear you."

"Who's in charge?"

"Garcia," Howard replied, and moved into the shadows of the house. Sam Garcia was the chief of the Alburquerque police, and if he was handling the case, it meant they were giving the murder top priority. The potential future mayor deserved nothing less.

Howard returned, motioned. "Don't touch anything," he said, the caution meant more for tía Delfina than for Sonny. He led them into the living room, a large area in Santa Fe adobe style with a large fireplace in one corner. On the mantel sat a row of large, colorful Kachina dolls. The large patio door facing east gave way to the patio. On the opposing wall hung a huge tapestry embroidered with the coat of arms of the duke of Alburquerque.

"Chief's in here with Simmons," Howard whispered.

Sam Garcia and Jack Simmons, the county sheriff, looked up. Frank Dominic was probably the most influential man in the city, so cops from both jurisdictions had showed up. As far as Sam Garcia was concerned, Frank Dominic lived in the city and the case belonged to the city police. The man was running for mayor, not for county commissioner. Jack Simmons thought differently. Cases as juicy as this one was bound to be didn't come along often.

Also seated in the large living room was a somber Casimiro, Dominic's right-hand man. Next to him sat a likewise quiet Al Romero, Dominic's numero uno attorney.

They were waiting for someone from the medical examiner's office, and all knew that shit was going to hit the fan the minute the examiner's report was made public. The fact that the victim was the wife of Frank Dominic made it front-page news. There would be a run for handguns in the gunshops as the public learned of the grisly event, a clamor for the murderers to be caught, perhaps a call for the police chief's scalp if the case wasn't solved quickly.

They looked at Sonny, but only the police chief rose.

"Mrs. Dominguez." Sam Garcia stepped forward to take tía Delfina's hand. "I am so sorry. Gloria was a wonderful woman—"

"Let me see her," tía Delfina said coldly.

"It's not pleasant—" He shook his head.

"I didn't come for pleasantries. I came to see my daughter," tía Delfina responded.

"As I explained on the phone, señora Dominguez, it is definitely a homicide. I'm sorry, I think it would be best if you view the body from the van outside. We have a video screen in there—" He turned awkwardly to Sonny. "Why don't you take Mrs. Dominguez out to the van—"

"I want to see my daughter," tía Delfina insisted, her voice rising, her gaze cutting through the chief.

The chief squirmed. He looked at Howard.

"I'm done," Howard said.

"Let her," a voice, and all turned to see Frank Dominic enter and stand by the large hallway entry that led to the back of the house. "Buenos días, Delfina," he said.

Tía Delfina turned to look at Frank, but didn't acknowledge him. The man stood as immobile as a statue, not a hair out of place, dressed in a three-piece dark suit, like he was ready to step out to do a campaign speech. No grief showed in his face. The silence in the room was heavy.

Frank Dominic's command cut through police regulations. The chief shrugged. "Howard, you take Mrs. Dominguez. We have to be careful about touching anything. . . ."

Howard took her arm and led her past Dominic, down the darkened hallway. Sonny started to follow, but his tía shook her head, nodding for him to stay. She wanted to view her daughter's corpse alone.

"Tough woman," Sam Garcia said, and looked at Sonny. "She shouldn't be here."

"Gloria's her daughter," Sonny reminded him. "She has a right."

Garcia frowned. Last summer Sonny had gotten headlines in the paper. The press had lauded him while criticizing the police department. A dentist, Sonny's dentist, had been growing marijuana up in the Sandias. A whole farm of it, with the latest technology, drip irrigation and solar panels.

The dentist's secretary had made a move on Sonny, so one night he found himself having a drink with her. She was mellow, and she told Sonny that if he ever needed good home-grown mota she could get it. "My boss grows it," she explained, telling Sonny the specifics of the operation.

The following day Sonny was having coffee with Howard, and he mentioned the elaborate setup. "I thought the chief would like to know the guy's a lousy dentist," Sonny said, and Howard smiled. There was a bust, and the newspapers made Sonny out as a hero in the war on drugs.

"The secretary wouldn't speak to me after that," Sonny complained later.

Chief Garcia broke the silence. "I feel like a drink. Damn! This is gruesome! Why are you here?" He turned his anger and frustration on Sonny.

"My aunt asked me to bring her. And Gloria *is* my cousin."

"I want you to keep out of this," Garcia continued. "Don't get involved. This is way out of your league."

"When did it happen?" Sonny asked.

Garcia just frowned and turned away.

"She was murdered 'bout midnight," Sheriff Simmons offered.

"Murdered," Sonny whispered. He still couldn't believe it. He kept thinking he was going to wake up from a bad dream, like he had awakened from the chain-saw nightmare, and Gloria would be alive.

"Cold-blooded murder," Dominic said

From the back of the house a high, keening cry echoed, then all was silent again. Tía Delfina had vented her grief in one long cry. The men in the front room turned, waited. No sobs followed, only silence.

Dominic cocked his head. "This is awful, damn awful. Yesterday she was alive, planning things, now she's dead. And the way it was done . . ." He shuddered.

Before Sonny could reply, tía Delfina appeared at the door. She looked coldly at Dominic, her face dark and expressionless. "Now you can have your way," she hissed.

"I know you don't like me, Delfina, but you have no right to—"

"To accuse you?" She arched her eyebrows. "We shall see," she said and turned to Sonny. "I want you to find whoever did this."

"I—" Sonny stepped forward, shaking his head, feeling the tension in the room. "Tía. The police will take care of this," he stammered.

"This man has the police in his pocket," tía Delfina said, looking at Frank, her anger rising, her wrath about to explode.

"We're in nobody's pocket!" Garcia replied, the vehemence in his voice surprising even him. "Mr. Dominic's right! You have no right to accuse anyone!" He shook his head but pulled back, afraid of the scene Delfina could create.

She hated Dominic, for her own reasons, and they were afraid she would come right out and accuse Dominic of the murder.

"My daughter was murdered!" She turned to Howard who stood behind her. He nodded. She turned back to Sonny. "I am hiring you to find the person who killed her! I have that right! My daughter is dead!"

She stood trembling, and Sonny reached out, thinking she would fall. "My daughter is dead," she kept whispering as he helped her to a chair.

"Tía, you're upset. Let the police handle this. You know Chief Garcia will do his best."

Howard brought a glass of water from the kitchen.

"Here, tía—" Sonny whispered. "Drink this."

"I'm all right," she said. She sipped, handed the glass back to Sonny, and covered her face with both hands. Sonny could feel the trembling of her body.

"Get her outta here," Romero, Dominic's attorney, whispered to Sonny. But tía Delfina refused to move; she was lost in her grief.

Dominic shrugged and turned down the hall.

Sonny looked at Howard. "Watch her," his look said, and he turned to follow Dominic.

"She always hated me," Dominic said, leaning against the wall. For a moment his composure broke, his voice was low and troubled, and Sonny saw a sheen of sweat on his forehead. "She's crazy, you know. Don't you go getting into this."

"Why?"

"Why?" Dominic trembled. "I'll show you," he said, and led him down the hall into the master bedroom located in the back.

The large bedroom, decorated all in white, was as neat and quiet as a funeral parlor. There was a trace of perfume in the air. The scent of garden flowers was wafting in through the open door that led to the patio.

The large canopied bed stood in the middle of the room. It, also, was all in white, and on it lay the form of the body, covered with a white silk bedspread.

"You want to see her?" Dominic asked, and for a moment Sonny almost said no. He remembered his father in the casket, remembered how much the sight had taken out of him, and he didn't know if he could face Gloria's dead body. Memories of their evenings together came flooding back. She shouldn't be dead, he wanted to scream. She didn't deserve to die.

Dominic went to the bed and pulled back the silk bedspread without hesitation. His wife had been murdered, and he could lift the sheet and not feel Gloria's spirit. Sonny felt a tightness in his stomach, he felt a breeze stir around the body as he stepped forward. The ashen, lifeless color of her face shocked him, but even in death her striking features revealed her beauty.

"They drained her blood," Dominic said.

"Drained her blood," Sonny repeated. He felt the hair rise along the back of his neck. The woman in his dream had tried to draw his blood with the saw. The nightmare had connections, complexity.

"Yeah. They cut open her vein and drained her blood. Crazies, Sonny, sonofabitching crazies!"

Sonny shook his head. Who would kill a woman and drain her blood? There was something diabolical in the room, an evil presence, he felt it.

He wanted to reach out and touch her cold cheek, but he hesitated. Whatever the spirit in the room was, it was swirling around him, making him dizzy. Cold sweat broke out on his forehead.

"Gloria," Sonny whispered, as if apologizing for her death, wanting to do something but feeling impotent in her presence.

"Only crazies would do something like this," Dominic said. "Drain her blood like some fucking satanic crap. God, what a time for something like this to happen!"

Cabrón, Sonny cursed. He was thinking only that this would ruin his mayoral campaign. He wasn't feeling anything except *inconvenience* over his wife's death! He reached for a chair, touched the wood, gripped it tightly to steady himself.

"Where were you?" he asked.

Dominic shrugged.

"Where were you?" he repeated, the sound of his voice creating a reality in the swirl he felt.

For an instant Dominic looked surprised, then scoffed. "What the hell difference does it make where I was! I don't have to tell you!"

"You weren't here?"

Dominic raised an eyebrow. "Don't pull the private investigator crap on me, Sonny! I don't owe you any answers!"

"You owe her mother!"

"Delfina? She hates me. Always did. I don't owe her anything!"

There was no love between the son-in-law and the mother-in-law, Sonny knew. Dominic wanted nothing to do with the barrio. He wanted Gloria's beauty and her family name, but not the familial connections.

The spirit filling the room with its heavy presence forced

Sonny to look again at Gloria. "Avenge me." The words filled Sonny's mind.

Had Gloria spoken? Did Dominic hear what he had heard? Her dark hair a swirl on the silk pillow framed her lovely, cold face.

"Why doesn't Delfina trust you?"

"She's crazy, that's why. People told her stories about me. Me and women. So she hates my guts. Hire you," Dominic laughed. "See how crazy she is? You find kids who run away from home, Sonny. You help divorced mothers collect alimony from guys who skip out. Or take dirty pictures like you did of the mayor and the boxer. But murder? Hey, let the cops handle it. This isn't like chasing after missing persons or cheating husbands. Whoever did this is dangerous."

Sonny's throat felt dry, constricted. He shivered. The cold presence of death pervaded the room. The voice was calling to him.

"I have to help her," Sonny said.

"Don't start fucking with me. I don't give a damn what Delfina says!"

Dominic's forcefulness battered Sonny. He felt weak, but it wasn't just Dominic's power, it was the force of the spirit in the room making him shiver. He took a step forward, again wanting to reach out and touch Gloria, but unable to. Something cold and heavy was enveloping him.

Any other time he could stand up to Dominic, tell him how he, too, despised him because of the way he treated Gloria, but he couldn't. Gloria's death had not seemed to affect Dominic, but it was sending Sonny into a tailspin, a vertigo he couldn't fully explain or shake off.

"Just keep out of it," Dominic said in parting. His voice carried the weight of a command. Then he turned and walked quickly out of the room.

Sonny was startled by Dominic's voice resounding through the house, shouting at the police chief, then the slamming of the door as he left.

Left alone, he walked slowly around the bed, staring at Gloria. He remembered when he was nine. His mother had sent him and his brother Armando to the store for milk. On the way home a neighbor's pit bull got free and attacked them. Armando froze, dirtied his pants, and waited to be ripped apart by the enraged dog. Sonny thought of running, felt his system pumping adrenaline, and tasted fear in his mouth, yet he turned to face the dog. He snatched a stick from the ground and struck at the dog.

He kept the dog at bay for few moments, but the dog was vicious and strong, and when it caught Sonny's stick in it jaws, it broke it in two. Then Sonny heard the report of a pistol. The dog yelped and fell dead. Sonny turned to see his father, the revolver he used in his night watchman's job smoking in his hand. It was the pearl-handled pistol of the Bisabuelo.

People gathered around him; his mother gathered Armando in her arms and carried him home. His father rested his hand on Sonny's shoulder.

"You were brave, hijo," his father said. Proud of him.

Perhaps that's when he knew that one day he would carry the Bisabuelo pistol, and he would have to help those in trouble.

That night he woke up screaming. The vicious dog had returned in a nightmare. It came growling through the mist to leap, fangs bared, at Sonny's throat.

"It's susto," his mother said when she held him in her arms.

She took him to a curandera in the valley, a woman from Mexico. The old woman talked to Sonny, and she prayed. She gave Sonny a candle in a glass jar, the picture of the Santo Niño painted on the glass surface, and she told Sonny's mother to burn the candle while they prayed together. That night they lit the candle, and the dark smoke rose in the shape of a dog. Both of them were sure they saw it. They prayed and the image of the dog disappeared and the smoke rose peacefully to the ceiling. After that Sonny forgot the incident, and he could sleep.

That's what he felt now as he looked at Gloria, the same fear he had felt when the dog attacked. But there was no candle to burn to dissipate the fear. There was something palpable in the room, something seeping into his blood. Something cold. Something evil.

4

Police Chief Garcia, the sheriff, and Howard entered the bedroom.

"You made Mr. Dominic goddamned mad," the sheriff said with a smile.

Sonny looked at Howard.

"Delfina's okay," Howard said.

"Damn her!" Garcia scowled. "Even if she is Gloria's mother! She can't make accusations like that! What the hell does she mean Frank's got the police in his pocket! Damn nonsense!"

"Maybe she knows something we don't," the sheriff drawled.

"Fuck off, Jack. I've got enough trouble here without your so-called witty comments."

"You've got trouble? We haven't even settled on jurisdiction yet—"

Garcia cut him off. "Well, if Delfina gets her way, we don't need to settle. She wants Sonny here to find the murderer. Elfego Baca rides again, eh?"

"Sonny looks for missing persons, not criminals," the sheriff replied. "So I suggest you take the case."

Garcia raised an eyebrow.

"Sure," the sheriff continued, "after all, Dominic's your friend, ain't he. He gets to be mayor and he's your boss. So you find whoever killed his wife. I wash my hands."

He was taunting Garcia, Sonny knew. The rivalry between city and county law enforcement had a long history.

"And, Sonny, if you want to find your cousin's killers, be my guest," the sheriff added, smiling. "Show Sonny around. Show him what he needs to know to solve the case." He poked Garcia in the ribs and whispered, "And while you're at it, tell him about the widow Glass case." He laughed. "Me? I'm getting some fresh air. In fact, I believe I'll just take a drive up to the Santa Fe Downs and see how the ponies are running. You want jurisdiction, Sam, you got it. I'm pulling my men out. Good luck." He tipped his cowboy hat and walked out.

"Sheriff must not be feeling well," Howard said.

Sam Garcia shrugged. "Just saving his skin. The case is ugly." He shook his head and looked at Howard. "You cleaned the place?"

"With a pair of tweezers."

"Where was Frank last night?" Sonny asked.

"Won't say," Garcia replied.

"Won't say? His wife was murdered. He's got to tell."

"And what if he wasn't home? Maybe he is sleeping around, but that don't mean—" Garcia stopped short. Tía Delfina's accusation had put him on edge.

"Sleeping around or not, he's got to tell you where he was," Sonny said. He knew Garcia and Dominic were old buddies. Maybe Garcia was trying to keep it from the papers. If they found Dominic was sleeping with another woman it would be on tomorrow's front page.

"Political consequences," Howard said.

The chief nodded. "The election's only weeks away! This is going to blow the city wide open! I need some air." He shook his head in frustration and turned to walk out onto the patio.

Sonny turned to Howard. "What do you think?"

" 'Bout you and this case?"

Sonny nodded.

"This is not your cup of tea. . . ."

Yeah, he had never been on a murder case. He had chased bad credit-card debtors, trailed missing spouses, and found guys that didn't pay child support. But murder, no. Still, Gloria's spirit was tugging at him. She wanted revenge. She deserved it.

For a moment he wished Manuel Lopez was alive. He could go to the old investigator, get some help, get advice.

"You should be thinking of law school, not chasing the kind of people who killed Gloria," Howard said.

"Maybe I owe it to her," Sonny insisted. "But I need help."

Howard's forehead furrowed. He couldn't refuse his friend, and within the limits of his job, he knew he could help.

"I'll do what I can. Come here," he said, and slipped on a plastic glove, then drew away the silk bedspread, revealing Gloria's naked body. Even frozen as she was in death, her muscles stiff with rigor mortis, she was beautiful. The contours of her curves flowed gracefully from head to long throat, to perfectly shaped breasts, her flat stomach, the mound of her sex between smooth thighs, the long legs ending in perfectly shaped feet, the pomegranate-crimson nail polish on the toenails.

Both men admired the beauty of the lines for a moment, both felt the waste. Howard pointed at the puncture on the left inner thigh.

"This was not a bungled break-in job," he said as he pressed on the cut to reveal the collapsed vein and artery. "Somebody came to kill her."

Yeah, Sonny thought, came intent on draining her blood. He felt sick from the fragrance, the burned candle wax, the oozing heat of the day that poured through the open door. He looked and saw the faint trace of a scratch around her navel, a bruise on her right temple.

What the hell did it mean, he asked himself, a knot forming in his guts. He leaned over Gloria, trying to identify the sweet fragrance that permeated the room. If he had eaten breakfast, he knew he would have chucked it up.

"They cut into the femoral," Howard said, pointing. "They raised the artery and vein and injected water through the artery. Probably used a plain water solution with a perfume. Lilac."

Yes, that was it, Sonny nodded. Lilac. The flower of the spring, the purple flower of the bushes that lined her driveway and her garden. When lilacs bloomed in April, the people of Alburquerque knew spring had arrived.

"They drained with a small hose or catheter at the vein. They knew their job."

"Why?" Sonny wondered aloud.

"Ah, that's the interesting question. They collected every drop; there's not a splash of blood in the bathroom, nothing on the toilet, nothing in the tub. They didn't wash the blood down the drain. They took it with them."

Took it with them, Sonny thought. They came to kill her and took her blood. Separated soul from flesh. Why? Crazies? Vampires? The evil brujas his neighbor don Eliseo often alluded to in his stories?

"They needed a pump," Sonny said to Howard, his gaze still fixed on the frozen body in front of him, the presence of death real to him, and its horror compounded by the images of him and Gloria dancing in her apartment long ago, she in her bare feet, her breath warm on his neck, his longing for her rising like hot, magnetic waves, a fever he had struggled to keep in check every time he touched her.

Howard nodded. "A portable electric with a five-gallon plastic container to collect the blood would fit in the trunk of a car. Or they could have used an old-fashioned hand pump. There's a few of those around, mostly as museum pieces. Before there were electric pumps doctors used the hand pumps. Same type of hand pump that was used to embalm the dead soldiers during the Civil War. During the early part of the war, they used to ship trainloads of dead Confederates down south without embalming them. You can imagine what that was like in summer, especially if a rail line was cut and the train stalled. So they begin to embalm on the field with hand pumps."

"So where's her blood?" Sonny interrupted.

"I suspect you won't find the blood," Howard said. Sonny looked up at him. "It's just a theory, but if they took the blood, my guess is they used it for whatever ritual they had in mind. Else why take it?"

"Ritual," Sonny repeated. So Frank wasn't far off speculating about satanic rumors. He cursed and turned to look around the room again. He had smelled wax the minute he walked into the room. He stared at the dresser, on which rested four candles in brass holders. It looked like an altar, the kind his mother had in her bedroom, but there were no statues of saints. Gloria came from a Catholic family, but she definitely wasn't into old-fashioned altars.

Howard followed his gaze. "The chief asked Frank about that. She never set up anything like that before. But there are prints on the candle holders, and I'll bet when I check them out, they're hers."

She prepared the altar herself, Sonny thought. Was that what Howard was driving at? He felt his stomach tighten as the cold and eerie presence in the room swept around him.

"Why four?" Sonny wondered.

"I've been saving this for last," Howard said. "Look." He pointed to her navel. The scratches Sonny had noticed now became the outline of a barely perceptible circle around her belly button. Four radiating lines extending from the circle, and when Sonny looked closely, he saw each line was really four lines.

Four lines up toward the middle of her breasts, four down toward her sex, and four out to either side.

"Damn," he cursed. They had scratched the Zia sun sign around her navel.

El ombligo. There was something very special about the ombligo. It was the connection to the mother. On Gloria's soft mound of a stomach the sign lay nascent, a red outline on her smooth, pale skin.

"The Zia sun," Howard said.

Sonny stared at the round symbol that circled Gloria's navel. The Zia sign was a sacred sign to the Pueblo Indians of New Mexico. It was the symbol of the Grandfather Sun, the deity of life.

The circle was the sun; the four radiating lines were the four sacred directions of the Pueblo Indian world. He knew some of the history of the pueblos. He went often to the dances at the pueblos. When he was teaching, he had taken his literature class on a field trip to a dance at Jemez. He made his students read *The Tewa World, Ceremony, The Man Who Killed the Deer,* Simon Ortiz's poetry, and Joe Sando's history of the pueblos. He encouraged them to learn the underpinning of the history that sustained life along the Río Grande. It was part of their history, their heritage.

He knew that on the West Mesa the ancestors of the Pueblo Indians had carved petroglyphs into the lava boulders, the escarpment of the once-fiery volcanos. On one of those monoliths he had seen the Zia sun symbol. It was now also used as the symbol for the state flag. Now Gloria's stomach was scratched with this ancient sign for the sun. The crazies who killed Gloria had put the sacred symbol to their own perverted use.

"Just a guess, but I'm sure Garcia's thinking the same thing. It looks like the work of a cult," Howard said.

If Howard was right about that, and this wasn't a random murder, it could mean Gloria had a hand in her own death. Had she let them in? Was she part of the ceremony?

He looked up.

"Some kind of sun cult?"

"Something like that. They knew what they were doing. Sonny, there's something else. . . ." Howard leaned forward and whispered. "I think she was pregnant."

Sonny felt a new weight added to the pressure he felt in his chest. Blood upon blood, and where did it end? Surely Howard was mistaken. She was nearly forty. She and Frank had been married nearly ten years, no children, and any kind of love they might once have had was long gone.

Howard saw the look on Sonny's face and reassured him. "It's just a hunch. I pressed here," he motioned to a spot between her ombligo and her sex, "and I'm no doctor, but I felt something. The autopsy will tell us."

Pregnant, Sonny thought. It didn't make sense. Did Dominic know? Her mother obviously hadn't.

The chief walked in from the patio. "Damn nice out there," he said, and pulled up a chair and sat down to stare at the body.

"You going to tell us about the Glass case the sheriff mentioned?" Howard asked.

The chief lit a cigarette. "Why not," he said, in a better mood now that Simmons was off his back. "Happened a year ago."

Sonny raised an eyebrow and thought back to recent murders reported in the papers, trying to find something that linked to Gloria. But he couldn't remember anything that seemed connected, anything involving the Zia sign or draining blood or cults.

"Dorothy Glass was a widow of the old man who bought the Sims property," Sonny remembered. "Architect. Left her a fortune."

Garcia nodded. "Turned up dead one day. The rumor was she had been mixed up with spiritualists who claimed they could contact her husband. I followed the lead, but it led up a blind alley. Hell, everywhere I turned I found spiritualists. Alburquerque's full of these people. And Santa Fe's worse. Did you know a con artist up there offers Jeep trips to places he calls spiritual vortexes? Yeah, for a hundred bucks you can be driven out to these places and get your soul cleaned. Damn, what's this world coming to!"

"Let me guess: the widow Glass also had the Zia sign cut into her," Sonny said.

The chief nodded. "I didn't report it. Hell, I didn't want the city in a scare! Fucking papers get hold of something like this and it only makes trouble. Papers love this kind of shit!"

"Did Dorothy Glass have her blood drained?"

The chief nodded.

"And she lived in this neighborhood?"

Garcia nodded again. "That's why it's scary. Two women, same area, same method. I don't like it."

"The Zia murders," Howard sighed, "yeah, the papers will love it."

"Hell, I get no complaints when winos and the poor die in the streets, but when the rich die, damn, that means anybody can die." The chief grew silent, morose.

"How many people would it take to do something like this?" Sonny asked, turning to Howard.

"At least two," Howard answered. "They must have worn cloth covers over their shoes, probably the type doctors wear in surgery. I picked up a few cloth fibers that don't match the rug. It's hard to tell, everything is so clean. One could have done it, but I figure at least two." He went to the sliding glass door and pointed to where it had been jimmied. "This is to make us think break-in."

"But you think she let them in herself. You think she knew her murderers?" Sonny asked.

Howard nodded. He pointed to the floor, which he had painstakingly combed for evidence. "They wore plastic gloves. Left everything spic and span. There's not a trace of anything."

"And the bruise?" Sonny asked.

"I think it's to make us think there was a struggle. But maybe she fell."

Howard was reconstructing the murder and fixing the pattern in his mind, Sonny thought. That's how he worked, and that's why he was so good at what he did. Since they'd met, Sonny had hung around Howard's lab. He was the best forensics man in the city. He took pictures and vacuumed the room for scraps, then put everything under his microscopes and made the smallest piece of evidence tell stories. Armed with only a microscope, Howard usually gathered enough evidence to help the DA get his convictions.

Howard looked at Sonny, then glanced at the chief. "I think there was some kind of ceremony here," he said quietly. "I think she knew the person or persons who killed her."

"Dominic's got dogs," Sonny remembered. Two big Dobermans.

"They're in the backyard, poisoned. Probably cyanide. The stuff is easy to get. A lot of ranchers use cyanide to poison coyotes. It can't be traced."

"They had plenty of time," the chief sighed. "They must have known Frank wasn't going to be home. They had time. Notice how carefully they arranged the body."

Yeah, Frank wasn't home, Sonny thought. That had been going through his mind. It made Dominic the prime suspect. That's why the sheriff had cut out. Let Garcia put the squeeze on his friend. Let Garcia take the toughest man in the city downtown for questioning.

"That's how I remember old widow Glass, lying on a bed of pine cones, peaceful. Like she was asleep."

"Sadistic bastards," Sonny cursed.

"It's going to be a tough one," the chief said, frowning. "I'd better get out there and talk to the press." He rose, walked to the door and turned. "Just so we understand each other, Sonny. I know she was your prima, and I know Delfina's upset. Hell, I would be too if I found my daughter like this. But we play no favorites. My job is to find whoever did this, and I'm going to do it. But you better stay out of this. Comprendes?"

Sonny nodded.

"You better get Delfina back home," he said, and went out.

"He's worried," Howard said. "It's going to be tough. There's so damn little evidence. If the press goes after him, it might cost him his job."

Howard gently pulled the bedspread back over Gloria. "In the prime of life. What a waste."

"Yeah," Sonny agreed, and felt a shiver. The dead body lay beneath the sheet, but the ghost of the woman lingered in the room. The spirit called for vengeance. Where is my blood? The ghost of Gloria Dominic cried. Sonny was sure he could hear the anguish of the dead woman's soul.

"Took her blood," he whispered.

Howard nodded. He sat and lit a cigarette. He passed the package to Sonny, and although he hadn't smoked in over a month, he took one and lit up.

"Brujas," Sonny said. "Don Eliseo still believes there are evil witches."

"Maybe there are," Howard said with a nod. "These are definitely not your friendly Tarot card readers."

Yeah, Sonny thought. And where was Frank Dominic last night? The man was going to have to come clean.

"They're into something that has to do with sacrifice. Like the cattle cases."

"Cattle cases?" Sonny asked.

"You know, the mutilations. Every year a case or two comes up. A rancher finds one of his steers slaughtered, the blood taken, the genitals or tongue of the animal missing. Flying saucers, the papers say, signs of a spaceship landing, aliens from outer space involved. There was a report about a flying saucer just last week. Then once a year, sure as Halloween comes around, there's a story in the newspaper saying it's satanism. But they don't get it right," Howard said thoughtfully.

"What do you mean?" Sonny asked.

"It's an obsession as old as humans on earth. The sacrificing of a victim to appease the gods. Now we're supposed to be more civilized, but it's still going on."

He paused and Sonny waited.

"We just had a cattle mutilation on the other side of the Sandias."

Sonny remembered the headline in yesterday's paper. He hadn't bothered to read the story; it all seemed so absurd. "Coincidence?"

"Maybe," Howard answered. "But in both cases, whoever does the killing goes for blood."

Sonny looked out the window and saw a line of policemen coming toward the house. They were combing the grounds, step by step, as far as the ditch road. He heard one shout and another hold up a bag of plaster. They had found tire tracks and were going to take a print.

He wondered about the container that held Gloria Dominic's blood. Where was it? How would they use it? Thinking this made his stomach spasm. He tasted bile in his mouth.

"The Aztecs used blood to feed the sun. They offered blood to the sun to ensure it would rise every day."

"Yeah?" Howard said thoughtfully. "There's a connection, sun symbol and blood. Maybe they offer it to the sun. Offer it to the flames for renewal. You know"—Howard leaned forward—"in the mortuary they flush the blood down the drain. They put the body on a cold slab and drain it, and the blood is just flushed away. Orthodox Jews don't allow that, you know. They want the blood that nourished them to go to the grave with them. The Egyptians used to gather all the organs and bury them with the body. Canopic jars."

Sonny listened. Howard's history lessons were usually right on. So, what if Gloria's blood had been offered as a gift to the sun? A gift to renew life? The ombligo was the center of the woman, circled by the sun, with four lines radiating out in the four sacred directions. Somewhere there was a pattern. He had to find the meaning in the symbols and trace it to the people who inscribed the Zia sign on Gloria Dominic's belly. How did they use her blood?

Sonny's stomach flared with acid. Maybe he should get some coffee, or breakfast. No, he couldn't eat, the image of Gloria's ashen face and the Zia sun carved on her stomach was too fresh, too poignant. The faint scent of lilac wafting through the house nauseated him.

There was little to start on, he thought. Look for the pump that had been used on Gloria. He looked at Howard.

"Was she dead when they—"

"I hope so," he answered. "Hey, man, you don't look good. You need some air, and I need to finish up here. If I find anything, I'll call you."

"Thanks," Sonny acknowledged. "I gotta get my tía home."

"I'll call you," Howard said.

"Thanks. Say hi to Marie."

"And you give Rita un abrazo."

Sonny nodded and walked back to the front room. Maybe Garcia was right, best leave it to the cops, he thought. But it was his cousin, his family, and familia ran deep. The Mexicanos of the valley came from extended families, and sometimes they fought and carried feuds for generations; but let an outsider attack one, and the clan was obligated to pull together. And there was the love he had for Gloria.

Damn, he cursed himself. This is Alburquerque, we don't have cult murderers here. This was still a cow town a few years ago. Sure we're growing, but we're not up to murder in politics.

The doctor from the office of the medical investigator had just arrived. Sonny sidestepped him and Garcia and went to his aunt. She was still staring into space, but the color had returned to her face.

"Tía," he said softly, taking her hand.

She looked at him and stood, and without a word she went

out of the house, allowing Sonny to lead her to the truck. She didn't speak until they were near her home.

"You have to find who killed my daughter," she said.

"The police, tía," Sonny tried to explain, but she wasn't listening.

"She had grown thin, she wasn't eating well," she continued. "Very upset, nervous. She went to the doctor, but he couldn't find anything. Gloria thought she had cancer, but it wasn't cancer, it was something else. She was depressed. Publicly, she was the active wife of Frank Dominic, a woman the city adored. Beautiful and talented. . . . But inside . . ."

Tía Delfina paused and took a handkerchief from her purse.

"I blame myself."

"Tía, there's no reason for you—"

"Yes, I blame myself. She didn't have a normal childhood. I was busy working, trying to support the family. You don't know this, Sonny, but her father—" She wrinkled the hanky nervously in her hand and touched it to her lips. "He drank. He used his family name to get free drinks from those he called friends. He was a very troubled man. . . ."

Yes, Sonny thought, I know.

"Gloria had grown so depressed. She had something inside she had to make peace with. She went to a woman, a healer. At first it was very good. She regained her health. She told me the woman had cured her cancer. I didn't say anything, I was happy for her. It wasn't cancer, but her depression the woman had cured. But later she grew more nervous. Frightened. The woman seemed to have a strange hold over her. She had helped Gloria in one way, only to possess her in another. The last time I saw her she said she had to get away from the woman."

"Did she tell you the woman's name?"

"No."

"Why did she want to get away from the woman? Was she demanding money?"

"I think so. They—"

"They?"

"There was a small group that met with the healer. Two or three. My group, she called them. They had found out something about her, something about her personal life that they used to threaten her. To reveal it would hurt not only her, but Frank. Maybe ruin his chance to be mayor. Not that I would care if the man dropped dead. Why her, and not him? Ay, my poor daughter. Never any peace in her life."

Her head dropped and she grew silent. "There's also an insurance policy. . . ."

Sonny waited.

"Gloria told me only a month ago. Frank had taken out an insurance policy on her. Two million dollars, Sonny," tía Delfina said, and looked at Sonny, and when Sonny took his eyes from the road and glanced at her, he saw Gloria's eyes.

Now his aunt had dropped a motive, and no matter that he couldn't picture Frank as a murderer, it was still there, pointing at Dominic. The man was running a very expensive mayoral campaign, of course he needed money. He dreamed of building canals throughout downtown, creating a Venice of the southwest with Río Grande water. He was vain and ambitious and he wanted, more than anything, the power to run the city.

Still, Sonny wanted to believe that even Frank Dominic wouldn't murder his wife.

"When money's involved, trust no one," the ghost of Manuel Lopez whispered, instructing him still. "You dig at the facts. People's motives will turn and twist you all sorts of ways, but the facts don't lie."

"It's not unusual—" Sonny said. People with as much money as Frank Dominic buy hefty insurance policies. The timing was coincidence.

"Find who did it, Sonny," tía Delfina said as he drove up in front of her house. His mother's car was parked in front; she was standing by the front door, and now she came quickly toward the truck.

"I'll pay you," tía Delfina said, and she took crumpled dollar bills from the small, black purse she had clutched all morning and pushed them into Sonny's hands.

"Tía, no—" He tried to push the money away, but his tía was insisting, pushing the tightly wadded money on him.

"Do it for Gloria," tía Delfina whispered and wrapped her chilled, thin fingers around his hands.

Tía Delfina quickly stepped out of the truck to be gathered up in her sister's arms. Sonny heard his mother sob. He got out of the truck and followed them to the front door, feeling awkward and useless in their presence, feeling the wad of bills in his hand.

"What can I do?" he asked.

"Nada," his mother said, turned, and reached out and embraced him. Her abrazo was warm, loving. "Ah, hijito, que horror. I heard everything on radio on my way here. Who would do such a thing? Who?"

Sonny had no answer. He looked at his aunt. She had her suspicions, and she had hired him to confirm them.

"I'll stay with Delfina," his mother said, and took her sister by the arm and drew her into the house. Sonny pulled the door shut.

His mother would take care of things, she was strong. Her eyes were wet with tears and her voice trembled, but she was strong. She would stay with Delfina and share the grief and whatever preparations had to be made.

He? What could he do? Nada! Pinche nada!

He walked back to his truck and kicked the tire. Nada! He looked up at the clear, blue sky. The heat of the hot June day was oppressive, but it didn't warm him. He shivered, opened his hand, and stared at the crumpled bills his aunt had given him. Old bills, bills that had sat for a long time in his tía's purse. No telling how long. They exuded the fragrance of the purse, perfume and lipstick, old coins, hairpins, tissue. He slowly undid the wad and counted two five-dollar bills and ten ones.

He laughed. Shit. Twenty bucks to find a murderer.

5

What the hell do I do now? Sonny asked himself.

Start from the beginning, Manuel Lopez said. Start gathering the facts. You've been hired, hijo, hired by a poor woman who only had a few dollars to her name, but her daughter's been murdered and you owe it to her to find out who committed the crime.

Yeah, Sonny thought, and I owe Gloria. He dialed Rita on his car phone and left a message on her machine. "Something very important has come up. I'll see you at the café later this afternoon." There was nothing else he could say. He felt drained, like he needed a day's sleep, but he knew he couldn't rest.

Facts, he thought, and the widow Glass case tugged at him. He drove to city hall, where he spent several hours reading police files, scrutinizing any murder that seemed even vaguely related to the Gloria Dominic case. He found nothing besides the Dorothy Glass case. But then, Garcia admitted he'd withheld details in that case; maybe he did the same in others. Newspaper clippings mentioned Dorothy Glass's eccentricities, and her wealth. Her friends said she had been depressed since the death of her husband, so it was written off as a suicide. And the chief had made sure no one found out about the Zia sign carved on her belly.

He finished going through the public files and decided to head for the library up the street. The media was running like a pack of excited roadrunners around city hall, trying to grab anyone on the case for an interview. Sonny dodged them as best he could. As he entered the solemn mustiness of the public library, he looked for Ruth Jamison.

She was an old friend; she and Sonny had attended Rio Grande High together. After high school, like many in the senior class, they drifted apart, but after he finished his degree at the university and started teaching, they met again. She had taken a job at the library, and he would drop in to find books of interest for the kids. They talked, and later he dropped in whenever he was downtown. She was a reader, too, so once in a while they had coffee and talked about books.

"After the kids are in bed, reading is all I do," she told him. Ruth had married right after high school, but her husband took to drinking and beating her, so she and the two kids moved out. She went on welfare, then got a chance to learn to be a librarian through one of the apprentice programs the city was running, and she loved it.

"They pay me to come and be surrounded by books." She smiled. "Imagine." She supported herself and her children, and her life centered only around her children and job.

A priestess of books, Sonny thought. He admired her, and she had a fondness for Sonny, a crush that lingered since high school days when he ran touchdowns for the football team and she cheered on the sidelines.

That hot June afternoon she gathered the newspaper clippings she could find on the Dorothy Glass case, and Sonny read through them. He also looked for anything on cults. One reporter had turned up an old hippie commune in the mountains, a relic from the sixties, founded and run by a man called Raven.

According to their story, Raven was the spiritual leader of the commune. Their religion was a curious blend of mystical beliefs, mostly a misinterpreted Pueblo Indian way of life. They took what they needed from the land, but the land on the east face of the Sandias was so bone-poor that the practice translated into poaching livestock from the local ranchers to keep the group in meat. The article also intimated that Raven was the father of the children of all four women who lived in the commune. No other men were mentioned.

Raven's philosophy included bits and pieces of Indian lore that he had picked up during the three years his group was encamped near Taos Pueblo. He professed a kind of free love, a pro-environment stance that centered around their mission to save Mother Earth from destruction by pollution.

The real find made Sonny hold his breath. Because Raven allowed no pictures of himself or his mountain compound, the newspaper had taken a picture from the air, and there, clear as could be, was the circular shape of the main building. Four rooms jutted out from the round building, creating a rough form of the Zia sign.

"Four wives, four directions, four rooms," Sonny whispered. "I need to talk to him."

A wino in the carrel next to Sonny awoke with a start. He had come in to get out of the heat and grab a nap in the cool, air-conditioned library. "I ain't done nothing," he muttered.

"Sorry," Sonny said, grinning. "I didn't mean you. Go back to sleep."

Sonny returned to his file. The people of La Cueva, the mountain village near Raven's commune, didn't care for Raven and his group; that much was clear from the ranchers who had been interviewed for the article. Someone was poaching their cattle, they complained to the reporter, and always right after an animal disappeared, the sweet aroma of roasting meat rose in the smoke that came from Raven's place.

Sonny felt the hair rise along the back of his neck. Something connected. But what? The cattle mutilations Howard had mentioned? That was a possibility. He found Ruth, who was never far away when he was doing research, and explained what he was after.

"There was a cattle mutilation in the Sandias reported just a day ago," Sonny said.

"Yes," Ruth answered. She pulled the paper. Sonny scanned the article. A cow with its tongue and vagina neatly cut away had been found on the ranch of José Escobar. Something similar to this happened once or twice a year somewhere in the state. The cops investigated and the paper did a story and that was it. But something about this incident bugged Sonny.

"Is there any more on this?"

"A reporter for the *Cattlemen's Journal* did a story on cattle mutilations recently," she said. "In fact, we have a folder on the subject." She dug through the cabinet file and came up with a stack of articles that went back ten years.

Sonny hunkered down and began to read, making a note of the time and place of each occurrence. There was usually one a year, usually in the early summer, and always in a different part of the state. The mutilations were always done with surgical precision; tongues were removed, vaginas cut from cows, and balls from bulls. Very little trace of blood was ever found. And not a single person had ever been arrested in a case that involved cattle mutilation. That didn't make sense, Sonny thought.

Now he remembered the year a bull had been found mutilated near Isleta Pueblo. It was while he was still in high school. The testicles were taken from the bull, the cuts were made with a surgeon's precision, and a large burned area was found near the bull. No car tracks were found, no trace of anyone going or coming, no meat taken, just the balls. The tribal cops were stumped, called in the FBI, and they found nothing. The tribal members of the Isleta Pueblo grew very upset; the thing smacked of witchcraft as far as they were concerned. The pueblo was closed off to visitors for a few weeks.

Sonny thought back to a couple of other cases he remembered from the newspapers. Whoever did a mutilation came in the dark of night, did the job, and disappeared. Usually mysterious signs were found near the dead cattle. The most common sign left at the scene was a burned area of grass or weeds, and the scorched area could never be identified as a gasoline or oil burn. Sometimes piles of rocks were left, signs that apparently held meaning only for the mutilators. No tracks of vehicles were ever found, which gave rise to the flying saucer theory.

Most of the articles reporting on the mutilations quickly turned into science fiction. If there was no trace of blood found, and no vehicle tracks, then the reporter, tongue in cheek, usually reported the rancher's story: little green men from outer space were into cow tongues, vaginas, and Rocky Mountain oysters.

Sonny laughed halfheartedly. Whoever did these things usually drained the blood of the animal without spilling a drop. The image of Gloria's pale, lifeless body floated before him, an image which haunted him. He had seen blood spilled in South Valley bars, but that seemed kind of normal when men got together to drink and arguments started.

Blood. That's what life boiled down to. Blood and spirit. They had separated body and soul in a gruesome ceremony. Separated her vital juices from her body, and left the pale, white shell. The only way to lay her soul to rest was to find the murderer, and find her blood.

He had felt Gloria's restless spirit in the room. Rest, it cried, I need to rest! Sonny, if you loved me, find my blood and allow me to rest.

Or was his search really to lay his own fear to rest?

"You cold, Sonny?" Ruth asked, and placed her hand on his

shoulder. Her perfume was sweet, mixed with book ink, amid the hushed whispers of the library. A book waiting to be opened, Sonny thought as he looked up at her. A long dress enveloped Ruth's warm body.

"The air conditioning," he explained.

"Hope you're not coming down with a summer cold," she said, and went off in search of more files.

Sonny read on. The ranchers interviewed in the newspaper stories usually reported strange lights or sounds near the time a mutilation occurred. "I thought it was an army helicopter," one old rancher was quoted.

"We seen lights flashin' at night," his wife added, "comin' and goin', kind of scary."

"It was a flyin' saucer, and it came right down behind the barn." The couple was from southern New Mexico, near Tularosa. "Then it lifted straight up. Ain't no plane or rocket over in White Sands that can do what that spaceship did."

A handful of people in the state actually claimed they had seen flying saucers. Ranches were isolated in the wide open spaces of the raw landscape, and people just saw things. The canopy of the Milky Way at night was brilliant and immense, and it was etched with falling stars. Coyotes cried, and the large and barren landscape of the state became a ghostly moonscape. Loneliness filled the nights.

Why, a rancher would ask when he found one of his steers or bulls mutilated, would anyone do a thing like this? If there was no trace of human activity where the mutilation took place, the rancher and his wife grew nervous and looked to the skies.

"Maybe it was the lights we saw last night."

"Maybe we're being watched from outer space."

The air force over at Kirtland had actually set up a special division to follow up on the sightings. But Sonny knew sure as hell the Kirtland boys wouldn't talk. They'd been storing nuclear bombs and high-level radioactive waste in the Manzano Mountains outside of town for a long time, but they had the city

duped into believing they were into nice, quiet peacetime exper-
iments. The Kirtland payroll was a big factor in city economics,
so nobody in city hall ever raised questions.

The nuclear waste was piling up. No end to it, he thought,
and people don't seem to give a damn. But he was aware of it.
Sonny was sure the cancer that killed his father had come from
his exposure to radioactive material. Sonny sighed, shook his
head, and returned to the article.

"Hell," one old rancher was quoted, "if it'd been poachers,
they'd've taken the beef. Don't make sense to poach a beef and
leave it to the vultures. It's the devil's work, that's what I think."

Devil's work, that's what don Eliseo would say, too.

"Seguro que sí, Sonny, there's diablos all around. They come
to pull a curtain over your eyes. So you can't see the Señores y
Señoras de la Luz."

Don Eliseo and his octogenarian friends had been telling stories recently. Strange things happened at night in the backroads
of the irrigation ditches. No, not kids going out to smoke dope
or sniff paint cans. The dogs barked, then whined, but they didn't
challenge the noises heard at night. Don Eliseo believed evil
walked the earth.

"Last week we found a big spot in the field behind Toto's
house," he had told Sonny. "Burned in a circle. No tracks. Just
the strange burn. And Toto's dog was dead. It's no good, Sonny.
Something evil has come to Ranchitos. It's right here with us."

In the old days the people of the valley believed that witches
came in the shape of fireballs. In the deep recesses of the river
bosque, the balls of fire gathered to do their dance for the devil.
Some believed sacrifice of roosters and chickens took place. The
witches danced with the devil, fornicated with the goats. The
imagination was fired by the unexplainable, or perhaps, Sonny
thought, by the belief in the spirit world. These very religious
people still believed the devil and his witches came to do their
evil work on earth.

His mother believed in those signs. "When we were children

growing up in Socorro, we saw the fireballs dancing along the river. Late at night they would come out. We could see them from our ranch. The old people said it was witches, and we believed. Mamá would take us inside to pray."

There are good witches, Sonny thought. A shaman served the tribe and did good, like Rita's friend, Lorenza Villa, a curandera who lived in Corrales. But there were those who did evil. Gloria seemed to have run into the murdering kind.

There was a postage-stamp-size article on the recent strange light that had appeared in the North Valley, near Ranchitos. So it wasn't just don Eliseo and his friends, Sonny mused. The local cops called Kirtland, but the air force swore it had no tests scheduled that day and no helicopters in the area.

They called weatherman Morgan at one of the TV stations, and he thought it was the aurora borealis, the northern lights. Dry heat bouncing off the atmosphere. There had been no rain since a few stingy showers in early May, and the heat and electricity in the air were playing tricks.

Sonny dug deeper into the files, trying to make sense of the cattle mutilation stories from around the state, working desperately, as if the search could nullify the cold he felt, the image of Gloria, his thoughts of his mother and tía Delfina sitting in the darkened house, feeling the grief which was so deep. He should get out of here and go to them. But what could he do?

"How's it going?" Ruth asked. It was nearly closing time.

"I was reading the cattle stories. Just going back a few years, I've found quite a few that occurred around the state. . . ." He paused. Around! That was it! "Can you bring me a state map? And thumbtacks!"

Ruth nodded and went off; she returned quickly. "Where can I pin this?" he asked. She cleared a bulletin board for him. He pinned the map on the board. "Around the state," he kept repeating, "around the state."

When Ruth handed him the thumbtacks, she felt his hand tremble. He looked at the notes where he had jotted the exact time and place of each mutilation, then he began to place a thumbtack where each incident had occurred. Tucumcari. Wagon Mound. Tierra Amarilla. Ramah. Quemado. A ranch in the Black Mountains. A ranch near White Sands. Picacho. Elida. And the most recent one on a ranch just the other side of the Sandia Mountains, twenty miles as the crow would fly, near the village of La Cueva.

Sonny breathed deep as he slumped back in his chair and gazed at the map.

"See," he said.

"What?" Ruth asked. She stared at the thumbtacks on the map.

"What do you see if you trace the thumbtacks?"

Ruth traced the outline. "A circle," she said as her hand swept round. "Except this one here at the Sandias. It's—"

"The center."

"And the four outside the circle?" Ruth pointed.

"The four lines of the Zia sun," Sonny whispered. The same sign that had been etched on Gloria's stomach. The Sandias thumbtack, in the center of the sun, was just where Raven's Zia-shaped commune stood. He *definitely* needed to take a ride up there.

"What does it mean?" Ruth asked

"A theory. Nothing but a theory." He glanced again at the article on the La Cueva mutilation.

I need to pay a visit to señor Escobar to check out that mutilated cow, and to Raven and his four wives, Sonny thought. His stomach knotted as the image of Gloria's cold body appeared superimposed on the map. Her navel was the center, her arms and legs spread out in the four directions.

"You okay?" Ruth asked, concerned.

"I'm fine," Sonny answered, but he wasn't. Something had gotten under his skin in the death room. Some strange power was making him see images, confusing his thoughts. Frank

Dominic made sure I went into the death room with him. He lifted the sheet from his wife's body so I could see Gloria. Why?

"I'll keep these for you," Ruth said as she gathered the map and the files he had been reading.

"Thanks, Ruth," he said, and took her hand, warm and soft. "Keep it secret."

Ruth nodded. "You know what goes on between the researcher and the librarian is confidential." She smiled. Ruth, the guardian of books, was herself a closed one.

The news of Gloria Dominic's murder had been on the television they kept in the office, and she wondered if he was on the case. Sonny was trying to connect something, but she didn't press. She never did.

"It's like the sins confessed to the priest." She held her fingers to her lips. What she had learned would not escape.

She was standing close enough for him to smell her perfume. Her hair was done up, but one movement would release the pins, and her auburn hair would cascade over her shoulders. He needed to be held, he thought, by his mother as she held him when he was a child, or by Rita, whose love often lullabyed him to sleep, or by Ruth, who was warm and alive, not cold and dead like Gloria.

She's like a nun, he thought as he looked at her clear, gray eyes. She lives in a world of the sacred, in a sanctuary of books, whispers, spiritual thought, and great ideas.

She had hinted that she hadn't had a man since her divorce. "Too busy," she said once when they had lunch at Lindy's.

She took his hands in hers and sighed softly. He had never held her hand or touched her before, and yet the impulse had been there.

"You take care of yourself," she whispered.

"I will," he answered.

"Anything I can do?" she offered.

She was a good-looking woman, but she had been hiding

from the touch of a man, hiding her long, auburn hair, hiding behind the image of the librarian, hiding behind her glasses.

"Gloria Dominic was murdered last night," he said.

She nodded. "It was on the television news."

"She was my cousin. . . ."

"I didn't know. I'm sorry." She touched his cheek.

Her hands were soft and delicate, warm on the coldness he felt all over his body. He looked into her eyes and thought of Gloria.

Yesterday she was alive, warm, glowing with life, and now she was dead. Right now she was probably resting on a slab where one of the doctors of the office of the medical investigator was sawing into her. He would cut into her thigh and dig out again the femoral artery and vein to examine them carefully, and finally open her vagina to take samples of the dried-up juices that could be found there. He would open her womb and know for sure whether she was pregnant or not. And as he cut, the doctor would mutilate her anew, surgically opening up her most private parts and exposing them.

"It was ugly," he whispered.

Ruth sensed his anguish, touched his lips. "Oh, Sonny," she whispered.

He slipped his arms around her and held her, as if embracing her would make Gloria's haunting image disappear. She stood quietly, trembling in his embrace, his fear a new emotion that filled the moment.

He held her and felt the beating of her heart, then he smiled, said "Thanks for everything," and slipped past her and out the door.

6

His mind churning and his stomach raw from hunger, Sonny drove north on Fourth Street to Rita's Cocina. He needed to eat, and he needed to see Rita.

He flipped on his CB and found the police band was still buzzing with the Gloria Dominic murder, but there seemed nothing new on the case to report.

A thin veil of dust from the unpaved side roads hung over the valley, creating an eerie curtain. The heat of the June afternoon had climbed to 90, the twilight would last long, and the cool of evening wouldn't come till sunset. There was no prospect of rain to cool off the dry spell. The dull sky hung over the valley like a turtle shell, trapping the heat.

He swerved in and out of Friday-evening traffic, a silent ethereal flow that moved as an image in a bad dream. The traffic included shoppers going home, hurrying to the coolness of their swamp coolers or shade trees in the backyard. Working men who had spent all day under the blazing sun were now stopping at their favorite bars to cool off with a beer before heading home.

A few lowriders were already cruising toward Central, where they would join the summer-evening ritual, showing off their customized cars as they paraded from downtown to the K mart on Atrisco. The loud music from their boom boxes shattered the otherwise quiet air.

Summer had arrived, and with it the high desert heat that was dry and therefore manageable. But without rain the sky would remain immense over the valley, and the beauty would become oppressive.

The autopsy, Sonny thought, and on a chance he dialed the chief on his mobile phone. He was surprised when he was passed through. Sam Garcia was working late.

"Anything new?" Sonny asked, doubting he would get any information, but the chief was in an agreeable mood.

"We got a set of tire tracks from the ditch road along the back of the house," Garcia replied. "They look fresh. But who the hell knows, they could belong to a ditch rider. Medical investigator report's done. Shows there was no rape. . . . We interviewed all the neighbors, but they heard nothing. Dominic's house sits on a three-acre lot; someone coming in the back way wouldn't have been seen. And the dogs were silenced."

"Did the medical investigator find anything else?" Sonny asked. If Howard was right, the fact that Gloria was pregnant would be known by now.

The phone was muffled for a moment, then Garcia, "No, nothing. We questioned the gardener. Leroy Brown, black, male, from the San José area. He was working for the Dominics up to a week ago. So was the housekeeper, Veronica Worthy. Both were hired by Gloria. And get this, both were fired by her. People we've talked to say the Worthy woman was devoted to Gloria Dominic. But Brown . . . I let both go, for now. Right now the tracks on the ditch road are the only thing we have going, officially. But I think we'll find this is simpler than it looks, a disgruntled employee. That's the only reason I'm telling you all this, because I think the whole thing is going to be over before it really starts."

Someone behind Sonny honked angrily and broke the silence of the street. Sonny glanced in his rearview mirror and saw a couple of cowboys tailgating him in their high-riding, boss Chevy. They had obviously just left the local watering hole and were on the way to the next one up the street. On Friday nights, Sonny knew, the best rule was to let anybody who wanted to pass, pass.

Let them wrap themselves around a telephone pole somewhere down the road, Sonny thought. He sure as hell didn't want to tangle with them. It was getting so that a lot of crazy motorists carried weapons in their cars. Only recently, one had stepped out of his car to shoot another man over a simple traffic quarrel. Now these two cowboys were full of Bud and peering down at him from their high-riding truck, intimidating him.

It wasn't anywhere near deer season, but Sonny could make out two high-caliber rifles in the gun rack.

"Enough." Sonny frowned as he pulled off onto the shoulder of the road so he could concentrate on Garcia. The big four-by-four Chevy, riding three feet off the ground, barreled by. "I don't want to be a statistic," Sonny said, raising his middle finger in salutation.

"What?" the chief asked.

"Nothing. I don't believe it," Sonny replied. The chief was in a good mood, he was talking, but damnit! His theory sounded too simple.

"What the hell don't you believe?"

"Shutting this down by conveniently taking in some poor gardener who won't know what hit him, that's what!"

"Goddamn you, Sonny! I shouldn't give you the time of day! What makes you get so high and mighty?"

"Delfina hired me!" Sonny shot back.

"You're crazy if you agreed! I'm telling you, this isn't what old Manuel trained you for! This is murder, not missing persons!"

"I need the MI's report. Tell me, what else do you know?"

"Ah, shit," Garcia replied. He was pissed off, and for a moment Sonny thought he might hang up, but he didn't. "Okay, okay, the blow to the head didn't kill her. She was cut open and drained while still alive."

Sonny groaned. He had feared all day he would hear that, but he still wasn't prepared. A cold sweat broke over him; he felt nauseated.

He lay his forehead on the steering wheel. His stomach was in a knot; he felt chilled, but he was sweating.

"Like I said, this is going to be a shit case. The press wants to hang me on this one. Did you see the five o'clock news? You watch the paper tomorrow, they're going to cry for blood! People are scared stiff! 'Satanic cult,' the news said. Mayor called me in, she wants something done right now! I wouldn't get into it if I was you, I don't care if she was your prima."

The phone went dead. Sonny slowly lifted his head and looked up the street. The cowboys in the truck had sped out of sight, cars moved steadily up and down the street, and Sonny pulled back into the traffic. The bars and restaurants were busy; life had not changed on Fourth Street. The drive-up window at Isidro's Bar had a line of five cars. Mexican workers who had done dirty, heavy work all day now wandered in to drink a cold beer. Tonight they would dance. For a lot of these people, Gloria Dominic's death would be of little or no interest. People they knew died every day, and life went on. Life on the margin was rough, and on Fourth Street it was rougher. But it went on.

A black seed of fear had taken root in Sonny's stomach. It was now the size of a fist, with tendrils that reached out and squeezed his soul. Gloria's haunted voice cried to him.

He tasted bile in his mouth. His stomach was empty; he hadn't eaten all day. The revulsion he felt when the chief said she had been drained while alive fed his nausea.

"Fucking crazies!" he cursed and slammed his fist into the steering wheel. She had been alive!

He pulled into the packed, graveled parking lot of Rita's Cocina. Rita served the best Mexican food in the North Valley. Mostly locals ate there, but even the North Valley yuppies stopped by to eat Mexican food. A few people even wandered down from the Northeast Heights, Anglos who had learned to love Mexican food. They came to the valley if they thought a place was safe, Sonny knew, but tonight the North Valley was not a safe place. Tonight those who had inscribed the Zia sign around Gloria's navel roamed the dark streets of the valley.

He got out of the truck slowly and entered the restaurant. A soft voice called his name, a hand reached out to take his. He turned to face Rita and smiled. Her love was the medicine he needed tonight.

"Querida." He smiled and kissed her.

"I'm sorry, I'm really sorry. I know she meant a lot to you." Rita embraced him, felt the tremor in his body. "Ven," she said, and led him to the table that was always reserved for him. "I tried calling you after the news came on the radio. I've been worried about you."

"Sorry, I should have called you here," Sonny apologized as he slipped into a chair. He felt exhausted. Cold perspiration covered his forehead. The air conditioner, which on any other hot afternoon made the café a welcome haven, now made him shiver.

"It's terrible, Sonny, terrible. She was a good woman." She paused and looked at him. He looked drawn and pale. "Por qué?" Rita asked. "Why her?"

"No sé," he answered. He didn't know.

He held her hands and knew he was lucky to have her. Her black hair cascaded over her shoulders, her dark eyes shone with warmth.

Tonight she wore a bright fiesta skirt and a white blouse that revealed her soft, tanned shoulders, a tan that came from working in her garden. Her eyes were his mirror, and just now their concern reflected his distress.

She handed him a glass of water. "Drink." She sensed what he had gone through.

"Have you eaten?" she asked.

He shook his head.

She snapped her fingers and a waitress nodded; Sonny's special plate would be served in minutes. Rita got up and brought him a beer, then she sat across from him and held his hands. He had to talk about it.

"It was on the news," she said. "Everybody's talking about it. Why would they kill her? She was always helping people, and they killed her. It can happen to anyone," she said, and looked out the window at the ebb and flow on the street. "One never knows."

Sonny nodded in agreement. "La vida no vale nada, as the song says."

He sipped the cold beer. He hadn't had anything to drink all day, he remembered. He looked at Rita. Yes, death could happen to anyone, anytime, he admitted, and with that he could began to tell her the story, right up to the map on the wall and the connection he felt the case might have with the recent cattle mutilation at La Cueva. He told her about Raven and about the police chief's cover-up of the Glass case, and she listened attentively.

His hot meal was served, a large platter of the best Mexican food in town. As he ate, he talked, and the hunger to repeat each incident of the day was as voracious as his appetite. He scooped up the beans and red chile with the tortillas and tore hungrily into the rich chunks of carne adovada, the delicate pieces of pork marinated in red chile.

He talked compulsively, recalling each detail while attacking the enchiladas with his fork. The corn tortillas laden with cheese and chile and tender chicken disappeared as he talked. He splashed red chile on the rice and on the refried beans, and he tore apart more tortillas to scoop up the food. He drank another beer and ate until he could eat no more.

He ate to cover the fear he felt, but it did no good. Gloria's image would not let him rest. When he turned to look outside, her pale, naked body was reflected in the window.

"Qué pasa?" Rita asked, placing her hand on his.

"Nada. I'm okay. Good food, amor."

He smiled. He had finished eating, he felt better. He was trying to feel better, to be in control of himself. He prided himself for being in control, but Gloria's death had thrown him for a loop. Act normal, he kept telling himself. Hell, Bisabuelo Baca held off a gang of bad-ass Texan cowboys, this you can handle.

"Panza llena, corazón contento," he said, and wiped the sweat from his forehead. He felt warm now, better. He blew his nose into the paper napkin. "God, that chile was good."

Good enough to clean away the bad spirits, he thought. Rita's meals always made him feel better; just looking at her made him feel better. As he calmed down, he caught a whiff of the perfume scent in the air.

"What's that?" he sniffed.

"What?"

"Perfume. Something sweet. . . ."

"You noticed," Rita said, and extended her arm for him to smell her wrist. "It's cheap, but I liked it," she said. "Rosie Abeyta came by. She works so hard selling this stuff, I can never say no."

A frown crossed his face. The scent of the perfume awakened the image of Gloria. A nauseating, burning acid in his stomach made Sonny wince.

"Eau de Lila," she said.

"Lilac," he groaned, and jumped to his feet, knocking over the chair. He rushed out the back door into the alley. He reached the large trash container in time to lean over and spill the contents of his stomach. Everything came out, burning his esophagus and his sinuses, making his nose water.

Rita was right behind him. "Sonny, Sonny, amor." She massaged his shoulders with her strong hands. "Qué pasa? Qué pasa?"

He took out his handkerchief and wiped his eyes and mouth. "Sorry," he said through watering eyes.

"Are you sick?"

"They scented the water they used on Gloria with a lilac perfume," he said.

"Oh, shit," she cursed, and led him back inside. "I'll wash it off. That big meal didn't help. You need something simple, tea, and rest. . . ."

She made him sit, quickly had the table cleared and a pot of her yerba buena tea served. She went to the bathroom, washed off the perfume, and returned to find him sipping tea. His color was returning.

"Sorry about that." He grinned.

She put honey in his tea. "You need the energy."

"I feel like a sissy," he said, and looked around, feeling self-conscious.

"Susto," Rita said.

He looked at her. He remembered the pit bull of long ago, and the old woman who cured him. "Susto," she had told his mother. He and his brother had been frightened, shocked.

"What do you mean?"

"You were at her deathbed. Sometimes the soul is in the room. Her death was so horrible, there was no priest or curandera to help."

"Help?"

"When the soul is leaving the body . . . if it doesn't want to leave, it can get into someone who is near."

He looked at her. Rita knew the old traditional world of the Nuevo Mexicanos. For most common ailments she had her own house remedies, herbs and unguents. She didn't need Freud, she knew the symbols in dreams, and she knew how the people of the valley had used folk psychiatry for centuries. She had grown up in the tradition of the last curanderas who practiced in the valley. She had learned not only the remedies, she also had the gift of seeing into the soul. But this was too much, suggesting something of Gloria's soul had gotten into him.

"Got into me?"

She held his hands in hers. "That's what susto is."

"I loved her," Sonny whispered.

Rita nodded, squeezed his hands.

He looked into her eyes and felt her warmth. The coldness he felt was his soul feeling the horror of Gloria's death.

He had believed in evil since he was a kid. His mother took him and his brother to church. Sometimes when they played along the riverbank, he felt something unexplainable in the darkness of the bosque. La Llorona, the kids said, the weeping woman who haunted their late-night ventures.

He was a sophomore in high school when his father died, a victim of the cancer Sonny was sure was caused by the chemicals that had gotten into the groundwater of the valley, the nitrates and PCPs seeping down from the labs and the air force base into the water table. The oil companies had storage facilities in the area, and over the years oil and gas had spilled into the land. The earth was poisoned.

He had turned to Gloria for solace. After his father died, she was the only one he could talk to.

"There's something I have to tell you," Sonny said to Rita. Something he'd been wanting to tell her for a long time, but the moment was never right. Now he had to unburden the secret.

She waited.

"It was senior week, that last week of classes. We were all running around like crazy, partying, raising hell. I got wrapped up in it, got crazy as anyone else. Then Gloria called. She wanted me to come over that night. I skipped a party and went. . . . She was dressed up like she was going out. Really dolled up. I don't think I'd ever seen her more beautiful. 'I dressed for you,' she said. She wanted to be part of my graduation. I remember, she had lighted candles. That was the only light in her apartment. . . ."

He paused. "Go on," Rita said.

"She gave me presents, shirts, ties, belts, all sorts of things. Expensive stuff. We drank champagne and she made me open every gift. Like Christmas, she kept saying. Then we danced. She wanted to dance with me, she said, just that one night, then she would give me back to my friends. We had never danced like that before. Then she kissed me, and I realized all those times we were together, we wanted each other. We made love. It was the first time I made love to a woman."

He paused, then continued. "It was her gift to me. She knew I'd never had a woman. Holding her, being with her that night, it's something I can't describe. They say a man finds himself in a woman, becomes a man, and it's true. I felt the love of a woman for the first time. . . . That's what she gave me. Then she left. A few days later I got her note. She was in LA. I think it had something to do with that night. She knew we couldn't be lovers. We were cousins. I didn't care, I was ready to take the world apart for her. But she was gone. When she came back years later, she kept her distance. We both kept our distance. I could never give her what she gave me. . . . Now the only thing I can do is find whoever killed her."

He looked at Rita. Something in her eyes told him she understood. He had told her all about Angie, but never spoke much about Gloria. Now she squeezed his hands.

"I'll help," she whispered.

"You're too good," he said.

"And you need to rest," she replied, and rose. "Take some of this tea with you." She went to the kitchen for a thermos, poured some tea in it, and packed some tortillas and cookies. "Sip a little tea and try to nibble. You need something in your stomach."

"What would I do without you?" He embraced and kissed her.

"You would probably get in even more trouble," she answered, smiling. "Call me."

"I will." He kissed her again and went out the door into the fresh air that was finally seeping into the valley. He felt better. The tea and Rita's understanding were good. He remembered they had made plans to go out tonight, and he almost turned back to apologize. No, he thought, she understands.

He drove home on Fourth Street and turned on the dirt road that was La Paz Lane. The quiet of the evening had settled over the old farming community. People sat out on their porches. It was a hot night, and the coolness that came from the acequias and the irrigated alfalfa fields was refreshing. The hum of the cicadas droned in the twilight.

He was not surprised to see don Eliseo sitting in a rocking chair under the tree. He had a small fire burning, embers in which he burned dry cow dung. The smoke kept away the mosquitoes.

The old alamo still stood; they hadn't been able to bring it down. They had made a few cuts around the base of the tree, like beavers, but the tree had proved too tough. Chips of bark lay scattered on the ground.

Sonny parked his truck and got out. The steady call of the cicadas filled the descending evening. It was a pleasant sound, an integral part of summer. He walked over to the old man and sat down by him.

"Cómo 'stás, Sonny?" don Eliseo said. He was looking across his cornfield. Above them a sliver of the last-quarter moon, the discarded cut nail of an old bruja, shone weakly in the dull sky.

Sonny sighed and sat in the wooden chair next to don Eliseo. He breathed deep the cool air, listened to the grillos singing. Around them the last of the swallows searched for insects in a dance, then came the darting bats.

Don Eliseo rolled a cigarette while Sonny opened the thermos and poured a cup of steaming tea for the old man. "My wife," don Eliseo said, "may her soul rest in peace, used to sit here and watch the moon come over the mountain. I used to roll her marijuana cigarettes. For her arthritis. I always had a plant or two growing in the garden. God gave us the plants to eat and use for medicine, but now they got a law against them." He shook his head.

He handed Sonny the cigarette he had just rolled and began another. They sat in silence and smoked.

"On a hot day like today, you can hear the corn grow," don Eliseo liked to say. His cornfield was lush and green, three feet high, and yes, the plants groaned as they curled in for the night to sleep.

Finally don Eliseo spoke. "I feel like that old tree, Sonny. Dry, but still alive. The boys couldn't do it, Sonny. I don't blame them. Kids. They don't know the land and trees anymore." He slurped the hot tea.

Then Sonny slowly opened up and told the old man about the murder.

"Madre de Dios," don Eliseo said, making the sign of the cross when Sonny finished. "It's the work of the diablo."

"It's not the devil," Sonny said, "it's crazy people."

Don Eliseo sighed. "When I was a kid, they told the story of el hombre dorado, the man made of gold. A long time ago, the people said, he came up the Río Grande looking for the fountain of youth, just like the old Españoles. He was a strange man, burning with the desire to find the fountain of youth. The man looked in all the pueblos, he talked to the medicine man, to the old men. They all tried to tell him, there is no fountain of youth. Life and death are part of the natural cycle. The cycle of our lives is like the cycle of the seasons. Death must come. To seek eternal youth is to seek that which is not natural.

"They tried to warn him. Don't look for eternal youth. Accept nature. Evil people will come and promise you immortality, but in turn they will take your soul. 'I don't believe in witches,' the man said, and continued his search. He was possessed by his desire. And so evil witches came out of the darkness. 'We will give you immortality,' they said, 'if you give us your soul in return.' That is real evil, when someone wants to steal your soul," don Eliseo whispered, and paused to sip his tea.

Sonny listened intently.

"A man without a soul cannot live. Oh, you can exist, but you cannot live. Once the soul is captured and taken away by those who wish you evil, you're lost. The battle of good and evil is always for the soul. So the brujas promised the man what he wanted. They brought him gold. More gold than he had ever seen. Take this gold, they said. Gold will give you eternal youth. With this gold you can buy immortality. The man agreed. With enough gold I can live forever, he thought. He didn't know he had lost his soul. He belonged to them.

"They coated his body with gold. That's how he become el hombre dorado. All the people could see him coming, he was shining in the sun. But they stayed away from him. They knew he had no soul. That man still wanders the valley of the Río Grande, they say. Searching for his soul. Now there are many like him. They don't want to plant and wait for the harvest of the earth, they think gold can buy everything. But it's an illusion, Sonny. When you are enclosed in the gold, it's like being in a shell. Inside it's dark. The bad brujos block the light of los Señores y las Señoras de la Luz, they take the light which is the soul. It is the work of the devil."

Don Eliseo paused. Something in the cornfield moved, a swirl that danced among the corn plants, and for a moment the shrill continuous hum of the cicadas ceased. A breeze stirred.

"And me?" Sonny asked.

"It was evil that killed your prima. If these evil people think you're getting in their way, they will go after you. They will offer you things, they will mislead you, put false clues in your path, send you bad dreams, try to cripple your soul. They're dangerous, Sonny. Those who do this evil have been in the world a long time."

Sonny shivered and drank of the tea. "Maybe I can help with the tree," he said, and reached out and touched the scar on the tree. There was wet sap where the saw had cut into the bark.

"No, I'm going to leave it," don Eliseo said. "I was sitting here enjoying the fresco, and I fell asleep. I had a dream: when the tree dies, I die. So let it die a natural death. It's not the time."

Good, Sonny thought. The trees were the ancestors of the valley, just like don Eliseo. In May the female cottonwoods were thick with the clusters of green pods, and in June the tetones ripened and exploded with cotton. Each little flower of cotton held a tiny seed, the possibility of a new tree.

Even now, the cotton from the trees along the acequia was floating in the air. As sure as the seasons renewed themselves, the cotton from the trees came like snow each June.

When he was a kid, Sonny and his friends gathered the tetones and pelted each other. They used popsicle sticks to fling the stinging pods. It was a wonder they hadn't blinded someone. In spring the teachers at school prayed for the tetone season to pass, and prayed for school to end. When it did, the kids exchanged the school playground for the river, where they swam all summer. The green tetones exploding into cotton marked the beginning of summer, and the swimming season.

Sonny felt an itch; unconsciously he rubbed his stomach, around his navel.

Once, when he was seven, he had come unexpectedly on his mother as she stepped from the shower. She had covered her breasts and sex with the towel and stepped back into the shower, but not before he saw the ripeness of her breasts and the mound of her stomach, the small pit of her ombligo. He was not yet intrigued by the overwhelming questions that would come to him and his friends in the next few years regarding the sex of women, but he remembered her beauty. He dreamed of reaching out and touching her, but even as a child he sensed the inviolate mystery of her stomach, her womb. To touch his mother's belly would be a violation.

Don Eliseo put another piece of dry cow dung on the coals of the fire.

"They scratched a Zia sign around her ombligo," Sonny said, "the sign of the sun."

"Dios mío," don Eliseo said. "They defile everything. The sign of the sun is sacred. The sun gives us life, not death. Only brujos would put that sign of life on a dead woman's stomach."

Sonny shrugged.

"Concha and Toto found the place where we saw the light a week ago. We went to look at it and found feathers around the burn. Four black feathers. Like the feathers of the crows that come in the winter to roost in the alamos along the river. There's bad things happening, Sonny. Evil people doing these cere-monies. They don't use the feathers of the eagle to send prayers to the sun, they use the black feathers of death. Be careful with those feathers, Sonny. They can bring death. These people don't want their evil known, so they will leave things for you to find, false signs to lead you astray, warnings to frighten you away."

"They know about me?"

"Oh, yes."

"How?"

"Because every generation repeats the struggle between good and evil. You are a good man, Sonny. What gathers around you is destined to be. The time is changing, new ways come to the world, and those who do evil multiply."

Sonny shrugged. Sometimes he didn't understand the old man.

"In the old days," don Eliseo continued, "we called them bru-jas. Men and women who did black magic, fornicated with goats, prayed the Black Mass. Ah, that's what the people said. They are really people who have destruction in their hearts. Things don't change. Now maybe they drive to work in fancy cars, wear nice clothes. They work all over the city. The surface changes, Sonny, underneath the evil intent remains."

He paused. He was looking in the flickering tongues of the

fire, into the embers, as if reading Sonny's fortune. He was so still Sonny thought the old man had fallen asleep.

"I'd better get some sleep," Sonny said.

"Yes. Get some rest. Cuidao."

"Gracias." Sonny turned and placed his hand on the old man's shoulder. "I'll be careful."

He walked across the street to his little house. A couple of night crickets had crawled through the torn screen of his kitchen window; now they chirped shrilly at each other. A song of love in the dark. Sonny smiled. It was good luck to have grillos in the house, his father used to say. A house that has grillos singing doesn't have black widow spiders lurking in dark corners. When he turned on the light, the grillos grew still.

The house was stifling hot. He had forgotten to turn on the swamp cooler. He opened all the windows and doors, then went into the kitchen to listen to the messages on his answering machine. Rita had called three times. She must have started calling as soon as the news flashed on TV. An old rodeo friend from Mountainair had called to tell him he was on his way to Vegas, he had two women with him and a tankful of gas in a 1980 Cadillac he just bought: would Sonny like to go?

His mother's message was also engraved on the squeaky tape. "Sonny," she cried, "Oh, mi hijo. . . ." She sobbed. "Delfina just called. Gloria's dead." Then a moment of sobs. Sonny felt the shock again, as if just hearing the news for the first time. "I can't believe it. Who? Who would do such a thing? I tried to call you . . . I called Armando. I tried to call Mr. Dominic, but I couldn't get through. Ay, hijo, cuídate. I love you. Call me."

She must have called right as I was picking up tía, Sonny thought.

The next message was a muffled voice he didn't recognize. "Stay away or you will die! Stay away!"

Who? Sonny wondered.

At the end of the tape, Howard. "Found something. Give me a call."

He dialed Howard's number.

"Sonny, glad you called. Just got the autopsy report. She wasn't raped."

"Yeah, I talked to Garcia."

"I smell something fishy."

"Qué?"

"The autopsy report," Howard answered, smacked his lips. "Excuse my chewing, but my cousin just dropped off a bucket of his famous barbecued ribs. You called just as I was getting started."

"What about the autopsy?"

"I'll know more on Monday, but an intern did it. My hunch is Dominic called the MI and asked for a specific doctor to do the autopsy—"

"You still think that she was pregnant?"

"Maybe."

"Come on, Howard, why would they rig the autopsy?"

"Just a hunch."

"Why think so wild?"

"What if Gloria was pregnant, and what if there was a way to tell it wasn't Dominic's. . . ."

"Oh, shit," Sonny groaned.

"Anyway, enough theory. We found some tire tracks in the ditch road behind the house. Something else. I found an earring. A little, handmade earring made of copper. It's in the form of the Zia sign. And there's a feather dangling from it—"

"A black feather like from a crow," Sonny interjected.

It was Howard's turn to pause. "Yeah."

Sonny scratched his stomach. The crickets in the kitchen were chirping again.

"It bothers me," Howard continued. "These people were too careful, they couldn't have overlooked something like this. It had to be planted, but why? Off the record, maybe it was even the cops who put it there, maybe it gives them some way to close this case quickly."

They will leave clues to mislead you, don Eliseo had said. Sonny pushed the kitchen window curtains aside. The old man was sitting by the tree. He would sit there late into the night, perhaps his friends doña Concha and don Toto would drop by to visit, and they would sip wine and tell stories. They would talk about the murder of Gloria Dominic and the bad things that were coming to their valley.

"Someone's trying to lead us along a false path," Sonny said quietly.

"Yeah."

"Thanks, Howard. Good night."

"Buenas noches."

7

Sonny flipped on his tape player and poured himself another cup of tea. He opened the cupboard where he kept a bottle of bourbon, and poured a shot into the tea. Then he sat back and listened to the romantic strains of the Juan Arriaga symphony. The melody floated out the window into the summer night. He had been listening to the Spanish composer all week.

Glancing out the window, Sonny saw don Eliseo still sitting under the protective branches of the tree. He felt happy the tree would stay. A few weeks ago a young constable had tagged the tree and declared it a public nuisance. The tree was dead, it was going to fall, he said, and it might hurt someone. A windstorm could bring down the dry branches and endanger passersby. Don Eliseo insisted the tree was alive, it was just resting. The dry, dark buds, which clung like brittle cockroaches on the branches, would bloom, leaves would come, the old man said. Just wait.

"You cut it or we cut it," the young deputy threatened, "and if we cut it, we send you the bill."

Don Eliseo, who had lived in the valley all his eighty years, chased the young man out of his yard.

"Qué sabes tú?" he shouted. "Nada! The roots are alive! You don't bury somebody just because they got a weak heart, do you? Pendejo! It's going to get green, you watch!"

"It's June!" the deputy shouted as he drove away. "Look!" He pointed around to the other cottonwoods along the irrigation ditch. They were green and glistening, the tetóne pods were ripe. The grapelike clusters were already bursting, letting loose the cotton that would drift for weeks on the summer breeze, catching on the bushes, powdering patios, roads, everything. Cotton from the female cottonwoods, the alamos of the river, the unofficial tree of the city.

"Maybe the pendejo was right," don Eliseo later told Sonny. "The tree is like me, bien seco. Time to cut it down and let it rest. You get old, the juices stop flowing. El Coco lives in the tree, Sonny, but even El Coco gets tired of living."

"El Coco?"

"Sure, the Cucúi. A tree spirit. Lives in the bosque of the river. Each tree has a spirit, mi hijo. . . ."

For the old man everything had a spirit. Tree, corn, stone, rain, clay. Everything was alive.

Since he had moved into the small rental across the street from don Eliseo's house, Sonny had watched as more and more of the old cottonwoods of the North Valley were cut down for new housing developments. Now don Eliseo's old tree had decided to die. Maybe it was sadness killing the tree, sadness as huge expensive homes covered the once fertile fields of Ranchitos.

"I grew up under this tree," don Eliseo sighed. "It's been in the family since my family settled here in Ranchitos. Sanamagon, there's been Romeros here since before the Indians kicked out all the Españoles in 1680. Before Alburquerque was made a villa in 1706, the Romeros were already raising corn here. There were trees, an alameda of alamos. The raices, Sonny, beneath the earth the roots of all these trees stretch far, connecting to other trees, until the entire valley is connected. You can't kill a tree and not kill the past. The trees are like the gente of the valley, sooner or later we're all related. Primos, Sonny, primos from the first people who came to the valley. Our raices stretch into the past. Our seeds are like the cotton of the trees, carried by the wind. . . ."

The old man grew passionate as he told his story. "The Indians from Sandia used to live here. Under this earth lie the adobes and stones of their old pueblos, the bones of their ancestors, the Tiguex. My father, and my grandfather before him, found bones when they plowed. Bones we took to our vecinos in the pueblo to bury again. Not put in the goddamned museum like the gringo antro-poligies. Our ancestors were real people, and they sat here and talked about their familias and planting corn and about the acequias. This tree was giving shade when the railroad first came to Alburquerque. How can I cut down my history?"

Sonny had been happy earlier in the spring when don Eliseo had pointed at one of the topmost branches where a few buds appeared ready to burst into leaf. "It's still got juice!" he'd said, smiling. "Give it time."

But there had been only a few spring rains in May, and now the relentless heat of early June scorched the valley. The buds seemed to wither; there were no leaves. Don Eliseo grew despondent. Then a spring windstorm knocked down a large branch on the north side, proving the village constable right.

Don Eliseo was one of the few old-timers who still planted an acre of corn on his land. Mixed in the corn were calabacitas, beans, watermelon, pumpkins. By July the entire neighborhood would be eating elotes, the fresh ears of green corn on the cob, and tender squash. Don Eliseo would set up a small stand in front of his house: Organic Vegetables. The new Anglos of the North Valley flocked to buy them.

"It's in my blood," the old man said, "The seeds I plant have been in this valley since before the Españoles came. It's Indian corn, Sonny, and it's going to be around long after all the new hybrids are gone."

Sonny looked out the window across the field of young plants that glistened in the moonlight. Don Eliseo was now standing in the middle of the field, listening to the heartbeat of the earth.

"My ancestors and then my father farmed this land," don Eliseo liked to say as he pointed proudly at his field of corn. "Beans, corn, calabacitas, and chile, that's all we need to survive," he said, then added, "but the old people are nearly gone, sold their farms to the ricos."

His voice was always sad when he spoke of the large estates that had taken the farming land of the valley.

"Matanzas were held under this tree, and the blood of the slaughtered animals fed the roots. That's why it grew so big and fat, and why it has lasted so long. They hanged a man here, from that branch." He pointed up. "In my grandfather's time a man murdered an Indian from Sandia Pueblo, and the sheriff got a posse together and found the man. They hanged him from that branch. My wife, que descanse en paz, and I would sit here in the summers and visit with our neighbors. In the fall we made the ristras de chile. We peeled and sliced apples, dried them on the roof, that's how we did it."

"Ah, la vida," Sonny whispered, and sipped the spiked tea. The combination helped calm his stomach. He thought of Gloria, how her life had been ended so suddenly, and he wondered if he was wasting his own life.

After he finished college, he had taught at Valley High School a couple of years, but he found the work confining and a lot of the kids not interested in learning. Then he hooked up with Manuel Lopez, a private investigator whose specialty was in finding missing persons. Manuel worked out of his home in the

North Valley, doing mostly insurance cases, but that same summer Manuel took Sonny into Chihuahua on a ransom case.

Two Mexicanos had kidnapped the young wife of a big car dealer in town, and the local cops had no leads. Manuel's lead came from the Mexicanos in the barrio. They whispered they had known the two desperate men who kidnapped the woman, and following the leads, Manuel took Sonny with him into Mexico. Like a hounddog, Manuel Lopez followed the men into the Chihuahua Mountains, found the place where they were hiding the woman, and rescued her in the middle of night.

There was a brief exchange of gunfire. The kidnappers, thinking they were tangling with Mexican federales, fled. The only person who had fired at them was Manuel.

The media had made a big deal out of the incident. Manuel's picture was splashed all over Mexican and New Mexican newspapers. Right behind him appeared Sonny and the car dealer's wife. The Mexican government had protested. He and Sonny had grabbed the woman and spirited her back across the border at Juárez. Her husband had paid them enough for Sonny to live a year, which he stretched to two.

Even after Manuel died a couple of years ago, Sonny's fantasies of future cases continued, but the recent work hadn't turned out to be as exciting. He didn't especially like looking for those who skipped out on banks or credit card companies, and even missing persons could be dull. Husbands escaping from the responsibilities of marriage; wives cutting loose like Thelma and Louise. Sometimes he hated to bring them back. People were looking for freedom, a breath of fresh air.

He wasn't the only one less than thrilled with his occupation.

"You're not getting any younger," his mother, like Rita, reminded him. "What are you going to do? Look for missing persons all your life? You have a college degree. Go back to teaching. At least you get a regular salary."

"Not much," Sonny replied.

"You've got your Bisabuelo's blood," she concluded, sighing.

Yes, he admitted, he was haunted by the stories of his great grandfather, haunted by the pistol he carried in his truck. In 1910, when he was in his early thirties, Elfego Baca had moved to Alburquerque to practice law and hire himself out as a private detective. The old-timers said he went around town dressed in a flowing cape, a mean-looking bodyguard at his side.

There was something of the showman in el Bisabuelo. He handed out business cards that read "Elfego Baca, Attorney at Law, Fees Moderate" on one side, and on the flip side "Private Detective: Divorce Investigations Our Speciality, Discreet Shadowing Done." Sonny had printed similar cards and kept them in his wallet just for fun.

He had read the history of Elfego Baca, the exciting days of the 1880s when the gringos were building New Town around the railroad station. The Mexicanos still lived over in Old Town, la Plaza Vieja, or along the north and south valley, where they farmed. It was a time of great change, great adventure.

"Damn city ought to build a statue to him," Sonny mused. Damn city didn't know its own heroes.

Ah, those were the days. Fighting it out with outlaws was more interesting than taking pictures of indiscreet husbands running around. Or indiscreet wives.

He looked out his kitchen window again. Don Eliseo had returned to put a piece of wood in the fire. He was waiting for his friends.

Don Eliseo is like one of the old, gnarled alamos of the river, Sonny thought. Rita is like the purple budding tamarisk, the salt cedar that grows along the river arroyos. Passionate, a lovely mauve in flower, with straight, burnt-red branches.

I need to be more like a tree, less like a tumbleweed, Sonny thought. But what tree?

Sonny sipped the last of Rita's tea and stared out the open window. Across the way he saw a customized '57 Chevrolet cruise to a stop in front of don Eliseo's place. Two shadows disembarked, two figures of the night who had crossed the River

Styx to come to visit don Eliseo. Sonny felt his heart quicken; he leaned forward.

"Eliseo? 'Stas ahí?" a hoarse voice called.

"Dónde a d'estar?" don Eliseo called from beside the glowing embers of his fire. The figures approached him. It was don Toto and doña Concha, don Eliseo's North Valley compadre and comadre. Sonny smiled and relaxed.

The old-timers on North Fourth called don Toto "El Chuco," because even though he was eighty, he still dressed like an old pachuco from the forties. He kept his double-soled shoes spit-shined, he wore his pants tapered at the ankles and slung low around his thin waist. He drank and danced in the North Fourth bars every Saturday night.

"La movida chueca," he said with a grin. He was once the terror of the gray-haired bingo ladies who gathered to play bingo on Tuesday afternoons at Our Lady of Sorrows, until Father Joe, who was no angel himself, had ruled the bingo game off limits to don Toto.

"Until you learn to behave yourself," Father Joe had pronounced the day he kicked don Toto out.

Don Toto had propositioned one of the younger ladies, seventy-year-old la Suzie, who powdered her face and added a spot of bright rouge and lipstick. She wore a blond beehive wig, which contrasted with her very dark complexion. She liked to swing her hips when she paraded up and down the aisles selling bingo cards. Don Toto had pinched her rear.

"Let me swing on your swing." Don Toto grinned. La Suzie liked the compliment, but her comadre Celestina, who was a real saint, reported don Toto to the priest. Some of the other ladies felt she was jealous because Toto hadn't propositioned her.

"Life's too short to behave, padre," don Toto said in parting and gunned his Chevy down Fourth to the nearest cantina. "Once a lover, always a lover," don Toto rasped as he bought drinks for all the women. He had no preferences, he chased them all.

"You and me are brothers, ese," he once confided in Sonny while they were having a beer, "we like las mamasotas. You're young, you can still get it up. Me, I modify!" He slapped his leg and laughed until he cried. "Modify! Get it!" And he laughed and coughed and lit a fresh cigarette. "I'm a modified lowrider!"

Doña Concha was the best-known wheeler-dealer on North Fourth. She'd had a small home near the acequia, an adobe that had been in the family for years, the remnants of large acreage her family once owned. Her husband had died years ago, but not before a prolonged illness siphoned off their savings. Concha couldn't pay the property taxes.

"That's how they get us, honey," she explained, "raise the taxes and make us sell. Look at Santa Fe. Good-bye to los pobres. Now it's the same here." She had to sell the house and most of the land to pay the bills. She kept the chicken coop in the back, which she converted into a very comfortable small place for herself.

"It's all I need, honey. No le pido nada a nadie. I'm independent. Let my kids do what they want, I got a life of my own."

She was the most independent Chicana in the North Valley, totally free to roam the streets, visit friends, and she was happy. She was nearsighted and wore thick glasses, and she bumped into things. She had been run into twice by a car while crossing the busy street, and when asked about it, she would smile and say, "The third time's the charm, honey. Cuando te toca, te toca."

She walked with a cane, which she used to swat mean Fourth Street dogs and naughty boys. She had outlived don Toto's and don Eliseo's wives, and now she had them to herself. She touched peroxide to her gray hair to give it a slash of red, which turned burnt orange. She wore falsies, cotton-laden bras that continually fell to her waist and which she continually pushed back into place. "If you got it, flaunt it" was her favorite saying.

"Party time," Sonny heard don Toto say as they pulled up chairs next to don Eliseo.

"Ya era tiempo," don Eliseo laughed.

Sonny smiled. They would sit and sip wine and tell stories in the coolness of the summer night. He glanced at his watch. It was still early, and he knew he couldn't sleep. His thoughts were swarming with images of the cattle mutilation, the mysterious Raven, and the Zia-shaped mountain compound where he apparently kept four wives.

But Sonny knew he had spent the day without really probing the most disturbing question: Frank Dominic.

He rose, took a quick shower, put on a clean pair of pants and a shirt, and went out.

"Sonny, come on over, honey," la Concha called. She was always happy to see him. Hitting eighty, she still dolled up on Friday nights to do the North Fourth bars with don Toto.

"Buenas noches," Sonny called back. "Can't. Got some business."

"Girlie business," la Concha called back. "I wish I was on your list, honey."

"You are, Concha," Sonny called as he got into his truck. "I think of you every day. Like my grandma."

"Grandma!" she complained. "Don't be so cabrón."

"Cuidao con las brujas," don Eliseo called as Sonny drove away.

8

Sonny drove into a North Val-
ley night filled with the fragrance of alfalfa fields being watered,
a release from the heat of the day. He drove across to Rio Grande
Boulevard and to Dominic's place. Dominic's Cadillac and BMW
sat in the gravel driveway next to a red Corvette.

Looks like the man's home, Sonny thought. And he's got company. Not a good time to knock.

Sonny cruised by slowly, checking to see if the cops were
watching the place, but no, Garcia's boys didn't apparently have
a stakeout.

"Garcia doesn't think Frank's a suspect," Sonny muttered as he
parked his truck a few blocks away and cut across a neighbor's
alfalfa field toward the house.

A horse whinnied in the dark, a dog barked; otherwise the
night was peaceful, filled only with the drone of the cicadas in

the trees. A Russian olive hedge covered his approach. A dim light shone through the back patio doors. Yes, the man's home, Sonny thought, and prayed Dominic hadn't already replaced his two Dobermans.

He made his way around the back, crouched, and slipped toward the large plate-glass patio doors. He peered into the dimly lighted room. Dominic appeared to be alone, sitting at his desk; the only light in the room was a desk lamp. Beside the desk sat a small suitcase. Dominic was on the phone, smiling as he talked. The sliding door was partly open; Sonny strained to hear.

Fucking cops aren't watching the place, he thought, and wondered if they had bothered getting copies of the telephone records. Who did Gloria talk to the few days before her death? Who did Frank talk with? Was Garcia, despite what he claimed, treating Dominic with kid gloves?

Sonny heard a car on the graveled front drive, then saw the glare of the car lights on nearby trees as it turned from the street into the driveway, the crunch of tires, then the slamming shut of a car door.

The ring of the doorbell made Dominic frown. He hung up the phone and disappeared into the dark foyer. Sonny jumped forward, pushed the open door, and entered. If he was going to eavesdrop, he might as well go all the way. He could hear the sound of loud voices in the entryway.

"We have nothing to talk about!" Dominic's voice rose, the irritation clear.

"We have to talk," the other voice insisted. Calmer, more measured.

A man's voice, Sonny thought, and glanced quickly around the room. The best place to hide was behind the large wall tapestry of the coat of arms of the duke of Alburquerque, a white oak on a dark crimson field. Dominic's crest. I feel like Polonius in *Hamlet,* Sonny thought as he slipped behind the handwoven tapestry. Hope I don't get stabbed.

"Didn't you hear me say we have nothing to talk about?"

Dominic said, then a muffled response to which Dominic answered, "Very well, come in."

"It is only proper, that I come to pay my respects," the second man began as the two moved into the room.

Sonny peeked around the tapestry's edge and got a glimpse of the handsome Japanese man. Dressed as sharply as Dominic in a three-piece suit, he looked like that Japanese multimillionaire who was trying to build a computer chip plant in Alburquerque. Akira Morino? Yeah, sure as hell, it was Akira Morino. Dominic's arrogant, irritable tone told Sonny the man wasn't welcomed.

"Respects?" Dominic scowled. "You have nerve, Morino."

Why so angry? Sonny thought. In the dim light he could see Morino's face. There was sadness written on the rugged face. Sonny remembered the news articles on the man. He had climbed to the top of the Japanese banking world, then he had gotten into computers. Akira Morino had cornered the market on the new flat liquid-crystal display screens, which, it was said, were going to revolutionize the industry. Computer screens of the future could be hung on a wall like a painting. Sony already had such a screen, but Akira Morino was promising the city fathers that he would bring his plant to Alburquerque. If Sandia Labs and Los Alamos Labs could deliver on the promising concept of "bubble memory," the central processing unit of a small computer could hold thousands of megabytes.

This can happen in Alburquerque, Morino told the papers and the Chamber of Commerce. He wanted to build a computer corridor that would rival California, and rival Intel, which had already poured billions into its Rio Rancho plant west of the city. The Alburquerque políticos and business community were betting Morino could get Japanese backing quickly and compete with Intel.

Now as they stood facing each other, Sonny saw they were an even match. But there was sadness on Morino's face, perhaps grief; there was none on Dominic's.

"I was very fond of Gloria," Morino said, as if apologizing.

"I don't want to hear about that," Dominic snapped. "What is it you really want?"

Fond of Gloria, rang in Sonny's mind. Early on, Dominic had courted Morino's money to finance the canal system he envisioned for downtown Alburquerque, and Morino refused him. Later the papers began to report that Morino was being seen around town with Gloria, accompanying her to social events here and there. Was it more than political maneuvering? Were Morino and Gloria lovers?

"All right," Morino said, "I'll get to the point. I want to know what happened."

Dominic's lips parted in a smirk. "Go to the police; they'll tell you what happened. Now if you'll excuse me . . ." He turned away but Morino grabbed his arm. Dominic spun and twisted his arm free, his face throbbing with anger.

"Don't touch me!" he snarled. He was ready to fight.

"I have been to the police!" Morino shouted back. "Your friend Mr. Garcia won't tell me anything! But you know what happened!"

Dominic drew a deep breath. "What the hell are you getting at!"

"Gloria's death was a tragedy. I have to know the truth. Or there is no rest—"

"No rest." Dominic leered. "Yeah, there's no rest for those who are guilty. You better leave, or I'll call the police."

Morino stared into Dominic's eyes. From where he watched, Sonny could sense the anger. A surge of hate flowed between the two men, a rage about to explode. Then Morino backed off.

"All right," he said, pulling himself away. "I cannot force you. But I'm going to find a way to make you tell the truth!"

"Out!" Dominic shouted, and if Morino had not finally turned and walked away just then, Sonny was sure they would have come to blows.

Sonny heard the front door slam, then the sound of a car driving away. Dominic cursed, then turned to the bar and poured a drink.

Sonny stepped out from behind the tapestry. Might as well stoke the fire while it's hot, he thought.

"Pour one for me," he said softly. Dominic spun around.

"What the hell are you doing here?" he gasped, a scowl crossing his face. Dominic didn't like surprises.

"Looking for Gloria's murderer," Sonny answered, and stepped forward.

"Playing detective! And you dare to break into my home!" Dominic said, and tossed down the brandy. "I don't care if you are Gloria's cousin, you have no right to come in unannounced. Now get the hell out, before I throw you out!"

Dominic was ready to explode, fired up as he had been by Morino. The two faced each other, and Sonny knew he could take Dominic. But he hadn't come to fight. Men like Dominic didn't talk when cornered, they fought. Sonny eased back. Try a soft approach on the sonofabitch, he thought, go slow.

"The door was open, so I walked in. What's there to hide?" Sonny said.

Dominic looked at him, then shook his head. He laughed. "I don't believe it," he said, "two crazies in one night."

"And one suspects you. . . ."

"You heard?"

Sonny shrugged. "A lot of people are going to suspect you," he added.

"Including you?" Dominic laughed.

"Yes."

"Screw you, Baca!"

"Where were you last night?"

"I gave a complete statement to the police this afternoon," Dominic answered, and stepped to the patio door.

"And you think that clears you—"

"Yeah, it clears me!" Dominic shot back. "But it doesn't clear you!"

Sonny took a step back. "What the hell do you mean?"

"Gloria told me about you two. All these years and you carried a flame for her, hated me. Jealousy consumes, Sonny, and it consumed you."

Sonny felt stunned. Gloria had told Frank about them. No, she wouldn't. "You're crazy," he mumbled.

"No, I'm not the crazy one. I've got an alibi. Garcia knows *exactly* where I was last night. But he doesn't know where you were! If he knew about the little fling you had with Gloria, how all these years jealousy has been eating away at you, then he might pull *you* in and ask *you* a few questions!" Dominic laughed and poured another drink. He was playing Sonny like a cat with a mouse.

Sonny clenched his fists, then relaxed. No, the man was insane and he wasn't going to fall for it, but damnit! How did he know about him and Gloria?

"How does Morino fit in?" Sonny asked, taking a deep breath to steady his voice.

"It was in the papers. Everybody knows he wanted a partnership with me. I didn't like his offer, so he started seeing Gloria. He became her, shall we say, escort."

"You were too busy."

"Gloria had a mind of her own," Dominic said, his jaws flexing, as if he was remembering her. "She came and went as she saw fit. I didn't like it—"

"But you were coming and going too," Sonny said.

Dominic forced a smile. "Smart boy, Sonny. But what was happening between me and Gloria has nothing to do with what happened last night."

A door sounded and he paused and glanced at the stairway.

"I can't stay here. Gloria—" he said. "Well, I'm staying with friends," he said, "So goodnight, Sonny," he said, and pointed at the patio door.

Sonny stepped to the door and paused. "Your friend, huh?"

Dominic smiled. "That's right, Sonny. We didn't have a happy marriage, so I had a friend, and Gloria saw Morino. Everything was discreet, until—" He paused. "But that has nothing to do with her death. Go on thinking what you like, just don't come around. Next time I'll call Garcia. Entiendes?"

They were interrupted by someone at the top of the stairs. "Frank?" the woman's voice said, then she came down slowly.

Sonny peered into the shadows, watched the golden-haired beauty descend. A young woman, no older than Sonny, dressed in a red evening gown, high heels, her long, blond hair flowing around her head like a halo.

"Someone here?" she asked, and stepped into the light at the bottom of the stairs.

Dominic's friend, Sonny thought. He recognized her, he knew he had seen her picture in the papers. But he couldn't place her.

"He was just leaving," Dominic said.

"Aren't you going to introduce me?" Sonny said, still trying to place the young woman. She was a beauty all right. The new duquesa for the duke of Alburquerque? Maybe Gloria had simply become too old at forty; she had lost the sheen of youth and Dominic was already working on a new trophy wife.

"Adiós," Dominic said sternly, and Sonny shrugged and stepped out the door. Dominic slammed it shut, locked it, and pulled the curtains.

Sonofabitch! Sonny cursed. Gloria's not even buried and the man's already hopping into bed with the new prize! A friend Garcia knows. Is that why he's buying Dominic's story? And accusing me! Hijo de su chingada madre!

He walked back to his truck in the dark, kicking at the clods of dirt and alfalfa.

Damn, he needed to talk to Rita, but her place was already closed, and feeling the way he felt, he wasn't good company. He stopped by the Fourth Street Cantina, found a quiet, dark booth in the back, and ordered a beer and a shot of bourbon.

He was going to drink until he could cry, somehow get the grief out. He needed to relieve himself of the deep sadness, or the fear he wouldn't admit. He was going to drink until they closed the bar or he got in a fight, anything to let go.

He looked at the full cantina, the booths packed with Friday-night party-goers. At the dance floor in the back, the musicians were ready to start a new set. He ordered another shot of bourbon and downed it, and a third right on top of the one he just had.

Two Mexicanos sat at the bar, nursing their beers and studying the floor for women. Sonny also turned his attention there.

Lord, there were too many good-looking women in the city. The Fourth Street Cantina was packed with women. Young women, middle-aged women, old women, all pickled in the passion of the dry, hot days of June. It was like picking apples: some had slight blemishes, others were perfectly formed, all were sweet to eat.

They had a special beauty, a special flavor, something they got from the Alburquerque water, some said, or from the hot chile that flavored every Mexican meal. Hot, spicy, good-looking ma-masotas, Chicanitas with Indita ancestors and with the spice of life in their blood. Mixed in with them were the Anglo cowgirls of the North Valley, saucy blondes who loved to dance country-western on weekend nights, drink beer, make love, and get home just before Daddy woke up.

The city was alive with women, and summer was the season of love. The wide, expansive sky that stretched from the face of the Sandia Mountains on the east to the rim of Nine-Mile Hill on the west was a blanket of love laid over the valley. When the summer thunderstorms swept across the valley, the energy of nature was unleashed; so was the need of the hot blood to be fulfilled.

Ah, Sonny cursed, and downed his shot of bourbon, I'm in no mood for a woman. Still, the rage he felt inside needed to burst out.

At the other side of the bar sat three cowboys. Two lanky guys and a big heavyset man with heavy, dark eyebrows. The thin men looked vaguely familiar, maybe he had rodeoed with them, maybe one of them was Joe What's-his-name, who ran the feed store up the street. But the big man wore a smirk on his face. He looked around the bar and seemed to sneer at the other patrons. He was built like an ox. He was ugly, Sonny decided.

A few more drinks, Sonny thought, and I'm going to tell him I don't like the way he wears his black hat.

Though he was drinking to forget, the more he drank, the clearer Gloria's image grew. He could smell her perfume, and suddenly the big cowboy with the big hat looked across the room at Sonny.

Who's the little fucker over there? Sonny was sure he had asked his friends.

Sonny stood up. "He sure as hell's looking for a fight," he said.

9

The following morning Sonny slept late. The bourbon with beer chasers from the night before, which normally made him sleep peacefully, hadn't. By the looks of the light glowing in the blinds, it was nearly midday. He pulled the pillow over his head.

The scuffle with the big cowboy hadn't helped anything. He had gone looking for a fight, and when he pushed, the big man pushed him back, right into the arms of Leroy Quintana, the bouncer.

"What the fuck do you think you're doing?" Leroy whispered as he drew Sonny away. Leroy was an old friend of Sonny's. "Go home," he ordered as he helped Sonny out the door. "You know better than to pick a fight!"

Troubled dreams filled Sonny's night, images that didn't make sense when he awoke. In one he saw an infant being born, the umbilical cord tied around the child's neck, the baby hanging and gasping for breath. Then a female figure, large and dark, a fat mamasota with huge breasts. Her gleaming eyes bore into Sonny just before she cut the cord with a sharp instrument. A flint knife. Sonny cried out.

He slipped from one nightmare to another, garbled images of distress. A dark chamber, his muscles taut with pain. He tried to move, but dark hands held him still. He was strapped faceup over a hard, stone bench that cut into his back. It was steaming hot, the stench was overwhelming, flies buzzed around him. Above him Aztec priests chanted in Nahuatl, an offertory. The door of the temple was outlined in light; beyond, he could see the valley of Mexico. Around him moved the dark figures of the priests. Eyes bored into his, a woman. The smell of blood clung to her body as she leaned over Sonny. She was squatting on him? Pissing on him? He felt the warmth of his crotch as she used him. He felt his own release, the slow flow of semen from his spent body, a brief, orgiastic bliss, then the woman held up the obsidian knife, pressed it across his stomach, opening his chest cavity around the rib cage. She reached in and ripped his heart out.

Sonny cried out, but there was no sound in the dark, stifling temple, only the woman holding the beating heart.

She held the heart aloft, offering the hot, steaming blood to the sun. A loud cry rose from the people at the foot of the temple, then men and women dressed as coyotes rushed forward to take the heart. Clan of Coyote. They took Sonny's heart to eat. He was becoming coyote.

The flint knife in the woman's hand dissolved into a steel blade dripping with blood. The coyotes devoured the heart, the blood drained into the earth, then Sonny sprouted wings and flew into the sky.

"Weird," Sonny mumbled as he tossed aside the pillow and blinked. "Where in the hell do those things come from?"

It wasn't good, he thought, analyzing his dreams. He was the baby? Birth meant facing the knife. The first event of life was being severed, torn away from the mother, then the cord was cut away, and life became an acid in which to swim. But there were two cuts. The second was the foreskin of the tip of the penis. Most male children got two cuts, the female only one.

"Not fair," he said.

No wonder we're marked for life. We've just been delivered to the world, and the doctor cuts off the foreskin. What do they do with the little piece of skin? Do we go around looking for it the rest of our lives? Is that part of our restlessness?

But I wasn't circumcised! Why wasn't I? Did la jefita spare me the pain? Told the doctor, leave it alone! You're not cutting anything from my Elfego!

Some of the women he had slept with thought it was a curiosity. Isabela, a young woman from San Antonio who had come to the Santuario de Chimayó on a religious pilgrimage, had run into Sonny right after his divorce. One drink led to another, so she interrupted her pilgrimage. Or she found the holy grail she was seeking. "Que bonito," she whispered as she pulled back the skin. "I've never seen one like this," she said. Her longing look made Sonny shiver.

Sonny blinked, shook his head, and slowly rolled out of bed. He stood up and walked to the phone to check with his mother.

"Hi, jefa, how are you? How's Delfina?"

"Sonny, I'm so glad you called. I stayed with Delfina last night. It's hard for her, but she's strong, very strong. I just got in. I still can't reach Mr. Dominic. We have no idea what the arrangements will be. What can Delfina do?"

"Frank will take care of it—"

"Yes, but when I couldn't reach him, I called the church, and the priest said there is no rosary planned. The same at the mortuary. I don't understand. It's sad. Sonny, I still don't believe it. Max came by to help—"

"Max?" Sonny searched his mind for the right face.

"You remember Max. Anyway, I'm going back to Delfina's. I

want to be with her. Ay, Dios, if we could only plan a rosary, call her friends. I can't get your brother, Mando. Have you spoken to him?"

"No, not yet." He hadn't talked to his brother in weeks.

"Hay que muchacho. I think he's out of town. What about Turco?"

"What about him?"

"Delfina won't call him, but he is familia. Rotten as he is. Shouldn't he be told? Will you talk to him? Gloria *is* his sister. Max is going to call, so I have to go. If I'm not home, I'm with her. . . . Dios te bendiga."

"I'll be over later."

He hung up the phone and felt his left foot tingle. He looked down at his bare feet on the linoleum. Did the tingle mean it was finally going to rain? Would the thin cirrus clouds that swept over the valley in the afternoons finally become the fat cumulus that brought rain?

Images of the nightmare returned. Rita would know what it meant, he thought as he headed for the kitchen. He needed coffee badly. He started the coffeepot and flipped on the radio. KBAD had the best Saturday-morning Mexican music. But not even the lively music helped dispel the images in the nightmare. Was the earth mother who cut out his heart related to the chainsaw vamp? She had cut the umbilical cord and carved the Zia sign on the baby's forehead. Like the old pachucos used to carve small crosses on their foreheads, pricking the skin with a pin and rubbing India ink into the cut; the homemade tattoo remained for life.

His father, Polito, had such a cross on his hand, in the soft cleft between the thumb and the first finger. "After the war there were pachuco gangs in every barrio," he had told Sonny. "What the hell, I was twenty, very macho. I belonged to the Five Points gang. We fought Old Town, Barelas, Martineztown. Those were good days. Good dances, and women. Hijo, the most beautiful women in the world are right here in 'Burque. Don't you forget that. They were coming from all the small towns in those days, looking for work. That's how I found your madre."

Diana. From La Joya. La Joya was a small village at the end of a dirt road south of Belén. Diana Jaramillo, de La Joya, was a beautiful name. A beautiful woman.

Don Eliseo's friend don Toto also had the cross tattoo on his forehead, faded by the years and wrinkles, but there nevertheless. If don Eliseo was a living symbol of the farmer of the valley, don Toto was the urban guerrillero, an old fighter of the streets, whose sign on the forehead meant resistance.

The forties were tough, Sonny thought as he headed for the shower. Usually he sang, but today he couldn't sing. He thought of don Eliseo and the old man's friends. The Second World War had brought change into the Mexicano communities. In LA the pachucos fought the racist navy sailors on the streets. Then and now, life was still not easy for Chicanos. But we learn a lot from the old ones, Sonny thought, we learn to fight back. Like my Bisabuelo, who took no caca from the Texan bullies.

But why these thoughts when he should be concentrating on Gloria's murder?

Nothing is wasted, Rita would say. Every dream is connected to your life and what will become of it. Ah well, he knew he couldn't order his dreams, but Rita was his dream interpreter. She would know.

He dressed and called Rita; her answering machine said, "Sonny, I'm going shopping. Coronado. Don't forget, the symphony pachanga is tonight. I guess it's not canceled, and I guess we're going. I know how you feel, so if you want to cancel, it's fine with me. Cuídate, amor."

He left a message for Rita saying he would pick her up at eight, then stepped out of his house into the dry, hot June heat. In the field of corn he spotted don Eliseo and don Toto. They were hoeing. La Concha stood by the ditch, hoe in hand, turning the water from the acequia down each row of corn. A swinging bag lady who hadn't forgotten how to use the hoe. The viejitos could drink wine all night and still get up with the sun to work.

Damn, Sonny thought, let me grow old like them.

"Buenos días les de Dios," he called a greeting.

"Hey, Sonny! Buenos días! Come and have coffee! Que coffee! Come and hoe!"

They laughed. They liked to tease him. Sonny was one of the few young people who paid attention to them. He sat with them at night and listened to their stories. He sometimes took them to watch the Dukes play, and he'd often drive them to their doctor appointments.

"Can't—I'm on a case!" he called. He got in his truck and drove to Barelas to have breakfast at Jimmy's Place on South Fourth. When Rita wasn't at Rita's Cocina, he liked to drive to Jimmy's, and today it was on the way to his mother's home.

The restaurant served Mexican food, and its specialty was menudo, sheep tripe thoroughly cleaned, cut in small pieces, and cooked overnight with dry posole corn. Served in large, steaming bowls with lots of hot red chile and oregano, the dish was a delicacy. It was the best food for those who woke up crudos, and Sonny still felt the effects of the prior night's bout of drinking.

He recognized the two men sitting at a table by the window. Ben Chavez and Frank McCulloch. Ben was a writer, Frank a well-known artist. They had a club called Hostile Elders, and since their retirement from teaching, they often met at Jimmy's to eat and talk about art, books, and movies. And women.

Sonny had taken a class in writing fiction from Ben Chavez when he was at the university. He stopped to say hello.

"Ah, Sonny." Ben smiled, stood, and shook hands. "Sorry about Gloria. She was a wonderful woman."

"Gracias," Sonny said, accepting the condolences.

"You know Frank."

Sonny said buenos días and shook Frank's hand.

"You taking up writing again yet?" Ben continued. "Took a class with me. About eight years ago, right?"

Sonny nodded. It made him feel good that Chavez would remember.

"You still doing investigation?"

"Yes."

"A writer is like a good detective, always looking for motives." Ben looked at McCulloch, who smiled but appeared unsatisfied with the comparison.

"Writers are pícaros," he replied. "The hell with motives, just write about what smells bad." And with that they launched into an argument about the role of the artist.

"Anyway, good to see you," Sonny said, excusing himself.

"Cuidao," Ben Chavez called in parting.

Sonny sat at a table near the window and ordered a bowl of menudo, which he spiced with diced onions, oregano, and red chile. The message in the dreams haunted him, and so he ate in silence.

As he ate, he glanced out the window at the slow-moving traffic. It was going to be in the nineties today. Hot. Heat rose from the sidewalk and the pavement.

Eating slowly and looking at the bright light, Sonny thought of the leads he had to follow. His "visit" to Dominic had raised more questions than it answered. And Morino. If the man had been seeing Gloria, then he might know something. And then there were the gardener and the housekeeper Garcia mentioned.

But first he had to pay a visit to his mother, find out what was being planned for Gloria.

He sipped the last of his café con crema y azúcar, wrapped the tortilla left on the plate in a napkin and stuck it in his pocket. It was an old habit. Sometimes on the run there was no time to stop even at a 7-Eleven for a sandwich and drink; then even a hard tortilla came in handy.

He paid his check, drove across the Barelas Bridge, and turned south on Isleta Boulevard. Isleta was the highway of the

South Valley, the road that connected the Indian Pueblo with the Hispano and Mexicano land grants that dotted the valley. Los Padillas, Pajarito, La Merced de Atrisco, home of the farmers from Spain and Mexico who had carved out their way of life in the earth of the Río Grande del Norte centuries ago. This was home, his stomping grounds as a youth.

There was a note on his mother's front door: *Sonny, I've gone with Max to see Delfina. Please wait.*

Who in the hell is Max? he wondered again as he let himself into the house. Without his mother the house was silent. The front room was dark, cool. Hand-crocheted doilies sat as ornamental pieces on her chairs and sofa. The large doily that covered the dining room table was her pride. After his father died, Sonny's mother went through a long withdrawal. Being attached to the man was hard on the Mexican woman. When the center fell away, the family hurt, and the woman especially.

Had he been of any help to her during that time? I was too young, Sonny thought. Sixteen. Struggling through high school and all that meant. But, Lord, the death of his father had left a vacuum. I never really helped Mom, he thought, and felt guilty as he walked slowly around the room, touching the things that belonged to his mother, feeling in each object a part of her. The Virgen de Guadalupe statue sitting over the television set, a votive candle burning. The doilies. Pictures of the family hung on one wall, the kitchen arranged in her pattern, aromas that were hers.

But hell, his father had died fourteen years ago. Had she, too, grown restless? What about this Max? And a year ago she had taken up word processing at T-VI. What for? he had asked her.

I want to do something, she answered. She had enough Social Security to live on, but she wanted something to do.

The kitchen glistened spic and span. He opened the refrigerator, peered in, but took nothing. He rubbed his stomach, feeling the itch that wouldn't leave him.

Something drew him down the hall to his mother's bedroom.

He couldn't remember the last time he had been in her bedroom. On her dresser rested bottles of perfume, lipsticks, her hairbrush and hand mirror, a photograph of her wedding day. Diana and Polito, a smiling bride and bridegroom. Other pictures of the family. He and Armando in Little League uniforms. One showing them with their first trout, caught in the Jemez when he was ten. Memories. His mother's fragrance filled the room.

The shades were drawn, the room was cool. He felt a sadness, something caught in his throat. I should see her more often, see Armando. Gotta stay together as family, he thought, and turned to flee the room and the tide of emotion.

As he stepped out the front door, a car drove up, a late-model Honda. A stocky, medium-size man with salt-and-pepper mustache and hair quickly stepped out and hurried to open the door for Sonny's mother. "Permítame, comadre."

Max, Sonny thought, a gallant Max. He hadn't seen a man open the car door for a woman in ages.

Sonny's mother stepped out, smiling. "Hijo," she called, and waved, but paused to acknowledge Max's courtesy. "Gracias."

"Hi," Sonny said, and kissed his mother, and she embraced him hard. He heard her sob and looked helplessly at Max, who looked back at Sonny and shuffled his feet. She clung to him for a moment, her abrazo of grief for Gloria, for her sister, but glad her son was in her arms. She still had him.

He smelled the shampoo in her hair. She had dyed her hair a light auburn, covering the gray. When? Had he missed it? She looked younger.

"Ay, hijo," she said when she could pull away and look at him, "I'm glad you're here."

"I was just about to leave."

"We've been with Delfina. Max, you remember mi hijo. . . ."

"Seguro que sí," the man said, smiled, held out his hand.

"Quihubole," Sonny replied.

Of course, Sonny thought, Maximiliano Contreras, a man who

had worked with his father. From time to time Max and his wife had visited his parents. Max's wife had died a few years ago, Sonny had taken his mother to the funeral. When had this happened? Max had called his mother "comadre," a close friend, and the smile on his face when he looked at Sonny's mother gave things away.

"Come in, I'll fix coffee," his mother said. "Mi pobre hermana, it's been a shock. There is no pain for a parent like that of losing a son or daughter. Come in, come in."

"I can't," Sonny replied. "I got a lot of things to do. I just wanted to know if there was anything I could help with. The funeral—"

"I guess Mr. Dominic is taking care of everything," his mother answered. "I tried to call, but I got only a secretary. Everything's taken care of, she said. But there's no rosary, nothing. It's not right, Sonny. Poor Delfina."

She looked at him with a pained expression. She wanted to help her sister, and things weren't moving according to custom.

"Did you ever get Turco?" Sonny asked.

"Yes, but don't mention his name. What kind of son is he? He doesn't see his mother. Do you think he cares? No. And you know what he's saying?" She looked at Max.

"He's accusing Frank Dominic of murdering Gloria," Max said.

"Delfina believes it. But it's not possible," Sonny's mother said. "Is it?" She looked at him, and he saw lines of worry around her eyes.

"No," Sonny replied.

How can things get so fucked up, he thought. He wanted to help his mother, offer consolation, be a man. Instead, he found himself looking helplessly from her to Max.

Sonny said nothing about Delfina hiring him. "I gotta go," he said, and kissed his mother. "I'll see what I can find out. I'll call you. . . . Good to see you, Max." He nodded and stepped toward his truck.

"No rosary," his mother called, "can you imagine? No rosary."

"You want me to come for you?" Sonny asked.

"No, Max will take us. It's a shame," she said, "a terrible thing."

Sonny started his truck and backed out of the driveway. As he drove away, he saw his mother wave, and Max standing next to her put his arm around her shoulder in consolation.

"Damn!" Sonny cursed. "Damn! No valgo maseta! I can't even take care of my own mother!" A strange jealousy mixed with the impotence he felt.

He called Howard as he drove back downtown. He wanted to know if the cops had gotten hold of Dominic's phone records, but Howard didn't answer. He went back to the library and spent the time hunting through files on Akira Morino.

"Dig," Sonny told Ruth, "all the way back to Japan if we have to. I want to know everything there is to know about this man."

Late that afternoon he went home exhausted, feeling like he was coming down with a cold. He almost fell asleep on the couch, but he didn't want the nightmares, and he didn't want to be late to pick up Rita. He got up, showered, put on his tux and the Tony Lama boots he reserved for dancing, then he drove over to Rita's. He felt drained, and he couldn't put his finger on the cause. He hadn't slept well, he knew, but it was more than that.

Seeing Rita improved his mood. She looked stunning in a low-cut burgundy evening gown. "Que guapa," he said, and kissed her. "Let's not go."

"Gloria?"

He nodded.

"All right," she agreed.

He looked at her. She had dressed carefully for the occasion, but she would do what was best. What more could he ask for? A beautiful woman who loved him. He felt like a world-class ass.

"No. Let's go. We promised we would, and we're ready, so let's go. The party will get things off my mind."

"You sure?"

"Vamos." He kissed her and walked her to the truck, where he opened the door for her.

"Por Dios." Rita smiled at the courtesy.

10

The lobby of the Hyatt downtown was full of City Symphony aficionados when Sonny and Rita entered. The music lovers, artists, and wealthy patrons of the city always turned out for the annual fund-raiser. Board members circulated in the crowd, greeting old friends and working the room for new contributors. It was an event that drew the city art community together. But this year the mood was subdued; the murder of Gloria Dominic had touched a chord of grief and disbelief in the city, especially the elite circles she traveled in.

"Feels like a funeral," Sonny whispered as they made their way through the crowd. The music of the string quartet hidden in a corner of the lobby did little to cheer things up.

"They need a mariachi," Rita replied.

Music and raising money for the symphony weren't the only

things on the minds of the symphony supporters, Sonny thought. Business will get done and politics hashed over. The upcoming mayoral elections were being hotly debated. Walter Johnson and the incumbent, Marisa Martinez, were in attendance, meeting old friends and pressing the flesh. Johnson, the old conservative businessman from the Country Club area, reminded friends that he was a longtime supporter of the symphony. Marisa reminded them she was spearheading the drive to build a new Performing Arts Center that would house the symphony. But she was fighting opponents who said the center would cost too much and serve only a few, so her ambitious plan was now an endangered project.

But the murder of Gloria Dominic was the most-whispered topic. Sonny could feel the undercurrents it created as they made their way through the crowd.

"Try to enjoy yourself," Rita whispered as she drew him toward a group of business acquaintances. A small group was gathered around Mike Gallegos, president of the Hispano Chamber of Commerce. Rita was a member working on the committee that was trying to build a Hispanic Cultural Center. The city had been founded by the Nuevo Mexicanos in 1706, and now, three hundred years later, there was still no organized way in which to show off their arts and culture.

The Chicano Arts and Resistance show at the Alburquerque Museum a few years ago had galvanized the Chicano community. Now the activism for the cultural center had moved out of the artists' hands and into the hands of the business community.

"The city fathers move too goddamned slow when it comes to showcasing our arts," Rita had complained. "And before anything will get done, we'll need to set off dynamite under Mike's ass. He spends most of his time kissing up to the gringos at the Rotary."

Mike Gallegos was the man many said was *the* up-and-coming político in the city. He was a handsome, young Hispano who seemed born to be a politician. He was on the city council now, and although he was letting this mayoral race slide by, he was already laying the groundwork to jump into the next one.

Mike and Sonny had attended high school together, but Mike had gone directly into college, then straight to law school at UNM, and now he spent most of his time on advisory boards and charitable causes around town.

"Hi, Rita. You're looking beautiful as ever," Mike greeted them. He presented his wife, Tiffany, and the cluster of friends surrounding them. "So how's business, Charlie Chan?" he said, and slapped Sonny heartily on the back. He laughed, and the group smiled.

"Fine," Sonny replied. He wasn't in the mood to trade barbs.

"I told Sonny years ago, when we were at UNM, let's go into business together. But did he listen to me? Oh no. Spent his time reading books. Then to top it off! He got into this chasing missing husbands business!"

"Darling," Tiffany interrupted, "Sonny does all right. Didn't he save the Dodge lady from Mexican bandidos?"

Sonny stared into her blue eyes. She smiled.

"Yeah, he did." Mike nodded. "You want a medal, Sonny?"

Sonny let it pass, smiling halfheartedly.

"Well, I thought it was romantic. I certainly wouldn't mind being saved by Sonny." Tiffany smiled, looking straight in Sonny's eyes.

Mike put his arm around her. "Okay, okay, so Sonny's a hero. I wouldn't tease him if I didn't like Sonny. Hell, we played football together. Remember, Sonny. You dropped a lot of passes then, too!" He laughed loudly.

"I remember," Sonny replied. Mike the quarterback. He always needed the limelight. Now Mike was making big bucks being a lawyer for the electric utility. The utility allowed him time to serve on the city council and be involved as a supporter of the symphony. But that was his style. He had been the back-slapper all through high school: student council president, senior class president, Boys State. The teachers treated him like a god; they predicted he would go far.

"So how's the grape business?" Sonny asked.

Mike's family had been produce distributors for generations, and Sonny knew Mike was very sensitive to the fact that his family trucked in grapes to sell while Cesár Chávez was boycotting the growers.

Sonny liked to remind Mike that the California farmworkers would be living in poverty, sleeping under plastic bags, and sick from the pesticides as long as the boycott wasn't supported.

"Making fine wine." Mike smiled and changed the subject. "We're sorry about Gloria. It's a great loss," he said, suddenly looking somber.

"She was a good woman," his wife agreed.

"Helped get Marisa elected, helped the Hispano chamber on a lot of projects," Mike added. "We're going to miss her. . . ."

The group nodded in consolation.

Tiffany asked Sonny if he thought there was a connection to the recent series of rapes in the Northeast Heights. Sonny shook his head, thinking about the coalition of women Gloria had organized to protest for more police involvement in the cases. She'd had to tone down her activities because of her husband's bid for the mayor's seat, but it hadn't softened her private opinions.

"The city is becoming too violent," she had told Sonny, "and much of it is violence against women."

"It adds a bitterness to her death," Rita said. "I mean, even if there's no connection, she's still a victim of the violence she fought so hard against."

"I heard you were there that morning," Mike said.

Sonny shook his head. "I took my tía to see her, that's all. I only know what's in the news—"

"Come on." Mike leaned toward Sonny in confidence. "This is familia," he said, indicating the friends around him. "Is it true what the news said? The way she was killed? Sounds like a damn cult or something. Or is Frank just smart enough to make it look like that?"

Before Sonny could respond, he felt Rita touch his arm. The group turned to see Tamara Dubronsky working her way across the room toward them. Dressed in an elegant black gown with diamonds glittering on her fingers and throat, she was the most dramatic-looking woman in the crowd.

"Darling, I'm so happy to see you," Tamara greeted Sonny, and he leaned forward to kiss her cheek. "Mr. Mike Gallegos, how pleased we are to have you and your lovely wife join us tonight. All of you." She smiled at the group and at Rita but returned her attention quickly to Sonny.

"My, you look more handsome than ever."

The women smiled. Tamara was right; dressed in his tux, his face tan from the sun, trim and muscular, and technically still eligible, Sonny always drew the attention of the women.

Tamara, too, was extremely alluring. Her eyes were dark, intense, mesmerizing, and she accented them with just the right makeup. She had the lithe body of a flamenco dancer, and she knew how to use it to best effect.

Everything about Tamara made a statement, including her intriguing accent. Some said it was Russian, others said Polish, still others said German. Nobody knew for sure, because Tamara Dubronsky did not talk about her past.

Sonny knew only the rumors about Tamara's past. It was said she had been born in Eastern Europe, in that marginal land created in the aftermath of World War II. She was intensely focused, and intelligent. She spoke Russian, Polish, German, and French. She was said to have been studying music when she met Peter Dubronsky, a widower who had been in Berlin on sabbatical from teaching Russian at the University of New Mexico. He returned to tell colleagues and friends that he had fallen in love, and although he was sixty, he proved his love. It took him a few years, but he finally got Tamara out of East Germany. He brought her to New Mexico, where they were married.

What everyone knew for sure was that three years after Dubronsky and Tamara were married, he died of a heart attack, leaving her a fortune in artwork. Using the family money left to him by his mother, Dubronsky had collected art since he arrived in New Mexico in the early fifties. He fell under a spell, he said, of the land and the people, and he wanted to safeguard the romance of New Mexico. The only way to save the past was by preserving its art, so he religiously bought the old New Mexican masters and as many Georgia O'Keeffes as he could.

He roamed through the northern villages and bought wood carvings, the old santero pieces of Barelas and the other native carvers. He bought old Navajo blankets, the black Santa Clara pottery of Martinez, anything he could get his hands on.

He had bought an estate in the North Valley large enough to hold all his artwork. There Tamara still lived, once a year splurging on a big party for the City Symphony, the rest of the time visited only by a small coterie of friends. Recently she had become more reclusive, moving her annual party to the downtown hotel, though she was, as always, an Alburquerque society regular. People whispered that she was part of a secretive group of women who were into psychic phenomena. Tamara herself said she was psychic. Many swore by her predictions.

Tamara claimed no country, but in New Mexico, she said, she knew she had arrived at a sacred and primal place on earth. She had given her soul to this tierra encantada. She now called herself a citizen of this land of the sun.

Tamara and her "powers" were always the subject of cocktail party conversation, and with some derision, but no one denied she had a gift for raising money. Elderly widows who learned of her powers were attracted to her, especially those who wanted to communicate with their departed husbands.

The last woman who had contacted Tamara for this reason was from the southern part of the state. Her husband had died and left her a large ranch, but life was lonely on the open space. She begin to hear the voice of her husband in the vastness of the arid desert. She sought out Tamara, and Tamara became her spiritual guide, the channel through which the woman spoke to her husband. He told her the City Symphony needed help, and that same afternoon the woman wrote a check for a quarter of a million dollars to the symphony. No one, especially not the symphony director, thought of asking what Tamara charged the woman for her services.

Looking at Tamara, Sonny remembered the first time he was introduced to her. Her grip was strong, and the flow of energy was like touching a low-voltage power line. There was an immediate sexual attraction that both recognized. Tamara's eyes were the eyes of a Gypsy woman, dark, holding him in their power. She had invited him to her home, and he had declined.

Had he been afraid of her? That's the question he had never answered for himself. She had sensed his lust, and so she seduced him by acknowledging his need. The thought of Rita had made him decide not to pursue the chemistry that attracted him to Tamara. But then, a woman like Tamara only came along once in a lifetime, he thought, and there had to be something wrong with a man who got an invitation from her and didn't respond.

Now when they met, even with Rita standing beside him, the sexual chemistry was still there, unresolved.

"Tamara." He coughed softly to break the tension. "You remember Rita." Rita had met Tamara once before and instinctively disliked the woman.

"How lovely to see you." Tamara acknowledged Rita with a glance. "Sonny, you pick the sweetest girls."

Sonny winced.

"He didn't pick me." Rita smiled coldly, putting her arm through Sonny's. "I give him the pleasure of my company, darlink," she responded, mimicking Tamara's accent.

The women in the group smiled. Good for Rita, the smiles said. Sonny was worth fighting for.

"You are wise." Tamara smiled and turned to Mike, unflustered. "Now if you'll excuse me, Mr. Mike Gallegos, I must take the very important Mr. Baca to meet someone," she said diplomatically, and led Sonny and Rita away. "It is a terrible thing about Gloria," she said as they walked away. "Terrible. We thought about canceling tonight, but I talked to Frank. He's so sweet. The poor dear is so distraught."

Frank, distraught? Sonny thought.

"Life must go on, I told him," Tamara continued, "and he said he agreed."

Tamara didn't pursue the subject. She led them to the center of the lobby, where a small group was clustered.

"I want you to meet someone who will be very important in your life," Tamara whispered. "I told you about my friend, Anthony Pájaro. I want you two to meet. He fights to save our Earth."

Anthony Pájaro, Sonny thought, sure. He was the leader of a statewide antinuclear group. Pájaro's group had been focusing their attention on the Waste Isolation Pilot Plant, the nuclear waste dump near Carlsbad. They were protesting the storage of high-level plutonium waste at the facility. The Department of Energy storage tests at the WIPP site had been barred, and it sat empty. Millions of upkeep dollars poured into the storage facility, but the DOE couldn't proceed.

Recently the tables had turned. The Senate had approved the test run of a large truck carrying radioactive waste from Los Alamos to the WIPP facility in a couple of weeks. The run was headline news, and every antinuclear group in the state was reenergized.

"Would you like to meet him?" Tamara asked.

"Why not," Sonny said, glancing at Rita, who nodded in agreement.

Tamara pushed through the crowd, and Pájaro turned to greet her.

Sonny expected to meet a "back to nature" environmentalist with a thick beard full of ticks from sleeping in the forest. Instead, the man who turned to smile at them was lean and handsome. He had dark, penetrating eyes, a hawk nose, and polished black hair, which he combed back and tied in a ponytail. He was dressed in a tux, but instead of the usual black bow tie, he wore a gold medallion around his neck. It was a beautiful large piece, round, inscribed with the Zia symbol.

"Tamara." He smiled in greeting and kissed her cheek, but his eyes remained on Sonny.

"Darling," Tamara said sweetly, "I am so glad you could come. I want to introduce you to Mr. Sonny Baca, whom I've told you about. And his lady friend, Miss Rita Lopez."

"Sonny Baca," Pájaro said, and took Sonny's hand. "Any friend of Tamara's is a friend of mine. Anthony Pájaro, at your service."

The man's charisma was strong. He was approaching forty, Sonny thought, and was as trim and muscular as a runner. His black eyes bore into Sonny, and in them Sonny saw a zeal he did not see in most men. He was a man with a mission.

Pájaro turned to Rita and took her hand. "You don't know me, but I know you. I've eaten at your place. Best carne adovada in town. I worked around the Navajo reservation for a while, so I learned to love mutton and chile."

"Thank you," Rita answered.

"Nice piece," Sonny said, nodding at the gold medallion that hung around Pájaro's neck.

"Lovely, isn't it." He smiled and looked at Tamara. "A gift from a very special friend. But let me introduce my friends," he said, indicating the people gathered around him, and gave their names.

"Our wonderful group of warriors," Tamara said. "They fight against this pollution of the Earth." Her eyes flashed with genuine pride.

Ah, Sonny thought, he is also Tamara's lover.

"Tamara is one of our true believers," Pájaro complimented her.

Sonny sensed Tamara's enthusiasm. So Pájaro was her friend, and he wore the gold medallion with the Zia symbol, so what?

Was he getting so suspicious of the symbol that every time he saw it, it would remind him of Gloria? The Zia symbol, after all, was the most-used symbol in the state. Electricians, plumbers, medical groups, dozens of small businesses used it on their stationery, on their fleets of cars or trucks.

"You must be upset about the Senate decision to allow a test run," Rita said.

"Yes, we're getting ready for the battle again," Pájaro said, his look growing serious. "We're a small group, we have only one goal: to close down WIPP. Our reasoning is simple, but it will work. If the nuclear waste producers have no place to store their garbage, they have to stop producing it, right? During the cold war the whole world went insane producing plutonium. Now they want to shove that high-level waste down our throats. We resist. We're committed to saving Mother Earth." Though he addressed Rita and Sonny, the few around him nodded in assent.

Sonny thought of the various groups around New Mexico that had fought the storage of nuclear waste at the WIPP site in the underground salt mines near Carlsbad. The fight had gone on for years, in the courts and out.

He looked closely at the man and felt the fervor of a religious fanatic. His intense gaze reminded Sonny of pictures of saints he had seen, men burning with the divine spirit, or the eyes Goya painted. Eyes of the prophets of the desert, men of righteousness. Pájaro was more than a Greenie, more than an activist citizen concerned about WIPP trucks carrying nuclear waste down New Mexico roads. He was a very committed man.

"We're going to get this state up in arms," Pájaro continued. "On June twenty-first we'll have people blocking the highway from Los Alamos to Santa Fe. The DOE and the Senate has to know we don't want the test. To allow the test now is to open the door to WIPP!"

"That'll take some doing," Rita said. She, too, was studying Pájaro intently.

"We need all the help we can get," Pájaro said.

Sonny shrugged. "I've never been involved in the antinu-clear—"

"And yet your father died of cancer," Pájaro interrupted. "He was working in the GE plant down in the valley, and he died of cancer. Someone like you working with us could really get attention to the issues."

Sonny nodded slowly. How the hell did he know that? he wondered, irritated that the man would bring up his father's death. His father had been a night watchman at the GE plant in the South Valley, and the plant was a subcontractor to Sandia Labs. Who knew what kind of contamination seeped down into the South Valley watertable from the labs and the air base on the hill?

The radioactive junk had taken his father's life, Sonny was sure of that. He felt a kinship with those who fought for stricter control of the poison. Pájaro's group was the most strident. They flatly didn't trust the government, and with the recent release of information that told of injections of large doses of radioactive isotopes into hospitalized patients in the fifties, who could blame them?

"We've been keeping tabs on cancer occurring in the South Valley," Pájaro said softly, and put his hand on Sonny's arm. "We read the papers, make notes, pinpoint where the person lived and worked. . . . A pattern forms. Your father died of leukemia, right? Cancer linked directly to the poison the base has been dumping for years. Did you know that area in the South Valley has the highest rate of cancer in the city? The pollutants are there, man, we know it and DOE knows it, but everybody denies responsibility and nobody wants to clean it up!"

He paused, lowered his voice, and whispered in a confidential tone, "Hell, it's not just Los Alamos that has the garbage buried in its backyard, it's right here in your city! They have more shit stored at Sandia Labs than Rocky Ford! Why don't you join us? Join Nuclear-Free Earth," Pájaro said, "and you can make a difference."

Anthony Pájaro was a preacher, the chief priest converting those who hadn't yet seen the light. Nuclear proliferation and the entire industry that produced nuclear waste was the Armageddon he warned about.

"Any nation on earth can build a bomb," he continued, "or nuclear power plants, and the more that are built, the more nuclear waste is created. It's madness, Sonny, insanity. Everybody knows it's crazy, but nobody wants to be the first to admit it! We know we can't store the stuff! It remains radioactive for centuries! The only thing for us to do is stop producing the poison! Shut down WIPP!"

Sonny nodded. Yeah, the WIPP site was a temporary solution, they couldn't go on stockpiling radioactive waste forever. Mother Earth was being disemboweled; the caverns that were her womb were now poisoned with barrels of nuclear waste. She was impregnated with plutonium, the deadliest element known to mankind, but she would resist. She would spew it out, if not now, sometime in the future. She would thwart science and technology, and when she did, the catastrophe created would make Three Mile Island or Chernobyl look like a picnic.

"I don't usually get involved in these political things, either," Tamara said, sensing Sonny's reluctance, "but this is to save our state. Our Earth." She pressed Sonny's arm.

Yeah, that and after-hours with Pájaro, Sonny thought.

"Think about it, Baca. It's the feds and the DOE that're running this state! Cramming all the shit from Rocky Flats and Los Alamos down our throats. Now they want to store the Pantex junk here! All those nuclear bombs beings dismantled are sitting up at Kirtland! We don't have to take it!" Pájaro squeezed Sonny's other arm.

It was the kind of gesture a father would make, a touch that told his son to wake up. There's danger all around us, wake up! It was the reaching out of brother to brother, drawing Sonny into Pájaro's confidence.

"Maybe," Sonny replied. "Look, we can talk later."

A television news crew working the event had gathered around them.

Pájaro smiled. "Yes, let's talk sometime. But there's not much time. The test is already scheduled for June twenty-first. We need to move fast. Nice to meet you. *Ciao*, Tamara," he said, and kissed her cheek. "Miss Lopez, a pleasure." He smiled at Rita and turned to face the reporter who pulled at him.

"He's a gifted man," Tamara said, "you two would work well together. He's going to bring this state to its senses. Now, if you will excuse me, darling, I have other people to see." She smiled and kissed Sonny's cheek. "Enjoy the party. Good night," she said to him and Rita as she moved away to greet others.

"A circus," he said, and turned to Rita.

"A good lecture," Rita said, and took his hand as they walked toward the bar. She stopped. "But you know, he really means it. He thinks WIPP can be made to fold up and go away. He's intense and he's handsome, and he has a cause. You can see women gravitate toward him. . . ."

"You, too?"

"I've never met a man as handsome as you," she said, smiling, "until tonight."

"Should I be jealous?" Sonny said.

"No. He's good-looking, intriguing, charismatic. And he has a cause. Some women are drawn to that."

"But not you?"

"No."

"Why?"

"He can be dangerous," she replied.

"How?" Sonny asked.

"When anyone wants something as bad as he wants to get rid of WIPP, they're dangerous," she said, and squeezed his hand. "Now, get me a glass of wine and I'll let you take me home tonight."

"Con mucho gusto," Sonny replied, and turned to the bar.

11

The next morning after he showered and dressed, he put on his last pair of pressed jeans and a clean cowboy shirt with pearl snap-on buttons. After he slipped on his boots, he put on his silver and turquoise bolo tie. His father had given him the bolo the Christmas before he died. He had bought it from a Navajo man, John Chavez from Cañoncito.

As Sonny looked in the mirror, he realized for the first time the design of the tie suggested a Zia sign. The silver leaves radiated in the form of the four sacred directions, and the turquoise in the middle suggested the bright New Mexican sky. He looked closely, and there in the center was a nick of gold. The round sun.

My imagination, he thought as the phone rang.

"Sonny. Jack Randall, NewMex Life. Sorry to call you so early—"

"S'all right," Sonny replied. He had done some work for NewMex Life and Jack Randall was apt to call at all hours.

"I just found out you're related to Gloria Dominic."

"Cousin."

"God it's a horrible crime. But I'll get to the point. A few months ago we wrote a two-million-dollar policy on Gloria Dominic. And the beneficiary is—"

Frank, Sonny thought. Red flags waved in his mind, more furiously than when tía Delfina sounded off about the insurance in her grief.

"The coincidence is . . ." Jack let his thought trail off.

"Yeah," Sonny agreed. So why tell me all this? He knew a case like this wound up with Equi-Fax, the investigative arm of the national insurance companies.

"Dammit, Sonny! I wrote the application. Gloria Dominic was as healthy as a horse. Two million seemed reasonable. . . ."

"Was she pregnant?"

"Pregnant? What makes you ask a crazy thing like that? At her age?"

"You didn't have your doctor check her?"

Randall groaned. "It was Frank Dominic, for crying out loud! His wife! Look, I need help."

"Like?"

"Work with Equi-Fax. You know Frank and the family, you know the turf. You know if I can get a suicide, knowledge beforehand, anything! We can go to court. I'll give you ten."

"It wasn't a suicide!" Sonny felt the anger rising.

"Maybe, maybe, but I need something! Frank's going to fight me in court! Even a settlement's gonna cost us!" Jack shouted back. "I need a break!"

"Dirt—"

"God, yes! It's going to be a dirty fight! Frank's tough! Fucker's got us by the balls, and I'm caught in the middle!"

Sonny smiled. Pendejo, did you just learn that about Frank?

"I can't."

"Why?"

"I've got a client."

"Frank?"

"No, a nice old lady who has an interest in the case. . . ."

"Who?"

"Confidential."

"So what? As long as it's not Frank, I don't care."

"Sorry, Jack, but I can't."

"Okay, okay, but if you change your mind, I need your help. I'll double the price."

Twenty grand? He'd never even dreamed of making twenty grand on any investigation. It was a temptation. But he wasn't into selling his services to look for dirt, not on Gloria.

"No, sorry."

"Don't say no. Say you'll think about it. You've got my number. You find anything and I'll buy it."

"Adios," Sonny said, and hung up the phone. Tía Delfina gave me twenty bucks to find Gloria's murderers, but twenty bucks won't buy a week's groceries. A couple of lunches maybe. But he had been hired, and he would stick with his tía, for Gloria's sake. For his.

He needed to talk to Gloria's housekeeper, and to Leroy Brown, Dominic's ex-gardener. He flipped through the yellow pages and jotted down the number and address listed for Veronica Worthy. Leroy Brown's number appeared under Zia Lawn Care. It had a San José barrio address. Sonny dialed, waited. A rough voice answered.

"Leroy Brown?"

"Speaking."

"My name's Sonny Baca, I'd like to talk to you."

"Not doing lawns anymore," the man answered. "Lemme give you the number of a friend—"

"I want to talk to you about Gloria Dominic."

There was a pause. "You police?"

"No, a friend."

"Already told the police everything," Leroy Brown said, and the phone went dead.

"Well, I'll just have to go by after the funeral and talk to Leroy in person, whether he likes it or not," Sonny said to himself. He put on his dark blue jacket and black cowboy hat. He looked in the mirror, removed the hat, and slapped it against his thigh. He needed a new one, something more dressy, a straw Stetson for summer.

He tossed the hat back on the dresser. He wouldn't wear one today. Hell, he'd just have to take it off in church. The kind of crowd that was going to be at Gloria's mass didn't wear cowboy hats, especially not one as dusty as his.

He went out and called buenos días to don Eliseo. The old man was sprinkling the grass in front of the house.

"Vas al funeral?" don Eliseo called.

"Sí."

"Que descanse en paz." Then he added, "I'll water your grass. Va estar bien caliente hoy."

Sonny thanked the old man, got in his truck, and drove to Rita's. She was sitting on her porch steps. Roses lined the porch, surrounding her, filling the morning with their perfume. The flash of a green-throated hummingbird flitted from one rose to the other, then rose quickly and was gone.

"Buenos días." She stood and greeted him.

He took her in his arms and kissed her. "You're as beautiful as a hummingbird," he whispered.

"That's nice to hear." She smiled. She picked up the four roses she had cut. "For Gloria," she said.

He smiled and smelled the roses. The aroma was subtle.

"Gloria's ghost is in my dreams. . . ."

"You should see Lorenza," she suggested as they got in the truck and drove south on Fourth.

Lorenza Villa was a friend, a curandera who had returned to

the old teachings of the healers of the villages after having completed a degree in nursing and counseling. Later, she studied in Mexico with curanderos. Deep stuff, something even Rita didn't discuss much. Something that had to do with the nagual, the animal spirit of the person.

"I might—"

"She can help."

Sonny glanced at her. She was dressed in a black skirt and white blouse, and she wore a scarf across her shoulders, not the rebozo that she often wore in the cool evenings but a small dark scarf.

"I guess," he said, and he wondered why the image of Gloria wouldn't leave him. Was she calling to him? He was sure he had heard her voice when he viewed her body.

"I had flowers sent to the church," Rita said.

"Thanks," Sonny said, "you think of everything. So why these four?"

"The four sacred directions," she answered. "I've been thinking. If those who murdered Gloria are using the Zia sign as their signature, they are misusing a sacred sign, a sign very significant to us. They're taking its power away from us. We have to fight back. The four is sacred. It's also a feminine number. We can't allow it to be used by those who do evil."

Yes, Sonny thought, and opened the door of the truck for her. She's right. The Zia sun is sacred, a deity of the Río Grande pueblos, the Tata Sol of the Chicanos. A sacred symbol, a living reality worth fighting for.

On the way to the church, he told her about Howard's theory, that it was possible Gloria Dominic was pregnant when she died, and Rita sighed and murmured a prayer.

"Dios mío, it only gets worse."

The police had cordoned off the streets around the church. Parking was difficult to find, so by the time they entered the church, the mass had already started. They walked slowly down a side aisle looking for seats until Sonny spotted Howard. In here, Howard motioned, and he squeezed the people down the row to make room for Sonny and Rita.

"Quíhubole," Howard whispered.

"Qué tal?" Sonny answered.

At the altar the archbishop was conducting the mass. He and the attending priests were attired in gold-brocaded robes. One of the altar boys swung the censer, and wisps of sweet incense curled upward.

Frank Dominic had spared no expense, Sonny thought as he looked at the altar, where a profusion of flowers spilled around the gold coffin.

The mystery of Christ, Sonny thought, el Cristo de don Eliseo, el Nazareño de los penitentes of Chimayó, the God of his mother, was born, died, and rose again. Ritual. The event was relived in ritual; by re-creating the event, the participants could enter the mystery, be cleansed by experiencing the birth and death of Christ.

"And on the third day he arose from the dead. . . ."

The morning was warm, and even though the doors were open, the packed church was stifling. The sweet perfumes of the women and the smell of wax and incense thickened.

From where he sat, Sonny had a good view of the mourners. The city's most-powerful business leaders, attorneys, bankers, congressmen, and of course, all the city hall políticos were in attendance. All wore their grieving faces, all were dressed in dark elegance. The women wore sedate summer dresses or dark suits. Even at the mass for the dead, those who had wealth showed it off.

Everything about the funeral was precisely orchestrated. From the moment Gloria was pronounced dead, Dominic's office staff had taken over, the services were quickly planned, and all the important people of the city called. No small-town rosary for Gloria; Frank had pulled out all the stops. Her death was turned into a precisely orchestrated social event.

Across the aisle sat Sam Garcia and his wife; in the front row sat the governor, a senator, and a congressman. Even Dominic's nemesis, Marisa Martinez, the mayor, sat with her father.

In the front row Sonny spotted his mother, in black. Next to her sat his tía Delfina. Next to his mother sat Max. Solid, hombre de la tierra, hombre del South Valley, Max. Maximiliano. A hard worker, a man of the valley. In some ways he reminded Sonny of his father. A short, stocky man; curly peppered hair; dark, thick eyelashes. Puro manito, puro Nuevo Mexicano. A sort of stoicism filled those men, Sonny thought. They were men who took care of their families. In spite of all the hard times, the dirty work they had to do just to survive, they carried an inner peace.

He glanced at Rita. Her eyes were closed, praying, or listening to the eulogy the archbishop had launched into. Beauty emanated from her face; an aura of beauty.

I should marry her, Sonny thought, quit fucking around. Forgive me, Father, I thought "fucking around" in church.

Lord, all the training he had received during catechism had taken. Confess every sin. No sinful thought is too small. God sees all, hears all, knows all. Remembers all.

"There in the house made of luz, casa de luz, en la mañanita, when the sun comes over the mountain," he heard don Eliseo's voice. "Casa de luz! The Lords and Ladies of the Light come to fill the house with light."

Sonny groaned. He felt someone watching him and looked across the aisle at Tamara Dubronsky. She smiled, a dark, seductive smile. She wanted him, she was waiting. Maybe he would take her up on that, sooner or later—

He smiled and at the same time felt Rita's elbow in his ribs, pulling his attention back to the service.

Sonny turned his attention to the mourners at the front of the church. Dominic sat with friends, solemn faced. He was dressed in black, impeccable as always, not a hair out of place. The blonde was not in sight.

What about Turco? Sonny thought. Probably too busy running drugs into the South Valley to bother with his sister's funeral mass. Just as well. A big man, ugly, with a scar across one cheek. He had a soft, moist handshake. Even though she had taken care of her mother over the years, Gloria had cut all her other ties to the barrio, and she had nothing to do with Turco.

The archbishop's voice rose above Sonny's troubled thoughts. He spoke of the charitable work Gloria Dominic had done for the community, and how he could always count on her to help Catholic charities. Gloria Dominic had given so much of her time to help the poor and the homeless.

Sonny stared at the casket, the gold gleaming with the refracted light from the stained-glass windows. St. Mary's had beautiful stained-glass windows, and the morning sun shone with brilliant blues.

Sonny's stomach churned at the sight of the bank of lilacs flanking the coffin. Lilacs, the flower of the city, the bushes that graced the estates of the rich as well as the front yards of the poor, symbol of spring, renewal, and he never again would be able to appreciate their scent. The purple lilac, rich and deep, lining walks and gardens everywhere, the color inextricably mixed with the spring-passion of the city, flower of transformation from death to life, blooming in the dooryard, like a poem he remembered by Whitman, renewing fertility of the earth, was now, for him, the flower linked to death.

The archbishop's speech was long, the heat and fragrance overwhelming; Sonny wondered if he would have to get up and leave.

"She was a giving woman," the archbishop intoned, the eulogy interminable. Sonny half listened. His gaze stopped on the stained-glass window on the east wall of the church. The circle of the dove, the Holy Spirit, was ablaze with the morning sun. From the circle radiated the four arms of the cross, divine love, a symbol as old as Christianity, older. It came from the earliest recesses of man's awakening to consciousness. The circle was unity, the four points met in the middle.

The four sacred directions, north, west, south, and east. The sun rose in the east, climbed to the zenith, then died in the west. It traveled to the underworld to rise again in the east. Gloria's soul should be traveling through the underworld, to rise on the third day into heaven. Instead it lingered on Earth. A spirit of disquietude.

One had to die before one could rise again, that's what his catechism had taught him. His New Mexico brand of the Catholic faith was something he had tried to lose. But the questions lingered: What was death? What was the soul? Why did Gloria hover in front of him, even now when the archbishop was trying to prepare her soul for rest?

If her soul didn't rest, was it doomed to wander the Earth forever?

Sonny looked again at the stained-glass window. The round sun, the four radiating lines. Four arms of the cross. Four seasons, the graces of the Río Grande. Four sections of the mandala. Four prior Aztec ages, and we live in the fifth. Four directions of the Zia sign on Gloria's body. Four wings at Raven's compound. Four women to die?

"Sonny!" Rita whispered as the priest ended the mass and the mourners stood. The funeral director's assistants quickly wheeled the casket down the aisle, not waiting for Gloria's mother. Dominic followed, staring straight ahead. They moved quickly toward the front door of the church.

The mourners filed out of their pews and followed the casket out into the bright sunlight where the hearse waited. Friends pressed forward to give Frank Dominic their condolences.

Sonny, Rita, and Howard made their way to the door and paused at the top of the steps, looking out over the dense crowd and the casket as it was loaded into the hearse.

"They're moving fast," Sonny said.

He looked for his mother and tía Delfina, but they had not come out the front door. Apparently they had not been asked to ride to the cemetery in the mortuary limo. There was only one car, and that was for Dominic.

"A lot of people," Howard said, and slipped something into Sonny's hand. Sonny held the copper earring out for Rita to see, watching it glisten in the bright morning sun.

"This is the earring I found by the tire tracks behind Frank's house. It was probably planted."

"Looks like it's made from copper," Sonny replied.

Howard smiled. "This is copper, but I traced the type to a shop in Old Town. Zia Southwest. The owner buys earrings made from shell casings from women who come in once a month from somewhere up in the mountains."

"I'll check it out," Sonny said, and looked carefully at the earring. It was the Zia sign with two black feathers dangling from it.

"Any more news on the autopsy?" Sonny asked. He was looking at the scene near the hearse. The casket had been loaded, but the crowd kept Dominic immobilized as people pressed around him.

"We'll never know if she was pregnant," Howard said, and hesitated. "She was cremated last night."

"What?" Sonny turned to look at his friend. "What the hell are you saying?"

"Not even the archbishop knows," Howard whispered. "I was calling the mortuaries to ask about the kind of pumps they use for embalming. Montoya didn't want to talk to me, but I found an old friend. You remember Rudy Griego?"

Sonny nodded. A high school friend who had married into the Montoya family.

"He made me swear on a stack of Bibles, then told me they cremated the body right after the autopsy. . . ."

Sonny looked at Alfredo Montoya, the stocky man who was officiating at the funeral. He was running his assistants like a general, trying to move Dominic into the limo. Alfredo Montoya had turned a barrio mortuary that buried poor Chicanos into a million-dollar business. Now he served the rich Catholics, regardless of ethnic background. Catering to Frank Dominic was a political necessity.

"The sonofabitch," Sonny whispered, anger stirring in his guts. Now he was sure Gloria had been pregnant. Why else would Dominic pull a stunt like this? "All this is just for show, worse than I thought."

"Have you talked to Leroy Brown?" Howard asked.

"Soon as this is over," Sonny answered.

"You better hurry. Garcia is about to go for a quick arrest," Howard whispered.

Sonny cursed himself for not getting on this sooner, instead of gathering information at the library on Morino, who wouldn't even give him the time of day.

"Why him?"

"Garcia's determined to close the case. The tire tracks we found in the road behind the house will be traced to him, even if—"

"Even if the tracks don't fit," Sonny said.

"Why not? Garcia's gotta get the news media off his back, so he needs to arrest someone. The old, trusted gardener who was fired by Gloria, they will say, returned to kill her. The news will shift back to the mayoral elections, and Frank Dominic, who was ten points behind before his wife was killed, will garner enough sympathy votes to squeeze past Marisa Martinez and Johnson."

Sonny frowned, rubbed his forehead. His friend was into a wild scheme, but Sonny knew by now he was usually right.

"Look," Rita broke in, pointing. "Turco."

So he did show, Sonny thought. Took time off from running drugs to pay respects to his sister. Nice homeboy.

They watched as Turco, a big, heavyset man in a mauve shark-skin suit, pushed his way through the crowd toward Dominic. Then he reached out and grabbed Dominic by the collar before the funeral director or the cops could react.

"You bastard!" he shouted. "You killed my sister! You killed her!"

The startled people surrounding Dominic fell back.

"Turco!" Dominic cried. He wrestled himself free of Turco's grip and fell backward. Three police officers grabbed Turco and pulled him away. It took all three to restrain him.

"You killed my sister! You killed her!" he kept shouting.

Montoya and his assistants, caught temporarily off guard, now responded by pushing Dominic into the limo and speeding away, leaving a shocked crowd behind.

Sonny looked around for his mother and tía Delfina, wondering if they had seen the attack, but he couldn't spot them in the crowd. Probably they had wisely left with Max out a side door.

"Why the show?" Sonny wondered.

"He's up to something," Howard replied.

"But Garcia already questioned him and let him go." Sonny frowned.

"Anyway, talk to Leroy Brown," Howard suggested. "Garcia's spooked everybody, but maybe the old man will talk to you. Their case is thin, Sonny." He paused. "Garcia's reassigning me—"

"They know you talked to me."

Howard nodded.

Sonny put his hand on his friend's shoulder. "Don't get in trouble for me, compa. We have to get to the cemetery," he said, and took Rita's hand, calling "Adios" to Howard.

"Qué piensas?" Rita asked as they drove to the Sunset Memorial Cemetery.

"I can't believe Dominic could get away with secretly cremating her. Then this whole charade with a coffin!"

"I guess it keeps him high on the suspects list," Rita said.

"Very high."

Sonny drove into the cemetery and up the graveled lane to the lone hearse. Two men were pulling out Gloria's coffin. Max had also just pulled up and was helping Sonny's mother and tía Delfina out of his car.

In the limo parked off to the side sat Frank Dominic. He was peering at the proceedings from behind the tinted windowpane, but he made no move to get out.

A TV van was parked behind Dominic's limo, but the crew stayed inside. If Dominic didn't get out, there was nothing to film.

"Sonofabitch can't even bury her," Sonny cursed as they got down from the truck. He took Rita's hand and approached his mother.

"Hijo," she said, and embraced him, then turned to embrace Rita. Her voice was tremulous, her eyes wet with tears. "It was a beautiful mass. . . ." She looked toward the limo where Frank Dominic sat, then at the mourners who had gathered. She turned, took tía Delfina's arm, and walked briskly toward the hearse and the open grave. Max shrugged and followed them.

Only a dozen or so mourners had shown up, mostly women who had worked on projects with Gloria. One of the priests from St. Mary's who had assisted at the mass was officiating. He, too, waited nervously for Frank Dominic to alight from the limo and join the small group of mourners.

Less than an hour ago the rich and powerful of the city had crowded the church to hear the archbishop eulogize Gloria. Dominic had planned the mass, invited the guests, and got the archbishop to deliver the eulogy. All great drama, everything calculated to garner sympathy and votes.

But the burial didn't count. Now there was only the priest and a handful of friends. They gathered silently around the coffin, and the priest intoned prayers, blessing the coffin with holy water. Overhead the sun climbed toward midday. The lawn and trees of the cemetery lent the ceremony an aura of peace.

Sonny looked at tía Delfina. His mother stood next to her, sisters, both dressed in black, two handsome women from the La Joya. Max stood by them. His mother needed a helpful man like Max. Where the hell are Mando and me when she needs help? Sonny thought. Mando hadn't even come to the funeral.

Rita glanced at him. She squeezed his hand. He looked at her, then back at his mother, Max, and his aunt. Under the immense bright sky there was something pitiful about Gloria's burial, something missing.

The priest was done. He went to tía Delfina and whispered a few words; then signaling to the altar boy who had assisted, he walked quickly to his car and drove away. Dominic's limo followed behind. The few mourners who had gathered bowed their heads and also walked to their cars and left. Sonny and Rita, his mother, Max, and tía Delfina were left alone with the two mortuary attendants.

"It's done," Rita said.

"No." Sonny shook his head. They had not viewed the contents of the casket, not viewed the ashes. He looked at the attendants standing near the hearse. They, too, were ready to leave.

"Open it," he said.

They looked at Sonny in surprise. "What?"

"Open the coffin."

"Can't," the man answered and looked at his partner.

"Sonny, what are you doing?" he heard his mother ask.

"Open it," Sonny repeated, stepping forward. "Or I will."

The attendants glanced nervously at each other. They hadn't expected this. There were no orders from Montoya.

"Who are you?" the younger of the two asked.

"Familia," Sonny replied.

The young Chicano shrugged, looked at his partner. "Why not?" he said. It was normal for the casket to be opened so the family could get a last view of the departed.

"Okay," his partner replied, and reached into the hearse for a key. He opened the coffin and partially lifted the lid.

"There." Sonny stopped him. He did not want tía Delfina to see the ashes. Or worse, an *empty* coffin. She wouldn't understand.

Sonny knelt and looked into the shadow of the coffin.

A white vase nestled in the white silk lining, the vase holding

Gloria's ashes. He remembered that when he had seen Gloria dead on the bed, he had felt the impulse to touch her, to place his hand on her stomach, to make some kind of connection with the woman who had meant so much to him. Now he reached into the coffin, ran his hand up the cold vase to the lip. He touched the dull, gray ashes that had spilled onto the silk lining. He ran his fingers through the ashes, feeling the fragile, glass-like texture. When he withdrew his hand, the white film of ash covered his fingers.

He looked up at Rita, and she handed him the four roses, which he took and placed next to the vase. He stood up, turned to the attendants, and nodded.

The man let the lid drop and locked the coffin. Then he pushed a button that turned a small motor which lowered the coffin into the grave.

Tía Delfina picked up a handful of fresh earth and threw it on the coffin. The others followed suit, tossing fistfuls of earth on the coffin. The sound was the sound rain makes on tin roofs during summer thundershowers. The ritual reminded them that they, too, would one day return to the earth.

"Okay?" one of the attendants asked of no one in particular, and they removed the apparatus that had lowered the casket, loaded it in the hearse, and drove away. Two workers who had stood in the background began the task of filling the grave. At first the shovelfuls of earth pounded on the coffin, then they became soft thuds.

12

Sonny and Rita drove south on Broadway toward the San José barrio. Rita had insisted on coming with him to see Leroy Brown.

"Josie's running la Cocina today," she said, sensing something on his mind. "I wonder if Frank knew she was pregnant?"

"Probably," Sonny answered.

"And then the question, was it his?" She spoke softly, as if to herself.

"Yeah," he replied, "Gloria and Frank had no children, she's seeing Morino, and suddenly she's pregnant."

"Que 'scándalo, eh. A Japanese-Chicano baby who looked nothing like Frank. . . ."

They passed in silence through the neighborhood that lay along the railroad tracks, inhabited almost exclusively by Chicanos and Blacks. Decades ago the men from San José had worked in the railroad yards, but when the roundhouse was shut down in the late fifties, the barrio fell onto hard times. The men and women of the barrio, ill equipped for the new technology that swept the region, struggled to support their families with odd jobs. They struggled to keep their sons and daughters away from the drugs that flowed in the streets.

Sonny sighed. Tía Delfina had told him she didn't trust Frank, but that was because she knew of his womanizing, knew how he treated Gloria. This was different.

He looked at Rita.

"I love you," he said, reaching out to take her hand.

"Ah, sweet music."

"It's not easy for . . ."

"For a man? You're a special man, not just any man."

"Thanks." He smiled. "It is sweet music."

At Las Palomas Bar he turned onto a side street and looked for Leroy Brown's address. The wood-frame house was dilapidated, like the others on the street, built originally for the railroad workers.

An old truck with weathered plywood sideboards was parked in front of the house. Zia Lawn Care was stenciled in faded letters on the door of the truck. Rita pointed.

"Yeah. Be right back," Sonny said.

"Can I come?"

"Better not. I don't know the man, so there's no telling . . ." his voice trailed. Rita could handle herself, but it made no sense to take her into a situation where there might be danger.

In the street a group of kids played baseball. Next door two Black women visited as they swept their sidewalks and watched the children. They paused to look at Sonny as he got out of the truck and approached the front door.

Sonny had to knock three times before the door was opened a crack. "What do you want?" a stern voice with the hint of a drawl growled.

"I want to talk to Leroy Brown," Sonny answered.

" 'Bout what?"

"I'm Sonny Baca, I called you. I want to talk to you about Gloria Dominic."

There was a silence.

"May I come in?" Sonny asked.

The door opened and a Black man about sixty looked out at Sonny through the screen door. His face was wrinkled, his hair speckled gray.

"I don't want any trouble, I just don't want any trouble," Leroy Brown said. He wasn't inviting Sonny in. "You police?"

"No, I'm . . ." Sonny paused. "I'm not police. Gloria Dominic was my cousin. I need your help," Sonny pleaded.

"Help?" Leroy Brown said sternly. "Can't help when it's the devil killing people."

"You think the devil killed her?" Sonny asked.

"Uh-huh. I seen it coming all along, before Mr. Dominic fired me."

"Frank fired you? You told the police that Mrs. Dominic fired you."

"No, I never did. He fired me. Five years taking care of his place, and he fired me just like that." He snapped his fingers.

"Why?" Sonny asked. The man was frightened and cautious, but he clearly had something he wanted to unburden.

"You really want to help Mrs. Dominic?" Leroy Brown asked solemnly.

"Yes."

"She was a fine woman. Treated me like a regular man. Black and brown didn't mean nothing to her. She helped people all her life. Then her brother start coming 'round—"

"Turco?"

"Yeah, Turco. You want to know about drugs, you ask for Turco. He should've stayed away."

"What did he want?"

"Money. That's all them boys ever want, money. Devil made money for them to play. I've been a hard worker all my life, Mr.

Baca. Worked with these two hands." He held up a pair of rough, calloused hands. "But those boys want easy money. Easy money come from drugs."

"Who else came to see her?"

"A lot of people came, they had a lot of parties." Leroy Brown rubbed his chin. "But I know what you're askin'. I read the paper. It was devil's work. It was the women."

"Women?"

"Yes. When the women come, Mrs. Dominic gave me the afternoon off. Next day I come to work, she'd be a different woman. Sad. Like she's in another world. You ask Veronica."

"The housekeeper?"

"Housekeeper? That woman never picked up a broom in her life."

"Do you know where I can find her?"

"I don't know and I don't care. Want to know the truth? I'm glad Mr. Frank fired me. That house was full of evil."

"Who else came? During these past few months? Did a Japanese man come?"

"You mean the big shot, Mr. Morino?"

"Are you sure it was Morino?"

"I told you, I read the papers," Leroy Brown replied. "The man is in the papers. Gonna build a computer plant, he says. He and Mr. Dominic talked. Right there on the patio, and I was minding my business, but I could hear. Didn't like each other. No love lost, I say. Then the Japanese man starts comin' back to visit Mrs. Dominic. It ain't for me to say what went on, but Mrs. Dominic was a lonely woman. You know, when Mr. Morino came around, she smiled, she was happy—"

He was interrupted by the squeals of a police squad car careening around the corner, followed by a second, and a third. They came screeching to a stop around Sonny's truck, lights flashing. Leroy Brown took one look and bolted. Sonny cursed under his breath as two cops ran past him, crashing through the screen door as they chased Leroy Brown. The chase didn't last long. The cops had also come through the alley and were waiting at the back door when Leroy Brown went flying out. He was in handcuffs in seconds.

"Sonny!" Chief Garcia shouted, lumbering up to the door. "What the hell are you doing here?"

"What's going on?" Sonny asked.

"I got me a prime suspect. What the fuck are you doing here?"

Two cops dragged Leroy Brown out the front door.

"Read him his rights," the chief said. Leroy Brown stood panting, sweating, his eyes on Sonny.

"You turned me in!" he gasped. "You said you wanted to help!"

"I didn't turn you in." Sonny shook his head. He turned to the chief. "What's the charge?"

"Taking him in for the murder of Gloria Dominic," the chief answered as two television vans came racing around the corner. "Here comes the fucking press. Take his ass in."

The cops hauled a shaken Leroy Brown away. The neighbors that had gathered, watched stoically, whispering to each other.

"He didn't kill Gloria!" Sonny protested.

The chief stuck his face in Sonny's and glared at him. "Who in the hell are you? An expert? The man was fired by Gloria. She told him to stay off the premises. The tire tracks we found in the ditch road in back of Dominic's place belong to his truck! And there's jewelry missing, a diamond necklace, Frank says."

Sonny groaned. How stupid did Garcia think he was? This was no disgruntled employee revenge or a petty theft gone awry. Anyway, one man couldn't pull off the draining of the blood ceremony alone. But Garcia was under pressure to make an arrest, like Howard said, because if a suspect is caught, it gets the story off the front page of the local papers.

"And you believe Frank?"

"Yeah." The chief smiled with satisfaction, then bowed slightly at Rita as she came up. "Nice to see you, Rita. I'll bring my wife by for that carne adovada you serve. Best in the city." He turned to Sonny. "I don't know what you were doing here, but if you had blown this arrest, I would've hauled your ass in jail and thrown the key away! Quit playing detective," he growled, and motioned to the lieutenant who stood nearby. Together they walked to the chief's car and sped away, the siren blasting a warning wail for the barrio.

"Damn!" Sonny exclaimed. Rita took his arm. A policewoman motioned for them to move on. The cops were cordoning off Leroy Brown's truck and home.

"Let's get out of here," Sonny said angrily, but he was stopped by a television reporter.

"Mr. Baca? Francine Hunter, TV Four. I'd like to ask you a few questions."

Sonny looked into the microphone the young, disheveled reporter had stuck in front of his face and shook his head. "I don't know anything."

"How did you know Mr. Brown was involved?"

"I was looking for someone to mow my lawn," Sonny answered with irritation.

He opened the door for Rita; Francine Hunter, followed by a stumbling cameraman, wasn't dissuaded. "We understand that Mr. Brown was fired by Mrs. Dominic because she feared for her safety. Is that true?"

"Ask the chief," Sonny replied, jumping into his truck and slamming the door shut, and even though the inside was hot as an oven, he rolled up the window. He looked at Rita. "You okay?"

"Yeah. But is he? What's going to happen?"

"They'll book him, but goddammit! Garcia knows he doesn't have a case! They made the arrest to get the press off their tails."

She nodded. "He doesn't look like a murderer."

"A murderer never does," Sonny said.

"So what do you think?"

"Akira Morino," he whispered. "Akira Morino could buy the

state of New Mexico and fly to Vegas to play high-stakes baccarat all in one day."

"Mr. Baca." The reporter tapped on the window. "I just want to ask you a few questions."

"They don't know when to quit." Sonny grimaced and started his truck.

"Garcia must know about the insurance policy?"

"Yeah, but he's not really looking for evidence to connect his future boss to murder. I need to talk to Morino. . . . But first Veronica."

"The housekeeper?"

"I got to Leroy Brown too late. Don't want to make the same mistake twice. I'll drop you off."

"Yes, I've got to make tomorrow's carne adovada. You are chasing danger. Ten cuidado," she said.

He dropped Rita off and headed for Veronica's, which was only a few miles from Dominic's, but in a poorer section of the valley. Here the houses were old, frame stucco or simple adobes. Old rosebushes, rosas de Castillo, hollyhocks, clumps of iris, small gardens with tomato and chile plants dotted front yards. The backyards contained an apple tree or two, room for the family's late-model car, perhaps a pen where a horse or sheep was grazed.

Veronica's house was especially run-down. It was one of the few two-stories in the neighborhood, and it stood by itself at the end of a dead-end street. Beyond the house lay the thick bosque of the irrigation canal, a young cottonwood forest full of river willows and Russian olives.

Sonny got off the truck and sniffed the air. An animal smell he couldn't identify touched his nostrils. A lot of people here kept chickens or horses in their backyards, but this wasn't the farm smell of cows or horses. It was something else.

He walked to the door and knocked. No dogs barked. He knocked again and waited a long time until the window curtains parted and a shadow appeared.

"Hello!" Sonny called. "Anyone home?"

After a while the door opened and a fat woman appeared. She was dressed in black. A large crystal dangled from a gold chain around her neck. Her black hair was pulled back in a ponytail. Her eyebrows were clearly outlined, her lips red.

"What do you want?" she asked coldly.

"I'm looking for Veronica Worthy."

"Yes. That's me."

"I'm Sonny Baca." He held out his hand, but Veronica didn't acknowledge it. "I'm here because of Gloria Dominic. She was my cousin."

"What's that got to do with me?" Veronica asked, the irritation showing.

"You worked for them, didn't you? I need information—"

"What kind?"

"May I come in?" Sonny asked. He heard women's voices drifting from some other room in the house.

"We're busy, Mr. Baca. What is it you want?"

"I need to know who visited Gloria before she was murdered. Who she called?"

Veronica shook her head. "I was not her secretary. It wasn't my business to know who she saw and called." She paused and her voice softened. "I don't mean to be rude. . . . It was a tragedy. I still can't believe it. We are mourning her today." She gestured behind her. "Mr. Dominic would not have allowed us at the funeral mass—"

"Why?"

"He is a very jealous man. You ask who came to see Mrs. Dominic? No one. She was cut off from her friends. Not even her mother visited her. She had to go to her mother's home to see her. *You* never came, not since I've been there."

It was true, Sonny thought, Frank Dominic's attitude had also kept him away. Perhaps the love he still had for Gloria also kept him at a distance.

"How about Mr. Morino?"

"He was the exception."

"Why?"

Veronica hesitated. "Let's say he was special."

"How special?"

"That's not for me to say." Veronica scowled.

"How long did you work for Gloria?"

"Only these past few months. She came to me with a problem. She thought she had cancer—"

"Cancer?"

"Of course, it wasn't cancer. She was haunted by nightmares from the past. I cured her." She gestured again behind her. "We cured her."

"And you went to work for her every day?"

"She couldn't be alone at night. I would stay with her."

"And Mr. Dominic?"

"He was always gone. Campaign parties, he said. But everyone knows there were other women. . . ."

"When did you last see Gloria?"

"A week ago. Mr. Dominic fired me and the gardener. Just like that. He didn't want anyone around his wife— Then she's dead. You figure that out."

"But Mr. Morino could see her."

"Mrs. Dominic insisted. Oh, she was strong when she needed to be. I heard their arguments. She would continue seeing Mr. Morino, she insisted. And there wasn't a damn thing Mr. Dominic could do about it. Maybe that's why he—"

She stopped and Sonny waited, but she didn't pursue the thought.

"I minded my business. I only tried to help her. When she saw Mr. Morino, she was happy. That's all I know. Now if you'll excuse me. We are mourning her. She was good to us."

She closed the door.

Sonny walked back to the truck and sat. The strong odor he had smelled when he arrived filled the air. He shivered. Spooky place, he thought. Spooky woman.

13

In the morning Sonny called Morino's office and tried to set up a meeting, but Morino's secretary put him off. Mr. Morino was a busy man, and just who was Sonny Baca? What was his business with Mr. Morino?

No appointment. He tried Tamara, in hopes she could make a connection for him, but she wasn't answering her phone.

Ruth called from the library. She had been gathering information from the Japanese news media and the Tokyo stock exchange, detailing Morino's rise to the top of one of the biggest computer companies in Japan. The information gathered from the Tokyo Stock Exchange and faxed to Ruth's desk at the Albuquerque library shaped the profile of an adventurous Japanese entrepreneur. She read parts of them to Sonny over the phone.

In the eighties the young Morino had made a fortune in banking, then diversified into computers and liquid-crystal display panels. With Morino at the helm, the company sent its tentacles around the world and knocked many American companies out of the competition. He was married, two children. Faxed newspaper clippings from Japan showed only one family picture, but in his worldwide travels as point man of his company, the other photos always showed Morino with an attractive woman at his side.

A frustrated Sonny decided it was time to head up into the Sandia Mountains and check out the cattle mutilations, and Raven's place. He had let it go too long. The whole thing was growing as stale as three-day-old tortillas.

So he cruised east on I-40 through Tijeras Canyon with Juan Arriaga's Symphony in D blasting on his cassette player. He wished Rita was with him, but she had lost a cook at the restaurant and needed to fill in.

I-40 cut through the Sandias. Beyond lay the wide Estancia Valley, the llano of the eagle and the nopal, a wide expanse of land and sky. Mexican symbols repeat themselves here, Sonny thought, but the Estancia Valley was no Valley of Mexico. Perhaps just as well. New Mexico didn't need Mexico City's overpopulation and smog pollution.

As he drove, he poured hot coffee from a thermos and munched on a cold tortilla. He hadn't slept. He had spent the night tossing in and out of nightmares in which the sun rose like a gigantic Zia sign, then there was a rain of dark feathers. Crows darkened the sky, swooping in to attack Sonny. In the middle of the turbulence, he reached out and touched Gloria's stomach, and she turned to smile at him. He awakened with a cry, drenched in sweat.

The village of La Cueva lay nestled in the juniper- and piñon-dotted hills on the eastern slope of the mountains. It was one of the last old Hispano villages left intact. Many of the other villages had become ghost gowns, or like Cerrillos, they had been converted into artists' colonies, or suburban subdivisions, as Anglos who worked in Alburquerque discovered they could live in the rugged privacy of the east side of the mountain and still commute easily to the city.

An old Nuevo Mexicano village, La Cueva clung to its roots, but as land prices soared around the old land grant, the weight of real estate taxes threatened to drive the villagers out. There was little work. A few of the old rancheros still ran cattle, but the ranches were so small and the land so poor that it was an effort just to survive. To remain on the land of their birth, many of the old people had to turn to welfare.

Happens all over the state, Sonny thought. When the traditional village culture is displaced, the people suffer. Chambers of commerce keep inviting development, and the speculators crush everything in their way to build homes for those who can afford them. Never mind that those who are already there can't.

"Water," don Eliseo always said, "they're going to run out of water. Just like the ranchers of West Texas. The aquifer will dry up . . . so will their dreams. . . . That's why they want what's left of our land here in the North Valley. We have the acequias."

And so the New Mexican diaspora from the villages continued.

Sonny turned off Highway 14 onto the dirt road that led toward La Cueva.

"If you move a blade of grass, you change the land. If you poison the water, someday you will have to drink it," don Eliseo said. "But the government don't listen when the poor complain. The government don't listen to los pobres."

Takes money to fight money, Sonny thought as he approached the village.

La Cueva was a dozen homes clustered around the church. Beaten-down barbed-wire corrals and old, weathered-wood outhouses were set at the back of each house. The small church shone with a fresh coat of white paint, blue trim on the door and windows, and today it was surrounded by trucks and cars. It was San Antonio's feast day; the small village would be celebrating with a mass.

Sonny parked and stepped out of his truck. A gust of wind

rolled down the dirt road. The dry hills baked under the June sun. There had been no rain since May, so the land was scorched. The wind swept across the dry grasses. Behind him rose the peaks of the Sandias, and to the east the hills of pine and juniper sloped down into the flat land of the Estancia Valley.

He looked at the cemetery next to the church. A few of the graves were decorated with faded crepe-paper flowers, reminders of Memorial Day. From the church Sonny heard the strain of a guitar and fiddle, then the doors of the small church opened and a couple stepped out, followed by the priest carrying a cross and the altar boy who assisted him. Behind them came the fiddler and the guitarist, followed by the dancers in bright costumes.

Ah, Sonny thought as he watched the colorful procession exit from the church, I haven't seen the dance of the matachines in a long time. The lively tune of the fiddle and the guitar cut through the air and dispelled the lonely moaning of the dry wind. Sonny watched the dancers. Each male dancer wore dark pants, a white shirt, and a tall mitre hat that resembled a bishop's. A fringe fell over the forehead and shielded the eyes. Pictures of saints or of the Virgen de Guadalupe were sewn to the front of each hat. Bright ribbon streamers and scarves fell from the back of the hat and over the shoulders. In one hand each dancer held a gourd rattle, which he rattled to the beat of the lively tune the musicians provided, in the other hand each held a palma, a trident made of wood and decorated with bright ribbons and paper flowers.

Behind the dancers came the parishioners who had attended mass, forming a line behind the dancers as they slowly made their way down the path, out of the gate of the churchyard, and down the dusty street. Two women carried the statue of the patron saint of the church, San Antonio. The statue would rest in the home of the mayordomos, the family that would take care of the church that year.

The scene made Sonny nostalgic. His father used to take him

and his brother to the dances in Bernalillo in August, when the village celebrated the fiesta of San Lorenzo.

Now, as he stood watching, something in the simplicity of the dance helped dissolve the dark thoughts that had filled his mind on the way to La Cueva. These people were surviving; they had their backs against the wall, but they were hanging on to their traditions. The deadly diaspora that had made many of their neighbors flee would not drive them out. Not until the last person forgot the dance of the matachines would their way of life end. The old men in the procession were like don Eliseo, guardians of the culture. When they died, it would be left to the young men and women to continue the traditions.

So Sonny was thinking when he felt a presence behind him and turned to face four sullen men. He had been mesmerized by the dance and hadn't heard them approach. Now he looked at the big burly men, ranchers whose brown faces were as weathered as the granite of the mountain. Mustachioed Chicanos, villagers, dressed in their Sunday-clean Levi's and cowboy shirts for mass. Three wore cowboy hats. One of them held a tire iron, one held a baseball bat. None spoke, they just stared at Sonny with suspicious eyes.

"Buenos días." Sonny nodded. The men didn't answer. The wind swept around them and wafted the strains of the guitar and fiddle down the hill where the procession headed.

Finally the man closest to him spoke. "Qué chingao buscas aquí?"

"I'm looking for José Escobar," Sonny answered.

The man broke into a grin. "Who the fuck are you, a cop?" he said with a glare, and took a threatening step close to Sonny. "Yeah, I think you're the pinche ley!"

"No." Sonny shook his head, realizing he was about to get his ass kicked. But he knew villagers didn't usually threaten strangers who came to mass and to watch the matachines. Something wasn't right.

The men with the tire iron and the bat walked slowly around

Sonny. Sonny glanced at the procession as they surrounded him. The parishoners were entering the house of the mayordomo. Too late to join the safety of the group, he thought, and looked again at the four men, and guessed he was just going to have to fight his way out. What taboo had he violated?

One man pulled a knife and snapped it open. "If you're not a cop, qué quieres aquí?"

"José Escobar," Sonny repeated.

The man with the knife laughed. He leaned down and slashed at one of the truck tires. The air hissed out. "There's no José Escobar here. Put your spare on and get the hell out of here," the man said. He put the sharp knife under Sonny's nose and backed him against the truck. "Or you might lose your air, like your tire."

The others grinned. One of the men, a thick, heavy man with thick shoulders and arms stepped forward. He wore a bronze bolo tie. "Qué quieres con José Escobar?" he asked.

"I heard there was a cattle mutilation on his ranch. I want to ask him some questions," Sonny said to the man.

"You with the fucking Cattleman's Association?" the man with the knife asked, still holding Sonny at bay.

"No."

"What kind of questions?" the heavyset man asked. Sonny's gaze fixed on the bolo tie: its design was the Zia sign.

"I want to see the cow that was cut up." Sonny shrugged.

"You want to know who did it?" he asked.

Sonny nodded.

"We know who did it," one of the younger men said. "But the fucking cops don't do anything about it. It was—"

"Shut up!" the man with the knife snapped. "We take care of this ourselves!"

"Looks like you haven't done a very good job," Sonny shot back. He was getting tired of the knife held in front of his face. One swift kick and the joker would be on the ground holding his groin and gasping for air. But there were four of them, and anyway, he hadn't come to fight. "I just want to see the cow that was cut up. It's important," he repeated.

The man with the bolo tie pushed the man with the knife aside. "Put away the knife, Alejandro." Looking at Sonny, he said, "I'm José Escobar."

"I'm Sonny Baca," Sonny said as he stepped forward and held out his hand.

José Escobar grunted. "So why do you want to see the cow?"

"Maybe I'll catch whoever did it," Sonny said.

"You won't have to go far!" the man called Alejandro said angrily. "Just go down that road to Raven's house. Sonofabitch lives off our steers. You tell whoever sent you that we're going to take care of this ourselves."

He pushed by Sonny and stalked down the hill. All but Escobar followed him.

Escobar shrugged. "The muchachos don't like strangers. Since the cow was cut up, everyone's nervous. They're tired of losing steers. What does it mean to you?" he asked.

"A matter of life and death," Sonny answered.

They looked at each other. "Sonny Baca," Escobar said. "Your picture was in the paper. You worked with Manuel Lopez?"

Sonny nodded.

"Paper said you're related to the old Elfego Baca?"

"Mi Bisabuelo," Sonny explained.

"Shit." Escobar smiled and stuck out his hand. "Elfego Baca was a goddamned hero as far as I'm concerned. Ponla 'ay." He stuck out his hand, and when they shook, Sonny felt the tough, coarse hand of a working rancher.

"Mis bisabuelos were from Los Chavez," Escobar said. "They knew all the families from Socorro. Tu sabes, they were related. Anda," he said, motioning for Sonny to get into his truck. "I'll show you the cow."

Sonny climbed into the truck. In the gunrack hung a .30-06. These ranchers were used to taking care of things on their own.

Escobar started the truck and they sped out of the village,

raising a cloud of dust in their wake. The dirt road wound through hills of juniper, piñon, and an occasional pine. Gullies and arroyos, scars etched into the flesh of the land, lay like wrinkles over the dry earth. The summer rains would fill the arroyos, creating flash floods that disappeared into the valley below. Not enough to form a river, though.

Long ago the valley may have been a lake. There were still salt beds on the road to Vaughn, salt beds that the first Españoles and Mexicanos who settled the Río Grande used to cure their meat. That's why the Abo mission had been established, to Christianize the nomadic Indians and to protect the salt beds.

"What do you know about Raven?" Sonny asked as they drove.

"He's a pendejo-sonomabitche-hippie who came here about four years ago. He and his women built an adobe house. He grows marijuana in the hills. I don't give a shit about that, but he has no respect for nothing. Está loco. You, what do you do?"

"Private investigating," Sonny answered.

"Just like your granpa, eh? 'Stá bueno. Takes a smart man to catch a crook. Us? We had no chance to go to school. I grew up here on this mountain, working de sol a sol. When I could pick up an ax, I had to make leña. Hard work. We had hard work all our lives," he said. After a pause he added, "Why are you interested in this chingadera?"

Sonny told him about Gloria's death. "She was my prima," he said.

"Ah, I'm sorry," Escobar said sincerely. "Sounds like crazies. La gente está bien loca, you know. Like killing my cow. Why? I ask myself? Why would anyone kill a cow and not use the meat? Doesn't make sense. They just took the culo. Why? And no sign of tracks, no blood, nada. Just a cut around the culo. Why?" he said in exasperation, shaking his head.

"Creatures from outer space," Sonny suggested.

Escobar laughed. "Could be anything. The boys think it's

Raven. The old people say brujas. Whatever it is, it's not good. And now look what happened to your prima."

Sonny looked out the window at the ridge on either side of the arroyo, a wide cañada they had entered.

Escobar reached under the truck seat and pulled out a bottle of Jim Beam. He handed it to Sonny. "Take a shot. The dead steer's up ahead. It smells like hell."

Sonny opened the bottle and took a swig. The whiskey burned his throat. He handed the bottle back and Escobar took a shot. "My father used to get up every morning and take a shot. Un pajualaso, he used to say. I never saw him drunk, but he had his shot in the morning. The old sheepherders used to do that. All this valley," he said, and pointed east and then south at the broad expanse of the Estancia Valley, "as far as Amarillo used to be sheep. Then the gringos came and planted beans. Now we have grass only for a few cattle. The land grant used to be big, now it's all broken up. I have to pay the Forest Service to run a dozen head in here. Think of it, I have to pay to run cattle on what used to be our land."

He took another swig and passed the bottle to Sonny. He drove in silence, as if mulling over his own words. "I got a theory," Escobar said.

Sonny waited.

"You know what I think?"

"What?"

"Could be the developers want to buy our land, so they hire someone to do things like this. To scare us, sabes? I think they hired Raven to try to drive us out. They think if they can scare the hell out of us, break us down, they can drive us out. If they get their foot in the door, cuídate! Then they jack up the price of the land, then the taxes kill you. It gets you either way, qué no?"

"Why would Raven do it?"

"For the money. He's crazy. The muchachos would like to kick his ass off the mountain. He brings trouble. Bad trouble. But you know what? The FBI sent one of the state cops to tell *us* to keep away from Raven. Why the hell are they protecting *him?*"

Good question, Sonny thought, and shrugged.

Escobar stopped the truck at the edge of a clearing in the sandy arroyo. Sonny sniffed, immediately catching the scent of the dead carcass.

Ahead of them, in the middle of the flat arroyo, lay the hump of the dead cow. The sides of the arroyo rose fifty feet on either side, cliffs spotted with juniper, piñon, and yucca, with a few ponderosa pines at the top. A flock of crows were feeding on the carcass, joined by a couple of turkey vultures.

"I was gonna bring some lime and cover it," Escobar said as he got out of the truck, "but I got busy painting the church, for the fiesta." He slammed the door shut and the dark birds lifted with raucous cries into the nearby trees. They would wait to resume their meal.

Sonny looked at the dead cow. The stench was sickening; it permeated the hot, still air. Escobar took a handkerchief from his pocket, splashed whiskey on it, and covered his mouth and nose. He motioned for Sonny to do the same.

"The sons-of-bitches picked one of my milk cows," Escobar cursed as they approached the dead cow. "Whoever did it didn't take the meat, they just killed it. They drained the blood. There was a cut in her throat, just a little hole, like a needle. You can't see anything now. They cut away the female part, clean as a whistle. Why kill a cow for the blood and the culo? Crazy, no?"

Sonny nodded. "Did you find any signs?"

"No tire tracks. Whoever did it walked in, but left no footprints. My wife says it's brujería. They are crazy witches as far as I'm concerned." The frustrated Escobar shrugged, his thick eyebrows registering a frown. "I don't know. I don't believe in that stuff, but I see something like this, and . . ."

Large green flies glistening in the sun buzzed around the dead heifer. A dry breeze scurried down the arroyo. Even through the whiskey-stained handkerchiefs, the stench was unbearable. Sonny's stomach went queasy.

"When you found it, did you find any feathers close by?" he asked. He looked at the crows and the vultures that had flown to the nearby trees when they approached the cow.

"Feathers?" Escobar repeated. "Yeah, some black ones. Just the crows, I guess. I remember because some were right where they cut away the culo."

"Anything else?" Sonny asked as he begin to walk in a wide circle around the cow. He had a hunch, and when he found the first freshly turned stone, he knew his guess was right. Whoever it was had made a ring of stones around the dead cow.

"No, nada. Qué buscas?" Escobar asked from the truck, hanging back because of the stench.

Sonny pointed. "Did you see the stones?" The rough circle of stones had been placed around the dead cow. Someone not looking for it wouldn't see it. Four radiating lines spread away from the circle, one in each direction.

"I didn't pay attention." Escobar shook his head. "What does it mean?"

Ceremony of blood, Sonny thought. Blood, the cow's blood and vagina taken for a ceremony. Sacrifice. They will put signs in your path to mislead you, the words of don Eliseo resounded in his mind. They will lead you into their darkness. Something wasn't right. Sonny shivered. Suddenly he knew he had walked into a trap.

"Cuidado!" don Eliseo said, his voice a warning in the wind that swept through the trees and down the sandy arroyo.

"I've seen enough," Sonny said, and started toward the truck, walking confidently, trying to show no fear, but sure now that he was being watched. He could feel his sweat prickling, and smell the danger, like a coyote can smell the scent of man. Up there, on the ridge, and dammit! he had walked in cold! He thought of his pistol, his Bisabuelo's Colt .45. Back in his truck in La Cueva!

He was halfway to the truck when a shot rang out. It whistled past his ear, so close he thought he felt the heat of the bullet. He hit the ground and rolled against an old, dead piñon tree stump. A second shot rang out and with a thud embedded itself into the tree. Sonny hugged the earth and the tree stump as close as he could. If he sprinted for the truck, he doubted he would make it. The sniper had him pinned.

He looked up at the ridge of the north side of the cliff. There was a glint of metal, then another shot. The dirt exploded near Sonny's feet. The sniper was going to play cat and mouse with him, knowing he could blow Sonny's brains out when he wished. Sonny thought he heard laughter. He looked toward the truck for Escobar. The rancher had disappeared.

Another shot rang out and spit up dirt in front of Sonny's face. The rifleman had him trapped and in range. The next shot would split his head open.

Thoughts of his mother flitted through his mind. He thought of Rita; he should have married her, had kids, gone back to teaching, pushed tacos at the restaurant in the summer. He was no Elfego Baca! He wondered how the old lawman would get out of a mess like this, but he knew the Bisabuelo would never be caught out in the open, unarmed. And he, Sonny Baca, had waltzed right into the danger.

In those short seconds he saw his life before his eyes, old friends, scenes, the pungent smell of red chile in his mother's blender, the garlic, diced onions, corn tortillas sizzling and float-ing as they were dropped into hot grease, gang fights, people he had loved, known, Gloria, countless encounters, dreams, Rita's body glistening with sweat and love, her voice, the excitement that rushed in his blood, then a pack of coyotes running along the river bosque, calling his name, and in their midst the creak-ing cart of la muerte, doña Sebastiana, her smiling skull of death, ribs exposed, withered leatherlike breasts clinging to her bony chest, stringy hair, her calling his name now and notching her arrow to the bow, laughing as she let loose the whistling arrow of death, sibilant as his prayer, "Padre Nuestro que estás en cielo, santoficado sea tu nombre. . . ."

He thought of all the times he wanted to be a hero, save someone, save himself in a confrontation against the enemy, against evil, and knew that he didn't have that violence in him.

"Pray for me now and at the hour of my death—"

His words and thoughts were scattered by the thunderous report of a rifle exploding near the truck. The report echoed across the arroyo, frightening the crows anew.

While the sniper was busy with Sonny, Escobar had been out of sight because he was sneaking his rifle from the truck. Sonny glanced up the incline to the junipers where the sniper hid. Escobar's shot kicked up dirt near the juniper the sniper was using for cover. A second explosion followed, and the bullet hit the tree trunk, sending bark shreds flying. A figure sprang up and ran, disappearing into the trees.

Escobar laughed. He came from around the truck holding his .30-06. "I hope I got the sonofabitch in the ass." He smiled as he looked at Sonny. "Did you see that cabrón run? You okay?"

Sonny got up slowly. His legs trembled, he was afraid he might have wet his pants. He looked down.

Escobar walked to him. "Someone's trying to kill you."

"Yeah," Sonny nodded, "and for a minute I thought you—"

Escobar's worry frown creased the lines on his forehead.

"I guess I owe you one," Sonny said. "Gracias."

"De nada." Escobar shrugged, went to the truck, and brought back the bottle of Jim Beam. He handed it to Sonny. "Take a good shot," he said. Sonny took a big swig. The strong, hot whiskey calmed his nerves. Yeah, whoever had shot at him had intended to kill him. Escobar had saved his ass.

Escobar scanned the ridge. "Let's get the hell out of here. That no-good sonomabitche might double back."

They drove back to La Cueva and passed the bottle of whiskey back and forth, so by the time they reached the village, they were mellow.

Escobar told Sonny about the time he got shot at by a guy that had it in for him because he fucked his sister.

"Well, I liked the girl. She was nice, and she got in my truck and we went to a dance over in Madrid. So I had a few to drink, and we got a little hot. Not just me, her too. We went outside, in the truck, and I start humping. Then I feel something cold on my ass. It was her brother, and he's holding a shotgun. I jumped out of the truck, pulling up my pants, and the guy swears he's going to kill me. I wet my pants!" He laughed.

Sonny laughed with him, but inside he felt the anger. Someone had tried to kill him, and he wasn't going to let the bastard get away with it.

"I'm going to pay Raven a visit," he swore under his breath.

"Cuidao. That brujo can fly," Escobar said cryptically.

14

"Mira." Escobar motioned as they got out of the truck. Someone had changed the punctured tire. "You see, the boys aren't all bad. They just have their backs up to the wall."

Sonny nodded. He'd still have to pay for a new tire, but he understood about anger, and he knew there was plenty on the eastern slope of the mountain, where there was nothing for young men to do except wash dishes in the tourist restaurants or pump gas in the gas stations over in Moriarty. Some tried to hold out by running a few cattle in the dwindling scrub land, but the odds were so against them that anger took on a new meaning. They had their backs against the wall all right; they knew the ways of their fathers were dying. Still, they kept up the church, the fiestas, and the dance of the matachines. They tried to keep their familias and their community intact.

"Come in and join the fiesta," Escobar said.

The tables had been set up in front of the church, and they were covered by the dishes of food the people had brought. The procession had returned from the mayordomo's house, and the women had set out the food for all to eat. The musicians were playing a polka and an old couple was dancing. People clapped to the beat, encouraging the old man and woman as they stomped to the music. Children chased each other in a game of tag around the cemetery.

"Gracias," Sonny answered, "but I have to see Raven. Y gracias for saving my life."

Escobar shrugged. "You have a gun?" he asked.

Sonny nodded and shook Escobar's hand, wondering how he'd be at actually *using* his gun.

"Mucho cuidado," Escobar said, and tossed the Jim Beam bottle they had shared into Sonny's truck. "You might need another shot," he said with a smile. "Come anytime. And listen, don't turn your back on Raven. Or the women."

"I won't." Sonny waved and jumped in his truck.

"You know," Escobar whispered, "the first day of summer is almost here. The brujas start doing their evil work."

First day of summer, Sonny thought as he headed down the dirt road that Escobar said led to Raven's place. He would have liked to stay and eat and dance and get to know Escobar's people, but inside, the churning anger called for him to get to Raven.

So the mutilations were made around the cycle of solstices and equinoxes. Did they offer the blood to the sun, as Howard suggested? When the days of the summer solstice approached did Raven's group drain a cow of its blood and cut away the vagina for their perverted summer solstice rites? It was almost June twenty-first, when the sun would reach the farthest northern point in its journey and stand there for a day before beginning its journey south. An important day in the cycle of the seasons; sacred for those who marked the sun's path. Were they offering blood to the sun?

Sonny's truck bounced down the washboard road, raising a cloud of dust that settled on the piñons and junipers.

Sonny was convinced Raven was the one who had tried to kill him. Maybe he was getting close to something Raven didn't want known. Feeling the bullets sputtering around him had tightened the knot of fear in his stomach. He had actually felt the presence of death, and it had made him giddy for a moment. The thoughts that filled him those few seconds were incredibly clear.

He had felt doña Sebastiana close to him. The Nuevo Mexicano thought of death as a comadre, one of the familia, a godmother who came to visit from time to time, came unexpectedly.

"You ever think of death?" Sonny had asked don Eliseo.

"Every day," the old man replied. "It's natural. . . . To think of death makes life real."

"Does it frighten you?"

"No," don Eliseo replied. "Don't you see, la muerte is a Señora de la Luz."

"What?" Sonny protested. How can death be one of the Ladies of the Morning Light who brought life?

"Dressed in white, her arrow is a shaft of light. She strikes you, and you are not dead, you are filled with light. Don't you see, Sonny, there is no death! There is only the clarity we all seek. The illumination. That is why we Mexicanos don't fear death. She releases us into the light!"

"Ah," Sonny groaned, "when am I ever going to understand?"

"In time." Don Eliseo smiled.

Just ahead Sonny saw a clearing and an adobe house. If he had followed Escobar's directions correctly, this was Raven's place. He braked the truck to a screeching halt, turned off the ignition, and opened the glove compartment. He took the pistol and its well-worn leather holster. He jumped out of the truck and strapped on the holster, checked the pistol. At close range the .45 was as deadly as a rifle. Its shiny pearl handle had Bisabuelo Baca's name engraved on one side, eleven notches on the other. Now let Raven try something, he thought, and looked around.

Dark pines surrounded the place, creating an eerie feeling. Piles of sun-bleached cow bones and deer skulls lay scattered around the place. Bunches of black crow feathers hung on poles around the adobe house, swaying in the hot breeze. Two savage pit bulls near the house had charged when Sonny got out of the truck, only to be yanked back by the chains that kept them tied to posts.

Raven keeps his dogs mean, Sonny noted. He smelled the air, instinctively searching for scents that might warn him of lurking danger. It was an evil place, not good, the dead odors in the air told him. He felt the hair along his neck rise as he walked cautiously toward the adobe building and called. "Raven!"

There was no answer. The wind swept across the clearing and raised dust; it moaned through the pine tops. Sonny took off his hat and wiped the sweat from his forehead.

What if Raven was still in the forest? Armed. He cursed himself for being foolhardy. The anger inside had made him expose himself again.

"Raven!" he called. The enraged dogs charged again, snarling and rising up on their hind legs as they tugged at their chains.

A young woman appeared at the door, shaded her eyes to look at Sonny, then stepped out and spoke harshly to the dogs.

She was dressed in buckskin beaded with symbols, the old primal signs lifted from petroglyphs. A Zia sign in gold on her chest. Blond hair curled from beneath her head scarf. Her eyes were bright blue, shining eerie in the sunlight.

"What do you want?" she asked, unsmiling.

She was measuring him, Sonny figured, his gaze resting on the one earring she wore. A brass Zia sign with a black feather hanging from it.

Was this one of Raven's wives? Sonny wondered. "I'm looking for Raven," he said.

"Raven ain't here," a voice behind her said. Sonny turned and faced the second woman. She had come around the building from the western side. She was thin and disheveled, and she was followed by two of the thinnest and sorriest-looking boys Sonny had ever seen. These people are starving, Sonny thought.

This woman was also dressed in tattered buckskin. Soot covered her face.

"Don't tell him anything, Sister," she said to the younger woman.

"Get the hell out of here!" a third voice cursed, and Sonny turned to see a third woman appear from the eastern wing of the building. "You're on private property!" she snarled. She looked as thin as the first two. A baby, maybe a year old, clung to her. She moved toward the lunging dogs, to let Sonny know she would let them loose if he came closer.

"I need to talk to Raven," Sonny insisted.

What kind of a leader was Raven, he wondered, who kept these women, his followers, maybe his wives and the mothers of his children, starved?

"Call Sister!" the third woman said to the young girl.

"I'm here," the fourth woman spoke as she appeared. She was large and stout, not starved like the others. She was dressed in a leather dress with lots of beads, and her complexion was dark, made darker by black paint or soot smeared around her eyes. She wore a beaded headband with feathers, and in her right hand she carried a wooden staff, the top of which was crowned with a Zia sign, feathers, and rattlesnake rattlers.

Veronica!

"We meet again," Sonny said, and looked around. If there had been other members in this cult, they were apparently long gone.

Veronica glared at Sonny. "We know you came to our mountain to cause trouble. This is a sacred place, and we don't want you here. Leave!"

Sweat trickled down Sonny's temples. The high, thin cirrus

clouds that swept over Sandia Crest didn't hold promise of rain. Around the dogs the flies buzzed. A crow called from a pine nearby and the women turned to look. Sonny put his hand on his pistol.

Veronica laughed.

"You better put that pistol away," she said, "or Sister will let the dogs loose. Ain't no pistol goin' to stop them," she snarled.

She had not been friendly at their first meeting, Sonny thought, but she had been polite. Dressed in black and mourning Gloria, she had presented an eerie picture. But now she had completely changed, dressed in dirty buckskins, covered with dirt. And mean.

"I need to talk to Raven!" Sonny insisted.

"What do you know about Raven?" Veronica said angrily.

Sonny hesitated. He knew nothing about Raven, other than what he heard from the ranchers about the blood being drained from mutilated cows, and that the shape of his Zia compound resonated to the way Gloria was murdered. And his suspicions about who had been shooting at him. It was a leap, but it's all he had to go on. A tenuous lead.

"The ranchers around here want to know about a mutilated cow."

Veronica grinned. "Shit, if they wanted to talk to Raven, they know where to find him. I think you're snooping. You saw the sign on the road: No Trespassing. That means you! This is sacred ground, and no firearms are allowed. You have to leave! We are here to celebrate the sun's journey. The day of the solstice is almost upon us. We have come to pray to the sun."

"Amen," the others answered, and all raised their arms skyward to the sun. The baby whimpered.

"Besides, you know Raven ain't here."

"Where is he?" Sonny asked.

"He's in jail. Sheriff Naranjo busted him yesterday. Just for growing a little pot. We use the sacred herb in our ceremonies, and the sheriff busted him!"

Sonny arched an eyebrow. Something inside told him he was about to feel very foolish. If that's true, he thought, then of course it wasn't Raven who fired at me.

His mind clicked as he retraced the steps that had brought him to Raven's place and the four women. Why would Raven, or one of his fellow cult members, shoot at him? He presented no threat to Raven, he only wanted to ask questions. But his thoughts were confused, and that's why he had taken crazy chances.

"Damn," he whispered.

Veronica laughed.

"Raven's not here, but his spirit is with us," said the youngest woman. "Hear the ravens of the forest crying?"

"Amen." The women nodded. They looked at the top of an old lightning-scarred pine tree where a large raven had landed. "He is with us," one murmured, her voice quivering.

"He's always with us. Jail can't hold his spirit," Veronica shouted.

The other three wives nodded. The one near the dogs reached down and grabbed a chain, and the starving pit bulls, sensing they might be let loose, snarled and strained at their chains. The children stared at Sonny as they cringed against their mothers.

"Ain't no jail that can hold Raven," Veronica spoke. "He comes and goes. He's always with us, guarding his mountain," she said mysteriously, and she waved the staff, rattling the rattlesnake tails, making the feathers flutter.

"Raven watches over us," she intoned, shaking the staff again.

He's a brujo, Escobar had said. He comes and goes. The large raven on the pine tree lifted furiously into the air and circled the compound, then it dove southward and disappeared.

"His spirit has come to cleanse the world," one of the thin wives sang.

Sonny turned to face the dogs, one hand on the handle of his pistol. If they charged, he had no choice.

"They'll kill you, mister," one of the thin boys said. He was warning Sonny to back off.

Sonny nodded and stepped back. They will mislead you, don Eliseo had said. He had come to the compound expecting to find Raven. Expecting to find whoever had been shooting at him, and he had been wrong.

"You put the Sun King in jail, but bars cannot hold him. Now you get off our land or we'll turn the dogs loose," Veronica threatened. "This is sacred land. This is our temple," she said, gesturing toward the large adobe compound.

"Come, sisters, back to our prayers," she called the women, and marched back into the round adobe house.

The others followed her lead, returning inside. But the young woman remained.

"She means it," the young woman whispered, "if you don't leave, she'll turn the dogs on you."

Sonny looked at the thin woman in front of him, his best chance for a break. If he worked fast. "Did you lose your other earring?" he asked.

She shook her head. "Only wear one." She smiled.

She was lying. Sonny could see both ears were pierced.

"Do you ever go into the city?" he asked.

"Only with my sisters," she answered. "I'd like to go more often," she said in a whisper. She glanced nervously over her shoulder, took one step toward Sonny, then hesitated. "Raven is everywhere," she said, and rubbed her hands nervously. She glanced in the direction the big black bird had disappeared.

"Are you afraid?" Sonny asked, sensing an opening. She wanted to talk, that's why she stayed, and he heard fear in her voice.

"There's danger," she whispered, looking at the dusty ground.

"But you said he's in jail."

"Don't make no difference. He's going to bring the warmongers to their senses! And make me the new Earth Mother!"

Sonny could barely hear her whispered words. Bring the warmongers to their senses? What the hell was she talking about? The new Earth Mother? Was the fat woman the present Earth Mother? Did they take turns? One at a time the wives got fed, became the fat woman for Raven's pleasure?

"You mean you will marry Raven?"

"I am to be the Earth Mother of the new year," she answered.

So that's it. Four wives for Raven, one Earth Mother at a time. That's how he kept them together. Sex figured into every cult, sooner or later. The leader was not only the messiah, he was the father, the progenitor, and having sex with him was bedding with the Sun King. The two other thin women had been holding young children. But not Veronica. Had she failed to produce a child in her year as Earth Mother?

"Take this," she said to Sonny, and nervously slipped a thin blade from the pouch at her belt and handed it to him. It was a surgical knife.

"Where'd you get this?" he asked. The blade was covered with a dark stain. Blood?

"Don't ask questions, just take it," she whispered.

"Who are you?"

"I grew up in the North Valley," she whispered, and cast furtive glances toward the house. "I came last year to live in the house of the Lord of the Sun. I was born again into the way of the Zia sun. I gave up my old life, got a new name. But it's lonely here. It's dangerous. . . ." Her voice trailed. "They call me Dorothy."

Holy enchiladas. Sonny shook his head. The youngest woman had been given a name that was the same as the woman killed a year ago—Dorothy Glass. Five women would have disrupted the sign of the Zia; one would have had to go. Were the wives sacrificed one by one? Would a new wife appear, renamed Gloria?

Dorothy suddenly turned and fled, disappearing into the dark forest.

Sonny looked at the knife she had handed him. Stainless steel, but dull. He wrapped it in his handkerchief. It probably didn't amount to anything, but he would let Howard check it out. Or maybe she really wanted out of the cult, and this was her message to him. More likely, she had been allowed to talk to him to give him a false clue.

He turned to go just as a gust of wind whipped up, a dust devil that swept across the clearing and made the feathers and gourds rattle. The gust moaned in the pine trees, then moved away.

Even if the surgical knife Dorothy gave him was a false clue, her fear was real.

15

Sonny climbed slowly into his truck. He felt exhausted. The young girl, Dorothy, troubled his thoughts. He stuffed his pistol and the knife into the glove compartment. Of course the knife didn't have Gloria's blood on it. Or could it?

He felt angry, at himself and at the pathetic women, their imprisonment by Raven, the thin children with their pleading eyes. Could Dorothy walk away if she really wanted, or was Raven's hold too strong? These sorry-looking women, out-of-date flower children, were descendants of the hippy communes in Taos in the seventies, but they never moved on. Instead, they found Raven and his message, and now they were his slaves. Raven had cast a spell over the women. What did he promise? Salvation? Sex? Both?

So the women worshiped the annointed leader, they would

follow him to any ends. Raven, the Sun King. The women fell under his control, until their wills were bent to do his bidding, because one at a time each could become the Earth Mother, the mother of his children!

Sonny reached for his car phone. The reception was garbled. Was it the place that interfered with the signal? Maybe the large, white rocks that encircled the place? Ah, he'd wait till he was in the canyon to call Howard.

He backed up his truck and headed down the mountain road. It had already been a long day. He wanted to talk to Rita, and he needed to talk to Frank Dominic. And he knew he should pay a visit to Raven himself. Maybe he should forget the deal he made with his tía Delfina. Let the cops handle the homicide. He had followed a false trail up the mountain and nearly gotten himself killed.

The chief may be right. I'm out of my league, Sonny thought.

"You're doing it for Gloria!" he told himself angrily, and another voice within reminded him Gloria was dead, there was nothing he could do about that, and he might as well leave the case to the police.

"You're not your great-grandfather," the voice said. "You're not Elfego Baca! You've never even fired his pistol! You keep it oiled and ready to use, you keep the ammunition ready, but you're afraid to use it! Afraid to use the pistol of Elfego Baca!"

"No!" he responded to the taunting voice. "I'll use it if I have to!"

At that moment a Jeep Cherokee slammed against the side of his truck and sent it careening onto the shoulder of the road. Sonny cursed and tightened his grip on the wheel, fighting to keep the truck from flipping into the ditch.

He hadn't been aware of the Jeep bearing down on him, and the two men motioning angrily for him to pull over.

"Cabrones!" he cursed the men in the truck. Were they the bastards who had taken a shot at him?

"Pull over!" the man in the Cherokee shouted, waving a fist.

Sonny stepped on the brake and his truck went sliding on the gravel and came to a screeching stop in a cloud of dust. He started to reach for his pistol in the glove compartment, but the Cherokee had pulled alongside and the larger man was on him too quickly.

The big man shouted something as he opened the door and pulled Sonny out of the truck. Sonny struck at him, but his opponent was too strong. He swore and punched Sonny in the stomach, then hit him with a right cross. Within seconds he and his partner had Sonny pinned against the truck.

"Easy, Mike," the driver cautioned.

"He was reaching for a pistol!" the man named Mike gestured to the open glove compartment. "Don't ever pull a fucking pistol on me!" he cursed in anger.

Through watering eyes Sonny looked at the two men dressed in hunting fatigues and wearing black greasepaint to camouflage their faces.

"What the fuck were you doing at Raven's place?" the man asked, frisking Sonny, reaching for his wallet and opening it.

"None of your business!" Sonny yelled.

"It is our business!" the man shouted back. "I'm agent Eddie Martinez, this is agent Mike Stevens." He flashed his FBI badge in front of Sonny. "What the fuck are you doing up here?"

"I went to talk to Raven," Sonny replied. FBI? Just what the hell *was* going on here?

"You a friend?" the agent asked, looking at Sonny's driver's license and identification.

"I'm not Raven's friend." Sonny shook his head and wiped at his bruised lip.

"Sonny Baca. Holy shit! A goddamned PI."

The big man laughed. "Fucking dick thinks he's a hero just because he and Manuel Lopez found the car dealer's wife," he said to his partner.

"Yeah," Martinez sneered. "We heard the story. But that was

child's play. Now we're talking about blowing up a truck full of junk from Los Alamos."

Blowing up a truck full of nuclear waste? Sonny wondered. What the hell did he mean? Did the FBI think Raven was an environmental terrorist? Is that why they were up here, and apparently didn't want anyone else to be?

"Listen," Martinez said angrily, pointing a finger in Sonny's face. "Stay away from Raven! Stay outta here!"

"Who the hell do you think you're talking to!" Sonny lashed back, but Mike pushed him against the truck and held him while Martinez shouted the message in his face. "Stay away from Raven, Baca! You could get killed!" He slammed the wallet against Sonny's chest. "You understand!"

Yeah, Sonny understood. What if it was an FBI marksman that had fired at him in the arroyo?

"Stupid dick," Mike sneered as they backed away.

They climbed aboard the Cherokee and sped back up the mountain, leaving a cloud of dust in the thickening shadows of dusk.

Sonny shook his head and spit blood. "Cabrones!" he cursed, and gasped for breath. "Pinche FBI! I owe you one!" he shouted. "José Escobar! Where are you now! I need a drink!"

Then he remembered the bottle Escobar had thrown in his truck. He chuckled and felt the pain in his ribs. Bruised rib, maybe broken. He knew he was going to be sore for a long time. He tossed his wallet into the glove compartment and took out the whiskey. Just what I need, he thought, and turned and walked into the forest.

He needed to think. He knew he had screwed up. Just who the hell was Raven, and what did he have to do with the nuclear waste shipment the DOE was planning on moving from Los Alamos to the WIPP site?

"I didn't do my homework!" Sonny kicked at the ground. "Came running up here like a pendejo! What would Manuel Lopez say!"

Yeah, he didn't know diddley about Raven and he had gone busting in. Yes, he could've been killed. Maybe by Raven. Maybe by the FBI.

Around him the ponderosa pines rose tall and stately, a faint vanilla aroma exuding from their pores. A dry carpet of needles covered the ground beneath his feet. The forest was tinder dry. One careless match or a bolt out of a lightning storm and it would burn. Smokey the Bear would have to be alert. Just as the rest of the animals of the forest were alert. He felt their presence as he held his bruised rib and walked up the slope through the scrub oak until he found a protective spot under a massive granite outcropping. He guessed it was a den of a pack of coyotes. The smell was strong in the air, their pee and scent glands in the trees around the place, marking their home. They had heard him come, probably heard the noise of the fight down below on the road and moved out.

"Run coyotes," Sonny said to himself, and dropped gingerly to the ground, feeling the softness of the earth, resting his back against the cool boulder. He took the top off the bottle and drank, taking a long pull at the burning liquid.

"Ah." He smacked his lips, grimacing, closing his eyes. "Bad stuff."

He drank again and then took a deep breath, waiting for the bourbon to drive away the pain. The spot was ideal, away from the trails that hikers used. From here Sonny could look east through the pines and see the expanse of the Estancia Valley. The valley was the color of a lion in the afternoon sun.

He took another swig. He knew he had made a mistake by going to Raven's place without checking around. Damn! Why had he run off half-cocked? He heard Gloria's voice in the breeze that moaned among the trees. Gloria was drawing his strength, she wanted her revenge, but his mistakes might deny her that. And they might cost Sonny his life.

A raven called in the forest; the call went unchallenged. Around him the eyes in the forest were watching him. The coyotes weren't hunting, they were waiting to see what move Sonny made. On the ground around him ants scurried in their search for food. He looked closely and saw a moth, then a mariposa, a king butterfly with tiger markings. He heard the shrill cry and saw the flash of a hummingbird. A brilliant Rufus. The mountain was full of hummingbirds.

Sonny grew still, and the animals begin to move around him. A blue jay fluttered to the ground, then two. The forest had accepted his quiet presence and was returning to normal.

He drank again and closed his eyes. The pain in his ribs had subsided. The bourbon made him relax; he closed his eyes and slept. He saw images. Someone making a movie. Manuel Lopez sat at the director's chair, motioned for Sonny to strap on the gun of his Bisabuelo. The credits rolled. "*Solstice Day*, starring Sonny Baca." He saw himself walking slowly down the dusty main street of a village somewhere in New Mexico. Adobe huts, corrals, blacksmith shop, saloon. Cowering villagers watched from windows. He alone was to face the bad guy, who was dressed in a black outfit, looking birdlike in his movements. Laughing, calling like a crow. Raven!

Sonny reached for his pistol, but his hand froze to the handle. Four women appeared and spun a cord around him, immobilizing him. Cackling and crying they drew him toward the tall cottonwood that graced the middle of the dusty plaza. They were going to hang him! He tried to move, but couldn't. He cried for help and the youngest of the women stepped forward. The knife she held sparkled with sunlight. She cut the cord that held him, and blood streamed from his navel.

Rita appeared, rifle in hand. No, it wasn't a rifle, it was a cross. She held the cross up and the swarm of birds flew away. Rita rushed to him and placed a green herb over his wound. The blood stopped flowing. Rita had saved him, and now the townspeople, led by the schoolmistress, a lovely young blonde in a blue taffeta dress and blue bonnet, came out to congratulate them and pin the star of sheriff on his chest.

But the ceremony was interrupted by the appearance of Gloria's ghost, pale and wraithlike, beckoning to him. He turned and ran, and the ghost became a storm full of fury. Not even Rita could stop the spirit of the dead woman, which descended like a whirlwind. A ghostly devil within the whirlwind lunged at Sonny, cutting at him with the same scalpel Dorothy had given him. He ran in the dark, trying to hide, calling Rita's name, and still the pale image of Gloria pursued him.

She cried to him: "Hiiiiii-jo," and the cry was like the wind mourning through the pines. The forest had come alive with the spirits of animals, like it does during the peyote ceremony, foxes and coyotes crossed in front of his path, the trees swayed with life, a spirit animating everything.

Three of these spirits materialized in front of Sonny. Only their presence turned away Gloria's ghost; only their presence made the dark wind subside. Peace returned to the forest, but when he looked back at the village, it was deserted. Rita, too, was gone. The three coyotes lay at his feet and waited his instructions.

Sonny opened his eyes. Around him shadows filled the east side of the mountain. The sun was setting. He half expected to see the coyotes of the vision still sitting in front of him. He shivered, then rose slowly, feeling his cramped and aching muscles. The cool of the earth had seeped into his bones, and in spite of the images of the nightmare, he felt somewhat rested. He looked at his watch and realized he had slept late into the afternoon.

"Time to move," he said to the animal spirits in the forest, and made his way down to his truck. "Gracias."

He slowly coaxed his truck back onto the road and down the hill toward the highway, heading home. Once in Tijeras Canyon, he took a chance and called Sam Garcia, hoping to find out more about why the FBI was buzzing around Raven, and he got an earful.

"Sonny! You bastard!" the chief shouted. "I told you to keep your nose clean! Stay out of this case! You're just getting in the way. Stay off that mountain! Stay away from Raven! The bureau just called me! You've blown their cover! Next time I'm going to let them haul you in, or let them feed you to Raven's dogs! You got that, Sonny? Stay away! We know what we're doing!"

"Blown what cover?" Sonny protested.

"Never mind! Keep away from that side of the mountains. I'm warning you, Sonny, I'll let them throw you in jail!" Garcia's phone slammed dead.

"Up yours!" Sonny shouted in anger, and wished he could slam his cellular. Instead, he flipped the switch to off and cursed. "I'm a citizen! FBI can't kick me around!"

So Garcia knew what the FBI was doing on the east side of the mountains. He dialed Howard. "Howard?"

"Hey, compadre, you still alive?"

Sonny's ribs ached, his mouth was bruised and puffing up, but he tried to keep his cool.

"Barely. Ran into some trouble at the nest of a weirdo named Raven."

"He's no weirdo," Howard replied. There was a pause. "Is there a connection to Gloria?"

"I don't know," Sonny answered, "but it seems the FBI has his place covered. What do you know about him?"

"Raven isn't really Raven, of course," Howard answered. "Let me put it this way. He's got a list of aliases a mile long. Sometimes he's John Worthy, sometimes Worthy John. Sometimes he's John Bearman, other times John Black Crow. But he's very secretive, won't allow himself to be photographed."

"The tip came from the FBI guys, though. They said something about someone blowing up a truck from Los Alamos. I remember reading in the paper about an anti-WIPP group threatening to do something like that, but nobody took it seriously, did they?"

"Maybe," Howard replied. "For years Los Alamos Labs has been telling the public that they're only storing low-level waste. Contaminated gloves, boots, instruments, stuff like that. The environmental activists say they're lying, that there's a lot of high-level plutonium waste up there that the labs have kept secret. At one point they even built components for atomic bombs, but they kept it secret. Now the truth comes out, they do have a lot of high-level junk. Just like Pantex and Rocky Ford, and they need to get rid of it. So they're going to run a truck down to the WIPP site. Congress is allowing the labs to send a truck carrying junk to make a test run."

"When?"

"Next week. So the protesters are claiming Congress has reneged on the moratorium, and one run will open the gates of WIPP. The transportation of the nuclear waste material had been fought by every community in the state. Nobody wanted DOE trucks loaded with the radioactive junk passing through their backyards. But with Russia and the U.S. dismantling their nuclear warheads, the plutonium cores have to be stored somewhere. WIPP has a billion-dollar cave in the salt beds of Carlsbad ready to receive the junk. From low-level contaminated gloves used in laboratories to old nuclear power plant and nuclear submarine reactor cores, the amount of hot waste shipped to WIPP would grow in amounts never imagined by even the DOE experts."

"And the protest has begun again," Sonny said.

"Except now there's been a series of anonymous threats to blow up the truck. They figure if they can create a nuclear catastrophe, it will focus attention on the issue. Don't you read the papers?" Howard teased.

"I read about the threats, but I thought it was just the papers blowing things out of proportion."

"Well, obviously the FBI is taking it seriously."

"And they're watching Raven because they think he's behind it?"

"It's just a hunch, after what you told me just now. Officially, I haven't heard anything."

Sonny grunted. "How do you know so much about Raven?"

"I read the papers, bro. I try to keep informed—"

"Hey, I don't need a lecture," Sonny groaned. His ribs were aching, his nose was puffing up. All that time at the library reading about Morino and the cattle mutilations, and he'd missed the real news. He vowed not to flip so quickly to the sports pages to check the Dukes score in the future.

Sonny needed an aspirin, or a drink, maybe both. He touched his lip. It was cut and sore. Someday he was going to return the favor to Mike the FBI Gorilla.

"The bureau boys must have something on him to be so uptight," Sonny said.

"I figure they have an informant in the group, but that's just an educated guess. They tell Garcia very little. You know how it is, FBI thinks they're top shit and the local cops are yokels. Anyway, they have to take any suspicions about Raven seriously. He used to work in the mines in Grants. He's an explosives expert."

Sonny whistled long and low.

"Who else did you see up there?" Howard asked.

"Only four women. And the number one mama is the Dominics' former housekeeper. Veronica."

It was Howard's turn to whistle. "Ah, it's getting thick. Were there others in the cult?"

"Maybe, but they would've had to have been hiding in the woods—they weren't at the compound. But *someone* took a shot at me. If it wasn't the FBI—"

"Took a shot—" Howard paused. "That's not good news."

"I'm alive."

"Yeah, well. You okay?"

"Yeah, I'm okay. Listen, why would Raven, or anybody fighting nuclear waste, blow up a truck? That's just the kind of accident the environmentalists want to avoid. Blowing up a truck means a lot of contamination. What's the point in causing the kind of accident you're protesting?"

"That *is* the point. If he can create a mess, it will turn this country on its ass. If he has enough plastic explosives or dynamite to blow a dent in the truck's barrel, he'll contaminate a large area. It's publicity he's after, and if he can do any damage to the barrel, the country will be scared. Scared enough by a real disaster to stop any possibility of it happening again. Or something *worse*. Anyway, the guy's crazy, they say. Really on the fringe."

"He'll need plastic explosives, and if the bureau's on his tail, he can't buy any," Sonny said.

"Mexican dynamite," Howard replied. "We got wind there's a lot coming in, but no shipments have been intercepted."

Dynamite, Sonny thought, enough dynamite in the hands of an expert could blow up the World Trade Center. Much less would be needed to blow a hole through a WIPP container.

"So the FBI needs to catch him with the explosives in hand. In the meantime Sheriff Naranjo stumbles into Raven tending a patch of marijuana and hauls his ass in. The agency boys are already pissed off. Now whoever's helping Raven goes deeper into the Sandias, and the explosives are really hidden. Then you show up and interrogate the wives. Now they're afraid he might not even come back to the mountains."

"And won't lead them to the explosives," Sonny grunted. "How the hell was I supposed to know? How did we get into this? I can't be worried about crazy eco-terrorists when I'm trying to track down a murderer."

He leaned back in his seat and let the truck hurl down I-40 into the city. "Por Dios Santo," he heard himself say, an exclamation his father had often used.

He heard Gloria whisper the same words, looked up, and saw Gloria's body superimposed on the valley of the Río Grande, which spread out before him. If he reached out, he could place his hand on her stomach, right over her navel, which was the bright, red sun setting in the western horizon.

His hand fitted perfectly into the Zia circle, and beneath the soft mound he felt the throb of life, the heartbeat of Gloria's child, like a drumbeat. Calling to him. Revenge. Gloria's soul could not rest. Her journey through life had been suddenly interrupted. That's why her restless spirit pursued him.

"Sonny!" Howard's voice called him back to earth.

"I'm here."

"What I'm afraid of is that you have to worry about it. They're the same case."

Sonny felt a chill go through his aching body. Had Gloria met up with Raven in her environmental activities? Was she more than the usual wealthy, well-intentioned activist? Or had Veronica gotten her mixed up in more than Gloria bargained for when she went looking for a healer?

"Yeah," Sonny replied.

"I'll keep digging on Raven," Howard said. "Gloria deserves some justice. The evidence is so thin the DA can't keep Leroy Brown more than a couple of days."

"Yeah," Sonny acknowledged. "Bueno. Talk to you later."

"Take care, amigo."

16

Sonny clicked the phone off. He was driving down into the valley now, into the dry heat of the city. On the western horizon he could see the clear outline of the volcanos, etched against a band of soft, apricot light. The sun, which was setting like a brilliant red ball, created the band of soft light around the bowl's lip, the horizon. Above the band of apricot light lay a band of light blue, very clear blue that seemed an opening into another universe, and above that hung the gray-blue sky of twilight.

Overhead, a few mottled clouds reflected the soft color of the horizon. It had probably hit 95 today. A blanket of heat hung over the valley. South, toward the Manzanos, clouds rose, not rain clouds, not clouds with a dark underbelly, just the first signs of moisture from the south.

A high-pressure system sat over the Southwest desert, from

LA to the Texas line. The land cried for relief, cried for a low-pressure to move moisture from the south. The puffy clouds teasing the Manzanos and the Taos mountains did not yet contain enough moisture to bring the summer rains.

The outline of Mount Taylor near Grants disappeared as Sonny dipped into the valley. In the fifties they had mined the uranium out of the mountain, one of the sacred mountains of the pueblo world, and they had ripped it open for the uranium. And Raven had been there, helping with the destruction he said he abhorred, learning the secrets he would now use. Now the cold war was temporarily halted, and the Mount Taylor mines were closed. Now the huge tailing ponds full of uranium waste were leaking into the earth.

Stories were told of Navajo shepherds who let their sheep drink at the huge ponds around the lake, and many died. Mutated lambs were born in spring. The waste left over from the mining of uranium was poisoning the earth. Now Raven was going to create a bigger radioactive pile. His lunatic plan could contaminate half the state if it worked, and even if it failed, it could destroy the right-minded antinuclear campaign.

In a city park off the interstate, a summer-lot baseball game had already started. Sonny remembered the Dukes were playing tonight. Tacoma. He had planned to take Rita. El Gallo was pitching. Young kid, but he had been blowing the competition away. Poetry in motion. Sonny had met the pitcher at a party. They had a couple of beers and talked baseball. Sonny wanted Rita to see him pitch before the Dodgers moved him to LA.

But he couldn't enjoy a game, not now. He slipped in a cassette and the Texas Tornados' corridos filled the truck. Coasting down the slope of I-40 into the Río Grande valley, he had time to think.

The Zia sign was going to plague him until the case was solved. The powerful, positive image of the sun, symbol of the state flag, god of life, grandfather of all, now perverted by those who scratched the sign on Gloria Dominic's stomach. Now the beauty of that life-giving image was associated with death as far as the city was concerned. The media was making a lot out of the symbol, playing up the rumors that Gloria Dominic's murder was a cult murder. Sonny feared those rumors were going to prove true.

The Zia sun, the positive symbol of the sun, giver of life, the grandfather whose path in the sky was daily observed by the medicine men in the pueblos along the Río Grande, was now a symbol of murderers.

Humans have always used symbols to unify the group, Sonny thought. Sun worshiping had a long history, and even those who did not think of the sun as a deity had ingrained in their psyche a very positive human response to the orb that brought warmth and light. Yeah, Raven had found the perfect symbol to serve his evil needs. The season had become the Zia Summer, a summer of fear, a summer when ghouls came to drain the blood of Gloria Dominic, and the life in her womb.

He remembered the case of the pregnant woman who had been abducted a few years ago. A woman who wanted a baby had kidnapped a pregnant woman and taken her up to the mountains, where she strangled the woman and performed a crude cesarian. She removed the baby with a beer bottle opener. People with deep desires were driven to the bizarre.

He thought of his mother and he dialed her number.

"Sonny," the welcoming voice answered.

"Mom. Cómo 'stás?"

"Why haven't you called me! Where have you been, malcriado?"

"Mom. I got busy. How are you?"

"Bien, bien. Y tú? How's Rita?"

"Fine. Did Armando come by?"

"Mando? That lazy brother of yours. No, he didn't come. He only comes when he needs to borrow money. He's got a new girlfriend now. A little gringita from Amarillo. He spends his time running around with her. Ay, Dios, Sonny, I worry about him."

"He's okay," Sonny tried to reassure her. "Listen, do you remember me . . . you know, when I was a baby?"

"Of course," she answered.

"When I was in your womb?"

"Of course I remember. That's something a mother never forgets. Especially when she carries twins. Heavy? Oh, Lord, you two were heavy. You came easy, but Mando came kicking. But why are you asking?"

"I was just thinking. . . ."

That's what he wanted to know. What she felt. But it didn't ease the disquietude he felt; instead, it reminded him how much he had grown apart from his mother. How little he saw her. How little he saw his brother.

"So how are you?" he asked.

"Spending time with Delfina. Ay, que mujer, she's strong. You know we didn't visit that much, before. Now that we've been together, I begin to understand what she's been through. I feel there's something she wants to tell me, but she just can't come out with it. She does talk about Frank. She blames him. You don't believe he—"

"I don't know," he replied, hesitating, not wanting to tell her all he was uncovering. She'd just worry.

"I don't know what to do. Max said to try to put it out of my mind. Go back to T-VI and finish my classes."

Data processing. She was taking classes. But she didn't need to be a data processor, Sonny thought. She didn't need a computer course; he wanted to think she still had everything she needed at home. But of course, she had her own life.

He took a deep breath and said, "I'm glad."

His mother was slipping away from him, like the romantic, almost overwhelming emotion of the song that echoed in his truck: Freddie Fender singing "Lonely Days and Lonely Nights." Had her days and nights been lonely since his father died? What had been her needs during the last twelve years? He didn't know. The thought made him sad.

"Armando's drinking again," she confided. "He has his office in the bar. He and his gringita. She's his secretary, he says. He wants to set up his own used-car lot. Mando, I said, get a job. A regular job. You're thirty, when are you going to settle down? That goes for you, too. Rita's a good woman. Marry her. Go back to teaching school. You want to spend your life chasing men that don't pay child support?"

"No."

"You're like your Bisabuelo. Not happy unless there's something exciting going on. Maybe I shouldn't have let your father name you after him. His name stuck on you."

"It's a good name."

"I know, m'ijo. Your father blew his top when your first-grade teacher couldn't pronounce Francisco Elfego Baca. Because her tongue tripped on Elfego, she started calling you Sonny. He raised hell with them. He went to the principal and said you call him Elfego Baca. That was his great-grandfather's name. Do you think they listened? Oh no. They put Sonny on your report card. It stuck. I told your father, está bien. It fits him. Sonny, like sol. Your father never agreed. 'The gringos even change our names,' he used to say."

The sun, he thought. The bright New Mexican sun. "I gotta go," he said.

"Cuídate, m'ijo," she said. "Don't you start drinking like Mando. Bring don Eliseo to visit. Bring Rita. Que Dios te guarde."

Que Dios te cuide, Sonny thought. His mother always ended their conversations by entrusting him to God's care. So did don Eliseo. They knew the world was full of danger, evil men and evil things, and so they entrusted those they loved to God's care.

This afternoon he had come close to buying the farm. He could still hear the whine of the bullets and feel the dirt spitting into his face. Someone had tried to kill him, and had come very close. He could be dead. The ante had been raised.

A sudden awareness of who he was and what he had done

and not done in life flooded over him. The thought of death makes the authentic man, he remembered reading. Unamuno. No one read Unamuno anymore. How in the hell had he wound up with that paperback of the Spanish philosopher's work? Ruth? No, he must have picked it up at Salt of the Earth Books. At least once a week he visited the bookstore and thumbed through the used-book cart looking for a discarded gem.

Yes, the dark streets of the city throbbed with death. The city was growing, expanding, flexing its muscles, envying Denver's wealth, never pausing to ask how it could take care of all the new immigrants it welcomed. Entire subdivisions sprouted on sandhills seemingly overnight. The city was looking for its character, its heart, and as it grew, it reflected the violence of the society. The peaceful, rangy city of his childhood was no more. Its violent statistics mounted, as they did everywhere else, and today he had almost become one of them.

He could be lying dead now, the flies buzzing over him like they buzzed over the dead cow. But it wasn't his time, it wasn't his time. Maybe being close to death taught one to savor life. That's what the philosopher meant. You come close to death and you only have yourself to face. That wisp of an essence inside. The real Sonny Baca. Maybe facing up to what happened at Escobar's ranch would teach him not only how deep fear could run, but something about himself.

His left foot ached as he clutched the truck into a lower gear and turned off the interstate and headed north on Río Grande toward Dominic's. He made a vow to see his mother more often. They had to stay together as familia. He had to see his brother, too. Pull him out of his bar one Saturday night and take him to see the Dukes play. Maybe go up to the Jemez and go fishing. Do something together, like they did when they were kids. It was hard to keep family together when they spread out over the city. Each person got into his own thing, change came with the distance, and soon familia and friends were forgotten. What the hell did he and Mando have in common anymore? Nada. They were brothers, but they might as well be strangers. Their father's death had left a vacuum, and Mando was still trying to fill it. He wandered from one used-car lot to the next, changing jobs like he changed women.

Maybe it was that sense of familia he was missing, Sonny thought, and his thoughts turned to Rita. Maybe he should marry her and stop running around. Become a taco pusher, help her run the business, join the Mike Gallegos gang at the Hispano Chamber of Commerce. . . . Ugh, he thought, enough was enough.

The city he knew when he was a kid had changed. Change was inevitable. But something else had seeped in with the change, or maybe it had always been there and he had been too young to see it. The rift between the cultural groups seemed to grow.

"No doubt about it," Sonny thought, change had come to the North Valley. Most people knew little of don Eliseo's kind of love of the earth, of the memory that ran through the roots of the plants and trees and the water of the river. They knew little of don Eliseo's prayers, his saints, his visits to Sandia Pueblo to pray to the deities of the pueblo, his daily prayers to the sun.

Different groups knew so little of each other. "The ricos," don Eliseo said, "can do anything. They spend a fortune on stopping the bridge project. Why not give the money to the kids who can't afford to go to college? As long as people live apart from each other, there will be prejudice," don Eliseo said. "That's the way the world is. Watch out for the hombres dorados, Sonny. They promise everything, but they have no soul."

The old man made sense, even gave him insights into his feelings about Gloria's murder. She was good, she did charitable works, and evil came and claimed her. Maybe she didn't have the time to be filled with the light of the Señores y Señoras de la Luz. Maybe her soul hadn't ascended into the arms of the Lords and Ladies of Light, and it still roamed the Earth. Her soul was haunting him.

Tears broke out in his eyes, and he felt a heavy depression come over him. He wiped his nose, sniffed. "Damn!" he whispered. "Keep the thoughts straight," he said, and shook his head. "I gotta think straight. Thirsty. Why am I so thirsty?"

"Mira," don Eliseo had said when he showed Sonny where rainwater dripped from the roof onto the sandstone patio.

"You know how long the water has been dripping from the roof? Since 1693. This casa de adobe was built by my ancestors after the Españoles and Mexicanos of the area came back after being driven out by the Pueblo Indians in 1680. Over three hundred years ago this adobe house was built. . . ."

Sonny looked at the large piece of sandstone. Those centuries of water dripping had worn a smooth depression into the stone.

"Water dissolves rock. It is the most powerful element on the Earth. Look at the valley the river has carved. Water, m'ijo, is the blood of life."

Sonny pulled a handkerchief from his pocket and blew his nose. Images and memories threatened to overwhelm him. He shut off the sad corrido on the tape. "Think!" he said to himself. "Think straight! Get hold of your thoughts!"

Frank Dominic was squeezing blood from the valley. He wanted to build "Venice on the Río Grande." He wanted to turn Alburquerque into one of the fabled Cities of Cíbola. He wanted to build a canal close to the river, following the river bosque. A new city stretching from Isleta Pueblo on the south to Alameda on the north. Casinos everywhere. The puritanical view of the west was dead. The newcomers aren't going to be entertained by the old fiestas or Indian corn dances, nor by mariachis for Cinco de Mayo. The new immigrants wanted *action*.

You think Denver's booming, Dominic said, make me your mayor and I'll build you a city the likes of which you've never imagined! I'll bring back the grandeur of the Spanish past! There will be jobs! Money pouring in! A new Camelot!

"Camelot of the desert," Sonny cursed. The city would run out of water long before Dominic's wild plan got off the boards.

Whoa, take it easy, Sonny stopped himself. What the hell's gotten into you. You're arguing with yourself. Try to focus. Think of Gloria. It's for her you're doing this. Did Gloria's murder have anything to do with that bigger battle taking shape in the corridors of power? With Frank's desire to be mayor? What did Gloria know?

As Sonny pulled in front of Dominic's place, he counted a dozen cars parked in the driveway. So the sonofabitch is finally home, Sonny thought, and he's got company. Again. As he walked to the door, he noticed the license plates. The white Volvo sported a New Mexico license plate in back and a U.S. senator vanity plate in front. The blue Toyota Land Cruiser plate announced it belonged to a congressman. The Washington políticos were in town, and Dominic was entertaining them.

Sonny felt a sour taste in his mouth as he rang the doorbell and waited. How could he be so tormented by Gloria's ghost, and Dominic be back to business as usual?

A woman appeared, a housekeeper. She looked at dusty, sweaty Sonny, noticed the bruise on his face but said nothing. She nodded for him to enter the large foyer, then she disappeared, and moments later Dominic appeared. When he saw Sonny, a shadow of irritation crossed his face.

"What do you want?" he said coldly.

"I gotta talk to you," Sonny replied. He felt grimy in front of the impeccably attired Dominic.

Dominic shook his head in disgust. "I have company." He motioned toward the patio, where his guests were gathered.

"We have to talk," Sonny repeated, and he pushed by Dominic and walked into the living area. Sonny glanced at the patio at the senators, the governor and his wife, other business leaders Sonny didn't recognize.

"Somebody shot at me today."

Dominic's brow furrowed. He looked closely at Sonny. "Where?"

"Up in the Sandias."

"What were you doing?"

"Looking into Gloria's death."

Dominic's eyes flashed with anger. "I told you to stay out of—" He paused. "You think I . . ." A slow, long-practiced smile crept across his face. "If I wanted you shot, you wouldn't be standing here."

Sonny nodded. Yeah, the sonofabitch had a point.

"Where were you that night?"

"When Gloria was murdered?" As Dominic pondered his answer, a grin filled his face, and he said, "I was with another woman. Is that what you've been waiting to hear? Now you have it."

"Who?" Sonny asked.

Dominic laughed. "You're playing detective, getting shot at, and you don't know that?"

"No, I don't know! But I sure as hell can find out!"

Dominic glanced at the patio, and Sonny followed his gaze. The blonde he had seen the night Morino visited Dominic stood talking to the governor.

Now he placed her. He should have recognized her then; he'd seen her pictures in enough newspaper articles. Jerry Anderson's daughter. Anderson had developed Sandia East Estates and the Four Hills Piñon Ridge against the side of the Sandia Mountains. He had pumped enough money into the last election to elect a Republican governor, and when the electric utility had been nearly bankrupted by its president, Anderson had been drafted by the new board to get it back on its feet. What Frank Dominic was to downtown, Jerry Anderson was to uptown.

His wife, Cheryl Whitson Anderson, was English. Jerry had met her in England, liked her sense of class, and married her. She turned out to be about as boring as an English breakfast as far as Alburquerqueans were concerned, all accent and no salsa. They had one daughter, Ashley, a beautiful young thing, a city debutante. Everybody knew her. She had been homecoming queen at the university, outgoing as her father, a young woman who had beauty and wealth. She was everything the mother wasn't.

That was the woman who had come down the stairs, the young woman in the red Corvette. Now she was presiding over the cocktail party as if she'd been doing it for years.

"It's no secret," Dominic said. "She came to work at the bank last summer. . . . I don't have to explain. It just happened, that's it."

Okay, Sonny shrugged, so Dominic was screwing someone half his age. It was no skin off his nose. If Jerry Anderson found out his daughter was sleeping with Frank Dominic, he would probably kill the man. Or maybe he knew, and from one hombre dorado to the other, it was okay. The power struggles took place both in the boardrooms and in the bedrooms: lose one, win another down the road.

"It was all over between me and Gloria, everybody knew that. She knew it. Maybe there was never anything there. We were, as they say, good business partners. She did her thing, I did mine. Anyway, Ashley will tell you I was with her the night Gloria died."

"Alibis can be bought," Sonny interjected.

Dominic stiffened. His dark eyes flashed fire. "I tried to level with you, Sonny. Because of Gloria. I don't have to tell you a damned thing. It's time for you to leave." His jaw muscles tensed.

Okay, Sonny thought, I've touched the right nerve. I might as well probe deeper.

"Will she testify in court?"

Dominic nodded. "Court? You've gone off the deep end, Sonny. Really playing detective, aren't you. Is it Delfina's idea to have you bothering me? Both of you are so wrong. Ashley told Garcia she was with me—"

"Ah, what a neat little arrangement. Papa Dominic likes the young woman, and Garcia gives his blessing and, more important, keeps it quiet. And Gloria is forgotten. Is that it?"

"That's enough!" Dominic replied.

"You really don't want Gloria's murderers found, do you?"

Dominic straightened a cuff, touched his gold cufflink, and glanced out the door where his guests waited.

"You're boring, Sonny. I used to think you were a bright young man. Gloria bragged about you. But you're boring. What happened to Gloria had nothing to do with my interests."

"You knew she was pregnant," Sonny said, taking his chances.

For a moment Dominic looked as if he were going to strike out. The blood vessels along his temples throbbed. Then he shook his head, calmly, but his eyes gave him away.

"Pregnant? Where the hell did you get that? You've dreamed up some wild stories, haven't you? Or maybe you get the stories from Delfina. Come, come, Sonny. You know the old woman hates me."

"Was she pregnant?"

Dominic slammed the desk in front of him. "Damn you! You keep insisting on the most ridiculous— All right, I'll tell you! You really didn't know Gloria, did you. I'll share a secret. We couldn't have kids. She was hurt when she was young. She had scars. Oh, they didn't show, but they were there. She didn't want children, so she had her tubes tied. Now you come up with this crazy idea."

"Tubes tied," Sonny repeated.

"She was abused as a child, and she couldn't get rid of the nightmares. In fact, they were getting worse. She was reaching for help. . . ."

Dominic paused, and for a moment he dropped the mask of power that protected him. For a moment he was a man feeling a mixture of past emotions he had once shared with his wife.

"They abused her, Sonny, her own. . . . They hurt her deep inside."

Sonny hesitated. The feeling of sympathy for the man gave way to a feeling of helplessness. He knew he couldn't trust Dominic, and he knew Dominic had enough money and influence to buy a doctor's statement that would prove Gloria was incapable of bearing children. Dominic could buy anything! Yet the flash of emotion seemed real.

"I—"

"I think you've said enough," Dominic cut him off, scowling. "You really didn't know Gloria, and you dare to come here with wild stories. Who are you really working for, Sonny? The opposition? Yeah, maybe that's it. You know there are a lot of people in this city who would do anything to beat me! Both Marisa and Walter Johnson would love for you to go to the paper with a story like this! You know that, don't you?"

Sonny nodded, hesitantly. Yes, he knew.

"Yeah, we're days away from the election and they would love to pin something on me. What's done is done, Sonny. Gloria's dead. I know she would want me to go on. We had gone our different ways, but she had faith in me. She *knew* what I could do for this city! If I get elected, I'll be in the position to change this city. The people you see here"—he gestured toward the patio— "also trust me. They share my vision. They want to move on. Gloria's dead and no one can bring her back. The gardener has been apprehended, and everybody wants to put Gloria's death behind them. People want to forget about the killing! Get on with their lives! Don't you get the message?"

Sonny felt his fists clench, a shudder pass through his body. Dominic's business interests wanted the world to be neat and clean, an environment in which the Río Grande could be diverted to build a Dominic Disneyland with water canals and boats for tourists and casinos for gambling. They wanted what happened to Gloria swept under the rug. Howard was right: the cops had arrested Brown and the case would be put on a shelf, then it would die.

He felt beaten, confused by Dominic's persuasion and his own conflicting feelings.

"Yeah, I get the message," he said. "But I'm not going to stop digging. I'm going to get whoever killed Gloria! I owe it to her!

I'm not stopping just because some unsuspecting gardener's been arrested on trumped-up evidence." He turned and walked out of the house, slamming the door behind him.

He thought he heard Dominic's gloating laugh behind him, imagined he heard Ashley Anderson walk up to Dominic's side and laugh with him. "Nothing at all like his old bisabuelo," Dominic would say.

It hurt to get into his truck. He was sore all over, his ribs were badly bruised. Some day, he thought as he sat in the truck. He wished he had a cigarette, but he had promised Rita to quit. Rita, that's where he needed to be. To tell her what happened, to have her heal him.

Sonny looked at his trembling hands. A gray sheen covered them. He rubbed his fingers and thought he felt again the fine texture of the ashes he had touched when he reached into the urn that held Gloria's ashes. The glassy texture, something like the wings of doves crumbling beneath his touch.

Frank was right about one thing. Sometimes he wondered if he knew anything at all about Gloria, about who she was after she came back from LA. But he did know the dark secrets of her past. As a little girl, Gloria grew up poor and tormented. Her life had been a nightmare. She had told him part of the story. One night in her apartment she was particularly sad, she drank a lot of wine. She cried. Sonny held her.

"It started when I was thirteen," she said, "and there was nothing I could do. I slept in a small room at the back of the house with my brother. One night my father came home drunk . . . he came into my room. I was too frightened to resist. I remember the pain, that's all. Everything else I've blocked out. I thought of him as a devil sent to punish me. Because I was a woman. For two years he used me when he was drunk, and there was no one I could turn to for help. I think my mother knew but pretended not to. And my brother knew. They said nothing, did nothing, and I, too, learned to be silent. Silence, Sonny, all I knew was silence. I let the creature enter me. I felt I was to blame. I grew ugly inside. Then my brother came on to me one night, and something snapped. I scratched his face as deep as I could, and I ran out into the night. I didn't know where I was going, I only knew I had to get away. I found a man, he took care of me. But in exchange for a place to sleep, he also used me. I was only fifteen, and I was already a whore. They made me a whore. That's what I thought I was, for so long. . . ."

Is that why tía Delfina hired me? Sonny thought. She wanted to make up for the years of abuse that had fallen on Gloria? She was haunted by the crime she had allowed in her home?

Around him the slow, enveloping darkness of summer was seeping through the valley, bringing the slow dance of soft shadows. A first-quarter moon came over the Sandias to hang over the valley. A nighthawk flew from the river, its darting flight a thing of beauty. Sonny pushed a button on his radio. At the Sports Stadium the Dukes were warming up to face Tacoma. In the peaceful old settlement of Ranchitos, don Eliseo would be sitting down to his simple supper of tortillas, beans, a chile stew with meat. The Lords and Ladies of Light had blessed the valley with another day of life, and the old man would give thanks.

Sonny sniffed the air. The coolness of the river wafted across the valley. Respite from heat. Still no smell of rain in the air. Only the green, sperm smell of cottonwood leaves.

He thought again of Rita, and he realized his thoughts weren't organized. They were running, like coyotes in heat, along the dark bosque of his mind. That wasn't good.

Slowly and painfully he put his truck in gear and headed toward Fourth Street and Rita's Cocina.

17

Sonny awakened hugging the pillow. Consciousness came slowly as the gray-pearl light of dawn filtered through the haze of his sleepless night. He had been dreaming that he was making love to Rita, a voracious love, a consuming, sweating, groaning type of love, wild with animal fury and heat. She whispered in his ear, "Make love to me!" She coaxed him and pressed her moist body against his. He groaned with desire, his body tense with the need to enter her and find release.

"Make love to me, amor," she cried. He had never felt her so aroused. Her strong hands caressed his back and kneaded his shoulders. Her fingers moved down along his stomach and to his sex, touching him tenderly, but do what she would, he remained flaccid.

All night he had been haunted by images of her naked body,

her moist curves. Her long dark hair flowing around him, the perfume of nopal blossoms, intense reds and purples, the white yucca flower rising into the blue sky like bells on a staff, the desert blooming with love. Her dark eyes were full of love, her nipples erect and lovely as dark peach blossoms, her thighs a warmth of flesh pressing against him, and her lips hot when she kissed him.

She kissed his mouth and face, his ears, his throat, and down his chest to the flatness of his stomach. Her fingers touched every part of his body, but he couldn't respond! The lovemaking only created frustration, a pain he couldn't release.

Soaking wet, Sonny moaned and opened his eyes. Damn, it wasn't even daylight! Outside, the morning jubilation of birds filled the air.

He turned on his back. The nightmare, he thought, was a reflection of what had happened last night. He had gone to Rita, but for the first time he hadn't been able to make love. She had been waiting for him, dressed in a red chemise and panties. Candles burned on her dresser, the soft aroma reminding him of childhood visits to church, mass and its solemnity, the Kyrie Eleison being sung by the chorus of women at the back of the church. The red of roses filtered through the room. Cans of cold Bud sweated in the ice bucket, and his favorite chicken tacos smothered with green chile were waiting for him.

"God, I'm tired," he said, and told her about his visit to Raven's compound and to Dominic's as he undressed. He needed to bury himself in her, allow her love to wash away the bad day.

"Yes," she whispered, "I'll give you a rubdown. You can rest. . . ."

"I don't want to rest"—he kissed her—"I want you."

He unsnapped his shirt and admired her as she reclined against the satin pillows. "And I want you." She smiled and pulled the lace ribbon of her top, revealing her round, inviting breasts.

"Your bruises," she said, softly touching his lips, which had puffed up.

"The hell with my bruises," he answered. Then he paused. Somewhere he thought he smelled the fragrance of lilacs. He felt sick.

"Lilacs?" he said.

"No, no lilacs. I got rid of that perfume," she replied. "Come." She held out her arms. She was in the mood to be loved.

He finished stripping, lay beside her, and kissed her. The taste of her kisses would wash away the scent of lilac. He loved the smell of her body when they made love: a deep, satisfying earth smell, like the fragrance of chamisa after a rainstorm, like tortillas cooking on the comal. Home, warmth, excitement. But when Rita drew him into her arms, nothing happened.

The image of Gloria in his mind hung over him like a veil, her touch cold, and he recoiled from it.

"You're tired," Rita whispered.

He slipped on his back and groaned. What the hell did it mean? He rubbed his stomach and felt the itch that had been bugging him for days. He scratched softly, the round circle, the four radiating lines, the sign of the Zia. He looked at the candles. The wax smell filled her bedroom, mingling with the lilac scent. He thought he heard the cawing of a crow.

Rita lay her head on his shoulder. "Rest," she whispered, and caressed his chest.

Sonny stroked her soft, round stomach and traced a circle tenderly around her navel. He touched the soft rim and paused to let his finger feel the dip in the center. She was the only woman whose navel he had ever caressed, he thought, and the thought surprised him.

"I don't know what's happening!" He looked down at his naked body and felt ashamed. He pulled the sheet over himself. "Today I was coming down I-40 and I just started crying. It was a mistake to go see Frank, I mean I just couldn't think straight. . . . I actually felt sorry for the bastard!"

"You loved her. She was the first woman you knew as a young man."

"I didn't think I'd take this whole thing so hard," he confessed, afraid his voice might break.

He turned to look at Rita in the dim light.

Her hand caressed his chest; he reached to squeeze it and felt his heart pounding.

"You're too good to me," he said, and held his breath. The candlelight created swaying images on the wall. Gloria's silhouette hovered there.

"What if she was pregnant twelve years ago, after our one night? After we made love?" he said hoarsely.

There, it was out, something he had not been able to say, or even to allow himself to think. What if there was a child created that night? It had haunted him. He looked at Rita. She sighed.

"There's no way to know," she whispered, her dark and lovely face looming over his. "But now the child she was carrying when she was murdered is haunting you. Some child spirit has returned. A young soul of the universe that wants to speak with you. You have to see Lorenza. She can help."

Lorenza would know what to do. She had gone to Mexico to study with brujos. She practiced a kind of indigenous shamanism, in the way of the good brujas, those called curanderas in the New Mexican villages. They had a way of healing, a way of knowing.

Don Eliseo often talked about the old ways of healing, but he didn't practice. He was content to muse on the meaning of the old traditional teachings. And Rita didn't practice the way, even though she grew the herbs used for the remedies.

"You think so?" Sonny asked.

"Yes."

"What's wrong with me?"

"Susto," Rita replied.

Susto? Sonny thought. Fear. Fear has gotten into me, it's draining me.

"I never felt fear like this before."

"This isn't like being afraid of a fight or one of those bulls you used to wrestle. This is Gloria's spirit. Her spirit was in the room with her body. Perhaps it's now in you. If she was pregnant, there's also the spirit of the child she was carrying. The lost child, the child you believe could also be yours, in a larger sense. A child's soul is trying to come to you, to help you, but it doesn't know how. It has something to tell you. Lorenza's the only one I know who can release the susto, release the energy Gloria and maybe her child are creating. It's in you, Sonny, like a shadow."

Yes, Sonny thought, and scratched his stomach. Etched around my ombligo, the Zia sign.

"I'll go see her."

"Good," she said, and slipped out of bed for a bottle of almond oil. She massaged his back. The gentle caresses took out some of the fatigue and he felt better.

"I don't need Lorenza, just you," he said when she finished. She served him a cold beer.

"You need to eat," she said. She put on a robe and warmed the tacos.

He sat back and let her do her ministering, sure that he had only to eat and rest and he would be all right. He was tired, but the love of this wonderful woman was all he needed. He ate greedily, eager to regain his strength.

He smacked his lips. The pleasant sensation of the hot chile tingled in his mouth; its subtle essence lingered on his lips. Every man should be so lucky, he thought.

"Delicious. That'll fix me up." He grinned and moved to her side.

She kissed him and caressed him softly, but the sexual energy he had always taken for granted just didn't light up. She drew him to her bosom and whispered again that he had to rest. She sang a lullabye, the soft words a hum that lulled him to sleep. It was a short sleep, and the only image that appeared was that of a child. The child was running with a pack of dogs in the forest, but when he looked closer, he saw the animals were really coyotes.

He awoke with a start.

"You okay?" she asked.

"Fell asleep. I'd better get going," he said, and reached for his pants.

"You can stay," she offered, but he knew she needed to rest. Tomorrow was Monday and her work weeks were long. He, too, had things to do. He had to go back over the territory, organize it like Manuel Lopez would organize. Be methodical. Get over the feeling of confusion.

"Gracias," he said as he slipped on his shirt, pants, and boots. "You need your rest. I'll call you. Sorry about—"

"There's nothing to be sorry about!" she snapped back. "You know that. But promise me you'll see Lorenza."

"I will," he said. He bent over her and kissed her. "You're great. Thanks for everything."

"Try not to worry about it," she whispered, but she knew that telling a man like Sonny not to worry about impotency, momentary as it might be, was like talking to the wind. "You need rest."

"I'll rest."

"Promise?"

"Scout's honor."

Rita laughed. Sonny hadn't lasted a month in the scouts.

He drove home and listened to messages on the answering machine, then he slipped out of his clothes and tried to sleep. For a long time he listened to the drone of the grillos in the trees, the dream-time music of summer locusts. He dozed in and out, disturbed by his restless thoughts. Just before dawn he finally slipped deeper into sleep, and images of a large black bird haunted the visions. Raven feathers swirling in a dark wind, a dust devil, the kind that swept across the llano on hot days, remolinos del diablo, the old people said. The devil riding in the whirlwind. He raised his right hand, crossing his thumb over his first finger in the form of a cross. The giant, dark bird covered the sun for an instant, then there was an explosion, and the shape of a luminous mushroom cloud rising in the sky.

He started, groaned, limped to the window, raised the blind, and looked across the dirt road. In the mother-of-pearl light before sunrise, don Eliseo was standing in the middle of his cornfield. The young corn plants were three feet high and growing inches each day. Don Eliseo stood among the plants to greet the morning sun, waiting for los Señores y las Señoras de la Luz to come with the sunrise, flooding the valley with light, nourishing both corn and old man.

Don Eliseo rose every morning before sunrise to greet the sun. Each morning he turned toward the east and bowed respectfully as the sun rose over the mountain, asking the sun to bless all of life.

Sonny looked into the gray sky. Wisps of clouds raced towards the Sandias, mauve stripes, strings of rosy pearls. There was some humidity in the air, the signs of the premonsoon low pressure. Dew clung to the grass and the corn plants. Moisture beginning to push up from Mexico, enough to tinge the air and tantalize those who prayed for rain.

The day would be hot and brassy. The rainy season of summer was approaching, but the anvil-shaped, dark-bellied clouds of rain had not yet begun to gather over the Sandias in the afternoons. Until the rains came, the clouds were stingy, virgin rain clouds whose blessing never touched the earth, clouds that dissipated under the intense June sun.

Stress, he thought, stress. He didn't need to see Lorenza Villa, he needed rest. A steady diet. Vitamins. A mega dose of C. Cod-liver oil.

"Don Eliseo!" Sonny called out the window, "Buenos días le de Dios."

"Hey, Sonny, how's it hanging?" the old man called back.

How in the hell did he know? Sonny thought, smiling weakly to himself.

"Ven a tomar café," don Eliseo called, and he moved from the cornfield toward his tree. A large pot of coffee was brewing on the coals of the barbecue grill, the strong aroma wafting through the neighborhood. Don Eliseo made coffee the old-fashioned way, just dropped handfuls of grounds right into the boiling water and let it simmer. It was the strongest and best coffee Sonny ever had. During the morning neighbors stopped by to visit with the old man and taste the coffee.

Under the cottonwood stood a wood crate, his rocking chair, and two extra chairs for don Toto and doña Concha.

Sonny slipped on his jeans. The scalpel Dorothy had given him still rested on the dresser. He had to get it to Howard and find out if the dry stains were human blood, though he wasn't sure he wanted to know the answer.

Shirtless and barefoot, he walked across the street to greet the old man. Don Eliseo had watered the grass in his front yard and the yellow rosebushes that hugged the adobe walls of his house. Rosas de Castillo, the small yellow roses first brought by the Españoles up the Río Grande valley.

"The rosas are blooming," Sonny said.

"Those bushes have been here since I can remember," don Eliseo said as Sonny limped to a chair. "Smell the earth, Sonny. In the morning, before the sun rises, you can smell the earth. Es la aroma de la madre tierra."

Sonny inhaled. The morning before the sun rose was the most refreshing coolness he knew; it was pure and deep. The green of don Eliseo's garden filled his nostrils.

"Why up so early?"

"Bad dreams," Sonny said with a shrug, sat and sipped at the strong coffee.

"I watered your grass yesterday," don Eliseo said. "Sun would have burned it."

"Gracias." Sonny nodded. He had been too busy to care for the small patch of green around his front door.

"Your landlord only comes for the rent money. What does he care about the grass? Ay, and no sign of rain."

June was as dry as vengeance. In the trees the cicadas that had hummed all night were silent. Don Eliseo's yard, with its garden of corn, flowers, trees, and bushes, was an oasis of coolness. Like his ancestors before him, he watered from the acequia, the irrigation canal that ran along the back of his property.

Yes, here it was cool, as was the river valley, but the heat of the day would evaporate even that freshness when the sun rose.

It would be the kind of day that drove roofers to drinking. Plenty of flat roofs on the adobe homes of the city, but on days without rain there were no leaks, and no leaks meant none of the emergency calls they loved to get on rainy days. They grew morose, gathered in bars to console each other, drank too much, looked to the sky, and prayed for rain. Then the rains would come and they'd get the calls, but they couldn't work while it was raining, so they drank some more.

"Sad men," Sonny said.

"Qué?"

"Just thinking. . . . No rain," Sonny said. The old man nodded.

"There's a dance over at Sandia Pueblo. Dance for rain."

"Don Eliseo," Sonny changed the subject, "can I ask you a personal question?"

"Sure, Sonny. What are friends for?"

Sonny cleared his throat. How in the hell did one ask questions like this? "Did you ever have any trouble with your wife?"

"No." Don Eliseo shook his head. "She was a good woman. Que descanse en paz."

"I mean, about making el amor, you know—"

"Oh, I was pretty good at that, Sonny. In my day. It's part of nature. A man is like a rooster. Once he learns to mount the chicken, he needs it every day. You know, we never ask the chicken about all this. When I got older and I was no good at that business anymore, my wife said 'Gracias a Dios.' Sometimes we learn our lessons too late, qué no?"

"But when you were the young rooster, you always—"

"Came through? Never failed, Sonny. A man adds up fifty years of mounting the chicken, a half-century, Sonny. That's a lot of practice. Pero todo se acaba," he added sadly. "If you throw me in the river, I can probably still swim, but if you throw me with the chickens, forget it."

"What about someone like me?"

"You?" Don Eliseo cocked his head and looked at Sonny. "You got Rita, what more do you want?" Don Eliseo studied Sonny's worried look.

Sonny nodded and looked down at the ground, and it dawned on the old man.

"With Rita?" don Eliseo said incredulously.

Sonny nodded glumly. He wanted to say it wasn't his fault.

"Híjola, Sonny, with Rita? Maybe I better give you a few lessons," he chuckled, and slapped his thigh. Sonny's look told don Eliseo it wasn't funny. He sipped his coffee. "I don't mean to laugh, Sonny. It happens. You're working too hard."

"It's something else. . . ."

"But you don't believe in the brujas," don Eliseo reminded him. "In the old days if a woman wanted to make sure the man only paid attention to her nest, she took a little of his hair from his private parts down there to a bruja. That hair can hold or turn a man any way the woman wants. Le hacía un mal."

"Cast a spell?"

"Sí. A curse, Sonny. Maybe they put a curse on you."

"Who?"

"The same ones who killed your prima."

He didn't believe in spells. "Only you believe in brujas, don Eliseo."

"I've seen enough to believe," the old man answered. "I saw a curandera cure a primo once. The man vomited up a ball of hair. The witch had taken a little of his hair and put the curse. The man was dying until la curandera lifted the curse. There's good witches and bad ones, as in all things. The world is good and evil. All the brujos I know here in the valley and up in the Indian pueblos, they're good people. Curanderos. They have the power to help people. It's the bad ones who hurt people."

"What do they want?" Sonny thought aloud.

"They want you," don Eliseo said, and Sonny followed the old man's stare and looked at his bare stomach. He had been scratching softly around his belly button. He saw the faint, pink outline of a circle around his navel. He was a marked man.

"Why me?" he asked with a worried look.

"Maybe you're getting too close," don Eliseo answered.

"Someone took a shot at me," he said, and told don Eliseo about his adventure at La Cueva. Then he turned back to the subject foremost in his thoughts, his lack of performance with Rita.

"Is there anything I can take?" he asked the old man. "Vitamins? Maybe some of those herbs you grow in your garden?"

Don Eliseo shook his head. "Sonny, you're too involved. Take a few days off and go fishing with Rita up in the Jemez. A day's rest and Rita will take care of everything else." He pointed to the newspaper on the crate. "I've been following the case. Page one, every day, the Zia murder. Did you ever talk to the brother?"

"Turco?" Sonny shook his head. "There's a big dope deal coming down, so he's hiding."

Fishing, he thought, that's how I should have spent my weekend. A day on the cool stream of the Jemez, and a fat rainbow trout hooked and fighting him, and later a lounge chair and a beer as the trout sizzled in the skillet. Fish were supposed to be good for the energy he needed.

"The papers mention the housekeeper. . . ."

"I talked to her," Sonny said. He told don Eliseo about talking to Veronica and then the surprise at meeting her at Raven's place in the mountain.

"She's a strange woman," don Eliseo replied. "She came to

Ranchitos a few years ago. You know how Concha goes to visit the new people who move in; she knows everyone. But the woman wouldn't talk to her. The rumors we hear are that this Veronica and her friends read the minds of people."

Doña Concha knew Fourth Street better than most. She spent her days wandering the streets and acequia paths from Alameda to Los Ranchos, as far south as Los Griegos.

"Psychics?" Sonny asked.

"Psychics?" The old man looked puzzled. "Brujas," he said.

Sonny looked down at the faint rash on his stomach. It was just his imagination that the rash formed a round circle. He had to get rid of that kind of thinking. Thinking they could put the sign of the Zia on him played into their hands. Yeah, but there it was, pink and itching.

"Mira," don Eliseo said. "Es tiempo de los Señores y las Señoras."

The first rays of the sun peeked over Sandia Crest, filling the valley with a dazzling light. Dawn shadows scattered as the brightness exploded.

A stillness filled the air as the first moments of scintillating light filled the valley, then the leaves of the cottonwoods quivered as the playful light came racing across the treetops and dropped to glisten on the leaves of corn. The entire valley seemed to fill with a presence, something Sonny thought he could reach out and touch.

"Los Señores y las Señoras," Sonny whispered, and held his breath.

The old man had told him about the Lords and Ladies of the Light who came with the sun, but Sonny had never been up early enough to share the event with don Eliseo. Now as the dance of light sparkled on the dew and the green plants, he felt the magical moment.

"Sí," don Eliseo replied. "Grandfather Sun is rising to bless all of life, and he sends los Señores y las Señoras down to earth.

See how they come dancing across the treetops, on the corn, on the chile plants, everywhere. . . .”

For a moment Sonny thought he could, like don Eliseo, see the brilliant, tall, and handsome Lords and Ladies of Light, who came as sun rays over the mountain to fill everything with light.

“Bendición,” Don Eliseo said, closing his eyes and turning directly to the strong light so the brilliance bathed his face. This was his moment of prayer. As the sun came over the mountain, don Eliseo greeted it, asking its blessing for all of life. He opened his soul to receive the light.

“Beautiful,” Sonny nodded, and he and the old man sat quietly.

It’s a dance, Sonny thought, a swift dance of light that descended on them. Like the first day on earth, the sun creating life, the sun sending its emissaries to touch every living thing. It lasted only moments, and yet in those moments, a transformation took place. Light replaced darkness.

Don Eliseo said his simple prayer. “Tata Dios, Sol que eres nuestro abuelo, bendición a toda lo que vive.”

“You pray to the Señores y Señoras?” Sonny asked.

“Yes, just as I pray to the kachinas and the santos. When my wife was alive, I went to church with her. Every Sunday we went to mass together. You know what I found out? In all those fifty years of going to church, not a single priest ever knew about los Señores y las Señoras de la Luz. Old priests, young priests, they came and went at our parish, but not one knew about this. They knew about Tata Dios, but they didn’t understand that Grandfather Sun is the giver of life. The light enters our soul and gives us clarity.”

The sun had cleared the crest of the mountain now, fully risen, and the play of light reached a climax that created the essence of a living presence around them.

“See the light shining on the leaves of the alamos, the maize, the grass, my wife’s roses. Everything they touch is alive!”

It took Sonny’s breath. Sitting by the old man as the sun rose was magical. It was real. Sonny could see the Lords and Ladies, see the forms of light that even now made everything shimmer with movement and light.

"Jesus Christ," he muttered.

"Sure," don Eliseo nodded. "The Cristo is a Señor de la Luz."

Sonny thought he hadn't heard correctly. "Qué?"

"The light fills a man up and it makes him a cristo. We can become like the Cristo. . . ."

Become a Señor de la Luz, Sonny thought, become godlike.

He looked across the field of corn, where the dance of light continued. The old man saw the Cristo in the sun, he saw the kachinas of the pueblos and the santos of the church.

Sonny felt the infusion of energy into the plants, the leaves soaking in the light, the penetration of the energy into the roots. It warmed his bare chest, his face, his arms. If he learned the way of his abuelos, he was sure the light would enter his soul. He remembered a prayer from childhood.

"My mother used to pray: "Quién llena esta casa de luz? Jesús. Quien la llena de alegría? María. Que claro se ve, teniendo en el corazón, a Jesús, María, y José. . . . Something like that."

"The prayer is to fill the house with light," don Eliseo said. "Every day one opens the window and doors and fills the house with the new light of day. Allow the Señores y Señoras de la Luz to also enter your soul."

The old man was describing his spiritual path. The prayers to the Lords and Ladies of the Light were so old that now only the medicine men in the Indian pueblos remembered them. And don Eliseo.

The old man opened his soul to the light, and the light filled his soul with clarity. It was there, trembling just beneath the old man's skin and bones, the essence of don Eliseo's soul.

Becoming god, Sonny thought. The Lords and Ladies of Light weren't just an abstract thought in don Eliseo's mind, they were real.

"Light," the old man whispered, "that's all there is. The light brings clarity."

"Yes," Sonny agreed. At that moment, when the dance of the dazzling, shimmering Lords and Ladies of Light was at its strongest, there was clarity. His mind was clear, at rest, absorbing light, communing with something primal in the universe, connecting to the first moment of light in the darkness of the cosmos.

"In the beginning was the chispa, the spark of imagination," don Eliseo intoned, his weathered, wrinkled face golden with light. "The chispa came to the womb of Madre Noche, the womb of time. The first light was born, male and female, and it was good."

"But what about evil?"

"It is an eternal struggle. On the one side the clarity of the Señores y Señoras de la Luz, on the other side the violence which destroys. Don't let yourself be trapped by darkness, Sonny. Pray to the Señores y Señoras de la Luz. Let the light fill your soul."

Sonny leaned back in the chair and breathed deeply. He closed his eyes and let the sunlight shine on him. The light penetrated, a soft luminous ball glowed in his chest, extended to his navel, enveloped him. His thoughts became dreams and memories. He didn't know how long the meditation lasted, he didn't care. He only knew that his soul had opened to receive the light. If there was anything sacred on Earth, it had washed over him. Then it was gone, and Sonny turned to look at the old man. A beatific smile filled his wrinkled face.

"How about another cup of coffee?" the old man said.

"Maybe it's this strong coffee you brew that makes us see things," Sonny joked.

"Maybe," don Eliseo nodded and poured them fresh coffee. "But when you feel the Señores and Señoras de la Luz come to bless life, you don't need anything else. When I was young, I used to do the peyote ceremony with my compadres at the pueblo. But when I got on the Path of the Sun, I found I didn't need the guidance of Señor Peyote. You only need to open your soul."

"The kids should know this," Sonny said. "They don't need drugs. Just being in the beauty of the new day is getting high, qué no?"

Don Eliseo nodded. "Our children have lost the way."

Sonny agreed. The children had lost the way. He had lost the way. But there was still time to recover. The old people like don Eliseo were still alive, still keeping the universe in balance. They had so much to share.

He thought of other times of the day or the season when the dance of the light took place. In early October, high in the Taos mountains when the aspen shimmered, gold leaves quivered with light. Then a person felt the light impregnating the leaves and trees. Or driving down in mid-October from the Jemez Mountains through the canyon. The red cliffs of Jemez caught and held the light of the golden cottonwoods. The earth had its sacred places.

"The ways of our ancestors were full of beauty," don Eliseo said. "They kept close to the earth, watched the sun and moon. And when they died, their spirits remained with us, in the light, in dreams. If the kids don't worship the ancestors, then what we created here on the Río Grande will die."

Sonny finished his coffee. It can't die, he thought, I won't let it. The thought renewed his strength.

"Qué haces hoy?" don Eliseo asked.

"Go out to that other world," he said.

"The world of the brujos," don Eliseo said.

"They're screwing around with the Zia sun."

"You have to fight evil. . . ."

"Yes," Sonny agreed, and they both stood. "Gracias por el café, y gracias por los Señores y las Señoras." He gave the old man an abrazo, impulsively, something he had never done.

The old man smiled. "You're a good man, Sonny," he said, returning the abrazo with strong arms, then placing his forehead against Sonny's forehead.

"The kiss of life," the old man said. The energies of their souls met for a moment, and the old man's light flooded through Sonny. He felt the old man's strength enter his body.

"Gracias," Sonny whispered.

18

Sonny hurried back to his house, afraid tears might well in his eyes. He showered and dressed, then drove to Garcia's Kitchen for breakfast. Garcia's served some of the best huevos rancheros and green chile in town. Sonny liked to sit at a window booth and look out on the traffic that moved up and down Central as he ate. Old timers from la Plaza Vieja frequented Garcia's, sat around, drank coffee, gossiped.

The gathering of the old men was an old custom. When the villages were small along the Río Grande, the center of the community was la plaza de armas and the church. There the old Mexicanos gathered to discuss the affairs of state. Warming their bones against southern adobe walls in winter and cooling off under the shade of the alamos in summer, the discourse of the old men was an essential part of the politics that ran the village.

Now the villages from Isleta to Bernalillo were swallowed up by the expanding city, but the men still found a place to gather to talk. In the mornings it was Garcia's or Duran's Pharmacy or the Village Inn Pancake House; in the afternoon they sat under the shade trees of the Old Town plaza and discussed the events of their community and of the world as they watched the tourists.

"Hi, Sonny," Rosa greeted him.

"Rosa, mi amor, when are you going to give me a chance?" he asked, smiling, and took the menu from her as he sat. Rosa was vivacious, an attractive woman, short and stocky with big breasts and a big smile. Sonny could tease her, and she gave as good as she got.

"Soon as my old man's out of town." She smiled and poured his coffee. "The usual?"

Sonny nodded.

"What's the usual?" the woman at the table next to him asked.

Sonny turned to look into a pair of bright blue eyes that smiled invitingly. She sat alone, wearing a bright blue summer dress, her blond hair teased up, her complexion white and smooth. Sonny guessed she was in her thirties.

An adventuresome tourist, Sonny assumed. Her kind didn't often stop for breakfast at Garcia's. They usually stayed at the Sheraton where they felt "safe." This lady was obviously out for a real taste of Alburkirk.

"Huevos rancheros." Sonny smiled.

"That's what I'll have," the blonde said to Rosa. "A ranchero with huevos."

Rosa bit her lip to keep from laughing. "Yes, ma'am." She smiled, glancing at Sonny. "You want him over easy or scrambled?" she asked, and the blonde said "Over easy" as Rosa hurried away to the kitchen, where Sonny knew she would burst out laughing and tell the cooks that the blonde had just ordered a rancher with balls.

"New in town?" Sonny asked, also trying to keep from laughing.

"We visit every summer. My husband sells kitchen equipment. We're at the Hyatt, but that's not real, you know what I mean?"

From the kitchen Sonny heard a roar of laughter. Rosa had just told her story.

"I know what you mean."

"I love Old Town. I'm going to look around. Any suggestions?" Her blue eyes were direct, inviting. She crossed her long legs, waited.

Sonny looked at her, felt the tug of the flesh. She was lovely, and alone. She wanted suggestions.

"Hmmmm . . ." he thought.

She waited, the crossed leg swinging softly.

"Well?"

Sonny cleared his throat. "Oh, there's a lot to see. Lots of shops, jewelry, . . ." he stammered.

"Yes, thank you." The woman in blue nodded. "I intend to do the shops." She broke off the conversation, sensing Sonny's reluctance, and turned back to her newspaper.

From where he sat, Sonny could smell her perfume. Her lips were painted candy red. A very nice-looking woman, attractive, and obviously in the mood. But not today, he thought, and tried not to kick himself too hard for turning her down. He consoled himself by looking out the window at Central Avenue and concentrating on anything but the woman in blue.

Central was the original Highway 66, which ran east to west through the city. Before the interstate was built, old 66 had cut through Tijeras Canyon and entered the city. It ran through town before it crossed the Río Grande and climbed up the long slope of Nine-Mile Hill. There it dipped into the Río Puerco valley, crossed the continental divide somewhere around Gallup, crossed the deserts of Arizona, and ended on the California coast. California, the land of dreams. The highway, too, was a road of dreams.

Route 66, a road of dreams, generations of dreams crossing the nation on the mother road. During the Dust Bowl era, the Okies had moved west, and Elfego Baca had stood somewhere near this very spot and watched the migration. The story was handed down the generations, how the Bisabuelo had helped an Okie family change a tire, paid for the repair, and given the man a few dollars for gas. Enough to get to Gallup.

The people here felt sorry for the dislocated, Sonny's father had told him. They often fed them, gave them food before they moved on to the dream of California. A few stayed. Cars broke down and some were forced to plant their dream in the Río Grande valley. Lean men and women with bony bodies and faces, trudging west to California, cars and trucks packed with all their worldly possessions, piled high, canvas water bags cooling as they hung over rearview mirrors or over the front of the radiator grill. Broke and without a dime, those who had no strength to continue on to the land of milk and honey laid down their load and learned to eat beans, chile, tortillas.

As they became learned in the cultural ways, some moved into the barrios, lost their prejudices against the Mexicans, started businesses in the booming downtown area, and now their grandkids were third-generation Alburquerqueans, as proud of the city as any Nuevo Mexicano.

Blacks who worked on the railroad, the cooks and waiters of the Super Chief, had brought their families and settled along Broadway, and their community thrived. Indians from the Pueblos and Navajos from the Diné Nation moved in and out of the city, creating a cultural cloth of many colors. Newer immigrants arrived, Japanese and Southeast Asians, more Mexicans, and those who fled the wars in Central America, each lending a new color and texture of fabric to the cloth, the woof and warp took on the earth tones of a Chimayó blanket.

The city was an intricately patterned blanket, each color representing different heritages, traditions, languages, folkways, and each struggling to remain distinct, full of pride, history, honor, and family roots. They were clannish, protective, often prejudiced and bigoted. Yes, the city was full of growing pains, bound to old political oaths and allegiances, lustful, violent, murderous when the moon was wild, drunk on lost loves. At the center they were all struggling for identity.

What will bind? What will bring us together?

"What?" Sonny asked.

"What you ordered," Rosa replied, sliding the plate full of eggs, beans, potatoes, and green chile in front of him. In a small dish came the just-baked corn tortillas. "Just like you like them, hot," she said with a smile.

"And here's your ranchero with huevos," she said to the woman in blue, serving the second platter and rushing back to the kitchen.

Rosa was devilish. Sonny smiled and looked at the blonde.

"Looks delicious," she said.

"The best in town," Sonny replied.

"I'm glad I took a chance." She smiled again.

"Provecho."

"Provecho?"

"It means enjoy."

"Oh, I intend to," she said, and ate. Sonny saw her eyes go full of tears as the first bite of hot chile burned her mouth. He expected a cry, a protest, but she only sniffed, touched her napkin to her nose and said, "Excellent."

She had spunk. She intended to enjoy. Sonny dug into his huevos rancheros. He ripped two smaller pieces from his tortillas, making little spoons with which to pick up the eggs, potatoes, beans, and chile. He glanced at the blonde and saw her cut gingerly with a fork into the food.

"Like this," Sonny wanted to tell her. "Here in New Mexico we are so rich that we use a new spoon for each bite we take. A piece of tortilla with which we scoop up the food." But he said nothing. Let it be, he said to himself.

He looked out the window. Across the way was Old Town, la

Plaza Vieja. From this spot, or one close to it, the Mexicanos of Old Town had seen the Okies and other displaced people of the Dust Bowl era travel west to the promise of California. Elfego Baca, too, sat here with his amigos and watched the westward migration of the poor. Watched displaced farmers, factory workers, those who built railroads and highways, women with families to feed, all colors and all kinds of workers, leaving the old to create the new in California.

Elfego Baca had also been witness to the migration west after World War II. The greatest boom the country ever experienced, the greatest change for New Mexico. The city was a migration point on the east–west road across the southern belly of the country, the oasis where travelers paused to fill their water bags and bellies.

Change came, new colors, new sounds, new threads, and the blanket extended itself to the foothills of the Sandias to cover the houses of gringos, south into the valley to cover the homes of the old Atrisco Land Grant settlers, north into the valley where the new estates of the ricos were being built. The cloth was the new society, a green oasis with cottonwoods fed by Río Grande water.

Sonny sniffed, blew his nose, smacked his lips, and felt the sting of the hot green chile, wiped the tears from his eyes. Great! The duende spirit of the Río Grande lived in the green chile. And in the red. Comida sin chile no es comida, his father always said.

Heat waves danced on the hot asphalt of Central Avenue. Across the road lay Duran's Pharmacy, which also served a hot chile verde stew with homemade tortillas. Next to it a summer-silent Manzano Day School brooded in the morning heat.

In the Old Town Plaza the summer tourists were already arriving to buy turquoise jewelry, paintings, arts and crafts, baskets, perfumes, candles, every imaginable Nuevo Mexicano item available. They would go to the nearby restaurants to eat New Mexican food, and write home about the hot chile that "blew them out." They would walk under the portal on the east side of the plaza and look at the handmade jewelry the vendors displayed, escaping the June heat for a moment in the shade.

They would enter the San Felipe de Neri Church, the church of the parishioners of Old Town, take pictures in the courtyard, take pictures in the kiosk of the plaza. Although many of the old families still lived in the community, Old Town was a thriving tourist museum that catered to the visitors, sold bits and pieces of the many-colored cloth, trinkets for those who browsed through on a hot summer day.

Frank Dominic wanted to change all this by building canals from downtown to Old Town. Sonny couldn't picture Venetian boats rowing across Central to Old Town. Venetian boats loaded with mariachi groups serenading the tourists who came shopping? Ah, the developers had gotten out of hand.

He looked out into the bright glare outside, and the traffic moving as if in a dream. He blew his nose again.

"Good chile," he said to the woman in blue. She was perspiring.

"I love hot chile." She smiled. "Really hot."

I bet, Sonny nodded, touched his napkin to his eyes. He didn't know what was gnawing at him. Why couldn't he tell this well-dressed and looking-for-excitement-in-funky-Alburquerque woman sitting across from him that he'd love to show her Old Town, the nooks and crannies the tourists didn't know. Nooks and crannies, yeah.

Because I have to see Lorenza. I promised Rita, he thought, and rose. "Enjoy yourself," he said to the blonde.

"I'll try," she whispered, blotting her lips. "Hot chile."

"Yeah," he said, moving to the cash register to pay his bill.

"What's the matter? Don't you like blondes?" Rosa whispered as she rang up the register and gave him change.

"I'm not the right ranchero," Sonny said lamely.

"Pendejo," Rosa chastized him.

He glanced one more time at the woman. That's life, he

thought, and borrowed the phone to call Lorenza. Yes, she was home and she was free. He could come by for coffee.

He drove north on Rio Grande, across the new Alameda Bridge and to Corrales. Once an agricultural community like the North Valley, the village was now a bedroom community for professionals who worked in the city. A few continued farming. There were fine apple orchards left, but more and more the place was becoming gentrified by those who could afford the prices of expensive real estate and custom-built adobe homes.

Lorenza Villa lived in a modest adobe home at the edge of the river bosque. Sonny knew she had been married, had two kids, both grown, but he didn't know much more. She did her thing, healing people, and kept pretty much to herself. It had been a year, Sonny guessed, since he had last seen her. He and Rita ran into her at the Kimo Theater at a play.

The thing Sonny always remembered about her were her eyes. They were dark, intense, no doubt the eyes of a woman who could see into other realities, but each eye seemed to belong to a different person. It wasn't a disfigurement, she wasn't cross-eyed, just a nuance of difference from one to the other.

When she opened the door, she smiled and stepped out to greet him, taking his hand in hers. Her grip was firm, warm.

"Sonny, I'm glad to see you. Come in."

She turned and led him into a small living area brightly done in Mexican prints and paintings. She was dressed in a white cotton gown, the edges embroidered with bright flower designs. Oaxaca, Sonny guessed. She was barefoot.

"Siéntate," she said, pointing to a comfortable easy chair. "Café?"

"Gracias," Sonny said, nodding. He watched her move to the kitchen counter, her walk graceful. She was a handsome woman, dark like Rita, long, raven-black hair falling over her shoulders, the high Indian cheekbones, full lips, full bodied. Not slim like the woman in blue. A trickster woman, Sonny figured, and a very good-looking one. Dark and lovely as a Río Grande Nefertiti. There was Moorish blood lapping at the banks of the river.

"How's Rita?"

"Good. Saw her last night. She suggested—"

"She called me." Lorenza smiled as she returned with coffee. "She's concerned. . . ."

"Right." Sonny relaxed. "So here I am." He smiled at her, letting his eyes take in her beauty. What a woman, Sonny thought. But how can she help me if I feel so attracted? Try to get the cabrón out of you! he chided himself.

"What are you thinking?" Lorenza asked.

He shook his head. "Nada." He lied.

"Sometimes talking helps," Lorenza said, and sipped her coffee.

"Yeah. Sure. Well, to tell the truth, Rita thinks I have susto. From Gloria. . . ."

"You saw her body?"

"Yes."

"Ah," Lorenza whispered, and Sonny felt drawn to her eyes. She was looking at him as if two different people were looking at him. Then she rose and walked to the window.

"The morning is beautiful. I was up to see the sunrise," she said.

Sonny followed her gaze, and in the brush of the river bosque he caught sight of a shadow. The movement became a form, a river coyote. Two more appeared, pausing to look toward the house.

Poised by the window, Lorenza looked like she might disappear into the shining sunlight, her white dress radiating light, her long, black hair glistening with light. Sonny wondered if she knew about don Eliseo's Señores y Señoras de la Luz. Was she becoming one? Was that the secret of the curandera?

"The coyotes watch over you," she whispered.

He was puzzled.

"Your animal spirit," she said, "watches over you."

He got up and went to stand beside her. The sun coming through the window was dazzling, and he wanted a better look at the coyotes.

"River coyotes," he said.

"When the animal spirit appears, it means they come to help," she said, turning to look at him, her eyes fixing him with a stare that held him immobile. "It implies danger. . . ."

She brushed past him and he caught a scent of her perfume, deep, like the aromatic piñon tree after a rainstorm, with other pleasant herbs, perhaps manzanilla . . . the scent of light, the warm comforting aroma of sunlight on her body.

Watching the coyotes, he remembered a story his father told. A man had been haunted by a coyote that came at night to prowl around the house. For months the man was allowed no sleep, and the man's rifle was useless against the ghostly coyote. Finally he etched a cross on a bullet. He took it to the priest and had it blessed. That night he shot the coyote, and in the morning he found spots of blood. He called his neighbors, and they followed the trail of blood to the house of an old woman who lived in the hills. They found her dead from a bullet wound.

Legends. Cuentos de la gente. The bruja could take the form of the animal, an owl or coyote.

Sonny sighed and went to Lorenza. He sat across from her and she took his hands in hers. She closed her eyes, and for a long time she just sat there, holding his hands. When she opened her eyes, she asked, "Do you know what a limpieza is?"

Rita had told Sonny about the cleansing ceremony.

"To cleanse . . ."

"A spirit has gotten into your soul. It has to be cleaned away."

"Spirit?" Sonny said. The stories of souls moving around were cuentos the old people told. Stories to scare the children on late-winter nights. To pass the time. Did Lorenza believe?

"Gloria's alma. The limpieza would clean it away."

"If her soul is in me," he questioned, "why would I want it cleansed away?"

"You loved her."

Sonny nodded. "She was the first woman I loved."

"No matter how much we love the person, when they die the soul must move on. The soul is on a journey, seeking its own light, its own clarity."

Ah, she did know don Eliseo's philosophy, or something close to it. The soul had to leave, to become a Señora de la Luz. But for some reason Gloria's soul didn't want to continue on its natural journey. It had fastened to him.

"Does she want revenge?" Sonny asked.

Lorenza nodded. "The soul has a reason for refusing to move on. It's in you, and that's what's troubling you. It could get worse. . . ."

Why would Gloria diminish him? She had been the one to teach him love. He would give anything to have her alive. But something had sapped his strength last night, creating a sense of growing depression, fatigue, not thinking straight. He wanted to find Gloria's murderers, and he had nothing to go on. A sense of hopelessness haunted him. And he hadn't been able to get it up with Rita. How could it get worse?

"Maybe I should do this limpieza," he said, and stood.

"It's up to you," she replied. "It takes a few hours."

Did he doubt her? Is that why he was hesitating?

"You decide," she said. "The old curanderas and sobadoras knew how to release the susto, release the souls of the dead. I've studied their ways, and I think I can help you."

Sonny was still hesitating when Lorenza spoke again. "There is a strong animal spirit acting against you," she said. "In the old teachings, the nagual is the animal energy of a person. We all have it. Someone is using their animal energy against you."

"How do you know?"

"I can see it," she whispered.

Raven, Sonny thought. That's the animal Lorenza is seeing. Or the animals that had killed Gloria. Human animals.

"The light oozing from you is so clear. You are being cut into, drained, and only because you have your own strength within are you able to keep going. It feels to me like you are a brujo within, a powerful but kind shaman, but one without training. You have not yet recognized your own power."

Sonny was embarrassed by what Lorenza was saying, and felt uncomfortable still at the thought of a limpieza, even if she and Rita were right about Gloria's spirit.

"Soon as I have time, I'll make an appointment," he said.

She walked him to the door. Sonny felt an urge to say something, but he couldn't think of anything that didn't sound banal.

"Thanks for the café," he said finally.

"De nada," Lorenza replied. "Before you go, come with me." She walked toward the bosque where they had seen the coyotes.

She walked softly, so silently she didn't stir the dry grasses of the path. Where the coyotes had stood, she pointed. On the soft sand lay the faint outline of the coyotes' prints. They followed the tracks into a densely shaded Russian olive grove. She stopped and searched carefully until she spied what she was after: fine strands of coyote fur, caught on a thorn.

She gathered the few hairs and held them up for Sonny to see, then turned to inspect the path again, as if looking for coyote nails or a tooth an old coyote might have lost on the river trail. Above the canopy of shade the sunlight was bright, warm. A drone of cicadas filled the green bosque; otherwise the place was silent. She took a small leather pouch tied at her belt, put the coyote hairs in it, and handed it to Sonny.

"Keep it safe," she said.

Sonny took it, nodded, slipped the bag into his shirt pocket.

He followed her back to her house, feeling for the first time that he was being watched. But they were alone except for a crow calling from its perch on the top of a dry branch of a gnarled cottonwood tree.

"Go away, diablo!" Lorenza cried out. "We're not afraid of you!"

The big bird lifted from the branch, crying angrily as it flew, circling the clearing, then disappearing over the treetops. Sonny remembered the large crow rising from the pine tree at Raven's compound. He looked at Lorenza, but she had already turned up the path toward the house.

Suddenly chilled, Sonny felt for the pouch in his shirt pocket, resting over his heart.

19

As Sonny drove south on Rio Grande, he thought of Morino. I gotta get to Morino. He knows something; that's why he went to see Dominic. Gotta get to him. . . . And Raven. Though he's not going anywhere now that Naranjo's got him in jail in Estancia.

On impulse, he picked up his cellular and dialed Tamara.

"You're in the neighborhood, darling," she answered. "What a wonderful coincidence. I was just thinking of you. Of course you can come. I am alone, I will expect you."

Okay, he would go see the mysterious lady. If anyone could help him get to Morino, it was Tamara.

The clear, dry heat of the day rose from the earth like the heat waves from volcanic magma. Humidity, 7 percent. The earth was seething with heat. He looked east toward the wrinkled face of Sandia Crest. The mountain was a dull, blue outline. He couldn't see the contours of the foothills or the canyons. Above him the blue bowl of the sky was dull, empty of clouds. Days like this, the paisanos dreamed of the Taos mountains, cool streams, green pine trees swaying in the breeze, cold beer.

Weatherman Morgan had forecast a few thundershowers over the northern Sangre de Cristo Mountains, but nothing for Alburquerque. A few clouds were gathering over Río Arriba, but nothing so far for Río Abajo.

Akira Morino had shown up in the city a year ago. He fell in love with the place and began to make plans to bring a big microprocessing plant into the state. The latest in liquid-crystal display panels, he told the Chamber of Commerce. Panels so lightweight they could be carried around the house and hung on refrigerators or vanity mirrors. A plant on the cutting edge of the industry, so advanced it would put Alburquerque on the map.

But Intel beat him to the punch, pouring billions into a gigantic expansion in Rio Rancho. The Intel Pentium chip was destined to run every computer in the world, and Morino's plans were sidetracked. Still, he stayed on, courting the business community, persuading, full of confidence and bravado, and promising to deliver the plant. He would, he insisted, move the computer age into the home in ways previously unimagined.

The Japanese build small computers, Sonny thought, because the islands of Japan are small. Landscape dictates character. But here we have lots of space. We don't need to walk around with a computer in our hip pocket. Forget their small is good. Give me big! Big trucks, big women, big horses, big mountains to climb!

Ah, dreams.

The old southwest was dead, or dying, taken over by Californicators living the Santa Fe style and staying in touch through fax machines. The once reclusive Villa de la Santa Fé had been "discovered" in the eighties. For those with money it became a place to escape to, a place for a second home for the LA crowd, a place to build new fantasies.

The new Southwest was dancing to the high-tech tune.

Morino swore he could put together the Japanese financial backing, and Marisa Martinez, the mayor, worked on putting together the bond and land package the city would offer him. If she could push the plan through the city council, it would win the mayoral race for her.

But Gloria's gruesome murder had shocked the city and soured business and politics. The idea of a cult had been picked up by the national news, CNN had run a story on the murder, and it had spread to the international headlines. The news stories concentrated on the horror of the case, playing up the role of a cult and highlighting the failure of the police to find those responsible.

The business interests wanted the case over with, hushed if need be. It wasn't good for business, and what wasn't good for business wasn't good for city hall.

Walter Johnson, the retired Country Club banker whom many had predicted couldn't garner enough votes for a run-off election, was now suddenly a front-runner. He was running on a "put the criminals in jail" platform and arguing the city needed a return to good old-fashioned family values, hard work, and the plain old business incentive of profit. He would fire Sam Garcia as police chief and replace him with someone who was tough on crime. It was familiar political rhetoric, but it still played well. Gang violence had come to the city in the past few years, graffiti spread, and now the city was gripped by a paralysis precipitated by the murder.

And Akira Morino had to know something about it.

Sonny turned off Rio Grande onto the long, graveled driveway that led to Tamara's home. The grand old house was one of the oldest estates on Rio Grande Boulevard. Built just before World War II, it was big and rambling, a failed attempt at a southern mansion on the Río Grande, Greek revival architecture that had turned Gothic. Set against the river bosque and surrounded by large trees, it was a dark and mysterious house. Although the grounds were immaculate, it had an aura of being deserted.

Sonny parked in front, got out, and wiped his forehead. Chingao, it was hot, but at least here a few weak currents of air from the river wafted through the hot air. He sniffed, distinguishing the smells that came from the wild bosque: skunk and traces of coyote scent floated in the still, dry air. The fragrance of flowering Russian olives. A trace of rain.

Yes, there it was, barely perceptible, but filtering in the breeze that came from the south. It was midday, and it wasn't dew or river coolness, it was a scent of rain. Overhead, mottled cottage-cheese clouds began to move in from the west, and with them the possibility of the first rain.

Sonny smiled. Maybe not the late-summer monsoon season of daily afternoon showers, but a good June rain. He knew the moods of the city swung to the moods of the weather. The desert people of the high, arid Río Grande plateau were like horny toads, they could go a long time without rain, but they paid the price. The dry electricity in the air created a tension within, a fiery disposition that put nerves on edge. There were more family arguments, more traffic accidents, more drinking bouts, more shootings, more graffiti splashed on vacant walls, and more anxious cops. People looked more often to the west in search of rain clouds. They grew envious as the nightly weather reports reported summer thunderstorms gathering over the northern mountains of Santa Fe and Taos.

Any trace of rain will do, Sonny thought as he pulled the rope on the bell at the door, a shiny ship's bell from an old Mississippi riverboat. Even a little shower to settle the dust, settle the destructive mood in the air.

"Darling, I'm so glad to see you," Tamara said with a smile when she opened the door. She held his hands and let him kiss her cheek. She wore an exquisite gold brocade robe that molded to the curves of her body. Pale but exotic, enticing as always, Sonny thought, admiring her sleek figure.

"You should visit me more often," she said as she led him into the expansive living area with a huge fireplace. The den was a museum, full of old paintings, Navajo rugs from the turn of the century, shelves full of pottery, santos.

"Please," she said, motioning to the large leather sofa. "May I offer you a drink?" A decanter of red wine and two glasses sat on the red cedar coffee table.

She poured before Sonny could say it was too early. "There is no housekeeper today, so I have you all to myself." She handed him the drink.

Sonny drank, the taste was dry, somewhat bitter.

"Peyote," she said with a wink, explaining the taste, and held up her glass in a toast. "To us."

"Salud," Sonny said, and sipped again.

"It quenches the thirst," she said.

She wore her long black hair pulled back tight, fastened with a gold clip. Her bright red lipstick glowed in sharp contrast to her pale complexion.

"Now tell me, to what do I owe this visit?" She drew closer, looking into his eyes, her breath warm on his face.

"I need a favor."

"Ah, Sonny, you mean you came only for a favor. How cruel of you."

"I—"

"Don't explain," she teased. "I understand. This very morning I awakened to thoughts of you. I must have known you were coming. You know why?"

Sonny shook his head.

"It is because you and I are old souls. Yes, we have lived many lives, we have known each other in past lives, and so we were destined to meet in this one. Our souls communicate with each other, and our bodies are the vehicles to transport us," she said, her dark eyes glittering, her perfume enveloping him.

"Where?"

"Into that moment of illumination when two like souls meet. Then we can truly peer into our past. There is a reason for us to meet," she whispered.

"Hey, I thought it was the man who made the move—"

She tossed back her head and laughed.

"Oh, you are so innocent. So caught up in your cultural ways. Darling"—she smiled and reached out to touch his hand—"you must put away those old ways, which only drag you down. We are special souls, Sonny, we have led special lives in the past. We can see into those lives by sharing the vital energy of our bodies, our auras." She paused and smiled. Her cool fingers caressed his cheeks.

"I can teach you how to connect to your past lives. . . ."

"And what would I see in my past?"

"The illumination of your past brings clarity. Understanding who you have been gives you energy to use in this life. The moment of looking into the past is a moment of immortality. You can never die, don't you see."

Illumination, Sonny thought. She offers her body and a glimpse into clarity. I can become a Señor of Light. She doesn't meditate like don Eliseo in the morning sun, she gets there through a good old-fashioned fuck.

She put her lips to his. He felt the flicker of her tongue on his lips. His own arousal surprised him, because he thought since he couldn't do it with Rita, the problem was going to last. But here he was, feeling the need to get it on with Tamara.

"I want you to make love to me," she said.

Sonny felt an ache, he wanted her, he admitted, surprised; somehow he needed her to get past the emptiness he felt inside.

"And Anthony Pájaro? I thought you two were—"

"Dear Sonny. How innocent you are. Anthony came to me a year ago. He asked me to help him. I do not want to get mixed up in politics, but I can't stand by and do nothing while the Earth is destroyed! I helped him raise money, that is all. It is no coincidence the three of us have come together. A greater fate has brought us here. We are three of a kind, you, me, and Anthony. You must understand that."

"I came to ask a favor," Sonny said, drawing back.

"Ah, back to that. You have only to ask." She smiled, pressing her hands around his.

"I need to talk to Morino, but I can't get through to him. Can you set something up for me?"

Tamara laughed. "Is that all you ask for? That can be arranged, Sonny."

She leaned forward and kissed him again, and this time Sonny didn't resist. He responded, tasting the wine on her lips, a warm surge of arousal.

She moaned and whispered, "Make love to me. I promise you a journey into a world you have not seen."

She rose and led him down the hall into her bedroom. It was a large spacious room in the back of the house. The round bed occupied the center of the room; beyond that Sonny spied the large sunken tub.

"This is the Sun Room," she said. "A room devoted to love."

"The tent of a desert princess."

"Yes. To make love here is to understand there is only one way into the past. Clarity lies only in the past lives. Most make love for the moment, satisfying the need of the present. But for me physical love has other purposes. It is a way into the past."

"And there?"

"You know who you were. You know your destiny. Everything becomes clear. You are young again."

"No." Sonny heard don Eliseo's voice from the shadows of the room.

"Why?" Sonny asked him.

"It is momentary."

"It doesn't last."

"Smart kid."

"But it's sure good while it lasts." Sonny smiled.

"No seas pendejo," the old man said.

"You are laughing at me," Tamara said.

"No, I was thinking of an old friend."

"Rita?"

227

"Her, too."

"I do not mind that she is your lover. You can come and see me when you desire. Love me once, and I know you will return."

"Probably so." Sonny nodded. He glanced again at the room, the inviting bed, then turned and kissed Tamara on the cheek. "I have to go. Will you help me reach Morino?"

She sighed, then smiled.

"Yes, I will call Mr. Morino. Come. I will see you out."

She led him to the door, holding his arm and speaking. "I know souls like ours must meet and unite. The day will come when you will realize that passion and lust are all the same. But there are some of us who can tap the potency of past lives and illuminate the lustful moment. I will wait for you."

"Good-bye," Sonny said, turned, and walked out. A current of hot air met him and made him shiver.

He got into his truck and headed for the freeway. The time had come to meet Raven. But a personal question haunted him: Why in the hell did he reject Tamara? And the woman in blue at Garcia's? Was he getting old? Or was it Rita? It was definitely getting serious. A few years ago, right after his divorce from Angie, he would have made love to any woman that offered. He loved women and he enjoyed making love to them. He prided himself on being a ladies' man. Then he met Rita one Saturday night at the Fourth Street Cantina, about two years ago. They hit it off right away. She had helped him find his house to rent, and between Rita and his new neighbor, don Eliseo, he began to learn North Valley ways, the deeper way of life they practiced.

He drove east on I-40 to Moriarty. Images of Tamara's bedroom appeared, mixing with the curves of her body. Her Sun Room, the room of love. From the round bed at the center radiated four lines of different-colored tiles, stretching out in four directions. Gold, blue, white, black.

The yellow tiles led to the fireplace. The opposite line led to a small, dry piñon tree with polished branches. The branches of the piñon were decorated with little ojos de Dios, simple adornments of colored wool woven in a diamond pattern on two dry branches in the form of a cross. The center of the diamond was said to be the eye of God.

Sonny had read that the ojo de Dios that the New Mexicans used were originally of Huichol origin. Prayer sticks. A way to enter visions. Now the ojos de Dios adorned every New Mexican home. The ojo de Dios also resembled a mandala, Sonny thought. It represented the four directions. From the center, God's eye looked out at the world. The eye of God could also be a center of contemplation, a place where the soul focused. The diagonal design of the ojo was a labyrinth that led to the center. And at the center, illumination.

The third line of tiles from the bed radiated to a stained-glass window on the southern wall. The thick, stained pieces of glass were another mandala. In the center of the four-leafed design lay the round, golden sun. The fourth line had led to the open bathroom, the large sunken tub, the erotic bath where the flesh was prepared for its flight.

Four lines, one center. The Zia sun.

"Damn," Sonny groaned, and turned on the radio and sang to the tune of the Mexican corrido to get the thoughts out of his mind. He turned south toward Estancia. The foothills of the mountains and the flat llano of the Estancia Valley were dry and withering under the summer heat. The tawny grass stretched as far as the eye could see. On his left a huge, dusty whirlwind swept across the hot landscape, picking up dust and tumbleweeds as it moved across the parched land.

We need rain bad, Sonny thought. The land of the Estancia Valley was a land of contrasts. The eastern foothills of the Manzano Mountains were ridged with arroyos and dark mesas. The pines of the heights gave way to scrub oak, thick green junipers, piñon, and that gave way to yucca and llano grass as the hills flattened into grazing land. It was ranch land, and barely good for that.

The old Nuevo Mexicano families of the villages along the slope, Chilili, Tajique, and Torreón, clung tenaciously to the land. Some rancheros still ran a few head of cattle, a few sheep. Before them the land had belonged to the nomadic Indians of the eastern plain, and maybe that was the truth of the land, that it had been molded for the nomad, not for the settled farmer or rancher.

Along the road grew clumps of sunflowers, snakeweed, the hardy Mexican hat, and the ever-present purple-blooming thistle. Cardo santo, the natives called it, good for back pain. All the cures in the world were right there, in nature's garden, hidden among the grama grasses. If one knew, as the old curanderas knew, how to use their secrets. They were gifts from nature, full of potency and magic.

In the old days the curanderas gathered the herbs and roots and used them in their medicine. Prayers to God and the healing herbs of the earth, that's what they used. He remembered the woman who had cured his susto after he was attacked by the dog. After his father died, the same woman had helped his mother. She came to the house and prayed over her, giving her an egg to hold in her hands. When the ceremony was done his mother cracked the egg and let it drop into a glass of water. There swimming in the white mucus and splattered in the blood veins of the yolk appeared the visible sign of her problem. After that she got better. Her energy returned.

Sonny glanced out the window. The wildflowers had gotten some spring moisture, enough to get them started, enough for the green fuse to hurtle its force into the bloom to create the seed.

But now the flowers and grasses of the llano lay shriveling under the June heat. Alive, but just barely. The flowers were like the people, they withstood the blows of nature: they would survive.

Long ago the Spanish Franciscans had set up the missions of Quarai and Abo in these lonely hills—to christianize the nomadic Indians, they said, but also to protect the salt beds that were so valuable for curing meat. Salt was like gold.

Then in the twenties and thirties the Okies fleeing the dust storms of Oklahoma homesteaded in the valley and tried to raise beans, like in the John Steinbeck novel. The corrido ended and Sonny slipped the Juan Arriaga tape into his player. The harsh earth of the Estancia Valley lent itself to epic drama, the stories of the people who came to conquer the land and were either beaten by it or adapted and learned to live in harmony. Still the people clung to the land, the sons and daughters of the old Mexicanos and the Okies and the new Anglo immigrants who set up lonely mobile homes on the open and indifferent land.

Looking for a place to call one's own, Sonny thought as the strains of the symphony lifted his soul into the clear blue sky. The rushing of the wind past his open window was a symphony he understood, something he felt in his blood. Viento. Wind. The llaneros had as many ways to describe wind as did the Eskimos for describing snow. The winds that came from the four directions were each unique, each brought its own type of weather. Wind was the constant companion on the open land.

There were dry winds and wet winds, male winds and female winds, winds for every mood, tormenting winds that drove people crazy, soft breezes that dried the sweat on the working man's neck, winds that brought no good, but always, the wind was constant. Yes, a constant companion, sometimes friendly, a kiss of coolness, sometimes deadly and raging as it swept across the land, swirling and raising sandstorms, driving giant hordes of tumbleweeds before it, pelting cattle and sheep, and dancing like a dervish devil around the ranch house, clawing at the tin roofs and threatening damnation as it banged loose, flapping tin on the roof.

When the winds came, the women shut doors and windows tight, and the people of the llano huddled inside, in silence, a pot of beans cooking slowly on the cast-iron stove, filling the enclosed space with their aroma. Then everyone spoke in hushed whispers; the men nervously waited for the wind to grow calm so they could walk outside and get on with their work. The women prayed that the devils riding the whirlwinds not enter their home, not stay, go away before madness came. Praying, silently, through pursed lips, waiting, listening to the cry and howl in the wind as if one of their daughters or sisters cried outside.

La Llorona rode the wind, the weeping woman rode the llano wind, she was sister to the wind, her keening cry was like the cry of the wind.

Sonny thought of José Escobar and his people, hanging on to the land on the eastern foothills. The land was all they knew, all they had, but the big ranches ate away at the small land grants, and the land developers for the past twenty years had been buying and dividing the land into one-acre plots and selling them to people from the city who came looking for country living. A cheap piece of land to call one's own was the dream of the new homesteaders, those who set up trailers on the barren land. A land dotted with trailers. They wouldn't last. The adults would get lonely, the children would grow up and leave, then the haunting, lonely sound of the wind and the emptiness would drive them all back to the city.

A clean, sultry smell filled the bright air. Thin clouds moved in from the southwest, high thin clouds that carried no rain but were the harbingers of the monsoon season. Cattle stayed close to the windmill water tanks. Overhead, two large turkey vultures circled. The constant wind swept mournfully across the dry grass. The land was quiet and empty.

Sonny squinted into the distance and wondered about the women who had survived the land and weather. First the Indian women, the nomadic Comanches, then the Mexican women of the Quarai and Abo missions, finally the gaunt-faced Okies. So many either went crazy or died dreaming of water. Water was the element of survival. Without water there was no life on the burning land. Life gathered around the oasis of the windmill tanks. Each new tribe added its bit of technology to the land and thus changed the landscape. Human life could exist only within the radius of the small oasis that men created.

They drilled wells and irrigated sparse fields of corn, pumpkins, alfalfa, just like over in the eastern part of the state and west Texas, where they were sucking the Ogallala Aquifer dry. They were sucking the aquifer dry, and now, ghost farms dotted west Texas, and so they would dot the ranches around Clovis and Portales and eventually the Estancia Valley. The wind would blow away the trailer castles.

That's why Dominic is so damn dangerous, Sonny thought. He wants to use the water of the Río Grande for his outrageous development, create a Disneyland for tourists, but he doesn't understand the balance, how the river and the underground water play in the scheme of things of the Río Grande basin. He wants to build an oasis out of Alburquerque. Canals, green beltways, flower gardens, the flow of fountains, canal boats carrying passengers from one casino to the next. Maybe Dominic had visited the Alhambra and the gardens of the Generalife, and he was bitten by the Moorish love of water.

What the hell, Nuevo Mexicanos who carried Moorish blood in their veins were idolators when it came to water. Water was the lifeline. Only by using the Indian acequia systems had the first Europeans and Mexicans survived in the northern villages of the state. People prayed for rain, implored the goddess of fertility. The Pueblo Indians danced for rain, prayed to the kachinas. People dreamed of rain, the life-giving rain. In the high, arid plateaus of New Mexico, rain, as well as the sun, was sacred.

It was so with desert people. They dreamed of what they did not have: bubbling fountains, running brooks, exquisite gardens, cool temples, rooms where the gurgle of water sounded just outside the window, rooms where one could make love, read books, enjoy a respite from the heat. From every room the lover of beauty wanted to hear the sound of running water.

The Nuevo Mexicanos understood Dominic's dream, because people of the high New Mexican desert didn't love heat and sand, they loved the oasis. A man of the desert could rest in the oasis and enjoy the beauty of women and the arabesques of Islamic art as his ancestors had enjoyed them in Spain, enjoyed the wisdom in books, the unending arguments of Jewish scholars, the whispered revolt of the Catholics, the love sounds of the warrior Arabs, but all this only if he could rest in a cool, refreshing place. The Arabic influence ran deep and brooding in the blood of the Nuevo Mexicano; it was the survival instinct that gathered the people to the pleasant gurgle of flowing water.

Or maybe Dominic had visited the gardens of Xochimilco in Mexico City. Imagined their grandeur before the Spaniards came. An entire civilization existing on gardens of flowers and corn, chile and squash, beans. Boats softly plying the canals as trade moved up and down Lake Texcoco. Alburquerque was to be the new Xochimilco.

I would like to see the Alhambra, Sonny thought. He had seen pictures of the buildings and the rose gardens. He wanted to explore Spain. Maybe to know more about that past. Moors, Jews, Islamic art. Things he yearned to know. In the library he browsed through a book of Goya's paintings, and he kept going back to it. There was something waiting to be revealed in Goya's often-tortured faces of his dark period.

Here, the truck stop is the oasis, he thought, and we have truck stop art. Rattlesnakes Ahead. See the Jackalope! Last Gas before Tucumcari. See Gopher Country. Stop at Clines Corner. Indian Jewelry, Cheap. And one old, barely visible Burma Shave.

What a poor excuse for culture! Still, the gas stations and cafés of small towns were where the traveler could fill his stomach and car, and for a brief time share a fleeting moment with other desert travelers. That was New Mexico, a land of watering holes. The wide horizons and the huge emptiness of the land wasted the spirit of the traveler. Families had to stop and rest.

Just then Sonny drove into Estancia. It meant Stopping Place.

Oasis. A dry, dusty dump of a town. Now Raven was cooling his heels in its jail. Sonny drove in and pulled up in front of the local bar, The Oasis. He smiled. The main street was almost deserted. A Jeep packed with hunting rifles sat outside the bar. Hunting rifles with high-powered scopes. In this country the ranchers usually carried .22 rifles to shoot coyotes, but these guys were armed to the teeth. A barely visible decal beneath the dust on the Jeep's bumper made him pause. It was the Zia sign.

Oasis also meant cold beer, and he decided to have a couple before heading over to the jail. Maybe he could pick up a little information from the bartender, he thought as he entered the cool, dimly lit cantina.

Two weathered rancheros sat at the bar, enjoying their beers. At the pool table a couple of mean-looking, stringy-haired Anglo men shot pool. Sonny guessed the Jeep outside belonged to them.

One wore a dusty, creased cowboy hat, the other a sweatband. It was obvious they weren't natives. What surprised Sonny was that one of the women from Raven's compound, Dorothy, was with them. She was standing by the table, smoking a cigarette and sipping from a bottle of beer. She turned to look at Sonny and smiled, a thin, ugly smile.

"If it isn't Sonny Baca," she said, and the two men playing pool stopped to look at Sonny.

Sonny ordered a beer. "Quívole. Qué hay de nuevo?" he asked the bartender.

"No, nada," the man replied as he set the cold, frosted beer on the bar. "Hotter 'n hell. Need rain."

The two rancheros turned to take Sonny's measure.

"What brings you to Estancia?" the bartender asked.

Sonny decided to test the pool players. He had a gut feeling. It looked to him like the four women and their children weren't the only ones tangled in Raven's web.

"I'm looking for a guy named Raven," he said loud enough for them to hear.

The two men at the pool table looked at the young woman, then at Sonny. There was a long, cold silence.

The bartender leaned over the counter. "You looking for trouble?" he asked.

"No." Sonny grinned, a friendly smile.

"Those are his compañeros. Cuídate," the bartender warned him, then shook his head and moved away to whisper to the two rancheros at the bar.

Sonny nodded his thanks and took a long drink from the beer.

The two men moved around the pool table. Sonny turned to face them. They were both bearded and mean looking, with close-set pale eyes. The big burly one had a scar over his left eye, the smaller one wore a grimy red headband. Both wore Zia earrings. Were they the sons-of-bitches who took shots at him?

"This is the guy that came looking for Raven at the compound," Dorothy said to the two men without taking her eyes off Sonny. By the sound of her voice, Sonny knew she'd had more than one beer to drink. Then addressing Sonny: "He's gettin' out this afternoon. You better watch out." She laughed.

"Shut up, Sister!" Scarface growled. "What the hell do you want with Raven?" he asked Sonny.

"I think he's FBI," Dorothy said. She wasn't the whimpering woman Sonny remembered.

"FBI," Scarface spit out, "fucking creeps are thick around here." He glared at the bartender. "You ought to keep them out of your bar, or you'll get a bad reputation."

"You have no business with Raven," the thin, weasel man with the dirty sweatband said. Both goons stood in front of Sonny with cue sticks in their hands.

"Get the fuck out or we'll throw you out!" Scarface spit.

"It's free country," Sonny answered, "last I heard." His adrenaline rose. He was sure he'd found the shitheads that had fired on him, and he was glad he had. He was ready for Scarface to attack first, and he guessed right.

"Smart-assed Mexican!" Scarface cursed and swung his cue stick. Sonny ducked and heard the woosh of the stick inches from his skull. He came up swinging, driving his fist into Scarface's stomach and following with an uppercut to the man's Adam's apple. Scarface groaned and reached for his throat, gasping for air. Sonny drove his knee into the man's groin and in the same motion pushed him into his partner.

Sweatband held his swing for a moment, and Sonny grabbed the cue stick out of his hand and drove it into his stomach, and in the same motion up into the man's chin. Blood poured from Sweatband's mouth as he toppled against the pool table.

Scarface staggered up, holding his throat, gasping. He was in no shape to move on Sonny, and the bartender's shout stopped the action anyway.

"That's enough!" He pointed a cut-off shotgun at the men. "You make a move and I'll blow you into Guadalupe County! Back off!"

Scarface and his partner backed off, nursing their wounds. They had underestimated Sonny, and they were not inclined to get blown to bits in a backwater bar.

"I'll get you, you sonofabitch," Scarface warned, grimacing. "I'm not going to forget this." They backed out of the bar, the door slamming in the wind. Dorothy hesitated.

"Thought you wanted out," Sonny said.

"It's too late," she said. "Raven gets out this afternoon. It's gonna blow." She looked into Sonny's eyes. Her bravado of moments ago was gone. "It's gonna blow," she repeated, and slipped out the door.

"You handle yourself pretty good," the bartender said as he uncocked the shotgun. The rancheros at the bar nodded in agreement.

"I'm not FBI," Sonny said.

"Didn't figure you were." The bartender smiled and poured him a shot of whiskey. "FBI boys wouldn't take on those crazies."

He was glad he didn't have to shoot, glad the young man had kicked the hippies' asses. "So what about Raven?"

"I think he and his friends killed one of José Escobar's steers over in La Cueva," Sonny answered.

The two rancheros nodded. They had heard about the mutilation, and anybody that was chasing down poachers was a friend of the cattlemen.

Sonny drank down the bourbon.

"This man, Raven, está loco," the bartender said. "Sheriff Naranjo has him in jail for growing marijuana. But he's a dangerous man."

"I know," Sonny said. "Thanks for the drink."

"De nada. You did me a favor by getting rid of those hippies. Be careful, eh."

"Yeah," Sonny said as he went out.

Sonny squinted at the bright sunlight when he walked out of the bar. It never failed, walking out of a dark, cool bar into bright sunlight was a shock to the nervous system. He glanced across the street where the Jeep now stood. They wouldn't mess with him, at least not for a while.

He walked down the street to the county courthouse. The main street of the sleepy town was nearly deserted, and yet he had the curious feeling that people knew he was in town. People watched him cross the street from shop windows.

By the time he entered the air-conditioned courthouse, the bartender had already called the sheriff and told him the young man who wanted to see Raven had kicked ass with Raven's buddies and sent them packing.

Sheriff Naranjo was waiting with a firm handshake when Sonny walked into the lobby.

"I'm Sheriff Naranjo. Heard you met Raven's boys." He slapped Sonny on the back. "I've been wanting to throw them in jail all week, but the FBI won't let me."

Sonny shrugged. "Sonny Baca," he said.

"Baca," the sheriff said. "From where?"

"Alburquerque. My father's family was from Socorro—"

"The Bacas de Socorro? Oh, por qué no dijites, hombre? Not from the Elfego Baca familia?"

"Sí."

"Well I'll be a sanamagon! Goddamnit, no wonder you didn't take any shit from the hippies! Elfego Baca. Pues, you got the blood of the old man. Come on in." He put his arm around Sonny's shoulder and led him into his office. "Siéntate." He offered a chair. "How about a drink?" He reached into a desk drawer and drew out a bottle.

"Gracias, just had one." Sonny shook his head.

"Coffee, cup of coffee. Maggie," he yelled out the door, "get this gentleman a cup of hot coffee. Milk? Sugar?"

"Black," Sonny answered.

"So you're from the Bacas of Socorro." The sheriff looked with pride at Sonny. "Chingao, hombre, there isn't a Chicano around here who doesn't know about Elfego Baca. You were working with Manuel Lopez. Found that Dodge lady in Mexico?"

Sonny nodded.

"Hombre, they don't make them any better than Manuel. I knew him when he first went into the business. He couldn't get jobs at first, but he proved himself. Bringing that woman out of Mexico was the toughest thing he did. And you were with him, damn."

A secretary with a dimpled smile entered the room with a cup of coffee. "Anything else?" she asked.

"No. Gracias."

"Anytime," she said, and went out.

"My familia was from Socorro County," the sheriff said when they were alone. "I remember my grandfather, and my father, telling stories about Elfego Baca. People thought that man was Robin Hood. One time, they say, a cowboy from Texas stole a plow horse from a farmer near Lemitar. You know those Texans used to come in and try to get away with all sorts of things. Muy abusivos. So your grandfather tracked down the cowboy, brought him back to the county jail. But instead of putting him in jail, he made the cowboy work a week for the old farmer. Made him plow and milk cows for a week to teach him manners."

The sheriff slapped his knee and laughed. "Piénsalo, one of those tough cowboys working as a farmer. Que insulto, no? But here's the good part. The cowboy fell in love with one of the farmer's daughters, so he married her. One of the best families in Socorro County came from that marriage. Coyotes, part Chicano, part Anglos. They're raza just like us. Just got the Anglo last name. Justice comes in different ways."

Sonny nodded. It never failed, wherever the old people recalled the stories of his great-grandfather, he heard a new one every time. Justice for his people, the Mexicano farmers of the Socorro Valley, that had been part of Elfego Baca's life, then there were the later escapades in Alburquerque. Someday he would write down all the stories he had heard about Elfego Baca, the Robin Hood lawman from Socorro County.

"What about Raven?" Sonny asked.

"I busted him for growing marijuana," the sheriff said, "but the FBI told me to let him go." He leaned forward and whispered. "They say he wants to blow up a WIPP truck. Doesn't make sense to me to let him loose. I figure they want him to lead them to the explosives. That's the only way they can prove anything."

"They can't trace the stuff?"

"Ah, he's probably buying dynamite in Mexico. You can buy it by the truckload and bring it up here easy, no records. If he packs it right, he can tear a hole into any WIPP barrel."

Sonny nodded. "Can I talk to him?"

"FBI won't like it"—the sheriff shrugged—"but why not. I'm going to have to let the sonofabitch out in a few hours when he makes bail. Not that I won't be glad to get the FBI off my ass. I'll give you ten minutes," the sheriff said. "Off the record, sabes?"

"Gracias," Sonny answered.

He led Sonny down a hallway to the cells in the back. "Got a visitor," he called to the man in the first cell. He was barefoot and bare chested, lying on the bunk in the dark corner of the cell with a backpack for a pillow. When he jumped to his feet and approached the bars, Sonny recognized the smooth way he moved, even before he focused in on the face. Around his neck hung the same gold Zia medallion he'd been wearing the last time they met, at the opera fund-raiser. Anthony Pájaro.

20

"Ten minutes," the sheriff said, and left the two men alone.

"Anthony Pájaro?" Sonny was too shocked to say anything more.

"Around here they call me Raven," Pájaro replied.

He laughed, his taunting laughter filling the silence of the cells around them.

Sonny shook his head. If I hadn't seen it with my own eyes, I might not believe it, he thought. Pájaro was the leader of the antinuke group, the leader who spoke in public, Tamara's lover, the well-dressed, poised, charismatic fighter of pollution. He was also Raven, the man who possessed four wives, who lived in the forest with his cronies and plotted destruction, feeding himself off poached livestock and starving his own children.

"Well, well, Mr. Sonny Baca." Raven smiled. There was something hard to his appearance, something deadly in his dark eyes. "So we meet again. Sorry I can't offer you a drink, but the accommodations are a bit slim. What brings you slumming? Last time I saw you, you had a beautiful woman at your side, and you were wearing a tux."

"You, too," Sonny responded.

Raven laughed. "This is temporary. In a few hours my attorney bails me out."

His mood changed as he looked hard at Sonny. "Heard you were snooping around my place, Sonny boy. I don't like that. You could get shot!" He laughed softly, deep in his throat.

Sonny remembered what José Escobar had said: Raven can fly, like one of those old brujos.

"I wasn't snooping, just visiting," Sonny replied. "I needed to buy a little dynamite."

Raven's face grew dark. "Ah, shit. Now you're talking like one of the FBI boys," he snapped. "You working for them? 'Cause if you are, you're on the wrong side!"

Sonny shook his head. Raven would not be easy to crack. He was too smart, he had been pursued by the FBI for too long. He was a cautious bird. Not a raptor, but a scavenger, moving from one kill to the other.

"They've been on my case since the Palo Seco nuclear plant in Arizona got its power lines blown up. I was in Taos They know that, but they keep bugging me. They plant a lot of what the government calls misinformation. I call it lies! They can plant stuff on you if you make yourself a social nuisance. You know that."

"Some of the members of your group think it's a social nuisance to stash dynamite. They're talking to Garcia."

Raven laughed. "No way."

"They're afraid." Sonny tested the waters.

"Afraid? Hey, I'm a peace-loving man."

"Afraid you might blow a truck—"

"People are crazy!" Raven shouted. "They make up stories! They twisted my words!"

He grew quiet, put his face against two bars, and whispered. "But just suppose it could be done. Isn't it better to blow up one truck and stop the proliferation of nuclear waste? Think about it. One WIPP truck goes up and it will scare the shit out of people. Maybe then they'll demand a stop to the madness. Yeah, one big accident, Baca, and we could have a nuclear-free earth!"

Would he really do it, Sonny wondered as he looked into the dark eyes of the man in the cell. Or was he crazy, spouting insanities? Raven was fed up with political solutions that hadn't worked. He and his group were tired of chaining themselves to gates of nuclear power stations, tired of community organizing, and tired of political rhetoric. Raven was ready to implement the ultimate solution: blow up a truck carrying nuclear waste. Create a holocaust that would make the world take notice.

"You blow open a container carrying high-level waste and it's going to kill a lot of people," Sonny said.

"That high-level waste already kills people! Did you ever think of that? Tons and tons of it all over the world. Don't tell me what kills people, Baca! The feds, DOE, Sandia Labs, Los Alamos. They kill people! They killed *your father*. They've been storing high-level shit in this state for forty-five years. Los Alamos has dumped radioactive water into the Río Grande. Sandia Labs has dumped right into the South Valley. Wise up, Baca, we didn't create the problem, we're trying to solve it. The DOE and the Defense Department have stockpiled nukes in the Manzano Mountains. All that stuff they're storing and dismantling is seeping into the water! At WIPP the barrels will be corroded by the salt! It's poisoning the earth! The old nuclear power plants in Russia are already leaking poison! North Korea is making nukes! How much more is it going to take to get people like you involved?"

Sonny didn't have an answer. He looked at the medallion hanging around Raven's neck. Round as the sun and inscribed with the Zia sun symbol. Heavy. The medallion of an ancient priest, or a modern cult leader.

"Like it, huh?" Raven smiled, sensing Sonny's attention on the medallion. He held it up and kissed it. "The Zia sun, giver of life, protector of the Earth!"

"The same symbol was cut on Gloria Dominic," Sonny said, the anger returning and mixing with the impotence he felt, making him giddy. He wished he had taken the drink the sheriff had offered. Help steady him.

"What's that supposed to mean?"

"Whoever killed Gloria Dominic cut the Zia symbol on her stomach."

"And you think—" Raven grinned. "You do have yourself confused with the FBI! You've been snooping around my place because you think I had something to do with that? That's not our thing, Baca. We're not into murder, we're into saving lives. Saving the spaceship Earth."

"Did you know her?"

"The Dominic lady?" He shook his head. "No, no, don't go making accusations just 'cause they found the sign of the Zia on her. I've got one on my jewelry. It's used everywhere. State flag uses it. Does that mean the state killed her? You're barking up the wrong tree, Baca."

"Why do you use two names?" Sonny asked. The man in front of him was Anthony Pájaro, but as he said, up here, meaning on the east side of the Sandias, he was Raven. The man seemed to move in and out of personalities.

"Pájaro's just a convenient incarnation, you know, someone to please Tamara. She's a real lady, you know, a great woman, a truly great woman. But me? Hey, I'm a mountain man. Tamara wouldn't have me around her and her fancy friends, but she'd have Anthony. She wouldn't let me fuck her, but she let Anthony!"

Raven burst out in a fit of laughter. When it subsided, he stared intensely at Sonny again, and the stare cut through Sonny

245

and made him shiver. Raven had become Anthony Pájaro to fund-raise, to put forth a good show, to become Tamara's lover. Did Tamara control him? Did she control Raven?

"You don't get it, do you?" Raven whispered. "You don't know what I can do?"

"Tell me."

"Ask Tamara. She can tell you about the power of this Zia medallion. Great power, Baca. The power to fly through the forest and see everything. Shit, I've got power you haven't even dreamed about." He scowled. "We're not playing for pennies," he said ominously.

Sonny had a long shot left, so he reached in his pocket and took out the copper earring Howard had given him and handed it to Raven.

Raven took it and looked at it. "My ladies make things like this to make a living. The FBI bought a few, now it plants them wherever they want. They can implicate whoever they want by planting false clues. Fucking Garcia helps them. Yeah, like the crazy stories in the paper. Murderers? Shit, the people I know aren't murderers. They want peace. They want an Earth free of nuclear weapons and waste. The FBI plants these clues. Falsehoods. Your friend at the police lab knows stuff was planted, doesn't he?"

Sonny nodded. Howard had warned him the earring was probably planted—probably by the police.

"Anyway, this one is made out of copper, and my ladies use shell casings. You're not dumb, Baca, you know what the bureau can do. Though in this case they're not even doing it *well*."

He handed the earring back to Sonny. "Give it to your lady. A gift from the sun people."

Sonny slipped the earring back in his pocket.

"The government's been feeding lies to the people," Raven said. "And you've been asleep. Time to wake up. Now they're sprouting a new lie. We're going to convert to peaceful uses, they say. Make plastic toys instead of plutonium. Can we believe anything they say? Only way to wake people up is to shock 'em."

"Shock them to death?" Sonny asked.

Raven looked at him, and in his look Sonny knew the man didn't care how he woke up those he thought were asleep. Idealism or insanity, it didn't matter what you called it, the man was going to go through with his messianic mission. He believed in it.

"It's a trade-off, Baca. Fight fire with fire. To remind everyone that the earth should stay nuke free. We're starting this chapter of the fight tomorrow with a press conference in the morning at Roosevelt Park. I'm giving fair warning to stop this disaster before it starts." He paused. "Or else, on the day the sun stands still, I'll go down in history as the man who saved the Earth!"

Sonny felt a surge of energy from Raven. The medallion shone on Raven's chest. Sonny could almost see his image in it. He pulled away, turned, and headed back to the sheriff's office.

"Fight fire with fire. . . ." Sonny mused, shaking his head.

The man was crazy. Blow up a WIPP truck and bring the world to its knees? Damn! But he had convinced himself he was doing it for only the best reason.

"Well?" Sheriff Naranjo asked. He had been waiting.

"How serious is his threat?" Sonny asked. He was still unsure. He had felt Raven's power, and he wondered how far this strange and charismatic man would go.

"I don't know," the sheriff replied. "FBI has to take any wild threat serious. The people around him are violent. Those two pendejos you met at the bar, they're crazy. And this guy, Raven, one minute he's loco like them, the next he's the most intelligent, smoothest talker you ever met. I can't figure him. I just want him out of Estancia."

"I can understand that," Sonny agreed as they walked outside into the bright sunlight.

"The highway from Los Alamos to Carlsbad is very long," the sheriff said. "FBI and state cops can't watch every mile."

"When does the shipment leave Los Alamos?" Sonny asked.

"June twenty-first. They're planning a big party. Governor's going to have the National Guard out, but that's three hundred miles of road to cover."

The twenty-first was Friday, Sonny thought, just days from now. But that was the FBI's concern, not his. Gloria was his concern, and he was still as far from finding her murderers as he had been when he started. Still, her death would pale in comparison to the havoc Raven could create. He thanked the sheriff and got into his truck. He had left the windows open, but it was still stifling.

A glint of metal made him look at the seat. He picked up an earring, looked at it closely. It matched the one Howard had given him, but this was made of brass. The real thing. Yes, anything could be planted on anyone at any time. Raven was right. Sonny slipped the earring in his shirt pocket and started his truck.

In the expanse of the searing llano the town was a speck, hardly alive. In a week who knew what it would look like? A ghost town, deserted because its inhabitants would have to move. Sonny turned over Raven/Pájaro's plan in his mind, wondering where the environmentalist and eco-terrorist's world overlapped with the bedraggled cult.

From the Jeep across the street, Raven's buddies were watching him. Dorothy sat slumped in the backseat. They must be waiting to take Raven home. Farther up the street two men sat in a Jeep Cherokee. The FBI boys, no doubt, waiting to tail Raven. There were a couple of other cars parked on the street; one of them followed Sonny back to Alburquerque. But were the occupants FBI or more of Raven's cohorts?

21

The next morning Sonny head-
ed for Raven's Nuclear-Free Earth press conference at Roosevelt
Park, near the university. Anthony Pájaro, alias Raven, alias God
only knew how many other names, was pulling out all the stops
in his fight against WIPP. The grassy knolls were jammed with
people. "Stop WIPP" signs proliferated.

Sonny parked his truck next to a black BMW. Tamara
Dubronsky's car. Sonny walked into the park and made himself
inconspicuous under a giant elm. There, from the outer fringe of
the crowd, he surveyed the festive atmosphere of the gathering.
Colorful balloons filled the air. People held antinuke signs: Anti-
WIPP, Pro Earth, A Nuclear-Free Earth. Like a political rally,
Sonny thought. The crowd was clearly caught up in the excite-
ment.

At a table at the center of the crowd sat the man himself. Not the crazy Raven Sonny had met in the jail cell, but his mask: Anthony Pájaro. He was smiling, greeting people. Select members of Nuclear-Free Earth sat at the table with him, but none of the cronies Sonny had tangled with in Estancia.

Other groups opposed to WIPP had come to see what Pájaro had to say. Most of the groups had early on resisted a coalition with his group, but it was June 19, only two days until the experimental truck loaded with dirty nuclear waste rolled out of Los Alamos to the WIPP site in Carlsbad. The coalitions against WIPP felt it was now or never for a concerted effort. Despite his dangerous ideas, Pájaro, they sensed, was the only one who could bring them together.

Sonny recognized friends from the South Valley group who were trying to get Super Fund money to clean up a huge, polluted area. He waved. A fleeting image of his father reminded him he still had unresolved business. Maybe when his case was over, he would join the fight again.

Clean Earth, he thought, who in the hell could be against a clean Earth? He scanned the crowd and recognized undercover city cops working through it. He saw people he knew, including the FBI boys who had worked him over the afternoon he visited Raven's compound. One of them spotted Sonny, nudged his partner, and frowned. Then they both disappeared into the milling crowd.

Sonny turned his attention to Raven. What a masquerade. As Anthony Pájaro, the man was sure of himself, exuding confidence as he shook hands with well-wishers. In his dark pants and white shirt with the ruffled collar, he radiated confidence. His raven-black hair was done in a ponytail. The Zia gold medallion glittered on his chest. Aggressive reporters pushed forward to get shots of him.

Rosa Guerra, a community activist from the South Valley, sat at Raven's side. She rose and her thin voice thundered in the microphone, greeting people, introducing the panel, explaining that they were gathered there to plan the biggest anti-WIPP rally ever held in the state of New Mexico. In just two days the WIPP truck would roll out of Los Alamos, and they were going to be there to protest. When she was done warming up the enthusiastic crowd, she introduced Raven.

"Now let's hear from the person who has been able to bring us together in our fight! A man who has just gotten out of jail, where he was imprisoned under false charges by those who would stop our fight! Anthony Pájaro!"

The crowd cheered as she handed the mike to Raven.

Raven's small group was enthusiastic, clearly under his wing. Today his job was to persuade the others to lay their bodies on the line and stop the truck from rolling. And if that concerted action didn't work, Raven had his own plan.

"Before I answer questions," he began, "I want to read a statement. Some of you know I just got out of jail. Yes, the so-called law of this state threw me in jail for my beliefs. This is supposed to be a free country, but if the cops want you in jail, they drum up charges. They claim I was growing marijuana. But they let me out of jail without charging me, so where's the marijuana I was supposed to be growing?"

"Maybe the cops smoked it!" someone shouted, and the crowd laughed and cheered.

Raven smiled. "Yeah, they want me in jail! Why? Because I'm fighting for a nuclear-free Earth! The FBI had trumped up the charges. They don't want me, and all of you, in Los Alamos on Friday when the WIPP truck loaded with high-level plutonium waste rolls! But we're going to be there, aren't we?"

The crowd cheered. He worked the crowd, turning to speak to each of the different groups present, urging unity of all the groups against WIPP. The crowd listened intently.

Sonny, too, was listening intently when he felt someone at his side, smelled the fragrance of a perfume he recognized.

"Darling." Tamara Dubronsky smiled up at him. She wore a white, flowing summer dress, a large straw hat, and dark glasses.

"How nice to see you," she whispered, peering over her glasses, leaning forward for Sonny to kiss her cheek.

"Buenas tardes," he replied.

"You are looking wonderful," she whispered. "This heat agrees with you." She slipped her glasses back on and turned to look at Raven. "Isn't he magnetic?" she whispered.

Magnetic? Sonny thought. Yeah. He nodded.

"You two are so much alike," she said.

He decided to find out just what she knew. "Me and Raven? Or me and Anthony?"

She smiled enigmatically and turned to listen to Raven.

"You are like a crystal, coated with all the superfluous trappings of your macho culture," she had told him when they first met. "Inside you are a sensitive person, a man who has a gift to share with the world. A view into your past lives would reveal so much. You are a man of the sun, the light within you is strong. Beneath the skin we are brother and sister. But you are afraid of the light. You need a guide to show you the possibilities. Let me be your guide. To truly know the truth you need a guide."

I have a guide, he'd thought. Don Eliseo. When he sat with don Eliseo in the garden as the morning sun came over the crest of the mountain, he had felt the beauty of the Señores y Señoras de la Luz. A mystery was revealed. A sense of clarity came from the sharing, no need to search past lives when the moment was so fulfilling. Clarity was in the moment lived.

And Rita was a guide. Being in her arms, he felt the layers of old notions fall away, revealing his real self. In her love he found his center; there he found peace, beauty, and strength. There was also a sense of knowledge, and yes, illumination. Love was a path. It was more than just the sex.

Maybe he was wasting his time here, Sonny thought. Maybe Raven really didn't have the guts to blow up a WIPP truck. Maybe the large barrel in which the nuclear waste was to be transported couldn't be blasted open. The containers had been designed at Sandia Labs, and each barrel was supposed to be impregnable. But no way Sandia had tested them against the dynamite charge Raven could rig up. If he could blow the container apart, or if he could just put a crack in it, the radiation would spread for miles in no time.

Raven finished reading his statement, and the reporters pressed forward with questions. He had handled himself well, Sonny thought, painting himself as the anti-WIPP hero, a man who wants to protect the earth and its people from high-level plutonium proliferation. New Mexico should not become a nuclear dumping ground for the nation, he said, playing on a theme many could agree on. He laid out his plan to bodily keep the trucks from moving. But he only vaguely alluded to the kind of violence he had in mind to back that action up.

When he was done, he raised his fist and shouted, "Power to the people! Down with WIPP!"

The small crowd responded with applause, and a resounding "Down with WIPP!" cry echoed across the sultry air. "Down with WIPP! Down with WIPP! Down with WIPP!"

"He is wonderful," Tamara said, taking Sonny's arm and leading him toward Raven.

Raven's groupies were gathered around him, congratulating him, but when he saw Tamara and Sonny approach, he turned to greet them. "Tamara," he said as he took her hand, watching Sonny out of the corners of his eyes.

"You were wonderful," Tamara said, beaming.

"Ah, Mr. Sonny Baca." Raven grinned. "Didn't think I'd see you again so soon. You ready to join us?"

"Not quite," Sonny answered.

"Some men are blind." Raven's look turned dark.

"He needs time," Tamara said.

"We don't have time," Raven replied, whispering something to Tamara as he kissed her cheek.

The crowd pressed around them, eager to talk to him, to ask questions, to plan details for the rally in Los Alamos, and he turned to greet them. For the moment he was in charge, the news conference had been a success: the Nuclear-Free Earth group now controlled most of the groups around the state. Individually, they had failed to stop the WIPP test shipment, but now, united, a new hope stirred. The excitement was palpable.

"Look around you," Raven said, "these are your neighbors, people you know. They've made a commitment to stop WIPP. Why can't you?"

Sonny looked at the crowd. How many around him knew Raven and Anthony Pájaro were the same man? He did nothing to hide the identities. Tamara apparently knew and accepted it. Did the others see it?

"Too busy to get involved," Raven said scornfully.

Tamara sensed the confrontation and took Sonny's arm. "The press is waiting for you, darling" she said to Raven. "You have done wonderful work today. Leave Sonny to me. Come, Sonny, walk me to my car."

Raven smiled. "Yes, perhaps you can *persuade* him. But there isn't much time left, Mr. Baca. Two days. Remember, two days. We want your body on the line when we close down the Los Alamos highway."

He laughed and turned to the news reporters who eagerly sought individual interviews for the six o'clock news.

"He has a way with people," Tamara said to Sonny as they walked out of the park. "He's the only leader they have."

"Who?" Sonny asked.

"Anthony, of course."

"And Raven?"

"You are playing word games with me, darling. Please don't. I trust Anthony, and I am committed to this cause because I know the evil of this deadly power. The cold war is only on hold, don't you see that. Madmen all over this world, from North Korea to Iraq, want to get hold of nuclear weapons. War will come, nuclear war, if we don't stop this madness. And with war, the Earth freezing over. . . ."

She paused and shivered, even though the day was hot.

"Yes, the scientists predict a cloud will cover the sun, a new ice age will cover the Earth."

"But the cold war *is* over," Sonny said.

"I don't believe it," she replied. "The governments have always lied to us. The arsenals are still immense. No, my dear, the world is still ruled by fear. The only way is to get rid of the weapons once and for all."

"Can I ask you about Gloria?" Sonny asked as they reached her car.

"Darling, you can ask me anything."

"She was seeing Akira Morino."

"They had become, shall we say, *attached.*" Tamara nodded.

"Were they lovers?" Sonny asked, and opened her car door.

"How well did *you* know her?" Tamara turned the question on him.

"Not as well as I thought," he admitted.

"I know she was an ambitious woman," Tamara offered. "In many ways she was the moving force behind Frank's plans. A very strong woman. I think she grew tired of his womanizing. Women like Gloria are not spurned easily. But in this case she didn't act quickly enough."

"What do you mean?"

"I wouldn't trust Frank Dominic as far as I can throw him," she whispered as she leaned forward and brushed his cheek with a kiss. "Very few in this city turn their back on him." She got into her car and put the key in the ignition.

"You don't think that he—"

"Dear boy, you tell me. You're the detective." She smiled.

"Did Anthony Pájaro know Gloria?"

"Why would he? This was not Gloria's cause."

"How about the rumors that Raven is going to blow up a WIPP truck?" Sonny said, deciding to gauge her response.

Tamara frowned. "Anthony doesn't believe in violence. This is gossip stirred up by the news media. They are trying to discredit his work. Anyway, I'm going to call Morino and put in a good word for you this afternoon, as you asked. Ciao," she said, and drove away. Traces of her sweet perfume mixed with the car's exhaust and dust.

"Yeah, hasta la vista." Sonny waved.

Where would it end? he wondered, getting in his truck and driving to Rita's.

On the way Sonny checked in with Howard, but nothing new had developed at the lab. Leroy Brown was still in jail, and the news media had returned its attention to the mayoral race. As predicted, Gloria's murder was slipping out of the public eye and into the police's back files.

Howard was no longer on the case. A man had been drowned in a South Valley irrigation ditch. He was found covered with a plastic sack covering his head, gagged and bound, a typical dope deal gone sour, and Howard was assigned to gather evidence.

"One of Turco's boys," Howard said. "Looks like the Juárez mafiosos have struck."

"The noose tightens on Turco. Gracias, 'mano."

"Take care," Howard warned.

"Ten-four," Sonny said, and drove to Rita's. He had the feeling he was being followed, but when he checked the rearview mirror, there was no tail in sight. Paranoid, he thought. He wasn't getting enough sleep, too much was crowding in too fast, and he felt lost in a quagmire without answers.

He told Rita his thoughts as they sat on her porch and enjoyed the cool of the evening. "Gloria Dominic's murder has moved to the back page," he said. "Frank is running his campaign as if nothing had ever happened. Garcia doesn't give a damn if the whole thing disappears and goes away. With Leroy Brown in jail, all is supposed to be safe."

What would Elfego Baca do? Sonny thought. Charge in and take command. Elfego Baca had been the doer. Legend had it that as a young man, el Bisabuelo had walked into Alburquerque from Socorro with Billy the Kid. They were fifteen or sixteen, two pimply-faced young men walking from Socorro into the big city of Alburquerque to seek their fortune.

Billy the Kid and Elfego Baca. It would make a good movie, Sonny thought. They were bone weary, dusty, and hungry. They walked into the Martinez Bar in Old Town, where Billy ordered the biggest meal on the menu for him and his friend. The ladies of the cantina joined them, and they danced and sang all night. Billy lined the bar with the free drinks for everyone—except Billy. He never touched the stuff.

Late that night when the time came to pay the bill, Billy winked at Elfego, secretly moved toward a table in a dark corner and lighted a stick of dynamite he had been carrying. He put it under the table and motioned to Elfego to grab his hat. Nonchalantly, he and Elfego worked their way toward the door. The explosion hurt no one, but it shook the bar and powdered black the faces of the ladies of the night and the many drunk cowboys. In the commotion the young Elfego and Billy scurried out the back door. That night, the two who had eaten and danced like kings slept in the straw of the livery stable.

"The most pleasant sleep I ever had in my life," Elfego was to write in his diary as an old man.

"I didn't see Billy again until March 28 of 1881," Elfego continued in his diary. "He was famous. Every man, woman, and child in New Mexico knew his name. Billy was being sent from Santa Fe to Mesilla to stand trial for the murder of William Brady, sheriff of Lincoln County. The train stopped at the Alburquerque train depot. I went down to see him. I knew all the city deputies, but I had a little trouble getting Tony Neis, the deputy U.S. marshal who was escorting Billy, to let Billy get off the train so he could have dinner with me at the hotel. I bought him a meal, and we talked about old times. Neis was armed to the teeth, because he was afraid of Billy, but I gave my word, and Billy gave his word, no funny business. We just wanted to talk. The restaurant windows were full of faces trying to get a look at Billy. As the Lord is my witness, I didn't know that a few months later he would bust out of the Lincoln County Jail and head for Fort Sumner, where he was finally gunned down by Sheriff Pat Garrett."

"Any ideas?" Rita asked, breaking into his drifting thoughts.

"How would you like to have lunch with Armando? My brother always knows what's really going on in the South Valley."

22

Howard had invited Sonny and Rita to the Juneteenth Celebration at the State Fairgrounds. "Do you good, compadre," Howard said. "Let's go chow down on some of Powdrell's famous barbecue ribs, fried catfish, and apple pie. A man does not live on enchiladas alone."

But Sonny declined. He was obsessed with finding Gloria's murderer, and it seemed he'd gotten exactly nowhere since he started. Though he needed one, he had no time for a night off. There was one source who was sure to know something, so he spent the night prowling the South Valley, looking for Gloria's brother, Turco. He followed Turco's tracks through the maze of dirt roads that criss-crossed the Five Points area, but he couldn't get close to the big jefe who controlled the South Valley drug traffic. Turco was running scared.

In the bars and Mexican cafés where people met, Sonny heard

a dozen different stories. Turco was reported hanging out at the house of such and such a friend. Or Turco was seen having a drink at one of the bars along Isleta or at the Aquí Me Quedo on Coors, but by the time Sonny showed up, Turco had always flown, if he had ever been there. Turco was moving constantly, sleeping at a different house each night. The heat was on. So why had Turco come out in the open at Gloria's funeral? Gloria had no love for her brother; in fact, the feelings had been quite the opposite. She hated Turco for what he and their father had done to her. Could Gloria have been blackmailing him? Did Turco attack Dominic to focus suspicion away from himself?

Sonny dialed his brother's number. A sweet voice with a Texas accent answered. "Mando's Used Cars, Jeanine speaking. Can I help y'all?"

Sonny smiled. The syrupy drawl belonged to Mando's current lady friend. Armando had met her in Amarillo at a used-car-dealers' convention. She was just divorced, for the third time, but she seemed to fit Armando just right.

Armando was running his used-car business out of the Ya No Puedo Bar. His phone was a pay phone near a back booth; he had a couple of junk heaps sitting in the parking lot. That was the extent of Mando's Used Cars.

Sonny sighed. Times like this he felt like his mother. He should help his brother, maybe just see him more often. His brother was adrift, still hustling, still part of la vida loca, the hard life of the streets in which many from the South Valley struggled for survival.

Hell, Sonny thought, maybe he's no more adrift than me. What do I have to show for my life? At least Mando seemed happy. Nothing got him down, and even though car dealing was a hard way to earn a living, he was honest. Mando kept clean. Sure he drank, sometimes too much, but he didn't do drugs.

His twin brother had an outgoing personality, people liked him, women liked him. He always enjoyed the company of a nice-looking mamasota. Jeanine was the latest in a long line.

"Hi, this is Sonny. Let me talk to Mando," Sonny answered.

"Sonny," Jeanine said sweetly. "So pleased to talk to y'all. Mando! It's Sonny!" she yelled.

Armando came to the phone. "Hey, bro, how's it going? Need a used car?" He laughed.

"No, my troca's running fine. Vamo' a'lonche.'"

"All right, bro. Dónde?"

"Jimmy's Place."

"You got it."

Sonny called Rita. Yes, she was ready. She had just hired a new cashier who had the lunch shift well in hand. So he picked her up, and they drove to Jimmy's Coffee House in Barelas. The place was packed as usual. The noonday conversations buzzed with local gossip and the latest mitote in city hall politics. People were interested in the mayor's race and, of course, the still-unsolved Gloria Dominic murder.

Jimmy cleared a booth next to the window, and they sipped coffee while they waited for Armando and Jeanine. Sonny told Rita about his visit to Estancia and his meeting with Raven. He didn't mention his visit to Tamara's.

When Armando and Jeanine made their appearance, it was a grand entrance. Armando was, in many ways, the opposite of Sonny. He was a few inches taller, heavier, outgoing. He came in shaking hands with everyone and pressing his business card on people. "Come and see me," he said, smiling at old friends from the valley. "Mando's Used Cars. 'Yo no mando, tú mandas!'—that's our motto. What you want, I can get for you! We treat you right. Right, Jeanine?"

And the red-haired Jeanine, whose signature was the tight pants and a tank top that bulged with her big breasts, beamed, "You bet!" Eyes turned to admire the attractive woman.

Mando greeted Sonny and Rita with warm embraces. "Cómo 'stás, bro. Good to see you. Sorry I couldn't make it to the prima's funeral. I was in Amarillo . . . I felt bad."

He gathered Rita in an abrazo. "Rita, you look beautiful as always. Really sorry about Gloria. She was a good woman."

"We are sorry," Jeanine added. "I didn't know her, but Mando said she was just so beautiful."

"This is Jeanine, my lady. At least one good thing came out of my trip to Amarillo."

"Hi, Jeanine." Rita smiled.

"Rita. That's a pretty name. So glad to meet y'all."

Armando always seemed to wind up with dumb, but very sincere, women.

"So I told Jeanine," Mando continued as they sat, "what's a nice girl like you doing in a dump like Amarillo? Come to 'Burque with me and I'll show you a good time."

"Yeah, great time." Jeanine winked. Maybe she wasn't so dumb after all.

"Patience, my love." Mando leaned to her and kissed her cheek. "You wait till Mando's Cars get going. We'll be rolling in the dough." He laughed, looked at the menu, and ordered the biggest combination plate available: enchiladas, tamale, tacos, beans, rice, red chile, and plenty of homemade tortillas hot off the comal.

"So when is this guy going to marry you?" Mando asked Rita.

Rita shrugged and replied, "And you?"

"Ah, Jeanine knows I'm not the marrying kind. But my little brother here needs to settle down."

"Little?" Sonny punched his arm. "So how *is* the used-car business?"

"Slow," Armando replied.

Jimmy came by to say hello. He and Armando were old friends, so he took good care of them.

Mando greeted the owner warmly. "Ese, Jimmy, cómo estás. You know my family. This is Jeanine, my secretary. Set up your best plates, hermano, we came to eat!"

"This is a treat." Jeanine smiled. "We don't eat out very often."

"Used cars aren't moving, but that's all going to change. I'm going to do for used cars here in the South Valley what Jimmy here did for tacos. Make them hot, make them sell, eh, Jimmy!" He slapped Jimmy on the back.

They exchanged pleasantries, then Jimmy moved on with his pot of coffee to serve his other patrons: businessmen and secretaries from downtown, small contractors from along the valley, and a few Anglos, all aficionados of the hot, homemade food Jimmy served. The conversations were in Spanish, English, and a blend of both: the Spanglish of the people.

Their plates were served, and Armando made small talk while they ate, talking about the Amarillo used-car-dealers' convention and how he and Jeanine met.

"I was modeling at Amarillo Shorty's booth," Jeanine exclaimed. "Shorty had us dress up in practically nothing. Know what I mean. Just little teenie-weenie bikinis."

"Us?" Rita asked.

"Me and Darlene. Darlene's a manicurist, but she was sleeping with Shorty. His wife found out, and the next she knew, she was fired. We were just trying to earn an honest buck. But it was embarrassing, sashaying around Shorty's cars in practically our bare asses. When Mando came along, I knew it was love at first sight."

"Lust at first sight," Mando said.

"It was Shorty's idea!" She nudged his ribs.

"Yeah, I know what Shorty had in mind," Mando teased.

"Not!" She slapped his wrist.

Sonny smiled. They clearly got along. But that was Mando's gift, he got along with everybody. He looked at his brother as he talked, listened to the voice he knew from childhood, felt the wide space that separated them.

Armando smacked his lips as he scooped up beans and chile with his tortilla. "Not as sabroso as yours, Rita," he whispered diplomatically, "but good."

"You haven't been to my place in ages," Rita reminded him.

"Hey, I don't get up to the North Valley too often. Too busy setting up the car lot."

"What he means," Jeanine said, "is we got no wheels."

Mando grinned sheepishly. "One car's got a dead battery, one has a flat. I had to borrow a car to get here. But this afternoon, we'll get the battery charged. Things are looking up, right Jeanine?"

"You bet," Jeanine agreed.

"So, what do you know about Turco?" Sonny asked when they had settled into their food.

"I ran into him a couple of days ago."

"Where?"

"La Granada. He's using the place as a hangout." He leaned across the table and whispered. "What do you want with Turco? Stay away from him, bro. The primo's bad news."

"He went to see Gloria."

"Yeah. So?"

"Right before she was killed."

"That's what they say. . . ."

"I need to know why."

"That's easy. Money. What else?" Armando leaned forward and whispered. "The word on the street says the Mexican mafia had brought a million-dollar dope shipment into the city for Turco to distribute. He sold the dope that came up from Juárez, and he was sitting on half a million bucks, maybe a million. Then he decided to gamble with it."

"Vegas?" Sonny asked.

Armando nodded. "Yeah. He threw a wild party. Charter jet, champagne, took half the city and a few legislators with him. It was a *big* party. He blew the money!"

Sonny whistled. "I heard about the dope deal, but I didn't know he had blown it. That's a lot of lana."

"Damn right it's a lot of lana! When the mafia came to collect, Turco was broke. His life wasn't worth a bean taco. So maybe he went to his sister for help."

Yeah, Sonny thought. If Turco had double-crossed los mafiosos de Juárez, sold their dope and took their money, they would be out for his ass. So that's why Turco was on the run, hiding here and there with old friends. But he knew, and everybody knew, that when the mafia came to collect, they did. Their money or Turco's blood, one or the other. Leroy Brown told Sonny that Turco had showed up at the Dominic house. The long-abandoned brother, the dope dealer, finally shows up begging at his sister's door. He needs money like he never needed it before, with the Mexican mafia after him. And Gloria had it, or could get it.

Sonny looked out the window. The peaceful, sluggish traffic of the hot summer midday floated on ripples of dry air. The surface of the barrio was pastel colors bright with sunlight, friendly sounds, and the smiles of the people. Beneath that surface lay the danger. Turco Dominguez was one of those dangers. In the barrios of the South Valley, you had to hustle to make a living. It was the same uptown and in city hall, Sonny knew, just more expensive, and the hustlers there wore three-piece suits.

Armando wiped the last of the red chile from his plate with the tortilla. "Great stuff." He smiled. Beads of perspiration lay on his forehead like glistening drops of dew. "Panza llena, corazón contento."

"What's that mean?" Jeanine asked.

"Honey, it means after a meal like this, we take the afternoon off." Armando winked.

"Oh, good." Jeanine smiled and drew close to him. "I wish I knew how to cook your chile, Mando."

"You do pretty well." Mando grinned. He pushed the bill toward Sonny. "Now maybe we can talk Sonny into investing in the new place I want to buy—"

"*We* want to buy," Jeanine corrected him. Mando laughed.

"I'm broke, Mando, same as you. If I had any money, I'd pay my own rent on time." Sonny smiled and pulled out his wallet. "But I'll buy your lunch if you tell me more about Turco."

"They have him on the run. There's a lot of guns from Juárez in the South Valley. The streets aren't safe, bro. You know Frank wouldn't let Turco step in his house if he knew about it, much less lend him money. But I think our cuz might have asked the Japanese man. He has money."

"Morino might have raised the money?" Sonny asked.

Armando shrugged. "Ah, Turco talks big. He dropped the man's name. Said that he almost had it, but the truth is he never got a penny. He came back to the barrio angrier than hell."

"Then Gloria was murdered," Sonny finished.

Armando shrugged. "These ain't penny-ante people, bro. There's high stakes involved, and our prima's dead. Add dos y dos and the answer is keep your nose clean."

Rita nodded in agreement and looked at Sonny. Would he take his brother's warning?

Sonny was thinking about Gloria. Turco had come to see his sister. He needed a lot of money to save himself. Dope was involved. But why would Gloria see Turco after all those years?

"Gotta see Turco," Sonny said.

"Por qué?" Armando asked.

"Why did Gloria even let him in? After all this time."

"Yeah, I know. I'm sorry about Gloria, bro. Sorry she died that way. But seeing Turco is dangerous," he cautioned. "You don't want to get caught in a crossfire."

"Thanks for the warning," Sonny said, "but I already am. He still dropping by La Granada?"

Armando nodded.

Sonny looked at Rita. "I know what you're thinking, and I'm going with you," she said.

"You two are crazy." Armando shook his head.

Sonny stood and dropped enough money on the check to cover it and the tip. "Adiós, bro. Keep in touch."

"I will, bro. Gracias por el lonche. Soon as we get our business going, we'll call you and take you to the Hyatt."

"Oh, that would be scrumptious," Jeanine said.

"Hey, we don't need the Hyatt." Sonny embraced his brother. "We've got Rita's Cocina."

"The next one's on me." Rita smiled and embraced both Mando and Jeanine.

"Oh, you're so great," Jeanine beamed. "People here are just so great."

"Glad you left Amarillo?" Armando laughed and put his arm around her.

"For sure."

"Take care of yourself," Sonny told his brother.

"Me? I'm not the one looking for Turco. You take care, bro."

They parted with handshakes and promises to see each other at Rita's.

"She was nice," Rita said as Sonny drove her home.

"Jeanine? Yeah, she fits Mando."

"You and Mando are so different, but you do have one thing in common."

"What's that?"

"Afraid of marriage."

Sonny smiled. "Gun-shy. Give us time, give us time."

"Oh, I will," Rita replied, and drew closer to him. "I'm beginning to like you," she teased.

"And I'm beginning to like you, mujer." He smiled.

"I just don't like the work you do, especially when it comes to dealing with people like Turco."

"Ah, he's no big deal. Dope dealers like Turco are chickenshits inside. They prey on the weak, play the middleman part, drive around in big cars, wear expensive suits, but they run scared. And Turco's running scared."

"Would Gloria really have given him money?" Rita asked.

"It does seem hard to imagine, but she was like that, very giving. She gave to charities, gave to every cause. What if Turco shows up, and she hates him for the abuse of the past, but instead of ignoring him, she turns and helps him. I wouldn't put it past her."

"Did she have the money?"

"Probably not. If she had gotten hold of that much bread, Frank would know."

"Morino?"

"He would really have to be interested to come up with that much money."

"And if there was money, Mando said Turco didn't get it."

"Yeah, so now there's a new motive. Assume Gloria raises the money. Who got it?" Sonny pulled up in front of Rita's Cocina. "Look, La Granada's no place—" he began, but Rita interrupted.

"No place for a lady. We've been there before."

"Once, and we left when the shooting started."

They laughed.

"I want to go," she said, and kissed him. "So don't argue. See you tonight."

"Adiós." He smiled and watched her walk into the restaurant.

Okay, if she insisted, she insisted. What the hell, Turco probably wouldn't show. They could have a few beers, dance, maybe clear his head. If any trouble started, they'd just leave. And later, back home with Rita, maybe he wouldn't be—

He shivered. Damn, he had to get over fear of impotence. It was a passing thing. Tonight would be different.

When he arrived home, he checked his message machine. One call was from Sears, where he had bought two tires on credit. His account was being turned over to a collection agency unless he called right away. The other was a muffled voice. "Mind your own business. You could get killed, stupid." The third call was from Tamara Dubronsky.

"Darling," she said, "I talked to Mr. Morino. Now call his office again, it shouldn't be a problem. Call me anytime. Ciao."

But as the machine clicked off, Sonny's mind was elsewhere, still on Gloria, Akira Morino, and Turco. The possibility of a lot of money between them that was now nowhere to be found. Something was finally beginning to click.

23

Later that evening Sonny picked up Rita, and they drove to La Granada Bar in the South Valley, one of the liveliest bars along Isleta Boulevard. The cantina was a meeting place for local Chicanos, stray cowboys, Indians from Isleta Pueblo, and the newly arrived Mexican workers who lived in the valley. The bar had the unsavory reputation of having the most homicides committed on or near its premises each year.

"Sure you want to go?" Sonny had asked Rita.

"You bet," Rita answered. "Let's boogie."

"You don't dance at La Granada, you dodge bullets." Sonny laughed.

Of course, the reputation of the place was exaggerated. Anyone who went looking for trouble could find it. But those who went to meet friends, have a drink, dance, and have a good time could enjoy themselves without provocation.

But Turco was a hunted man, and meeting him on his turf was chancy, Sonny thought as they pulled into the glass-littered parking lot. Pickup trucks and late-model cars dotted the lot, but no fancy cars. So Turco wasn't there, at least not yet. Sonny rolled down the window and breathed the night air, cool with the fragrances of the valley: fields watered, backyard corrals where some of the people kept horses, the rich smell of the cottonwoods giving up their day's aroma.

The music from within the bar punctuated the drone of the cicadas in the trees. The drone of the grillos carried a higher, more frantic pitch. Rain was on its way.

Sonny smiled. Rain would clear the dust that lay over the valley like a thin veil. He told Rita about his visit to Lorenza as they waited to see if Turco would show.

"She's good," Rita said.

"What if evil brujos were involved in Gloria's death?" Sonny asked. "What if she was involved with some kind of a blood cult, if she was tangled up with Raven's bunch?"

"There is something bad going on in the North Valley."

"But what?"

"It's like the stories Toto, Concha, and don Eliseo tell."

"You really believe their stories about brujos have something to do with Gloria's death?"

"It's there. And it's powerful. That's why Lorenza can help."

"How?"

"If the people who killed Gloria are brujos, you have to be prepared."

"How?"

"She knows."

"You don't?"

"I know herbs, remedies, massage for the man I love, but not the world of the brujos. Lorenza does. She learned her craft from brujos in Mexico."

"You mean she didn't study with the curanderas here?"

"She did, but most of the old curanderas here used prayers. They didn't want to mess with *real* brujería."

"Which is?"

"Getting into affecting the soul, laying a curse on a person. A person can fly, or the soul can fly, and it can change into an animal form. In Mexico it's called the nagual. Lorenza believes you can change form, you can change into that animal—"

Sonny sat up straight. A large car had just turned into the parking lot. Just as the conversation was getting juicy a large wine-colored Oldsmobile parked near the back door of the bar. A man got out, looked around, nodded. A heavyset man followed, then a woman. They walked quickly into the bar.

"Turco?" Rita asked.

"Yup. Vamos." Sonny got out and opened Rita's door. He thought of carrying his pistol, but that wasn't the kind of confrontation he was looking for. And anyway, a dope dealer would smell a gun a mile away.

The bar was packed when Sonny and Rita entered. Ladies' night and a dance contest, a hundred bucks to the winners, had drawn out the Mexican workers. In their just-pressed Levi's, cowboy shirts, and hats, men swirled around the floor with dark-haired morenitas in bright dresses. The juke box was blasting a Mexican ranchera. The mood was lively, happy.

Sonny and Rita edged their way to the bar. Sonny knew the owner from his old days in the South Valley. Mama Lucy had been a state legislator for years but retired to run the bar "I didn't really change careers," she liked to joke. "In Santa Fe we met at the Bull Ring or Pink Adobe," she said, naming two well-known watering holes where lawmakers cut deals over margaritas.

"Lots of margaritas and lots of promises," Mama Lucy boasted, "same as here," and she would point at her Granada clientele. "Except here the boys drink beer," she would laugh.

"Hey, Sonny, long time no see," the stout señora said with a smile. "How's it goin'?"

"Can't complain. You remember Rita," Sonny answered. He

ordered two beers and looked past the dancers to a booth at the back. Turco and his woman had settled down; their driver and bodyguard, a thin old pachuco left over from the fifties, stood near the door. Turco would have a drink, then move on. Sonny had to move fast. "And you?" he asked Mama Lucy when she returned with the beers.

"Same old thing." She shrugged and wiped the bar. The song had ended; there was a break as the dancers walked back to their tables.

"Come on, Lucy, how can it be the same old thing if there's an army in town and Turco's sitting in your back booth?" Sonny tested her.

"He pays for his drink like anybody else," Mama Lucy shot back. "Don't come around here looking for caca, Sonny! The caca's in the North Valley. I hope you keep it up there," she said. Her expression sobered and her eyes narrowed. She didn't appreciate Sonny snooping, that was clear.

"Nothing's clean," Sonny countered. He glanced at Turco's booth. "Not as long as pushers like Turco sit in your place."

"I got nothing to do with that business!" she replied angrily. "As far as I'm concerned, people like Turco are parasites. Right now the parasite had fastened itself to the Granada Bar, and there isn't a damn thing I can do about it. The sooner he moves out, the happier I am," she added. "I hope the damn mafia does get his ass."

"I gotta talk to him," Sonny said, and placed his half-empty beer on the bar. Mama Lucy reached out and grabbed his arm as he began to stand up.

"Don't try anything funny, Sonny. I don't want fights, and I don't want my place torched."

"Relax." Sonny pushed her hand away. "I came to dance, not to fight." Sonny smiled and grabbed Rita as the next ranchera blasted from the jukebox. He pulled her onto the dance floor and twirled her around the floor, stomping to the beat of the music, dazzling the other dancers who joined them. Loud cries of "Ajuas!" filled the smokey bar.

"We're gonna take the prize!" Rita shouted, enjoying the fast step. When they neared Turco's booth, she realized what Sonny had in mind. Sonny had swirled her toward Turco's booth, stopped suddenly in front of his cousin, who hadn't yet spotted him. Sonny smiled and reached forward to grab Turco's hand before the big man could draw back.

"Hey, primo, cómo 'stás?" Sonny greeted Turco with a smile.

Turco's eyes narrowed as he peered at Sonny. He was a barrel-chested man, thick, dressed in a snappy wine-colored suit, flashy. His dyed black hair was sleeked back with a shiny pomade, his face dark and pockmarked.

"Good to see you, ese," Sonny said, keeping hold of Turco's hand and pushing Rita into the seat opposite Turco and his woman.

"Órale." Turco smiled. He turned to his lady, a dark, attractive Mexicana, and explained, "Es primo."

"Quieres arm wrestle?" Sonny asked.

Turco had a reputation as one of the best in the South Valley, and with his broad chest, it was easy to understand why. Turco's body and face were like a chiseled Olmec statue, thick and ominous.

"No, chale." Turco pulled back, and Sonny let go his hand.

"This is my lady friend, Rita," Sonny said.

Turco glanced at Rita, nodded.

"Buenas noches," Sonny said to Turco's woman. The woman smiled. "Buenas," she replied, the Juárez accent clear. She was a border woman, tough enough to survive along the margin, or with dope dealers.

Just like Camela la Tejana of corrido fame, Sonny thought. They came across with their men, survived the double-crossing business, moved from one dealer to another, and eventually began to do business on their own.

Sonny turned and waved at the bar. "Hey, how about a round."

Turco looked at his woman. "Por qué no?" she said.

Turco's man at the door had moved forward, but when Turco shook his head, he relaxed and moved back.

"So how you been, prim?" Sonny asked.

Turco shrugged. His eyes looked tired, his face haggard.

"Pura joda," he said in a weary voice, glancing at the dancers on the floor, meaning life was hard, pura caca since the Juárez boys put a price on him. He was running and he was tired.

"Y tú, qué quieres?" He knew Sonny wanted something. Sonny had never given him the time of day, never would, but still, they were cousins and he had to treat him like familia.

"I need information, about Gloria. . . ."

Turco shrugged.

"Who killed her?" Sonny asked.

"Fuckin' Dominic!" Turco answered.

"Come on, Frank's a numero uno cabrón, but a murderer? No."

Turco pursed his fat lips, then stroked his thin mustache. He knit his brow, making his Olmec face darker, his dark eyes studying Sonny. There was nobody he could trust, not even the woman sitting at his side.

"You asked me," he glared, "so I told you. I think Dominic would kill his own jefita for ten bucks. Es un puto!" He spit out the words with disgust.

"You went to see Gloria just before she was killed," Sonny tested.

Turco didn't reply. He glanced at Rita, then back at Sonny. Beads of perspiration broke on his forehead, glistening in the strobe lights from the dance floor.

"You needed money," Sonny probed deeper.

"I don' know anything about her money." Turco laughed hoarsely, deep in his thick throat. "But I wish I had some of it. Eh, honey?" He said to the woman at his side.

"Claro."

"It wasn't Dominic," Sonny persisted.

"Pues, you think me?" Turco whispered. "You think I would kill my carnala?"

His words were menacing, Rita thought. She put her arm through Sonny's and shivered, even though the bar was warm with stale air and sweating dancers.

"Well, did you go see her?" Sonny asked.

Turco tensed. "Qué chingaos te importa?" he said angrily, then calmed himself as dancers nearby turned to look at him. "I didn't kill her, ese. But I should have," he scowled. "She was no good. Married the big man and forgot her familia. I was in the joint when the jefito died. She didn't even bury her father. What kind of daughter is that?" Turco said bitterly.

Sonny felt his jaws tighten, his teeth grit. The sons-of-bitches had tormented Gloria, and they expected kindness in return? He felt like reaching across the booth and strangling Turco, reminding him that it was he and his father who had ruined Gloria's life. But it wouldn't do any good. Gloria had written them off a long time ago, and so would he. He only wanted information; then if the mafia scored on Turco, he would dance at his funeral.

Turco stroked his hair, leaned close, and whispered. "She got too good for her people. She sold out. Got what she deserved, so don't come around asking questions, primo. You want to know who killed her, talk to Dominic. Or talk to Morino. Yeah, the pinche was shacking up with her. She turned out to be a puta."

"Puta!" Sonny blurted and grabbed at Turco's wrist. Anger seethed in his blood; he felt Turco flinch.

"Sí! She was Morino's puta!"

"A puta who had the money you needed, cabrón!"

"What money?" Turco replied, twisting his arm out of Sonny's grip. Then he hissed. "Don't play with me, Sonny. You know I'm in trouble! She said she would help. Yeah, the Jap was going to raise the money! But she didn't deliver! She kept it! I hope she burns in hell!" Both stood, and Turco's bodyguard drew close.

"She didn't deliver?" Sonny asked, feeling a tremble pass through his body. Was Turco telling the truth?

Turco cursed in Sonny's face. "The puta could've saved my ass! But she wouldn't! I'm glad she's dead!" He took his woman's arm and they went quickly out the back door, slamming it behind them.

"Damn him!" Sonny cursed and drove his fist into the table. He had come close to hitting Turco, taking him on for calling Gloria a whore, exploding with the frustration he felt. But Rita was with him, and the bodyguard opening up in the small, crowded bar would have meant danger for everyone.

"Ah, shit." He shook his head.

Rita touched him, he turned to look at her. "Don't let a pinche like that get the best of you." She smiled, moving into his arms.

"Yeah, you're right. I wish I could've killed him."

"He's a mal hombre," Rita said, a sigh of relief escaping her lips.

Sonny looked at her. She looked pale. He held her close. "You okay?"

"I almost peed in my panties," she laughed. "And his woman? Híjola, I thought pachucas like her went out of style in the forties."

Sonny laughed. "They're both creeps from the past."

"Was he telling the truth?"

"Gloria was kind. Maybe she could forgive even what they did to her. Maybe she did say, 'I've got the money. Come for it.' There is no other reason I can think of for Turco to show up at Gloria's after all the years."

"And Turco goes, but there is no money, and he kills her. . . . But then why make a scene at the funeral?"

"Turco can't go out of the barrio without being spotted. He moves from bar to bar, five minutes here, five there. He drives a big car, but he sleeps in the crummy back rooms of tecatos who will put him up for the night, the same dopesters he's afraid might finger him. He can't trust anyone. He has to keep on the move. The Mexican mafia wants their money, and he doesn't have it. He turns to Gloria, there's a promise, or at least he thinks she will help. . . . But she didn't have the money for him. He flies into a rage, kills her . . . later he thinks it should be easy to blame Frank."

"But Turco's probably not into draining blood."

"Right." Sonny paused. "I guess he could've hired someone—"

"But it keeps coming back to Frank," Rita whispered.

"Yeah."

"Or Morino.'

Sonny nodded.

"Did she have the money?"

"That's the sixty-four-thousand-dollar question."

Both grew silent. "So what do we do now?" Rita asked.

"We dance," he said, and he pulled her out onto the dance floor and held her tight as they swept back and forth to the tune of a Flaco Jiménez ranchera. "Forget Turco and Raven and Dominic and Morino!" he shouted. "Ajua!"

The others in the bar also felt the urge to dance freely. Turco was gone and the entire bar breathed a sigh of relief. Now it was time to enjoy the dance; no need to worry a gunfight might break out.

The dance turned into a wild, foot-stomping fiesta that lasted far into the night. Rita and Sonny competed for the dance prize, showing their stuff, moving up in points when "La Bamba" was played, moving down when a young couple did a polka that drew applause from all.

Hours later when they stumbled out of the bar, Sonny felt exhilarated. He enjoyed dancing, and Rita was a perfect partner. Her body fit his, he led her with slight touches, and because she was a good dancer, she was continually improvising, adding slight variations to the old steps. Other men watched with admiration when she danced, and that made Sonny feel good.

"We need to do this more often," he said as they walked to the truck. The cool summer-night air was bracing, a relief after the hot bar and dancing.

"Where to?" he asked, leaning to kiss her ear.

"Stay with me tonight." Rita snuggled against him.

"Not too tired?" he asked.

"Hey, you got the pump primed, Mr. Baca, now draw the water."

"Pues, vamos!" he laughed, and shot out of the parking lot.

To hell with the Zia curse, tonight he would make love to Rita. Taking the night off to dance had been good, just what he needed. Good medicine.

"Beautiful night," Sonny said as he drove into Rita's driveway and parked. Overhead the sparkle of the Milky Way lit up the dark sky, and around them the valley air was alive with the summer drone of cicadas in the trees.

"I feel rain on the way."

"Want to sleep on the porch?" she asked. "We can bring the rollaway out."

Sonny kissed her. "Anywhere," he said as he fumbled for buttons on her blouse. "Now. Here."

"Sonny," she protested weakly, "you want my vecinos to say I'm a bad woman. Come inside."

"The neighbors are asleep," he laughed as he jumped out of the truck. "I can't wait!"

As he stepped around the truck to open her door, he stopped cold. A rank odor filled the air, a bad animal smell. He felt his desire go cold, and an old instinct for survival take its place. Goosebumps covered his arms and neck; his senses felt the first shot of adrenaline. Someone had been here; there was threat in the air.

"Ugh, what smells?" Rita asked.

He looked around. The house was quiet, dark. The street was deserted; none of the neighbors stirred. The evil smell permeated the still night air. Sonny thought of his pistol, but that would only frighten Rita.

"Stay in the truck," he said as he walked toward the porch carefully. The odor grew stronger, a rancid smell.

"What is it?" Rita asked.

"Don't know." He stepped on the porch. The wooden floor creaked. "Hit the lights," he told Rita, and she flipped on the headlights. Sonny stood stunned for a moment. There, hanging from a porch beam, illuminated by the light of the truck, were what looked like two small sacks, dripping wet with blood.

24

"Shit!" Sonny cursed. Some sonofabitch had nailed the balls of a goat or a ram to the porch. Judging from the wet blood and smell, the testicles had been hung only minutes ago.

"Don't get out," he told Rita as he returned to the truck.

"What is it?" Rita asked. She was frightened.

He explained as calmly as he could, and took a pair of old leather gloves from behind the seat. Then he went back to the porch and yanked the balls off the beam. Disgusted, angry, and shaken at the thought that somebody could do such a dirty thing, he thought briefly of flinging the mess out into the street. No, that wouldn't do. He went back to the truck and tossed the smelly sacs in an old cardboard box on the bed of the truck, then the gloves.

"I can't believe it." Rita shuddered. "Should we call the sheriff?"

Sonny leaned against the truck. He thought he was going to throw up. "Just kids," he tried to reassure her.

"No, a warning," she answered.

"Yeah." They wanted him to know Rita was vulnerable. "I'll check the house. You stay here. Keep the doors locked." He took her keys, let himself in, and cautiously went from room to room, but he knew he wouldn't find anyone. Whoever left the warning was long gone.

"Looks okay." He waved from the porch, and Rita joined him. "You look it over. I'll clean up here."

She entered the house and he took the hose and washed the porch where the blood had dripped, cleaning away the disgusting smell. When he was finished, he went in and washed his hands in the kitchen sink.

"How does it look?" he asked.

"Fine. Doors are locked, nothing touched. They didn't come in the house, but—"

He held her. "I'm sorry this happened. I should have known they'd be following me. You're okay, just stay in the house. If you see or hear anything, call me right away."

"And you?"

"Gotta get rid of the mess," he explained. He needed help, and he thought of don Eliseo. He kissed her lightly. "Get some sleep. Maybe it was just kids doing something crazy."

"Kids don't castrate animals for kicks," she said, but she added, "I'll be okay."

"Don Eliseo will know," he said. It was all he could think of. The old man would know what to do.

He gave her a reassuring embrace. "I'll call you in the morning, amor," he said, and went out. He waited outside the door until she locked it. From inside she blew him a kiss.

He drove home, and as he expected, don Eliseo was sitting beneath the alamo. Two shadows moved around the small fire don Eliseo had going: don Toto and doña Concha. They waved as Sonny drove up. In the flickering flames of the fire, the three figures were three gnomes; just the three welcome duendes Sonny needed.

The smell of dry cow dung smoldering to keep the mosquitoes away touched Sonny's nostrils as he got out of the truck. The scent of the manure burning in the hot coals was a pleasant incense filtering through the summer night.

When don Eliseo's wife was alive, the neighbors used to gather on summer evenings under don Eliseo's tree to tell stories. They told the old cuentos of the people, folktales brought by their ancestors from Spain and Mexico into the Río Grande valley. They talked about their children, marriages and deaths, the local politics, and their crops. Los vecinos. Neighbors. For centuries the community was a vecindad in which people took care of each other. Now don Eliseo's wife was dead, and except for don Toto and doña Concha, all the old neighbors were dead or gone to nursing homes.

"Hey, Sonny!" Concha called as Sonny got out of the truck. She gave him a big abrazo. "How you been, cutie." She smiled.

"Come and have a drink," don Toto said. Don Toto kept one of the oldest vineyards in the valley, luscious grapes that had been brought by the first settlers and cultivated for centuries in the valley. He still pressed his own grapes and made his own wine.

"Whew, you been castrating goats, Sonny?" don Eliseo said, sniffing the air and looking toward the truck.

"Híjola," la Concha said, scrunching her nose. "Smells awful."

"Somebody cut the balls off a goat and hung them on Rita's porch," Sonny answered, and motioned to the back of the truck.

The old man frowned. Concha made the sign of the cross.

"What do I do?"

"Burn them," don Eliseo said, and hobbled to the truck. "Got a flashlight?"

Sonny took a flashlight from his glove compartment and shone it on the wet mess in the box.

"Híjola, they smell," don Eliseo said. He put on the gloves Sonny had used. "Mira." He pointed. "Red hair. It was an old red goat."

"Brujas," Concha whispered. "Why Rita?"

"It's a warning. Not for Rita," don Eliseo said. "For Sonny."

"I want the cabrones who did this," Sonny said in anger.

"Then you need to find an old, red goat that is having trouble walking," don Eliseo replied.

"Yeah, but a lot of gente keep goats and sheep in their back-yards," don Toto said.

Don Eliseo picked up the cardboard box with the mess, re-turned to his fire, and dropped the box into the coals. Then the gloves. "Put some wood on that, compadre. Burn away the evil."

Don Toto piled dry kindling on the fire and it rose quickly into a bonfire.

"En el nombre del Padre, del Hijo, y del Espíritu Santo," la Concha intoned.

"It's brujería," don Eliseo said.

Sonny shook his head. No, it had to be just a cheap, dirty prank meant to frighten Rita, not a curse.

"Brujas malas," Concha said. They had seen the signs all sum-mer, and just recently the strange lights in the bosque, a whining sound, and the morning after they found the burned grass in To-to's field. Something evil had come to stalk the valley.

Sonny rubbed his stomach. A warning, don Eliseo had said. Was it a prank? Did they plan to cut his balls off next? Or maybe they already had, symbolically, if his impotence was a curse, as don Eliseo had said.

"Who?" Sonny asked, his voice rising in irritation.

Don Eliseo's eyes glowed in the flames as he looked at Sonny. "The same people who killed your prima. You're getting too close."

Don Toto handed Sonny the bottle of homemade wine. He

drank, and the sweet taste washed away the bitterness. He felt tired and angry. The hocus-pocus was unsettling.

"Nothing we can do tonight. Get some rest," don Eliseo said. "You need to rest, get this out of your mind."

"You're right." Sonny nodded.

"We'll look around for that goat," the old man said. "If we find the goat, we find the brujas. Let us help."

"Sure," Concha assured him, "we know the valley. We'll find the cabrones who played this dirty trick."

"Yeah, don't worry, Sonny," don Toto added.

Sonny was overcome with their kindness. They knew he was stressed out, and they were trying to help as best they could.

"How about a ball game?" he said with a wink in gratitude. "Tomorrow night."

"Oh, that's great!" Concha shouted and kissed him.

"You sure?" Don Eliseo asked.

"Hey, we've been talking about going all summer. You said I need to kick back."

"All right!" Don Toto gave him a high five.

"We'll be ready," Concha said.

Sonny thanked them, said good night, and walked across the street to his house. He flopped on the bed, drained of energy. There was a slight ache in his foot. He slept, but the night was full of nightmares: images of the Zia sign, which became the rising sun of Japan. Voices spoke in dialects he couldn't understand, and a large, threatening figure of a dark raven flew down, eclipsing the sun, turning light to darkness, beating Sonny to the ground. Four dark spirits danced around him, rattling gourds and waving raven feathers. They tied him to the ground, spreading his limbs in the four directions. One cut with a scalpel, a bloody circle around his navel, then four lines. The last line went straight down to his penis, a faint pain throbbed between his legs, blood oozed, then a baby cried, protesting the pain of the circumcision, and the pale, ghostlike figure of Gloria Dominic picked up the bleeding child and cradled it in her arms.

Sonny awoke bathed in sweat, gasping for breath. He could hear the creaking fan of the air conditioner pushing only dry, hot air through the room. Water line must be plugged. He looked at his watch. Nearly noon.

"Santo día," Sonny whispered, tossing aside the tangled sheets. "I slept late," he chided himself. No, not slept, struggled through the weird nightmares. He thought of going for a jog, but he felt listless, lethargic. And besides, the sun was already hot in the noonday sky.

He went to shower and stood underneath the cold water for some time. Then he shaved, dressed, and called Ruth Jamison. He needed to know if the Dunn and Bradstreet report on Akira Morino was ready. "Yes," she said, "I think you'll be surprised."

As Sonny drove downtown, he went over what he already knew about Morino. The Japanese high-tech industrialist had been in the city about four months. He had rented the top suite of the Hyatt, a downtown hotel. His social life was full of luncheons with leaders from the business sector, the governor, the local politicians, senators, and congressmen. Evenings he often attended social events with Her Honor, the mayor. They were seen together at City Symphony concerts, plays, lectures at the university.

"It's good business," Marisa Martinez told the press. "Intel in Rio Rancho makes the chips, we make the flat panel display for computers. It's my job to show him what our city has to offer. We have a research center shared by the university and Sandia Labs. We can offer any new company a relationship to one of the best labs in the country. I have proposed to the city council a two-billion-dollar industrial revenue bond, a tax break on corporate state income taxes, and environmental and construction permits. We also have the state training fund. Through T-VI we can train workers faster than any other city in the country, including Rio Rancho."

"What about the water to run these plants?" one reporter had asked. "Intel is already drying up the water table. The people in

Corrales don't like what's happening. Our own state engineer warned us, our water table is falling. The underground supply is good only for twenty years."

"We have the water," Her Honor responded. "That is, if we can talk Frank Dominic out of his crazy plan to build canals."

Frank Dominic had been interested in Akira Morino's money when he first hit Alburquerque, but Dominic's plan was to channel the Río Grande into canals that would be lined with gambling casinos. He viewed Morino's high-tech plant as peanuts compared to his project.

Dominic had enough pull to have a special session of the state legislature convened in May, but much to everyone's surprise, it voted against the casino bill for the city. Conservative Republicans joined the Little Texas cowboy legislators from the southeast corner of the state in torpedoing the gambling bill. Suddenly the worm had turned on Dominic's bandwagon. Lawsuits against Dominic's corporation, which was buying Río Grande water rights, began to hit the courts, and Dominic's grand plan of building a Venice on the Río Grande ground to a standstill.

The Dunn and Bradstreet financial report did surprise Sonny. It turned out Morino was something of a maverick. He didn't play by Japanese team rules. He was practicing takeovers of weak industries in a Japanese financial culture that didn't prize the individualist, and the sad part was the gambles hadn't paid off. The Japanese economy was sliding into a recession. Akira Morino was in hot water back home.

"Sounds like he's on the verge of being fired by his board," Ruth had exclaimed as she put the report in front of Sonny.

"He's overextended," Sonny acknowledged as he read.

The evidence was clear, the local news reporters just hadn't bothered to dig it up. Akira Morino was holding on by a thread as chairman of the board. He was on the verge of being forced out by his own people. That's why he had shown up in Alburquerque, to try a grand-slam play. If he could get the city to donate the land for a new plant and bonds to build it, he could recoup his status back home. But could he deliver?

"He did the same thing in Mexico." Ruth pointed at the article from *El Diario.*

Morino had explored financial possibilities in Mexico, but nothing had worked for him. The blurred photos showed Morino standing on the steps of Los Pinos, next to the president of Mexico. Other photos showed him at Bellas Artes, attending the Mexico City Symphony and other social events, always with an attractive woman at his side.

"Looks like he has a taste for beautiful Mexican women, too," Sonny said. "Thanks, Ruth, you're an angel." He scooped up the articles and kissed her on the cheek.

"Are you going to the papers?" Ruth asked.

"Not yet." Sonny winked.

Outside the library, Sonny sniffed the air. There was a hint of rain as clouds struggled to rise over the Sandias. A front was coming in from the south. The approaching summer monsoon season was flirting with the Río Grande valley. Perhaps out on the eastern llano the quenching rains had begun. But they needed more energy, more Gulf humidity to create the towering thundershower clouds that would spawn the summer rains.

He dialed Rita. She was at the restaurant. She had slept peacefully. No, there was nothing out of the ordinary at home or at work.

"How about taking another evening off?" he asked. "Come watch the Dukes. I promised don Eliseo and his gang." She agreed.

Then he called Howard. "Howie, baby, the Dukes are playing. Let's take a night off."

"You're on," Howard answered. "El Gallo's pitching."

"And Seattle has Maloney, the heavy bat."

"Sounds like mano a mano."

"Ladies' night," Sonny said.

"Good idea. Marie's complaining I don't take her out often enough. Meet you at the beer counter."

"I'm bringing Snap, Crackle, and Pop."

Howard laughed. "Sounds like fun."

Sonny dialed his mother. "Sonny, Mando, I'm not home," the message on the answering machine begin. There was a pause, then "Max and I are looking at houses. Come to dinner Sunday." She sounded happy.

"Looking at houses?" Sonny exclaimed. "She's got a house! She doesn't need a house!" With Max? Wasn't she happy? He hadn't seen her since Gloria's funeral. Damn, I gotta see her more often, he blamed himself. Not right for a son not to visit his mother.

He drove home, climbed to the roof, and unclogged the air conditioner's water line. Then he begin to read through the thick file Ruth had collected on Akira Morino. When the house cooled off, he fell asleep, and when he awakened, he felt refreshed. Last night's images had not haunted his afternoon's nap.

He showered, grabbed a clean pair of Levi's and a Dukes T-shirt, and kept telling himself that the game would be good for him. The case had ground to standstill; his leads had all come up empty. Or was it him? Had he been beaten? Gloria's ghost cried for revenge, but he didn't know where to turn.

In the meantime he felt a tiredness in his bones. He knew he needed a break. He put on the jeans and T-shirt, a light wind-breaker, and instead of boots, his jogging shoes.

Yeah, he thought as he stepped outside, this'll do me good. Do us all good.

"Hey, Sonny boy!" Concha called from across the street where she and Toto sat with don Eliseo. "We're ready!"

They came hurrying across the street. Three duendes dressed in baseball caps, don Toto wearing an old third-base glove, Concha swinging a cracked, taped Louisville Slugger, don Eliseo carrying his faded Dukes banner.

"Órale!" Toto shouted, "Vamos a wachar los Duques!"

"I love El Gallo," Concha cried. "Almost as much as you." She greeted Sonny with a kiss. "How do I look?"

She was wearing a striped baseball shirt, something Sonny guessed she must have picked up in one of her trips to the North Fourth Goodwill Store. She had touched up her bright lipstick—candy apple red, she called it—and her falsies were a little skewed to the left, but they all whistled and told her she looked great.

"Like a Christmas tamale," don Toto complimented her.

"Oh, honey"—she pinched his cheek—"you're a real horny toad."

Don Eliseo and don Toto helped Concha into the cab, and they jumped in the back.

"Vamos!" they shouted as Sonny shot out of the driveway. "Ajua!"

Last summer Sonny had taken them to a couple of games. They had bought caps, "I Love the Dukes" buttons, and pennants. Sonny enjoyed watching them have fun.

Don Eliseo's sons showed up once in a while to check on the old man, and sometimes they took him to Sunday dinner at their homes, but the old man really didn't enjoy it.

"It's like they're not my sons anymore," he had confided in Sonny. "They don't speak Spanish, they live up in the Heights, their gringa wives just don't cook our food. No chile verde, no frijoles, nada."

Sonny understood. The boys had gotten educated and left the valley, married Anglo women, joined the great American dream in a Northeast Heights homogenized culture. It was happening all over, the change to an Anglo lifestyle, attention to work and green lawns on the weekend, kids in soccer or music lessons. In the process they forgot their Spanish language, grew ashamed of the old traditions, and they sure as hell didn't farm anymore. When they looked at their father's field of corn and vegetables, they wondered why the old man bothered.

They stopped by Toto's so he could refill his wine bottle, and by the time they picked up Rita, Sonny knew they were going to be late for the opening pitch. What the hell, it was summer and they were operating on Chicano time. The point was to enjoy.

"Hi, Rita!" they called.

"Hey, Rita, how's it going?" Concha asked, moving so Rita could sit next to Sonny. "How's your tacos?"

"Hot as ever." Rita smiled.

"Sit back here with us," Toto leered. "We'll show you a good time!"

"Sorry, don Toto, but I have a date," Rita replied. She knew don Toto's reputation, and she handled him as courteously as possible.

"Is Sonny scoring any points? Heard he was striking out," Concha needled.

"Sonny never strikes out," Rita replied seductively, moving close to Sonny and kissing him on the cheek. "Best batter in town."

"Híjola!" Concha shouted out the window. "Did you hear that? Batter up!"

"My mom's looking for a house," he told Rita as they drove. "With Max."

"Good," Rita answered.

"Good?" He glanced at her. Leave it to the women to stick together. "She has a house."

"Women need to fly from their nests sometimes," Rita suggested.

"Leave the gallinero," Concha added, grinning. "Especially when there's a new gallo in town."

"Yeah," Sonny mused.

His mother flying from her nest. He hadn't thought of the possibility. Now it was there, one more factor that he felt had to do with the dissolution of his family. Maybe she was lonely, and he just hadn't sensed it. And there was nothing he could do about it. He had called her to invite her to the game, but where else had he taken her all summer? Just to Rita's to eat a couple of times. Did he expect her to wait for him and Mando to come around once or twice a month and be satisfied? Ah, maybe this thing with Max was for the best. He was nice enough. She needed company.

The June evening was perfect, shirtsleeve weather that lingered as the sun sank in the west and coolness tinged the air. The bright stadium lights illumined the eager fans. They had come to see if the Duke's pitcher could hold the line on the Seattle batters. Howard and Marie were waiting at the beer counter.

"Sorry we're late," Sonny apologized.

"Hey, no problem. We're enjoying the beer."

"You know don Eliseo. . . ."

"Buenas tardes." Howard shook the old man's hand.

"Concha. . . ."

"Hi, cutie. This your wife?"

"Yes, this is Marie."

"Hey, you're real good-looking."

"Morenita de mi corazón." Toto took Marie's hand and kissed it gallantly.

"This is don Toto," Sonny said.

"Watch your wife around him," Concha whispered to Howard. "Come on, Sonny, buy us a beer."

"Okay, order up," Sonny said, and they loaded up with the large cups of beer, hotdogs, and peanuts, then went tottering down the aisle looking for their seats.

"Down in front," someone behind them complained as they settled noisily into their seats.

"Up yours!" Concha replied.

"Shh." Don Eliseo tugged at her. "Have respeto."

"Respeto for gorillas? He's probably escaped from the zoo."

Those around them laughed as the white-haired lady with the thick glasses and arms loaded with beer, hotdogs, and peanuts put the irate fan in his place.

Concha waved her pennant. "Come on, Dukes! Score a touchdown!" More laughter.

"It's base-boll," Toto said, slipped out his bottle of wine, and sipped. He wasn't a beer man. Besides, his own wine suited him fine.

"How about we go dancing after the game?" he said to Marie.

"Sure"—Marie smiled at him and batted her eyelashes—"if my husband comes."

Don Toto shrank, Concha laughed. "She got you that time, Toto. Howie's probably a home-run hitter, too, eh," she whispered to Marie.

"Home run every time at bat." Marie nodded.

Concha ribbed don Toto. "You're in the wrong league. Better go back to the viejitas at Saturday bingo!"

Don Toto shook his head. "Quiet. Let's watch the game."

Drinking beer and wolfing down hotdogs they settled down to watch the game, cheering loudly when El Gallo struck out an opponent.

"He's hot!" Concha jumped up and waved her pennant. "Hot! Hot! Hot!" Around her the crowd took up her chant. "Hot! Hot! Hot!"

"I never saw anyone enjoy a game more," Howard said.

"They don't get out much," Sonny replied. Then he told him what he had found out about Akira Morino from Turco. "I think she had the money on her," he concluded.

"So where is it?" Howard asked.

"That's what I'd like to know," Sonny answered. He emptied his beer cup. "I don't know a lot about Japanese culture, but he has a wife and kids back home. They overlook a lot of fun for the salary men after working hours, but not bastard kids. In Morino's position it would be the straw that broke the camel's back. The last excuse his board needs to throw him out."

"An abortion would have taken care of the complications," Marie suggested.

"Unless she really wanted a child," Sonny said. Is that what Gloria wanted?

"What if she was blackmailing Morino?" Rita said.

Sonny cocked his head. "What?"

"She's told Turco she will help him, right?"

"Right."

"So she needs to raise a lot of money. . . ."

"Morino's got the money, but Morino can't let it be known Gloria is carrying his child."

They looked at each other.

"So abortion is not a solution. She's never had a kid, now she's pregnant. She wants a kid, her child. But Morino would not want it known—"

"Possible." Sonny nodded. He hadn't thought of Gloria as a blackmailer, but why not? She was a strong, decisive woman. There was little love left between her and Frank, and suddenly she found herself pregnant, and the baby's father pressing her to abort it. But did she need the money for Turco, or for something else?

Howard interrupted them. "Mira."

They paused to watch Maloney. He was down three–two when he belted the home run, and the stadium went dead. "Damn," Howard groaned, "he gave him the fastball! Maloney's a fastball hitter and the sucker gives it to him!"

El Gallo turned to the crowd, smiled his broad Mexican smile, and shrugged. Next time, he seemed to say, I'll get him next time. How could the fans be mad at a guy like that? Even as Maloney rounded third, Concha and Toto jumped up and cheered for the pitcher.

"Gallo! Gallo!" they shouted, and the crowd took up their chant, on their feet, stamping on the bleachers and shouting, "Gallo! Gallo! Gallo!" So what if they were behind a point? It was only the fourth inning.

"The question is, would Morino give her the money?" Sonny asked as the cheering subsided.

"Yes. If he loved her," Rita answered. "Or was really scared she'd have that baby. There'd be no mistaking it wasn't Frank's."

"Was there really any money?" Howard asked.

Sonny shrugged. He didn't know. He told them about meeting Veronica and Raven.

"Did Raven know Gloria?" Howard asked.

"He denies it, but that's what I have to find out," Sonny answered.

"In the meantime," Howard said, "the scalpel you picked up at Raven's place? Blood of bovinus."

"Cow? I figured."

"One more thing," Howard said as they settled back to see if El Gallo could get his pitching under control. "Cops checked all the mortuaries. There's a new one up in the Heights, Dawn of Life. The owner has old mortician tools of the trade, a small collection. He had an old hand pump, the type morticians used to take out to ranches without electricity. And he reported it missing. No prints, nothing else taken, just the old hand pump."

The Dukes won the game, and Sonny drove his three exuberant friends home. By the time he got them there, they had mellowed down and were singing corridos. Don Toto wanted to continue the party, insisting the Fourth Street Cantina was open till 2:00 A.M.

Sonny, with don Eliseo's help, prevailed. "Everyone to bed," he said as he dropped each one off. "Party's over."

"Yeah, for us," Concha complained, "but not for you." She looked at Rita. "Ah, it's nice to be young. Batter up!" she cheered as Sonny and Rita helped her to the door.

"Hope so," Rita whispered.

25

The next day, Morino's assistant called and invited Sonny to a hurried and impromptu meeting. Sonny silently gave thanks to Tamara as he drove downtown.

Sonny pulled up at the stoplight in front of the Hyatt. It was nearly seven, the streets were empty, the downtown workforce had disappeared. Two homeless men stood looking at the people sculpture that stood on the sidewalk in front of the hotel. The long afternoon shadows tinged the air with nostalgia.

The light changed and Sonny found a parking space near La Galería. As he walked to the hotel, he passed the two homeless men, two out-of-luck young men, one Chicano, one Anglo. More and more the streets of the city were peopled by young, homeless men. They stood on street corners during the day and held up signs that read "Food for Work. God Bless You." They took handouts, loose change from the guilty at heart. Now they were probably on their way to the river, where they slept. During the summer they set up cardboard huts along the river bosque. Those camps were home at night.

Not much different from the migrants of the thirties, Sonny thought. The Depression. The new technology sweeping across the land created jobs for some, liberated some, and still created a class of untrained unemployed who couldn't lift themselves out of the quagmire.

Morino's office was a suite on the top floor. Morino's assistant, a young, very courteous Japanese man greeted Sonny. He looked as if he had just graduated from the Japanese equivalent of an Ivy League school, Sonny thought, except that this Ivy Leaguer was carrying a small automatic under his suit jacket. Sonny felt nervous. Had he entered the murderer's den?

"Ah, Mr. Sonny Baca. Very glad to meet you. Come in." He led Sonny into the receiving room. "Please sit." He smiled, snapped his fingers, and a Japanese woman dressed in a kimono appeared with a tray. Two small porcelain cups sat on the tray. The design on the cups was that of a dragon in a soft orange, almost an apricot color, the proverbial dragon rising into blue sky.

"Sake," the assistant said. The woman poured. Sonny took the cup she offered; then she set the tray on the table and withdrew.

"Please be comfortable," the assistant said. "I shall inform Mr. Morino you are here."

Sonny sipped the warm wine. It was mellow, a taste he wasn't used to, but good. He looked at the design on the cup and relaxed in the chair. The dragon on the cup was ferocious, bulging eyes staring out with fury as it rose along the curve of the porcelain cup. The dragon was the sun king in stories he had read. It rose from the depths of a lake and ascended into the sky. A sun god. A Señor de la Luz, Sonny thought, sipping.

The dragon was also the Quetzalcoatl of the Aztecs, the plumed serpent, the snake with feathers. As serpent he was earth energy, the intuitive side of the human psyche, with wings he could fly and partake of sun energy, the highest consciousness. Earth and sky met as one in this ancient deity from Mesoamerica, the intuition and the clarity don Eliseo sought.

Sonny remembered reading something by Ben Chavez. The dragon of the Orient and Quetzalcoatl were related. Maybe don Eliseo could be a Buddhist monk, or a shaman of the Russian steppe, a monk in Tibet, head shaved, thin body wrapped in orange cloth, turning the prayer wheel, living on beans or rice, letting the light fill him.

Quetzalcoatl was the god of illumination, civilization, cultivation, knowledge, wisdom. Lord of the Dawn. Lord of Light. He was the earth god who had become a Señor de la Luz. It was all there, just like don Eliseo said, and it wasn't a New Age theory. This knowledge had been part and parcel of don Eliseo's world for ages. In Catholic Spain, in Jewish Spain, in Moorish Spain, in the esoteric knowledge that swept from Egyptian history across the Mediterranean to meet with the "light wisdom" of the Americas, which was related to the Orient, which was related to . . . the round world.

The round Zia sun. The strands of light spreading around the world.

Gotta listen to don Eliseo, Sonny made a mental note. Who knows, I may be on the path to becoming a Señor myself. He chuckled. Nah, I like to screw around too much, he thought. Can't be on la movida and hope to become a Señor. La movida chueca, the urge to party, las ganas that drove men into strange bedrooms, the arms of women. Never satisfied, always glancing at the curves that came striding down the street, the breasts, the lips, the sensual smile, the invitation.

"You're not a computer," don Eliseo said. "You're a man."

Yeah, Sonny thought. I can choose.

He thought of Tamara. She used the joy of the orgasm not only for the moment, not only to get high, but to connect to the past lives, to reach for the light. Connecting to the past meant sharing in immortality, returning to the first moment in the dawn of time when the light exploded. There lay revelation. There lay the birth of don Eliseo's Señores y Señoras de la Luz.

But she used it to stay young. Vanity clothed even Tamara. Each new orgasm not only connected her to her chain of memory, it provided a sense of youth, immortality. That's why she dreamed of past lives, so she could live forever. In Tamara's chain of being, there was no room for doubt. She *had* been a princess in the court of the sun king, and history was replete with sun kings. Quetzalcoatl and the Chinese dragon were sun kings, even don Eliseo's Señores y Señoras de la Luz were children of the sun. The gods were reflections of the sun.

For don Eliseo, being filled with light meant understanding how the Señores y Señoras came into being. Clarity was a way of knowledge. The blessing of life they brought. They were the ancestors, and the spirits of the ancestors lived. They were prayed to, masses and rosaries were offered, on el Día de los Muertos you visited their graves, prayed, drank, took a picnic lunch to share with them. The ancestors were the santos!

Sonny looked into the cup. The warm sake had flowed into his veins. Should try this stuff more often, he mused. He finished the cup of sake and looked again at the design on the cup. Good stuff. A pleasant feeling enveloped him.

Like sex, thoughts could be a pleasure, he thought, allowing his mind to wander through the connections it was making. So, what if the original souls of the ancestors are still here, on Earth, all around. They came daily, spoke, entered dreams, could be called upon for help, and then you died and you became one. Went to visit los antepasados, the ancestors who had become pure soul. No more flesh, no more reincarnation, no heaven or hell, just pure light. Clarity. Then you joined the dance of the Lords and Ladies in the morning and came to bless life on Earth. That was a pleasant thought.

He put his finger in the cup and swished it around, put the finger to his mouth and tasted the last of the sake. Ah, good. Should he pour himself another? Maybe it would take away the nervous feeling he was trying to control. No, he needed a clear head when he spoke to Morino.

He placed the cup on the table and looked around. The room was in Japanese decor, subdued tones, screens, paintings of misty mountaintops, gnarled pines, paths disappearing into the clouds. Here Akira Morino greeted his business guests and outlined his plans. Supplicants came to be granted wishes by the king of technology, Sonny thought.

Just like the old patrón system of the state. The humble peons of the small villages used to approach the patrón with hat in hand, to ask a favor of the rich boss man. Los ricos dispensing favors. Sonny hated the system. It was petty and demeaning to the poor, to those without power.

"Fuck the patrones," he whispered, "and all the fucking políticos in Santa Fe who act like patrones!"

Maybe Morino was just another kind of new patrón, like the mayor when he was dispensing favors, like those legislators in Santa Fe who got elected and got a little power and became patrones, petty mafiosos, granting small favors here and there, but hoarding power and keeping the poor in check.

Morino had lived in Mexico, so he knew the culture. An interesting man, Tamara had said, extremely knowledgeable on many things. The man devours books. He's read about Elfego Baca and is surprised there's not a statue dedicated to this man in the city.

We don't honor our heroes, Sonny thought. Chicano heroes have been erased from the white man's history. Forgotten.

Sonny heard Japanese voices, turned, wondered what Morino would say, or deny, about Gloria. The more he learned about Gloria, the more he realized how much more there was to her than the part he knew. She knew what she was getting into if she helped Turco. She must have realized the possible consequences. Or was the money really for herself?

Morino entered the room, bowed, and greeted Sonny cordially. "It is an honor," he said, shaking Sonny's hand.

"Yes, an honor," Sonny said nervously. The man's presence

was overpowering. A guy like this doesn't break easy, Sonny thought.

"Please, let us be comfortable. We will sit on the terrace." Morino motioned, and they stepped outside. "From here the view is exquisite. I sit here in the afternoon, when it is cool."

The sun was setting over the West Mesa, its tongues of flame cast a bronze sheen on the evening clouds.

"Quite a view," Sonny agreed.

"Yes. Finally we have the relief of clouds. It will rain soon."

The assistant who had followed them onto the terrace placed the tray with the sake on the table and poured; then he disappeared. Morino handed Sonny a cup and bowed.

"I have come to love this city." Morino smiled, looking west, toward the green bosque of the river, into the suffused summer sunset turning a soft apricot color, orange, wisps of mauve.

"At night the lights glitter like diamonds. I have never been in a city where I felt so comfortable. It has become my home."

He spoke eloquently and with sincerity. Sonny followed his gaze and looked at the city. The last light of the day bathed the sky and valley in a soft glow. The summer evening air was pleasant, cool, and clear, a sensuous reward for those who had lived through the hot day.

"You are Gloria's cousin," Morino said, turning to Sonny.

"Yes," Sonny answered, nodding.

A moment ago Morino's voice had been bright and gay; now it was subdued, sad. Sonny remembered the night he had seen him at Dominic's. The man had been grieving.

"We have a saying. Here, in New Mexico, we're all primos, related one way or another," Sonny said.

Morino nodded. "Like Japan. We have been insular. So has New Mexico. You have been a nation unto yourselves for so long. Perhaps that is one reason I am drawn here."

"But a colonized nation," Sonny reminded him. "There's a difference."

"All nations are products of colonization," Morino said. "A

new migration comes and a new culture is layered on the old. Those who remember their past history dream of it as utopia, but it is not so. As much as I identify with your view, with your history, I also sense the inevitable movement of history. So I see the influx of migrations into this river valley as its strength. Now, New Mexico has been discovered, again. The Californians are coming in. People with money from Los Angeles—"

"The Japanese," Sonny said, and lifted his sake cup.

Morino smiled. "Yes, even we are tempted by this land. There's no retreating from that. You will continue to see this thing you call colonization, and in a small way, I am part of that change. But my contribution can be positive. . . ."

Sonny shrugged.

"I understand your reluctance." Morino smiled. "Right now you are thinking, 'They all say the same thing.' "

Sonny smiled, nodded, and Morino laughed. Morino emptied his cup of sake and poured again. "To our friendship," he said.

"To Akira, the morning sun," Sonny replied.

Morino looked closely at Sonny. "Ah, you've done your homework."

"The same sun which rises over Japan rises over New Mexico. We call it the Zia sun."

Morino arched an eyebrow. "I have lived in Mexico," he said. "I read the history of the ancient Aztec civilization. They were worshipers of the sun, and they made blood sacrifice to the sun."

Morino nodded and grew pensive. He sipped from his cup, looked at the display of colors of the afternoon sun, and mused. "The Aztecs were once a powerful people," he said after a moment.

"The technology of the Spaniards destroyed them," Sonny said. "The Spaniard had rifles and cannons, firepower. That same technology can destroy the Earth."

"That is one view," Morino said. "The other is that the nation of the Aztecs had become a nation unto itself. It had developed a high sense of consciousness, and it was no longer willing to learn from its neighbors. It could not respond to the Spaniards' onslaught because it could not understand the stranger. So, one may say, to not understand the stranger is suicide."

Interesting, Sonny thought. The man has thought through the conquest of Mexico. He has also thought through the final conquest of New Mexico.

"So I should understand you. . . ."

Morino smiled. "You said yourself, you've already done some homework. You want to understand the stranger, or the opposition."

"Yes," Sonny agreed.

"But opposition and competition are words we take from the world of politics and economics," Morino replied. "We need not be opponents. I take seriously the history of this area. I want to learn more about the people. There are beautiful traditions here, Mr. Baca, but if the people don't embrace the fruits of the new technology, they will disappear like the Aztecs. Perhaps we can find a common ground." He smiled.

"A common ground," Sonny repeated. Had it ever been so? Had the Anglos and the Chicanos and the Indians ever truly found that ground, or had the old patrón system simply been given a new twist, and those in power were still using those without power.

Morino nodded. "I believe the arts can be the bridge between the different cultures, a bridge between science and the desire to preserve the natural. My company will preserve the beauty of the land."

Morino turned to Sonny. "But I am a realist. I know it is not always the 'land of enchantment.' Men with evil in their hearts also migrate to the center. . . . Who do you think killed Gloria?" he asked suddenly.

"Why do you ask me about Gloria now? After avoiding me all this time?" Sonny asked.

"You want to find the person who murdered Gloria, and I

want to help you," Morino said.

"I've been working on that, and calling you to try to get some help—"

"I have grown cautious since Gloria was murdered," Morino interrupted. "I've had my men follow you. I am sorry, but you understand. Do you think the gardener the police have arrested is guilty?"

"No," Sonny answered.

"No, of course not," Morino said after a pause. "But the police seem determined—"

"To cover up certain facts," Sonny finished.

"Cover up?" Morino whispered, then he nodded. "Frank Dominic is a very powerful man."

"Yes, he is," Sonny agreed. "But so are you."

Morino shook his head and frowned.

"Don't be modest," Sonny pressed. "You snap your fingers and you can put your hands on enough money to help Gloria with whatever she needed. I couldn't do that."

For a moment Morino's hands trembled. He sipped his sake.

"You gave Gloria a lot of money just before she was killed," Sonny said, leaning forward, taking a chance. "But the police don't know that. I think when I find the money, I'll find Gloria's murderer."

Morino hesitated. He filled the cups again then leaned back in his chair. A breeze stirred and he seemed to shiver.

"So," he finally said, softly, as if in a confessional, "you found out about the money."

Sonny drew a deep breath and also leaned back in his chair.

"Her brother had asked her for the money, and she came to you. How much did you give her?"

"What I had in my safe, maybe a hundred thousand. No more."

"You gave it to her? Just like that?"

Morino leaned back and nodded, then in a whisper softer than the brush of wings from the nighthawk, he said, "I loved her. I truly . . ." Then he whispered again. "But it wasn't for her brother."

It was Sonny's turn to listen. He had assumed the money was for Turco. "He needed the money, Gloria was going to help him."

Morino shook his head. "Is that what you think, Mr. Baca? You are wrong. I will tell you the truth because I want Gloria's murderer brought to justice. And because . . ." He paused, and Sonny knew he was deciding how much he should tell. "The money was for Gloria. She was going away. She would be gone for a year, maybe two. During that time she would—"

"Have your child," Sonny finished.

Morino looked surprised. "Ah, you know more than I thought," he said, almost inaudible.

"I know she was pregnant when she was murdered. And the child was yours."

Morino sighed. "Our love bore fruit. But it was as much a curse as a joy."

"It complicated things."

"It affected Gloria very much. For the man, it is easier. But she had to make a difficult choice. I felt for her, I tried to help, but she couldn't decide. One moment she said she would have an abortion, the next she was determined to have a child. The decision was painful to her."

"Had she told Frank?"

"I think so. But during those last few weeks her mind was confused. She would swing back and forth. . . . When Dominic had the body cremated, I was almost glad. Glad I would not have to explain. Now I know I can't live with that lie. I have to tell someone. You were related to her, you are trying to find her murderer, so I'll tell you. Gloria did ask me for money, but she said nothing about her brother. She was going to go away, live out of the country for a while. We talked about her going to Brazil. . . . She was a lonely woman, Mr. Baca."

"Sonny."

"Thank you. I will call you Sonny. And you must call me

Akira," he said, and refilled their cups. "I have done business throughout the world, so one acquires an instinct. I know I can trust you." He raised his cup as if toasting the setting sun, the gathering gray clouds over the West Mesa.

"Gloria was special. A beauty that was deep. Perhaps the Mexican woman is like the Japanese woman. It is not only the beauty of the body that attracts, but some inner beauty. I was alone and far from home. The affair was good for both of us; it was fulfilling. But it could not last. There was something in Gloria that needed to punish me. I became the husband, or the father, she needed to punish. I do not wish to make excuses," Morino said. "I do feel I am much to blame for her murder. I wanted to help her. But there was something else, perhaps the real reason I gave her the money. She called me the night she was murdered."

"To blackmail you?" Sonny said.

"Such an ugly word," Morino answered. "Anyway, she called and told me she needed the money immediately. I got the money ready and she came here for it. I had never seen her so distraught. The woman was haunted. Like she was afraid she was going to die."

He paused.

"It was as if a strange power took hold of her. She knew when she was not herself. When we parted, she kissed me. She was dressed in black, as if she was going to a funeral. Then she said something that made me truly fear for her. She said she was afraid of her group."

"What group?" Sonny asked.

"She was involved with a group. People that read her mind, told her what was to happen in her life. I know very little—she kept these meetings very much to herself—but recently, each time she had a meeting with her group, she returned extremely nervous."

"Did the group have something to do with the money she needed?"

"Now, I think it did. She wanted to go away, she told me. To have the baby. Somewhere where the group couldn't reach her. 'They will take the baby from me,' she said. I felt her terror. I doubted if she really had anything planned. If she could get away, she said, she would be all right. Eventually she would return, and we could see each other again."

"Did she mention names?" Sonny asked.

Morino shook his head. "There were times when she seemed to be in a trance. 'I have been with my group,' she would laugh. 'We can see the future,' she would tease me one moment, then turn on me. 'There is no future for you here, Akira,' she told me. It was as if something took possession of her. I realized this group, whoever they were, had much power over her. She could get no help from her husband, perhaps that's why she turned to me. I mistook her need for love. Anyway, I feel I could have saved her."

"How?"

"I went to her home the night she was murdered, and had I been there moments earlier, she might not be dead."

"You were in the house?" Sonny asked, incredulous.

"Yes. I am speaking freely tonight because I, too, want the murderer revealed. If there is some way I can help find whoever killed Gloria, then you have to know. I know Mr. Dominic must have paid well to keep Gloria's pregnancy a secret. To erase everything," Morino said, "he had the body cremated. A few days ago I received a phone call. Someone very kindly asked me to drop all my dealings with the mayor, to forget about bringing the plant here, to go away and forget this city, or they would go to the press and expose Gloria's pregnancy."

"Who?" Sonny asked.

"It is easy to suspect Mr. Dominic," Morino answered. "It has to do with politics. If I can't deliver on the plant I have proposed, he blames Marisa Martinez. And if she loses the election, I fear for this city—"

Morino's face grew pale; he looked tired. "But I believe the call came from the group that Gloria feared. Maybe they know I was there the night she was murdered. I have thought since then, perhaps they were hiding in the house when I walked in."

The silence grew tense as Sonny listened to Morino's revelation.

"When were you there?" Sonny asked.

"I think a few minutes after she was killed."

"Alone?"

"Yes. You see, I felt the fear in Gloria when I saw her. She took the money and left me, but I couldn't rest. I decided to drive to her place. It was after midnight, the house was dark, the front door open. I called, then I let myself in. There were suitcases in the hall, as if she was going on a trip. Big travel bags. Four or five. I thought, 'Good, she is still home.'"

But there were no bags by the door by the time I got there, Sonny thought. They were no doubt gone by the time the cops got there, or Howard would have mentioned it. Had Dominic removed her luggage before the police arrived? So he wouldn't have to explain she was leaving him? Or had the murderers taken the bags?

"Go on."

"I called out to her. The silence in the house was unbearable. I could smell the perfume of lilacs, candles burning. I thought I heard a sound, like a person breathing. I called again and walked slowly to her bedroom. There was a light, the flickering of candles. I entered her room, looked at the bed, and there she was. I thought she was asleep. Everything was so neatly laid out. I went to her and touched her. She was dead."

Morino paused. It was not easy for him to talk about the death scene.

"I was shocked. She was as beautiful in death as she had been in life. There was no apparent cause of death, only the pale, lifeless figure. The body I had known as warm, the troubled woman who swung from love and charity to a woman possessed by spirits, was now cold. I still carry the sensation with me. I think it is the first time I have truly felt grief for a person. It was grief that covered my fear. If only I had come in time, I thought."

He paused and drew a sigh of relief. Akira Morino had seen the woman he loved and who carried his child on her deathbed, probably moments after she had been killed.

"I left quickly. I must admit I was frightened. I felt there was nothing I could do. She was dead, and I was panicked. I knew if I was found there, I would be accused. I got in my car and drove away, but as I pulled out of the driveway, Mr. Dominic drove in."

"Dominic? Are you sure?"

"Oh yes, I recognized his car, then his face was illuminated by my car lights. Perhaps he recognized me. It was a strange moment, captured in that frozen second. I stared at him. It was a haunting face coming out of the dark. I thought there was anger in it, or hate. I understand he's told the police that he did not arrive home until next morning. He is lying."

Sonny stood and walked to the edge of the balcony. Below in the shadows of dusk, the streets were deserted. He didn't want to feel sorry for Morino, but he did. He wanted to keep his emotions out of the way, but he found himself believing the man. Damn! He had seen the body of the woman who carried his child only moments after she was killed! And he had been unable to share his grief in any way. Until now.

Sonny turned and looked at Morino. "Why are you telling me all this now?"

"I know there is no reason why you should believe me," Morino replied. "I can only say that I loved her. I truly loved her. As you must have loved her."

What did Gloria tell him? Sonny wondered. Her image swept over him, not the frozen, cold image of her dead body, but of the night she made love to him, her fragrance, the warmth of her body, the sweetness of her whispers. Feeling the pain of the memory, Sonny feared his voice might give away his emotions.

"I could not live with this secret. I want to get to the truth, and so I have told you everything," Morino said.

Sonny believed the man, but he needed time to fit the pieces together. It was almost there, at the tip of his fingers, something palpable he could feel.

"You have trouble back home," Sonny said, and for a moment considered telling Morino about the paper trail he had accumulated. But why kick a man when he was down.

"Ah, my board is old-fashioned." He smiled. "We Japanese must stop making business with the world and then retreating to the safety of our culture."

"You, too, must know the stranger," Sonny said.

"Yes, we need to know the people we deal with. If I get my board to build the plant here, it is not just to make money, but to make ourselves anew with the richness we find here."

His head sank to his chest. Sonny stared at the man, feeling sorry for him. He had gambled a lot, on the new plant, and on his affair with Gloria.

But Morino recovered. He took a deep breath. "My favorite time of day," he said, looking out at the blue clouds now tumbling out of the west. The distant sound of thunder rolled in the clouds. Like a blessed trumpet sound, the sound was a benediction, the first thunder of the season.

"Rain," he said, "finally, rain."

Sonny sniffed. Yes, rain was gathering in the front rolling in, and the thunder was its precursor.

He turned to Sonny, bowed slightly, and shook Sonny's hand. "I have told you what I know. Please, find whoever killed Gloria. Buenas noches," he said, and turned and walked away.

His assistant appeared at the door.

Quite a confession, Sonny thought as Morino's assistant led him out. Who do I believe? Dominic or Morino? He went down the elevator and out into the street. As he drove home, the dark cloud overhead burst loose.

The roar of thunder filled the valley, and everywhere a sigh of relief went up. The ozone of the lightning flashes across the valley mellowed the tensions that had been so high. Hurried rain, falling fast and furious and sending people jumping across gutters suddenly full, and hurried flashes of welcomed lightning. The streets wore a sheen of neon lights as the summer rain covered the asphalt, and the people of the valley hurried home to find relief in love.

The newscaster on the radio said a slow-moving low-pressure system was moving up from the south, and it held plenty of moisture. At least two days of thick clouds coming up from the Gulf. Relief from the June heat was on its way.

Sonny smiled, then grinned, then laughed. He rolled down his truck window and let the cool rain splash against his face.

"Gracias a Dios!" he cried. Rain had come.

26

By the time Sonny got home, the clouds that had crept up from the south covered the valley; the sudden thunderstorm dumped fast, then became a steady drizzle drumming on his flat roof. Rita was waiting for him. She had prepared chicken enchiladas smothered in red chile, easy on the cheese, Sonny's favorite. Rice, beans, hot tortillas on the side.

She greeted him at the door and they kissed in the rain.

"Isn't it wonderful!"

"Beautiful! Beautiful like you!" He smiled and pulled her inside. "I feel like—" He paused, sniffed. "Chicken enchiladas?"

"I thought you'd be hungry." She smiled and led him to the table. "Eat first." She winked. "We have all night."

"You took the night off?"

She nodded.

"All right! Let's party!" He washed his hands, wiped his face with the towel, and sat down to eat. As he ate, he told her about his visit to Morino.

"Madre de Dios," she said when he finished his story, "imagine being in the room just after she was killed. He was in danger—"

"If he's telling the truth," Sonny reminded her.

"Ay, there's the rub, como dice Shakespeare. I've seen him interviewed on TV, so handsome, and so gentle."

"Gentle men also kill," Sonny said as he got up and took his dishes to the sink.

"Not the ones I know," she whispered, and hugged him.

"Let's not discuss anything that has to do with the case tonight," he whispered back. "Just you and me."

"Enjoying the rain." She smiled. "That's just what I had in mind."

He held her and looked into her clear brown eyes. "I love you, Rita."

"And I love you, Elfego."

"Let's—"

"Uh-uh. Dishes first. Remember, we have all night. I don't want to rush."

"I'll volunteer to do the dishes, and you—"

"I'll get ready," she said, kissing him warmly, her moist lips and the look in her eyes promising a night of love. "Don't take too long," she whispered, and disappeared toward the bedroom. They had promised each other that come hell or high water, tonight was theirs. And with the rain filling the house with fresh air and drumming on the flat roof, it couldn't have been better orchestrated.

Sonny smiled as he ran the hot water over the dishes. Then the thought crossed his mind that he still wasn't okay. Maybe he should smoke some grass. Like the spiked wine Tamara had given him. He wouldn't have had a problem then!

He finished the dishes and left them to dry in the rack beside the sink. He was feeling an urgency, and he didn't want to screw it up. It was going to be okay, he didn't need to smoke. He walked into the bedroom where Rita waited. She had put fresh sheets on his bed, showered, and slipped on one of his T-shirts.

"Got any mota?" he asked, surprising himself and her.

"No," she answered. "Do you want some?"

"No, just thought—"

He paused by the open window. Damn! Why had he asked?

"Qué piensas?"

"Enjoying the breeze," he said, stripping off his shirt. "The rain."

He looked out the window and enjoyed the coolness of the rain, the soft breeze of night stirring. Lord, it seemed like ages when they had last felt rain, heard thunder, smelled the fragrance of the hot earth as it gave up its rich aroma to the rain.

Rita came and stood beside him, wrapping her arms around him. They stood together, enjoying the warmth of their bodies leaning against each other. The sweet fragrance of rain and wet earth enveloped them. There was nothing like that smell in the high arid plateau. The desert earth was like a woman suddenly opened by the voluptuous caress of the lover. The rain and the earth mixed and rose within the thin veil of mist-cooled night.

The people of the valley understood and responded to the forces of nature that suddenly filled them with passion. Wide sky, clouds, rain, earth, lightning and its sound, the smells released were the essence of passion.

Across the way don Eliseo's cornfield was soaking up the moisture, the leaves of the cornstalks cupping the precious rain. Don Eliseo had watered the young plants with acequia water all summer, but there was no substitute for rain, the old man always said. The tall cumulus clouds of summer were feminine, woman-clouds, deities bearing the life-giving rain.

Soft, penetrating rain. Lluvia de amor. All night it would make a soft sound on the flat roofs of the valley. Each rain had a name. Manga de lluvia, falling dark and straight down like a sleeve. Or una manguita, a small sleeve. Lluvia de los corderos, the cold, spring rain of lambing season. In summer the monsoon that came to relieve the dry summer, and which sometimes turned into the "pinche rain" because it ruined cut alfalfa in the field, or a picnic, or a baseball game.

In July the tempestas de lluvia, lluvias fuerte, the thunderstorms of the summer, which came quickly and dumped everything in a few minutes. Those were the quickies of the high desert, the sudden rains that came with booming thunder and caused the floods. To make love during a thundershower was to make quick, hurried love. To be like lightning penetrating the earth.

In September showers moved in as sure as the state fair came around, and so people joked and called it state fair rain. There was a rain for every season, because rain was sacred, life-giving.

Now, this first rain was one of those unusual rains for the Río Grande plateau, covering the entire state with a steady drizzle. The gentle mood of rain impregnating the earth was like the semen oozing softly into the juicy darkness of a woman. A rain like this made the rhythm of love slower, long lasting, satisfying. The man's urges and his sperm changed as the seasons changed; the woman's needs and moistness also changed. The ozone of the lightning heightened the urge. The tumbling sound of the thunder that rumbled across the valley with a thunderstorm was the drumbeat of love, or lust.

Everything changed according to the weather; desire came and went according to the storms moving across the wide valley. The rain or lack of rain affected the way a woman cried out in love, affected a man's potency. Men and women lived in harmony with the rains that washed across the valley.

Rita's body is like the earth, he thought, enjoying her hands moving on his body, hearing her moan, a warmth and moistness ready to receive him. I am the rain. Our perfume of love will be the fragrance of rain and earth.

Rain from Mexico, tinged with the flavor of mangos, strong coffee, the call of vendors in the mercado. It was the soaking kind of rain the earth needed after the long, hot month of June.

It would lie like a blanket over the valley and the mountain, over the entire state for a few days, and it would renew the scorched earth.

"Amor," Rita whispered, and he turned and drew her to him.

"Rain at last," he answered her, and the sweet mixture in the room held her aroma, her perfume like the red cactus flowers of the desert, fruit flavor of the roses that grew in her garden, everything opening and exuding its soul to receive the rain, as Rita would receive him.

The flavor of the roses would change to sweet apricot as the rain kissed the petals, as the perfume of Rita's body would change when his body covered hers. The piñon scent of the incense she burned would mix with the sweat of love, and love would create meaning under the blanket of the cool night.

"How do you feel?" she asked, caressing his chest.

"I feel like making love to you," he replied, and they kissed.

"Ven," she said, and moved toward the bed.

He followed, thinking, I'm okay, I'm okay, everything's going to be just fine. He sat on the edge of the bed to take off his boots and pants. She reached out and embraced him. Her body made the hair on his arm rise, a soft, welcome tightness washed over his stomach and thighs. He breathed deep as he pressed his face into the cleavage of her breasts.

"Ahh," he moaned, felt his penis harden. Oh, Lord, he felt like the lightning in the sky! She the earth!

A strange scent mixed with the perfume of her body. For a moment he felt distracted by the candles. He looked toward the window and Gloria's image appeared. He cursed silently, fighting to keep his thoughts off the case, keep them on Rita.

"It's good to be alone," she whispered, trying to draw him out of his thoughts.

He looked at her. "Yes," he agreed. He looked at the window. The haunting ghost was gone. Damn, if I just stop thinking about the case! he thought. He slipped off his boots and socks, then his pants.

"Ready or not," he teased, and jumped under the sheet.

"Ready," she replied, meeting his embrace.

"Ah, you feel so good," he groaned, pressed against her and felt her body taut and ready.

She touched him and sent shivers tingling throughout his body. A moan escaped from his lips. It was going to be all right, yes, it was going to be all right.

A tapping at the window made Rita stiffen.

"What was that?" she asked, and drew the sheet around her.

"Nothing," he whispered, but paused to listen. He, too, had heard the tapping. "Only the wind, amor." He slid his hand under her T-shirt.

Rita moaned softly, relaxed for a moment, then sat up straight when she heard the second tap on the window. A squeaky voice called out, "Sonny, you there?"

Sonny groaned. Don Eliseo! "Sonny. It's us! Open!"

"Shhh," Rita whispered, and put her fingers on Sonny's lips. "He might go away."

But the beam of a flashlight outside the window revealed more than one person. Don Toto and Concha were with don Eliseo, and they were arguing loudly. They were drunk.

"Don't step on my shoes, Concha!"

"You got big feet, Toto!"

"Sonny, it's me!" don Eliseo said.

"Abre la pinche puerta," Concha hissed. "It's wet out here!"

"I'm asleep," Sonny said from under the sheet. Rita punched him. "Pendejo!"

"I hear you, Sonny. Abre!"

Sonny rose reluctantly and went to the window and parted the curtains. Outside in the drizzle stood don Eliseo and his two friends.

"I don't want any," Sonny said.

Concha laughed. " 'Cause you already got it, honey. We know Rita's in there."

"I'm sleeping—"

"Oh sí, sleeping! Hear that boys, our angelito is sleeping!"

"It's us, Sonny. Snap, Crackle, and Pop," don Eliseo cut in. He had been drinking Toto's Mad-Dog North Valley wine.

"Let us in," don Toto clammered. "We're all wet."

"Now?" Sonny said.

"We know you got Rita with you, Sonny, so don't act so innocent," Concha whispered. She held a flashlight, which she aimed at Sonny. "Ah, the evidence," she said, "he's empeloto!" The three chortled with laughter.

Sonny looked down, realized he was naked, and drew the curtain around him.

"If you got it, flaunt it," Concha teased.

"We found something," don Eliseo insisted.

"We been on the case, Sonny," don Toto said, and held a large magnifying glass to his face. Concha aimed the flashlight at him, and Toto's eye bulged in the light like a large oyster.

"We found the cabro sin huevos," don Eliseo said proudly.

Sonny's eyebrows arched. "The cabro sin huevos?"

"We found him!" don Eliseo said.

"What the hell you talking about?"

"It's true, Sonny," don Toto said, nodding vigorously. "Me la rayo."

Don Eliseo also swore. "May Tata Dios strike me dead if I lie," he said.

They've been drinking and playing detectives, Sonny thought, and the night with Rita was now an illusion. They would not let him rest.

He groaned. "The door's open," he said, and dove back under the sheet. "Snap, Crackle, and Pop," he said to Rita. "Drunk."

"Don't let them in," Rita begged, but it was too late. Concha's flashlight stabbed the darkness as they came stumbling through the front door and into the bedroom, pushing each other, and making jokes about old love affairs, and all together they tumbled into bed around Sonny and Rita. They smelled like wet chickens.

"It sure is good to see you, Sonny." La Concha grinned and shone the flashlight in Sonny's face. She pinched his cheeks. "You were always a good-looker, too bad you're so young."

"A good woman is never too young," don Toto crooned. He had found Rita; Rita pulled the sheet over her head and tried to hide behind Sonny.

"Who's your friend, Sonny?" la Concha asked, and winked.

"Rita."

"Rita, I didn't know you slept around" was Concha's snide remark.

"I don't! I just sleep with Sonny!" Rita retorted, and sat up. Instantly Concha flashed the light on her, and don Toto peered at her intently. "Ay, que cosas hace Dios," he said in lustful admiration.

"Oh, you got good taste," la Concha said, smiling.

"Listen to me." Don Eliseo tugged at Sonny to get his attention.

"Sleep with one, it's still sleeping around, qué no?" La Concha grinned. "Sonny, you feeling better? Can you handle it?" She punched Sonny in the ribs.

"Yes, I'm feeling better!" Sonny said, and gave don Eliseo a mean look. Was there anyone in the North Valley who didn't know his business now?

"This better be good," Sonny threatened. The old man's breath was sour with wine.

"We found it, Sonny! We found the castrated goat!"

"You've been drinking," Sonny said.

"Smart dude," don Toto said.

"We found the goat, Sonny!" Don Eliseo took Sonny's arms and pressed, his grip strong.

"It wasn't easy," Concha said, and straightened her bra. "But my compadre here made a big deal out of it, so we went looking and we found it! You want the pinche goat or don't you, Sonny?"

"Yeah, I want it." Sonny nodded. There was an urgency in don

Eliseo's voice. If they had really found the goat, that was a big lead. Right to the bastards whose ass he wanted to kick.

"Where?" Rita asked.

"At a house near the Ranchitos Road, back by the ditch," don Eliseo said. "The woman who lives there raises goats, and that's where we found the big, castrated red. Just like I told you, Sonny!"

Sonny was already pulling on his pants and fumbling for his socks and boots in the dark. The goat whose testicles were hung on Rita's porch! But why would some woman be bothering Rita and me?

Sonny paused and looked at Rita. Lord, he wanted her, and now this!

"But it can wait—" he said to don Eliseo.

"No!" don Eliseo replied. "I think they're going to get rid of the goat! Don't you see! The goat is a sacrifice. We've been watching them. These women keep coming out to the pen and doing all sorts of crazy things with the goat. Washed it, put ribbons on it—"

"Brujas," Concha said with a shiver.

"Sí, they're brujas and they're going to sacrifice the goat," don Eliseo said, his voice ominous in the dark.

"What do you mean, sacrifice?" Sonny asked.

"Don't be so tapado!" don Eliseo replied. "Don't you see? Tomorrow is the first day of summer!"

A summer solstice offering? Sonny thought. Holy caca! The goat is a sacrifice on the summer solstice! If what don Eliseo was saying was true, was Gloria, too, a sacrifice to the sun? But no, she had been killed before the solstice. He was making associations that didn't fit.

"They kill chickens, Sonny. Están locas," Concha added. "I've seen them."

"Call Garcia," Rita said, and pulled at him. "I don't like it."

"The women with the goat kill chickens?" Sonny asked. "Who are they?"

"The woman who lives there. She's there alone sometimes, then the others come. I've been keeping my eyes on them. They go to the chicken coop late at night. Son brujas, Sonny. I'm sure," Concha said.

"We watched them," don Eliseo said. "They came out and cut the chicken's neck. They offered the blood to the sun, just like the old Aztecas used to do."

"Pero los Aztecas used virgin blood." Don Toto grinned at Rita through his magnifying glass, fixating on her breasts. "Ay, que melones tan dulces," he said lasciviously.

"They kill chickens and roosters," Concha intoned, "and they smear the blood on their bodies. And the goats, Sonny, the goats. A long time ago the devil came in the form of a goat, and the brujas danced with him!"

Sonny shook his head. Concha was going overboard. He turned to don Eliseo.

"I think these brujas put the sign of the Zia on your prima. And on you," don Eliseo whispered.

Sonny pulled on his boots, Concha handed him his shirt. "You got good buns," she laughed.

"Do you think they are the ones who killed Gloria?" Rita asked.

"I got to go," Sonny said, and bent to kiss Rita.

"Call Garcia. It could be dangerous. Or let me go—" Rita started to get up again.

"No, no, it's okay. Garcia would just go busting in there. Scare them away. All I'm going to do is look around. You stay put. I'll be right back."

"Take a cold shower, honey," la Concha advised.

"Hurry, Sonny!" don Eliseo said anxiously, "If they sacrifice the goat, we got no evidence."

"I can stay with the lady," don Toto volunteered, and took Rita's hand.

"You come with us, Buster." Concha yanked him.

Rita swept the sheet aside to get up, then remembering she

was wearing only the T-shirt, she jumped back into bed. "It's crazy," she pleaded. "You can go tomorrow."

"I can't get no satisfaction," la Concha sang.

"You're drunk!"

"We may be drunk, but we found the cabro." Concha smiled. "Snap, Crackle, and Pop Detective Agency at your service."

Sonny hesitated. Rita wouldn't wait forever, and the cool summer night wouldn't last forever. He would rather stay in the warm bed with Rita.

"Yeah, Sonny Boy," Concha fanned herself with her flashlight, creating an eerie light on her wrinkled face with the red lips and thick glasses.

"We got them where we want them," don Eliseo assured him.

"I can stay," don Toto repeated.

"Ándale." Concha pulled him. "Leave the fooling around to Sonny. Ya tú no puedes." She laughed, putting the flashlight between her legs, and making a lewd gesture with it. "You need Energizer batteries!"

"I'll be back soon." Sonny kissed Rita.

"Let me go with you."

"No."

"Be careful."

"Keep the tortillas warm, honey," Concha said, "and the biscochito."

They laughed. "Que suerte la mía," don Toto sang, "comer sin tortillas, queriéndote así. . . . Que suerte la mía, dejar tu sopai pilla."

The three went stumbling out of the bedroom. Concha's light flipped and flopped as Sonny led the odd threesome through the door and into the wet night.

27

The three duendes jumped into the truck cab with Sonny, all jammed together like a pork meat burrito. "Ah, this is heaven," la Concha said, and pressed close to Sonny. "Nice and warm. Rita had you pretty calentito, eh, honey?" She winked and straightened her orange wig, which was wet with rain and smelling like wet straw.

As soon as they were bouncing out of the driveway, don Toto took out a bottle of wine, drank, and passed it. Each took a drink in the dark; lips sucked at the hot wine and smacked with gusto, until the bottle reached Sonny. Out of courtesy he took a drink, then wished he hadn't. The wine was hot and sour. He leaned out the window and spit.

"Chingao, don Toto, what did you do to this batch?"

"Hey, primo, it's good stuff."

"Makes you warm inside," Concha purred, and sang again, "Can't get no satisfaction."

Yes, Sonny thought, they had had a lot of wine to drink, but they had found the castrated goat, and that meant getting close to those who had left threatening messages on his answering machine. Ah, his mind was racing now, making the connections that had eluded him. These women made sacrifices, and Gloria had been sacrificed. Tomorrow was the summer solstice. . . . The day the sun stands still, that's what Raven had called it. Things were falling in place, finally!

Don Eliseo pointed the way, and Sonny obeyed. They followed the bumpy dirt road along the side of the irrigation canal.

"We can come in the back way," don Eliseo said, "That's where she keeps the goats. Pull over here," don Eliseo said, motioning to a vacant, weed-filled space. To the right ran the acequia, one of the old mother ditches of the North Valley. Bordering on it was one of the richest housing additions in the North Valley, the Bosque de Alameda home sites.

From here it was only half a mile to Rio Grande Boulevard, close to Frank Dominic's place, and just down the boulevard was the house of the late Dorothy Glass. From here someone could walk along the acequia path and enter Dominic's backyard.

Sonny pulled over and turned off the motor.

"This is it," don Eliseo said. Don Toto opened the door and he and don Eliseo tumbled out.

"Pinche zoquete," don Toto cursed, and wiped the mud from his pants.

"Tu ojete qué?" Concha laughed as Sonny helped her down from the truck.

"Cállense. You want to wake the dead?" don Eliseo cautioned. "We can walk," he said, and led them into the dark, thick brush under the canopy of towering cottonwoods. The rain was a thin drizzle, but enough to soak them.

"Que frío," la Concha complained. She shivered and held on to Sonny's arm.

Sonny knew the ditch road. Young high school kids came to smoke pot here. Lovers came to park. Used Rubber Lane, the local cops joked about the place. Over the years the cops had busted even more backseat romances on this road than drug transactions.

"Pinche yerbas!" Don Toto cursed the burrs that stuck to him.

The tall grasses and weeds were dry and sharp, and the rain had already formed mud puddles in the hard caliche earth. River willows and salt cedars slapped at their faces as the three duendes plus one worked their way through the thick brush.

"Shh," don Eliseo whispered. He was taking his job seriously.

"Can we stop for a drink?" don Toto asked.

"I need to pee," la Concha added.

"Shh," don Eliseo repeated.

Sonny could see the old man's bulk of a shadow in the dark and rain and heard the urgency in his voice. Yes, they had found something, the pattern was there. His old friends knew evil when they encountered it, and the woman who owned the goats, they believed, was evil.

"Aquí!" don Eliseo called, and stopped abruptly. Don Toto, Concha, and Sonny stumbled into him.

Don Eliseo had brought them around the back of a rambling adobe, one of the houses of the valley. Sonny could smell the goat smell in the rain. He cocked his ear and heard a bleating sound. He slid next to don Eliseo, and together they crept up to the side of the pen.

"Concha, your flashlight!" don Eliseo called.

Somewhere a dog barked. They were making too much noise, Sonny thought. He would have to get them out of there and take a close look at the place himself.

"At your service," Concha said, and passed forward the flashlight. Don Eliseo shone it into the pen. There in the corner stood a big red goat, sans balls. The cut was healing well, and if don Eliseo hadn't known what he was looking for, it would have been difficult to spot the wound.

"There it is, Sonny," don Eliseo said proudly as he focused the light on the red goat. "I told you it was a red."

"El cabro sin huevos," Concha whispered, and shivered.

"Que lástima," don Toto added, and fished out his bottle of wine.

Yes, there. it was, the castrated goat whose balls had been hung on Rita's porch to frighten him away. He was close to something evil, he could feel it in his guts. "She alone?" he asked, nodding toward the house.

"I think so," don Eliseo answered. "A bunch of others left when we were here before."

"Any dogs?"

"No, but the neighbors have dogs."

He had to get a look into the house, but it wouldn't work with Snap, Crackle, and Pop tailing him. They made too much noise, and there was the possibility of danger.

"It smells like hell," Concha complained.

"Take my truck back and go tell Rita I'll be a little late," Sonny said, handing the keys to don Eliseo.

"No, Sonny, we gotta stick with you. These people are dangerous. They're not amateurs," don Eliseo insisted.

"I'll be careful," Sonny whispered. "But Rita has to know I'm okay."

"Oh, he's worried about his honey," Concha crooned. "True love," she sighed, and struck a match to light the roll-your-own she had been working on while sitting against the goat pen, but the wet match only sputtered against the wet cigarette. Don Eliseo snatched the matchbook away from her.

"Que 'stás tonta!"

"I need a cigarette," she groaned. It had been a long night, and she was tired and wet. Detective work was okay in the day, but not at midnight in the rain.

"Get her home," Sonny whispered to don Eliseo, his tone meant to make the old man understand they were in the way.

"Ten-four," don Eliseo replied. "We better put Concha to bed before she catches cold," he said.

"I already got pee-monia," Concha said, and sneezed.

"Vamos." Don Eliseo motioned to Concha and don Toto. "We'll take Concha home, give her a glass of Toto's wine, and put her to bed."

"Oh, how romantic," Concha groaned. "I'm as wet as a chicken crossing the river, and these guys want to put me to bed."

"You'll live, m'ijita." Don Eliseo smiled and took her arm. "I'll call Rita, tell her you're okay," he said to Sonny. "Soon as I can, I'll come back and wait for you where the truck is parked. Okay?"

"Okay." Sonny nodded. "Thanks."

"Cuídate," the old man said, and punched his arm. "That woman in there, and her friends, are bad mujeres."

He turned and led Concha and Toto back to the truck, disappearing with much complaining and rattling of brush and weeds.

"See you later, Sonny," Concha called in the dark. "Be careful, honey."

Sonny waited until the noise of the three disappeared and he heard his truck start and drive away; then he turned his attention to the house. It was shrouded in darkness, an ominous shape in the mist. There was danger in it, he was sure. And perhaps the answer to Gloria's murder.

Then he thought of his pistol: still in the truck. He crouched and moved along the edge of the goat pen. He felt a tingle along his spine, the warning that danger was near. He turned the corner of the goat pen and moved in the dark to a small shed, then to the back door of the house. He turned the knob gently and the door opened. Damn, he thought as he walked into the dark, I should have kept Concha's flashlight.

He heard someone move in the dark, the rustle of cloth, but before he could jump back something crashed against his head.

He heard a loud ringing, saw flashes of light, and he lunged at his assailant as he fell. He scratched at a dark cloth and caught the whiff of lilac before he hit the floor and was enveloped in darkness.

28

Sonny awoke to a throbbing headache, darkness, and a tangle of cobwebs covering his eyes. Caked blood from his nose stuck to his mouth and chin. He kicked out at his tormentor but felt no resistance. He shook his head, the cobwebs fell away, but the throb in his head remained.

"Cabrones!" he cursed the dark. "Where in the hell am I?" he groaned. His arms were tied and stretched up to a ceiling rafter. His feet barely touched the floor. Whoever knocked him out had removed his shirt and hung him like a sheep ready for slaughter.

"Ah, pendejo," he cursed himself when he remembered walking into the house. "You walked right into it! 'Stúpido!"

When he spoke, the headache coursed through his head, like a bolt of snake lightning. He closed his eyes again, the pain subsided.

"I am sorry, Mother," he whispered, "you raised a dumb kid. I am sorry, Great-Grandpa Elfego, I disgrace your name. Your great-grandson is a pendejo."

He pulled on the ropes, but they only tightened around his wrists and cut into his numbed flesh. The beam he hung from was solid; the nylon rope would not break. The cement basement floor was damp and cold; his left foot ached.

His vision cleared and his eyes grew accustomed to the dark. Smells returned, and the overpowering smell in the dark room made him turn slowly to look at the figure hung next to him. At first he thought it was a man. But no, it was the big red goat. Its throat had been slit; the coagulated blood formed a pool on the floor. A few dark, fat flies buzzed at the cut.

"Chingao," Sonny groaned. "I'm next."

There was a small window, high on the wall behind him. He was in a basement and the window was a crawl space with a dirty, muddy pane.

I have to cut the rope, that's the only way out, he thought. He pulled again at the rope, then tried swinging his legs up, but his weight only tightened the rope at his wrists.

The stench of the goat filled the room, the air was damp and stifling. They're going to kill me, he thought, and felt a tremble along his spine. Being shot at in Escobar's ranch had scared the hell out of him, but there he could have made a run for it. Here he was tied and hung.

"Jodidos!" he yelled, and waited, but there was no answer. The headache struck again, and a wave of nausea that made him pass out momentarily.

How much time has passed? he wondered when he regained consciousness. He stood still and his head grew clearer and his eyes grew more accustomed to the dark. The only other thing in the basement besides him and the goat were the box shapes leaning against the wall in front of him. Suitcases. With a large gold monogram: "GDD." Gloria's luggage.

It took a great deal of concentration before he recognized the smallest form leaning against the wall. It wasn't a suitcase, as he first thought. It was a mortician's old-fashioned hand pump. The kind Howard said was used to drain Gloria's blood.

The flies buzzed around the goat's open wound. He had let a lot of people down, he thought. Manuel Lopez, for one, his mentor, who must be rolling over in his grave knowing Sonny had walked blind into such danger.

"Do things right," Bisabuelo Elfego said in the dark, "or the Texans will kick your ass. You know they tried to kick mine the first time I was deputized in Socorro. I held my ground for two days and two nights, and when they thought I was dead, I climbed out and took 'em in."

Now it was Sonny's turn to take them in, but unlike Elfego Baca's first battle at Frisco Plaza, he couldn't walk away. He knew he should have called Howard or Garcia. Now it was too late.

Don Eliseo and his cronies would be putting Concha to bed by now, well into another bottle of wine, arguing and telling stories and finally falling asleep. How long would Rita wait for him to return? If she gave up and went home, she wouldn't find him missing until late in the day. By that time he would be in the same condition as the goat.

His eyes had adjusted to the dark now, and he spied a small table near the goat. Something glinted on top of it. A knife! The knife they used to slice the goat's throat, still covered with blood. It was the same knife they would use on him!

"Unless," he thought, and he heaved himself up, grabbed the rope in his hands, and begin swinging. He swung closer and closer to the table, until he could slip his feet under the edge and pull. The table jerked toward him, teetered momentarily, then both table and knife clattered to the floor.

"Chingao," he cursed. Could he reach it now? He swung again, reached out painfully with his feet as far as he could, and finally touched the knife and drew it a few inches forward. The bloodied knife scraped along the floor. He swung again, pulled it closer, until he could grasp it in both feet, but he couldn't hold the gory blade between his boots.

"Take off your boots," Bisabuelo Elfego said in the dark, and Sonny spent the next five minutes slipping his boots off. When that was done, he could grasp the blade with his toes.

He heard voices somewhere in the dark. They were coming; he had to hurry.

Using all his strength, he raised his legs upward, even though the ropes cut painfully into his wrists and hands. He knew he had to free himself fast. He had only seconds left, the voices were nearer. They were coming for him, las brujas don Eliseo feared, Gloria's murderers.

He strained as he lifted the knife between his feet up toward his hands. With the remaining energy and his entire body trembling, he slipped the knife from between his feet to his right hand. His quivering hand grabbed the knife and he let his feet drop to the floor.

"Ah," he breathed in relief, sweating, feeling the buzzing of the flies around him. Awkwardly, he began to saw at the rope around his wrists.

The voices grew closer, they were outside the door now. Free and armed with the knife, he might be able to make a fight out of it, even if he was outnumbered. But the knife would be useless for defense if he was still strung up, like the goat. He cut furiously, felt one strand of rope snap. It was working, he smiled, but as he changed the blade to his left hand, it slipped from his grasp and clattered to the floor again.

"Damn!" he cursed, and looked up to see the door open and two women enter. A fat figure stood outlined in the light of the doorway. Beside her a smaller woman. He tugged at the rope, but it held. They looked at Sonny and approached cautiously. They wore long, black gowns, and each wore a yellow mask on which was painted the sign of the Zia sun.

"Look," the thin woman said as she picked up the table, then the knife.

"Stupid! I told you not to leave it there!" the large woman cursed.

They've come to do their surgical work on me, Sonny thought, and struggled. The nylon rope only bit deeper into his wrists.

"He's okay," the thin woman said, and touched the knife to Sonny's stomach. "He ain't going anywhere," she laughed.

"Yeah," the fat one said, and checked the ropes, satisfying herself that they would still hold. A sweet, almost putrefying smell of lilac oozed from her. She spoke in Sonny's face: "You know too much, Mr. Baca. I'm going to cut your balls off." She laughed and took the bloodied knife from the thin woman. Sonny felt his stomach contract. He knew the voice. There, pressing the knife against his skin, stood Veronica. Gloria's "healer."

"Not now," the smaller woman said. She drew close to Sonny. "We gotta wait till sunrise. Sacrifice his blood to the sun of the summer solstice."

"Yeah," the large woman answered. "But I'd like to cut his balls off right now and be done—"

"Not me," the thin woman laughed softly. "He's too good-looking. Wish we could have a little fun with him before you do your operation."

She caressed the flat of Sonny's stomach. "Come on, Sister, let's cut him down and have a little fun."

"You're crazy!" The fat woman shook her head. She drew close, the knife ready to strike, and again her friend held out her hand.

"Wait till sunrise. We got our orders," the small woman said, hugging Sonny. "Oh, he is gorgeous. I liked him the first time I saw him."

"Damn you!" the larger woman cursed. "I say we do it now and be done with it! He's been trouble from day one."

The small woman looked up at Sonny. "The sun needs blood on the solstice day. I tried to warn you, now it's too late."

"Yes, you did, Dorothy," Sonny replied.

"He knows your name!" the larger woman hissed.

"So what," Dorothy said, and took off her mask. She looked intensely at Sonny. "It don't do you no good, does it? You shouldn't've mixed in any of this. Now, you got about an hour before the sun rises—"

The fat woman laughed. "The Zia sun has reached its journey to the north. Now it returns to its home in hell. All will die as winter approaches. The black sun is angry. It wants the blood of a man, the blood of a warrior. Only blood will appease our sun on this solstice day."

"Is that why you murdered Gloria?" Sonny asked.

"Murdered!" the fat woman spat out. "She went willingly to serve the glory of the Zia sun."

"Bullshit!" Sonny shot back. "She was running away."

"She was crazy!" Dorothy responded angrily. "No one can leave us!"

"Shut up!" the fat woman shouted.

"What difference does it make!" Dorothy said defiantly. She ran her fingers on his stomach, outlining a circle around his navel. She put her arms around his waist and softly kissed his navel.

Sonny felt a chill.

"You horny bitch," the fat woman cried out, grabbed her, and pushed her away. "We came to mark him, not fuck him!"

She raised the knife and quickly and deftly cut the circle of the Zia sun on Sonny's stomach, just deep enough to draw blood, blood that oozed from the circle and the four radiating lines.

"There," she whispered, "you're marked for death. Your sacrifice will give the sun the power it needs."

She pushed the smaller woman toward the door.

"One question, Veronica!" Sonny called.

The two women turned to face him.

"Now ain't he smart. He knows your name, too," Dorothy chuckled.

"A lot of good that will do him," Veronica replied. She walked slowly to Sonny, pulled off her mask.

A surge of anger swept through Sonny as he strained at the rope. This was the woman who had killed Gloria.

"Why did you kill her?"

Veronica leered. In the dim light shadows played on her bloated face. "She was a willing sacrifice—"

"Bullshit! You murdered her!" Sonny cried.

"No one leaves the cult of the sun! No one!" Veronica shouted back, holding the knife at Sonny's throat. "What do you think we are, Sonny boy? Amateurs? You think we're playing games? We've been following you. We know where you've been and who you see! You're going to find out that this isn't a game!"

He thought she would lunge, stick the knife in his throat, cut as she had cut the goat. Instead, she hesitated.

"We thought you would be a worthy enemy," she whispered, drawing close. "But you don't understand Raven's power! You don't know that on this solstice we have signed a pact to bring down the world! It's bigger than you think, much bigger! And the time is at hand. Come," she said to Dorothy, turning away. She paused at the door and stuck the knife into the door frame. "There's an hour until sunrise. We must finish preparing for the ceremony. One hour, Sonny, and you join the goat. And Gloria." She pushed Dorothy out, closing the door behind them.

The room grew dark again. Sonny looked down at the blood oozing from his throbbing belly.

"Damn!" he cursed. He hated himself for having walked into the trap, and for being unable to free himself. And most of all he hated not understanding what she meant. She had confessed to killing Gloria, but the intimations in her words pointed at something bigger.

He struggled against the ropes, swung up and kicked, and the beam creaked with his rage and weight but did not give. The ropes only tightened deeper into his wrists, bringing a numbing pain that coarsed through his arms into his shoulders.

"Elfego!" he called on the spirit of his great-grandfather, "I need you!"

29

Moments later, his call was answered by a rap on the small window.

Sonny turned, a shadow appeared at the small window, then a hoarse whisper. "Sonny?"

"Quién es?" he answered.

The window creaked, gave way, then a body slid through the small opening and landed with a thump on the floor.

The shadow groaned, rose, spoke again. "Sonny?"

"Rita?"

She was instantly at his side, hugging him, pressing herself against him, then she felt the blood that oozed from his stomach. "You're bleeding!"

"I'm okay," Sonny replied. "Shhh." He motioned to the door. "The knife," he whispered.

"Where?"

"Stuck on the door. Hurry!"

She peered into the dark, went to the door, and pulled the knife from the wood. Then she went back to him, and reaching up, she cut the rope in one stroke.

Sonny dropped to his knees, his legs weak and his wrists aching and numb. She knelt beside him, steadied him. "Amor," she said as she cut away the ropes at his wrists. "Are you all right?"

"Alive." He groaned with pain, and allowed her to hold him momentarily in her arms. Both looked up at the dead goat hung from the ceiling.

"How did you—?" he asked, feeling her warmth and breathing deeply the rich, warm smell of her hair and perfume.

"Don Eliseo." She pointed out the window and helped him to his feet.

Rita helped Sonny pull on his boots, then steadied him as he rose and they stumbled to the window. "Dame la mano," don Eliseo whispered.

"You first," Rita said, and gave Sonny a push out the small window. Don Eliseo grabbed Sonny's hands and pulled, then both quickly helped Rita out.

Gasping for breath, they stood against the side of the house, shivering in the cold drizzle. Rita pressed against Sonny, protecting him from the rain. "Gracias a Dios," she whispered.

In the east the first light of dawn was a soft gray in the cloud-covered sky. Within the hour the women would come back to drain his blood.

"Vamos," don Eliseo said, throwing his jacket over Sonny's shoulders and pulling both of them away. He led Sonny and Rita back over the trail through the dense Russian olive trees to the acequia, and without incident they reached the spot where he and Rita had left the truck.

Don Eliseo opened the door and helped Sonny and Rita get in. Then he nimbly went around to the driver's side, got in, and started the truck. He turned on the heater. "Be warm in a minute."

"They were going to kill you," Rita whispered.

"Just like they killed Gloria," Sonny answered. "I was their sacrifice to the sun."

"Sanamabiches don't know anything about the sun," don Eliseo said angrily. "When it rises, we give it our prayers, not blood! We offer cornmeal, pray to the Señores y Señoras de la Luz, but these crazies take blood!"

"Human blood," Sonny said, nodding. An hour later and he would have been like Gloria. Like the cabro. Sin huevos. Sin vida. Sin nada.

"Gotta get you bandaged," Rita said, taking off her scarf and pressing it to his stomach. Her hands and arms were bloodied from his wounds.

Sonny looked across the field at Veronica's house. Now, in the light of dawn, he recognized it, even from the back. It lay quiet in the gray rain, but inside he knew Veronica and Dorothy and others were preparing for his death. It wasn't a house of the rising sun and light, it was a house of death.

Veronica's ominous words clung to him like the chill of morning: "It's bigger than you think." Bigger than murder.

"They want to create a world of evil and chaos," don Eliseo said, as if in answer to Sonny's thoughts.

Sonny slumped his head against Rita's shoulder, and she held him as they drove through the morning drizzle homeward. Feeling was returning to his wrists. He closed his eyes.

Had Raven anointed Gloria to be his next wife? She came back from the group meetings disoriented, Morino had said. When she found out she was pregnant, she tried to get out. The thought made him shiver. In trying to leave, she had broken the cult's primary rule, and for that she had to pay with her life.

"Gracias," Sonny mumbled as don Eliseo drove up in front of his house and stopped the truck. They helped him in. The first thing he did was to dial Howard. If Garcia could get there before

Veronica and her assistants in death found Sonny was gone, he could pick them up along with Gloria's luggage and the pump. He told a sleepy Howard what had happened.

Then Rita helped him take off his clothes, put him into a hot shower, then dried him and made him lie down while she bandaged the cuts. Still shivering, he put on the dry clothes she offered.

Don Eliseo had made coffee. He offered Sonny a cup with a shot of brandy in it. Sonny sipped the strong liquid.

"Garcia will take care of Veronica and her cronies, but I've got to find Raven. Try to stop him." Inside, he knew he wanted to get Raven for what he did to Gloria. Veronica was the one who did the cutting, that was certain, but had Raven been there? Had he given the order to drain Gloria's blood? Raven needed the money to finance his plans, and they knew Gloria had it. Reason two why they killed her.

"Won't Raven be showing up at Veronica's for the sacrifice ceremony?" Rita asked.

"I don't think so," Sonny replied. "More likely he leaves the dirty work to the women. There's something bigger, Veronica said. I think she means Raven's going for the WIPP truck."

"The news last night said the anonymous threats continue. You mean Raven has decided to blow up the truck, period, forget nonviolent protests?"

"It's summer solstice day, the day all their energies have been focused on. Raven knows the east side of the mountains like the back of his hand. That's probably where he is right now, waiting for the truck, setting up explosives."

"Doing the work of the devil," don Eliseo said.

"Call Garcia. The police will stop the truck," Rita suggested.

"Not on my call. I've got nothing concrete to offer. The fact that Raven's out there is known by the FBI. The question is, can they find him before he blows the truck?"

"What can we do?" don Eliseo asked.

"Get help from someone who knows the mountains."

"Escobar," Rita said.

"He's our only hope," Sonny replied, and dialed Escobar. The ranchero was an early riser, he was up, and yes, he would help. But there wasn't much time left. The truck was leaving Los Alamos that afternoon. If they didn't find Raven by sunset, it would be too late.

"We'll find him," Sonny said, "we have to. I'll be there in an hour." He hung the phone and turned to Rita.

"I'm going with you," Rita said.

"Too dangerous," Sonny tried to dissuade her.

"I got you out of the slaughterhouse. How can it get worse?" she answered. "Besides, I have a vested interest in your health."

"Grab some jackets," Sonny said, going to the closet where he kept his rifles. He took out his .30-30 and a box of cartridges. "We're going hunting for Raven. Stay near the phone," Sonny said to don Eliseo as he and Rita hurried out the door and into the truck.

"Ten-four!" don Eliseo called back. "Dios los bendiga."

Sonny waved and gunned his pickup toward Fourth Street and then east on the interstate. The streets were puddled with the rain; the gray mood was dismal.

Don Eliseo checked in. "Sonny, Concha and Don Toto just got here—"

"I was afraid of that," Sonny said.

"—with hot menudo and a gallon of wine. Don't worry, Snap, Crackle, and Pop at the battle station!"

Sonny flipped on the radio. The early-morning news chattered with the big event: a load of high-level plutonium waste was leaving Los Alamos for the WIPP site. In spite of the rain, the ceremony was going on as scheduled. The governor and senators were there; so were hundreds of protesters.

"That puts the truck in Raven's territory near dusk," Sonny figured aloud.

Raven's territory spread along the eastern side of the Sandia Mountains, somewhere from Galisteo to Moriarty. A lot of road to cover. The low-hanging clouds, the weather news announced, would blanket the state all day. The state cops wouldn't be able to have their plane in the air.

"Where?" Sonny asked as they drove. "Where?"

The radio stations broadcasting from Los Alamos were interviewing lab personnel involved in the nuclear waste transfer. No, the rain wasn't a factor, the director of the labs commented. The truck was designed for all sorts of weather. The emphasis was on safety. The huge, barrellike container in which the nuclear waste was housed had been tested over and over at Sandia Labs. The transfer was perfectly safe.

What about the protesters? he was asked.

The state cops would keep everything under control, the director assured the listening audience. In the background Sonny could hear the hecklers as the director spoke.

"Even a head-on crash wouldn't create a spill," the director insisted.

"What about dynamite? The threats we've heard from someone who's going to try to dynamite the truck?" the reporter asked.

"We have state police and national guardsmen along the road from here to the WIPP site," the director answered. "We want to let the people of New Mexico know that they have nothing to be concerned about. We foresee no problems. The governor has called out the guard; the state police are patrolling the route. People should remain calm. We are asking motorists who drive the designated route that was published in the newspapers not to use those routes today. Just as a precaution."

"The man doesn't want to talk about explosives," Sonny said, and lowered the volume on the radio. "But when they were making plutonium for bombs at the labs, they insisted they weren't. Makes you wonder who you can believe."

"That's why Raven, or Pájaro, has such a following," Rita said. "People are fed up with government lies. Does Raven have the dynamite?" she asked.

"I'm sure he has enough to punch a hole in the barrel. I don't think it's going to blow like a bomb, but the blast, if placed right, could leak a lot of radiation. A wide area of contamination. People will be killed, and more poisoned. . . ."

He paused and thought of the eventuality. What he had read on the possibility of such an event wasn't good. The contamination would last for centuries.

"It would create international news. That's what he wants."

The telephone buzzed, and Howard answered Sonny's hello.

"We got here just in time," he said. "Your lady friends were running out the front door when we drove up. Veronica's in custody. But no Raven."

"I didn't think you'd find him," Sonny replied. "He's going for the truck."

"Where are you?"

"On my way to José Escobar's place. Rita's with me."

"Ay caray, be careful. We got Gloria's bags and the pump. And in Veronica's bedroom, believe it or not, a nurse's certificate. It looks genuine. I've only glanced at things, but there are old check stubs from a Taos hospital. Apparently she did nursing to keep the group in food when they ran out of poached meat. Also, a gallon of water perfumed with a cheap lilac cologne."

It fit. Veronica had enough knowledge to do the killing. No wonder the wound on Gloria was done expertly, and the traces of blood nonexistent. She knew how to clean up after herself. But now there was enough evidence to indict her, Sonny hoped.

"Has she talked?"

"Nope. She's not saying anything. The DA's here. There's enough to hold her."

"She knows who else was in the room when she killed Gloria."

"Yes. It's just a matter of time. Garcia will get it out of her."

Yes, Sonny thought, they had the murderer, but would she implicate Raven? Or Tamara?

"Just as you predicted," he said. "They were into sacrifice, using the blood as an offering to the sun."

"And today they offer up the WIPP truck. Even if you find him . . ."

He knew Howard was thinking what he was thinking. If Raven blew the truck, the plutonium poison would bathe everything and everyone anywhere near it with a dangerous dose of radioactivity.

"You need me there?" Howard asked.

"I figure José Escobar is our only hope. He knows the area. Stay by the phone, though."

"Ten-four. Y buena suerte."

"Thanks, we need it."

"By the way, Garcia said thanks."

Sonny smiled. So the chief now had the real murderer in custody and he broke down and said thanks. A good sign.

"Anytime," Sonny said, and turned his truck off the interstate and up the road that led to Sandia Crest, then he turned east into the scrub forest of the eastern slopes of the mountains. The thin, gray drizzle hung over the mountains, creating a dark mood, a sense of impending doom.

José Escobar reflected the same mood as he invited them into his house and introduced them to his wife, Tomasita. Sonny told them what he knew.

"We should probably start at his place—"

"But he pulled out," Escobar said. "The women and the kids are gone. Disappeared. The FBI was thick as moscas, Sonny. They searched the place. What makes you think you can find him?"

"We have to," Sonny answered. "He's going for the WIPP truck today."

Escobar shrugged. "What can we do? From Los Alamos to Carlsbad is three hundred miles. A lot of empty road."

"What would you do if you were Raven?"

"I don't know. . . . Maybe set off a false alarm. Blow a little dynamite someplace, then strike when the cops are in the wrong place. I'd do it along the foothills, so I could get back up the mountain. . . . That's still a lot of road. Sanamagon, it's like looking for an honest politician in Santa Fe." Escobar frowned.

"We have to try," Sonny urged.

Escobar nodded. Yes, they had to try. He went to the closet and took out plastic ponchos.

"Dónde?"

"It has something to do with the sun," Sonny explained as he took one of the ponchos Escobar offered. "Today is the summer solstice, the first day of summer. He's got dynamite. He's going to blow up the truck. Dynamite equals fire. Everything has a meaning for Raven, so the place he picks to blow the truck will have a meaning. Everything relates to the sun. He acts according to the cycle of the sun."

"I figure he's hiding along the road. I talked to Rocky Page yesterday, the state cop who patrols this side of the mountain. He said they plan to have fifty cops out, headquartered at Stanley."

"Stanley?"

"Only a gas station and a post office. It's Bruce King country," Escobar explained as he opened his gun rack and took down his deer rifle. "If the FBI can't stop Raven and his locos, how can we?"

He slipped cartridges into the chamber, paused to look up at Sonny. "What if he blows the truck? What about the radioactive stuff?"

"Raven's not suicidal. He'll be wearing protection," Sonny replied. "But we won't. . . ."

He gave Escobar a reason to back out. Even a small leak after the explosion could release a lot of high-level radioactive plutonium, and exposure of that intensity meant almost certain death by cancer and leukemia down the line, especially for those in the immediate vicinity.

"I gotta do what I can to protect my land," Escobar said. He looked at Tomasita. "And my familia. Raven knows this country. He can get the dynamite to the road without running into the cops."

He turned and spoke to his wife. She had packed sandwiches for them, slices of cold roast beef in tortillas, and she filled two large thermos bottles with coffee. The house grew silent, only the steady sound of the dismal rain sounded on the tin roof.

"Que vayan con Dios!" she said when they were ready to go out. "Do you want to stay here?" she invited Rita.

"Thank you, thank you for everything, señora, but I have to go with them." She stood by Sonny.

"Pray for us, vieja," Escobar said, and put his arm around his wife. "If ever there was a time to pray to your Virgen de Guadalupe, it's now. Take out every santo you have, pray to them. Y sí, no. . . ." He shook his head. He didn't want to think about the truck blowing up and the damage the radiation would do.

"If any of the muchachos come by, tell them we're looking for ese cabrón Raven. Adios." He kissed her, then he turned and led Sonny and Rita out the door into the rain.

The back road to Stanley was already a quagmire. The caliche earth had turned into a thick, gooey paste. The ruts of the road were punctuated with rocks, making driving a test for Escobar. He had insisted they use his four-wheeler truck, and he was right. Without it they wouldn't have been able to move. The rain was steady now, a gray sheet that cut visibility to a few feet.

"First good rain of the season," Escobar said.

"And it plays into Raven's hands," Sonny added despondently. No state police planes in the air. No FBI choppers patrolling the state road.

The back road between Santa Fe and Edgewood was crawling with state cops. The national guard and the state police had a road block on the outskirts of Stanley, but Rocky Page, the state policeman who peered into the truck, knew Escobar.

"José, what are you doing out in the rain?" he asked and glanced at Sonny and Rita.

"Hunting," Escobar grinned. "And you?"

"Hunting? Estás loco! Don't you read the paper? The WIPP truck's coming through today. Look, if you don't have to be out, it's safer off the road."

"Trouble?" Escobar asked, playing the innocent.

Page nodded. "Well, a bunch of protesters blocked the road for a while, but they've been cleared out. The governor's cut the ribbon, and the truck's rolling. But you never know. Best stay off the road."

"I had a few of my steers cut a fence and get out," Escobar said. "A neighbor said they headed this way."

"Okay, okay," Page said. "Don't say I didn't warn you." He wasn't about to give a cattleman looking for stray cattle a hard time. He waved at the cops at the roadblock and they cleared Escobar.

"Gracias," he acknowledged, and drove south toward the interstate.

They drove in silence, looking, thinking, peering into the heavy rain. This was the first of the monsoon rains that came from the south, and it was welcomed by the ranchers. The rain would save the summer range; it also gave Raven cover to do his dirty work.

They reached the interstate and turned and drove back to Galisteo, a small village south of Santa Fe. Once an old mining and ranching village, it was now an artists' colony. Along the road they passed national guard vehicles and state police cars, but they weren't stopped again.

On this stretch of road the foothills of the Sandias were low mesas and arroyos that sloped down into the Estancia Valley. Small bridges spanned the arroyos. All of the gullies were already carrying runoff water from the mountain.

"The bridges are perfect cover," Rita mused. Time was running out; she felt the tension building.

"But which one?" Sonny asked.

"Too many," Escobar said. "Too many places he can hide. A man could move for days in these arroyos and mesas, in and out of the juniper and piñon. Cops don't have a helicopter up. You can't use dogs in this rain."

"Yeah, even the weather's on his side," Sonny said. He needed something concrete, and nothing was turning up on the road. Raven could be hiding behind juniper trees or a boulder along the road, down in a gully, or under a bridge, laughing at them as they passed by.

They turned and drove back toward the interstate, sipped coffee, listened to the Los Alamos news on the radio, and looked intently into the rain. They grew tired of driving back and forth, and as the hours slipped away, each grew more tense.

Begin at the beginning, Manuel Lopez always said. "Let's check his place," Sonny spoke, tired from the tension and the driving.

Escobar shrugged and turned up the mountain to Raven's compound. The dirt road was muddy and full of ruts, and it was slow going, but they had no other lead to follow. An hour later they pulled into Raven's compound. It was deserted, an eerie silence clung to the wet pine trees. They got out of the truck and hurried past the stone-marked cemetery and into the adobe building.

Both men carried their rifles, and Escobar packed his flashlight. Inside, an empty, hollow silence filled the large round room. Four doors led into the four smaller rooms that completed the dwelling. Inside, the adobe was exposed; it had not been plastered or painted. Rita shivered.

"Dirty," she said.

"Just like a raven's nest." Escobar shrugged. "A raven steals everything he can get hold of."

Mixed in the wet smell of earth and the dusty clutter on the floors, Sonny thought he smelled the fragrance of lilacs. He remembered the day he came to Raven's place. Yes, the aroma of the lilac perfume had been in the air even then. Veronica's.

Escobar shivered. "There's a bad feeling here."

Sonny stepped carefully through each room, taking a stick on the floor to poke through the trash: old newspapers, plastic flowers, the bits of brass the wives had used to make earrings and bracelets, feathers, beads, colored glass, and crude paintings apparently done by the children. The elemental signs of Raven's world were everywhere: fire, the Zia sign, a green earth, Down With WIPP signs.

He paused and held his breath when he found the Forest Service maps.

"Estos?" he asked as he picked them up and dusted them.

"Forest Service maps," Escobar explained. "Go to any forest station and pick these up."

But Raven knew the mountain and the foothills, so why the maps? "Let's have a look," Sonny said, and spread the maps on the earth floor.

Escobar shone the beam of his flashlight on the maps.

"East side of the mountains," Escobar shrugged. "But nothing on them. No marks."

"Where are we?" Sonny asked.

Escobar found the La Cueva Land Grant map and pointed. "Here's the village, here's my ranch, right here would be Raven's place."

Sonny marked an X. "And Los Alamos?"

"Not on this map. You need more sections. These maps are for the east face of the Sandias."

"Where's the highway?"

"Over here." Escobar pointed.

"These are roads leading down to the highway."

"Mostly old logging roads," Escobar said.

"And these?"

"Arroyos."

"He could follow an arroyo to the highway and never be

RUDOLFO ANAYA

seen," Sonny said. "He would go east toward the rising sun on the day of the summer solstice. The sun would stand still."

He looked at Rita. "On the day of the summer solstice, the sun stands still, then begins its journey south," she intoned.

"The explosion will make fire, the sun standing still," Sonny kept repeating, the mantra increasing the tension he felt.

"It's here," he whispered, and looked closely at the names of the arroyos on the map. "Arroyo del Oso, Calabazas Arroyo, Arroyo de las Gallinas, Arroyo del Sol—"

He stopped and felt his heart skip a beat. "That's it!" he shouted, and looked up at Rita and Escobar. "Arroyo del Sol!"

"Yes!" Rita cried.

"Can you find it?"

Escobar looked at the map and nodded. "Sure. I know it."

"How much time?"

"We have go back down to Sandia View Road to catch the highway, then to I-40 . . . maybe an hour and a half. Cops are out, so we have to go slow."

Sonny looked at his watch. "We don't have that much time!"

"There's an old road along the arroyo. So from here to the highway is half an hour, but even in my four-wheeler, we could get stuck."

"Let's take it!" Sonny shouted, grabbing Rita's hand, and they rushed out into the fading afternoon. Sonny guessed that the WIPP truck from Los Alamos had already passed Santa Fe and was nearing Galisteo, and Raven was waiting for it under the Arroyo del Sol bridge. The summer solstice bridge. It was just a guess, but it was all they had to go on.

"No radio," Sonny said as they piled into Escobar's truck. They were using the four-wheeler to get through the mud, but that meant they couldn't call the state cops. It was up to them to get to the bridge across the Arroyo del Sol before the WIPP truck.

348

30

The afternoon darkened as the cloud-shrouded sun dropped westward and disappeared behind Sandia Crest. Escobar gunned the truck for all it was worth, sliding and sloshing down the mountain, then cutting across an old logging road to the Arroyo del Sol. He stopped the truck at the side of the arroyo and turned on the headlights. The wide, sandy arroyo was running with red, churning water.

He turned the truck and followed the old lumber road along the side of the arroyo, weaving around the junipers and boulders that dotted the arroyo's edge. If Sonny was right about Raven's use of sun symbology, they would find him at the bridge where the road crossed the arroyo.

"He's going to be armed, hasta los dientes," Escobar said as he tightened his grip on the steering wheel and fought for control, grinding in low gear down the muddy, treacherous road. A false move here and even the four-wheeler stood a chance of slipping into a rut and getting hung up.

Sonny checked his .30-30. It was ready.

"There's a pistol in the glove," Escobar said to Rita. If it came to a gun battle with Raven, she, too, needed protection and a pistol was easier to handle. "It's loaded."

Sonny opened the glove compartment and dug through old papers, found a bottle of whiskey, a hunting knife, then the small-caliber pistol. He took it, checked it, and handed it to Rita.

"Use it if you have to use it," Sonny said. Rita nodded. He checked his own pistol, Bisabuelo's old pearl-handled .45.

Just then the road ended. A huge log lay across the ruts they had been following. Escobar stopped the truck.

"Holy tacos," he cursed. "The Forest Service screwed up again!"

"No way around," Sonny said, rolling down the window to get a good look. The headlights of the truck illuminated the large ponderosa pine lying across the road. The three of them couldn't move the huge log, and the four-by-four couldn't go up the steep hillside full of piñon and juniper trees.

"How far are we from the bridge?" Sonny asked, ducking his head back inside the truck, wiping the rain from his face.

"About a mile," Escobar answered.

"I'll go on foot," Sonny said, grabbing one of the ponchos.

"Wait!" Escobar replied.

He was looking at the arroyo and the foot of water it carried. From here down to the bridge, it would stay mostly flat and sandy. He knew the truck could handle it, but he also knew the way the arroyos could rise quickly when the rain off the mountain hit with full force.

"The truck can make it!" he shouted. Raven would have helpers, and he couldn't let Sonny face them alone. "Vamos!"

He threw the truck into low gear and turned it down the sloping side of the arroyo. The truck skidded sideways on the wet sand, straightened out, and went flying into the gully. It landed with a teeth-jarring thud in the muddy waters. Rita groaned.

"Sorry." Escobar grinned, as he kept the truck in low and aimed it down the arroyo. He had driven mountain roads and arroyos all his life, so what difference did a little rain make?

The truck shot forward, slipping and sliding in the current created by the rain. The clouds above them had grown thick and dark, and the water funneling down the arroyo was increasing in volume.

"It's going to get worse," Escobar said, and fought to keep the bouncing truck as steady as he could.

Sonny nodded. The way the rain had suddenly cut loose meant the arroyo could become a raging flood at any moment. If they didn't get blown to pieces or toasted by radiation, they might drown. Drowning actually seemed preferable.

They fishtailed and rattled down the arroyo in silence, knowing that if they had miscalculated, Raven would have a clear shot at the WIPP truck. Each prayed silently.

"Highway up ahead," Escobar whispered, and turned off the lights. He didn't want to come up suddenly on Raven and get blown out of the saddle.

Through the falling rain they saw the flashing red lights of the state police escort on the highway. The escort moved slowly as it approached the old wooden bridge.

"That's it!" Sonny exclaimed. Just behind the state police car rose the huge bulk of the barrel-laden truck.

"My rifle," Escobar said, and rolled down the window.

Sonny passed the .30-06 across to Escobar, who pointed it out the window and released the safety.

"There's the bridge," Rita whispered.

"Raven's here," Sonny replied. He could sense him.

"Sí," Escobar answered. He had hunted long enough to know when the prey was near. "How many with him?"

"One, maybe two," Sonny guessed, remembering Scarface and his partner from the Estancia bar. Or maybe he was alone, because when it came to actually blowing up a WIPP truck, most likely not many of Raven's followers would volunteer.

The water rushing down the arroyo propelled the truck forward. They were sliding from side to side now, as if on a boat.

"Ready?" Sonny said to Rita. She squeezed Sonny's arm.

"Ready." She slipped the safety off the pistol.

Just behind the state cop, flashing yellow lights glittering in the rain, the WIPP truck appeared, a huge shadow in the mist, the huge barrel it carried rising like the hump of a prehistoric monster in the dark. Plutoniosaurus. Inside the belly of the beast lay the hot, high-level radioactive waste, now only minutes from the bridge. The lead state-cop car slowed down. Had they seen Escobar's lights before he flipped them off? Had Raven?

Just ahead of them, crouched behind a giant boulder about four hundred feet from the bridge, Sonny spotted two shadows.

"Raven!" he pointed.

Raven and Scarface were dressed in bulky outfits, lab suits to protect them from the radiation, and the boulder would protect them from the blast. The sonofabitch isn't taking any chances, Sonny thought. Raven was going to blow the truck, then dash back up the mountain. It wasn't a suicide mission.

Escobar floored the gas pedal.

"You take the guy on the left!" Sonny shouted, and cocked his pistol.

Raven and his helper heard the truck and turned. They had been so intent on watching the approaching WIPP truck that they were caught by surprise. One pointed and the other man jumped for the rifles leaning against the boulder, but he was slowed by his bulky suit.

Escobar flipped on the lights and stepped on the brakes. The truck fishtailed in the mud and water and went crashing toward the two figures, illuminating them in the drenching rain. Sonny saw one man reaching for a rifle and the other, probably Raven, holding aloft a small black box: a small radio transmitter that was no doubt wired to the dynamite.

Scarface had time to reach his automatic rifle and get off one shot. Sonny shouted a warning and pushed Rita down on the seat as the truck windshield burst into a million pieces of glass.

"Cabrón!" Escobar cursed as the truck slid to a stop. He opened fire, and Scarface tumbled into the muddy water. "I'll get him!" he shouted.

"I'll take Raven!" Sonny cried, jumping out of the truck. "It's over!" he shouted, aiming the pistol and moving toward Raven. "Drop it or I'll shoot!" He grabbed at the man and ripped away the protective covering from Raven's head.

"You're too late!" Raven shouted, looking over his shoulder at the bridge.

"Drop it!" Sonny shouted again, and Raven cursed and struck at Sonny with the transmitter. With one blow he sent Sonny's pistol flying into the water.

"I'll kill you!" Raven cursed, striking another blow, which sent Sonny reeling.

On the bridge the lead state police car had skidded to a stop. The state cop had seen Escobar's truck lights in the arroyo and heard the burst of gunfire. He stepped on his brakes and jumped out of his car, pistol in hand. The big semi carrying the huge barrel full of nuclear waste skidded and slammed into the police car as the driver hit the brakes. It choked to a stop, a sitting duck in the middle of the bridge.

Sonny made a leap for Raven. Both went tumbling into the rushing water of the arroyo, and the transmitter flew with them. They rolled, then rose, slugging at each other, fighting for the transmitter, which eluded both.

"Damn you!" Raven shouted. Another well-placed blow made Sonny stagger. Again Raven scrambled for the transmitter. If he could push the switch, he could still detonate the explosives at the bridge.

But the transmitter disappeared in the darkness, swept away by the current. On the bridge armed policemen were already calling orders. With the transmitter lost and police swarming around the bridge, Raven's plan was spoiled. He turned and ran toward the boulder and the automatic rifle.

Sonny found his pistol in the mud, picked it up and aimed.

"Stop!" he shouted, and Raven turned momentarily.

They faced each other, panting for breath.

"You don't have the guts, Baca!" Raven shouted, inching toward his rifle.

"Shoot!" Sonny heard someone say, and thought it was the voice of his Bisabuelo, Elfego Baca, telling him to protect himself.

Sonny pulled the trigger, but his pistol, full of mud, misfired.

Raven laughed. Illuminated by the searchlights from the bridge, he had nothing to lose. He grabbed his automatic and aimed, and a small explosion sounded. Not the thundering staccato of an automatic, but the whimper of a .22.

Sonny saw Raven grab his arm and wince as he dropped the rifle. Out of the corner of his eyes, Sonny saw Rita standing firm, holding the small pistol in her hands.

The wounded Raven cursed and ran up the arroyo's incline. Sonny followed, tackling him as they reached the top. They rolled in the mud, both groaning and gasping for breath.

The rest of the state police cars had come to a stop behind the truck, and a state police SWAT team and FBI agents were swarming toward them, the searchlights from their trucks and cars illuminating the scene.

"Put your arms up!" a loudspeaker blared. "Drop your weapons and put your arms up!"

Another radio crackled: "Move the truck! Move the truck off the bridge!"

The truck driver rolled down his window and peered out. "Move the car!" he shouted at the cop he had rammed. "I can't move! Get the fucking car out of the way!"

"Don't shoot! Don't shoot!" Escobar shouted as armed police came running toward them.

He held up his hands, hearing at the same time a sound he

knew well. He turned and saw, illuminated in the car lights, a six-foot wall of water come crashing down the arroyo, picking up his truck rolling it down the arroyo like a toy.

At the same time two FBI men tackled him and sent him sprawling. Rita ran toward Sonny.

Other policemen shouted for her to stop.

"You blew it, Baca!" Raven cursed above the roar of the water, his face contorted with rage. He scooped up a piñon club and struck at Sonny. Sonny ducked once, twice, then stood facing the wounded Raven.

"It's over!" Sonny shouted. "Give it up!"

"Go to hell!" Raven cried and struck again at Sonny.

Sonny ducked and Raven's momentum carried him past Sonny and over the edge of the arroyo. Sonny reached out to grab him, but the only thing he caught was Raven's medallion. The chain broke and Raven plunged into the water. The wall of water that had picked up Esobar's truck and sent it bobbing down the arroyo now swallowed Raven.

Rita reached Sonny just as Raven fell. Together they saw him rise once, crying out in defiance; then he disappeared into the swirling darkness.

The cop car in front of the truck had moved off the bridge. Now the truck followed, moving forward across the bridge. Just then the ground shook as the thunderous explosion lit up the night. The transmitter must have bounced against a rock somewhere down the arroyo.

Rita and Sonny hit the ground, holding on to each other as the fireball rose over the bridge and rained debris on them. They were far enough away from the bridge so the worst they got was the mud splattering around them.

When the air cleared, Sonny helped Rita to her feet. "You okay?"

"Okay," she answered. "My ears are ringing."

The air was thick with a cloud of acrid smoke. The wooden bridge that once spanned the Arroyo del Sol was no more. But the WIPP truck had cleared in time and was safely rolling down the highway. Around them figures of state cops rose groaning, dusting themselves from the dirt and mud that covered them.

"We made it," Sonny said, embracing Rita.

"Gracias a Dios," she answered.

Sonny opened his hand and Raven's gold medallion glittered in the light from the cars.

Both shivered as state police and FBI agents surrounded them. They had seen the struggle at the edge of the arroyo, and they had seen Raven disappear; then they, too, had been flattened by the explosion.

"You got him, Baca! You got the sonofabitch!" Somebody slapped Sonny on the back. Sonny looked at the face illuminated by the headlights. Mike, the FBI agent who had worked Sonny over the day he visited Raven's place.

"The fucker's going to wind up buzzard bait when the water settles," his partner, Eddie Martinez, said. He aimed his flashlight at the angry arroyo.

The flood had hit with fury, but it wouldn't last long. As soon as the rain clouds cleared the Sandias, it would subside.

"Governor's gonna make you a fucking hero," Mike said, his wet face grinning in the light.

"Hero!" Sonny shot back. What the hell did the bastard know about being a hero? All the anger he'd felt from the time he saw Gloria's dead body came rushing over him, and he hauled back and hit the agent.

Mike reeled from the blow. He put his hand to his mouth and spit out blood. "What the hell was that for?" he asked.

"I owed you one," Sonny reminded him.

Mike glared at Sonny, then slowly smiled. "Yeah, you did, Baca. Sorry about roughing you up. You got my fucking vote now, if it makes any difference."

"I feel like doing the same," Escobar complained.

"Hey," Mike held up his hands. If Sonny's blow had staggered him, Escobar's would floor him.

"We apologize," Eddie explained, "we didn't know what was coming off."

"My troca!" Escobar moaned. "My pinche troca's in the pinche arroyo!"

"We're sorry about your truck," the agent said apologetically.

"Ah, the troca wasn't worth a damn!" Escobar retorted, "but my whiskey was in it."

Sonny looked at Escobar, then at Rita. They put their arms around each others' shoulders and laughed.

"Your whiskey?" one of the agents said, and they too laughed.

"Hell, we can take care of that," Eddie nodded, and someone appeared with a half-full bottle of Jack Daniel's. The agent opened it and handed the bottle to Escobar, who handed it to Sonny.

Sonny took a swig, then passed the bottle to Escobar, who took a long pull. He passed the bottle to Rita.

"To Escobar's troca!" She smiled, lifted the bottle, and took a drink. A new round of laughter filled the air.

In the headlights of the cars, the bottle was passed around, the cops and FBI and DOE agents taking turns, celebrating that the catastrophe had been averted.

Sonny hugged Rita as they stood in the circle and passed the bottle. Each new pass deserved a new toast.

Tonight the earth will not be burned by the deadly heat of radiation, Sonny thought as he peered through the dark and rain toward the wide Estancia Valley, and tomorrow the sun would shine, and after the rain, the slaked earth of summer would green again.

Time and again, the seasons came and renewed the Earth. The drought was broken and now the grasses of the land would green up. Across the broad expanse of land, the leaves of grass would feel the blessing of the rain. Plants and animals and the families who struggled for survival would give thanks.

In the meantime radioactive waste continued to pile up in Rocky Ford, Pantex, Los Alamos, and Sandia Labs, and so the scientists made plans to store the junk at the WIPP site, and other places. One of the Indian tribes had already petitioned the state for a license to set up a nuclear storage facility on their land. The storage of radioactive waste had become big business.

I don't want it in my state, Sonny thought. Not in this land that nurtured my ancestors, nurtured the dreams of don Eliseo. If there was one thing don Eliseo had taught him, it was that the Earth was alive. A soul throbbed beneath its flesh. The soul should not be burned and shriveled by the works of man.

But the deadly waste was here, and it was here to stay. It's life would outlive generations of the Río Grande valley. His children's children would live with the consequences. Somewhere it had to stop. Somewhere men and women had to come to their senses and stop producing what they could not control.

Raven had tried. Fight fire with fire, he said. Scare the world to its senses. Three Mile Island and Chernobyl had not been enough. Show them what a terrorist could do.

But Raven had another agenda, a darker, more evil plan. Chaos was his god. Violence his end. Raven envisioned the end of the world, and his cult coming into power in the new world. That's what Veronica meant. The struggle was bigger, the stakes greater than just tonight on the bridge.

"Qué piensas?" Rita asked. She sensed his quiet mood.

"Just thinking," Sonny replied. "Let's go home."

"Yes, it's time to go home," she agreed.

31

Sonny sat on Tamara Dubron-
sky's patio and watched the sun rise over the mountain.

The Señoras y Señoras de la Luz came flooding over the valley,
the bright light turning every dewdrop into a scintillating crystal, and igniting in Sonny a radiant emotion that overwhelmed
him with its beauty.

"Ahhh," he sighed.

He shivered as he felt the warm sun on his face, and gave
thanks to the old Abuelo Sol as don Eliseo had taught him.

"Bless all of life," he whispered, then leaned back in the patio
chair, closed his eyes, and allowed the light to bathe his face.

The energy of the sun warmed his body, seeped into his soul.

Overhead the sky was as clear as if last night's thunderstorm
had never gone through. True, the air was hazy with humidity,
but otherwise there wasn't a cloud in the sky. Maybe by after-

noon the sun would warm the land and the great clouds would rise over the mountains again.

He looked at the mountains. The humidity lent a bluish cast to the outline of the Sandias. That's all he could see, the blue outline of the mountains, as if they were cut out of the sky and one could step through their outline into another dimension.

Clear sky, outline of mountains, the green of the valley dazzling with light. That's all there was.

Someday I will practice becoming a Señor de la Luz, he smiled. He flipped on his Walkman and let the Symphony in D major by Juan Arriaga fill his pores.

This man is bad, thought Sonny. More New Mexicans should know his music. The Mozart of Spain, a homeboy from the old country.

Sonny let the stirring music drain the tensions from his body. He thought about Raven and his watery death. The flood had hit like a train, washing away everything in its path, but like all arroyo floods of the high arid country, it would subside as the rain subsided. The cops were already searching for his body.

Sonny wanted to be at Tamara's at sunrise to tell her about Raven, and to finish the unfinished business. So without awakening Rita, he had dressed and tiptoed out of the house. He wore a blue cowboy shirt with pearl snap-on buttons, Wrangler jeans, and his good boots. It had taken a long, warm bath to wash away last night's mud and grime, but after that he had slept soundly in Rita's arms.

Except for the questions that kept repeating: Had either Tamara or Raven been in the room when Gloria was killed? Were they, too, responsible for Gloria's death, along with Veronica? And where was Gloria's blood?

Raven's medallion rested on his chest. He caressed the texture of the bas relief Zia sign. The gold was cold to his touch. The Zia sun is good, don Eliseo had said. Make it good. Don't let those brujos use it for their evil.

Gingerly, he touched his stomach where the cut of the Zia

symbol was a recent, painful reminder of his brush with death. After his soaking bath last night, Rita had sprinkled osha powder on the cut and rebandaged it. Did Grandpa Elfego have a woman like Rita to help him?

What a woman. Last night on the arroyo, she had saved his life. They made a good team. Sonny and Rita, Private Investigators. Beats making tacos. No, she was too much her own woman to give up her restaurant. She liked what she did and she did it well. But she worried about him running around the city in the dark of night, meeting people like Raven and Tamara.

"Tough way to make a living," she had whispered last night as she slipped into bed.

Nancy Drew and the Hardy Boys never had it like this, he agreed.

He looked at the flowers that surrounded Tamara's flagstone patio. Bright roses and rows of petunias glistening with dew. On the edge of the patio sat a cloisonné vase. Washed clean by last night's rain, the vase was a deep blue, with a large burst of orange in the center. As he looked closer, he saw the design was the Zia sun.

He thought of Gloria. Gloria's soul haunted him; even now he felt her strong presence. He sat up straight and looked around the garden. She was here! He listened, thinking he had heard her voice, thinking he could smell the lilac perfume of her death.

Maybe he should see Lorenza Villa again, have her do the limpieza she had recommended. The traditional way to get rid of susto was to have a curandera clean away the fright.

No, he told himself. Get ahold of yourself. Gloria's not here. Couldn't be. Or could it? Maybe she was haunting those involved in her murder.

He touched his stomach and felt the fresh wound Veronica had cut into his flesh. "It will heal," Rita said, but the thin, barely visible scars would remain. He would carry the mark of the Zia all his life.

He stretched his legs. The left ankle felt good this morning.

The storm was past, the pressure had changed. Life was good. As long as the Señores y Señoras de la Luz came daily to bless life, it was good. Still, he felt uneasy, fearful of something he couldn't explain.

He knew he needed to delve deeper in don Eliseo's old ways, the traditions the ancestors had honed to perfection in the Río Grande valley. The old people knew there was evil in the world, and they knew how to take care of it. Lorenza Villa was a link, so was don Eliseo and his Lords and Ladies of the Light, so was Rita, so was his mother, so were so many people. . . . Him? What was he a link to? Had he lost the way and didn't know it?

Evil messed up the equilibrium of the soul, jumbled the internal harmony. Evil disoriented and weakened the person as it captured the soul, shut the spirit in a dark prison where it could not pray each morning to the Lords and Ladies of the Light.

Fragmentation of the soul. Like a fine porcelain vase, the soul could break, and few knew how to fix it. Only those who believed in the soul could help put Humpty-Dumpty together again.

We live in the era of la gente dorada, the people covered with a sheen of gold, Sonny thought. The beautiful people of Hollywood, television, movies, caricatures surrounding themselves with luxury, coated with a gold sheen but empty inside. Even here in the North Valley we have those who cover themselves with the sheen of gold, all over the city we have the hombres dorados, men of empty promises.

"Mira, Sonny," don Eliseo said. "This place where we live is special. It is a sacred place. That's why our vecinos from the pueblos have lived here for so long. That's why people come here. But what attracts the angel attracts the diablo."

Raven was such a diablo. A strange disquietude swept over Sonny. He would feel a lot better when Raven's body was found. Raven was a man who could fly, and even now his spirit was out there, calling to Sonny.

Sonny shivered. What about WIPP? For a few jobs and a federal investment in the state, the people had created a trash dump for plutonium. Now some of the Indian tribes were thinking of storing the stuff in their backyards. The radioactive waste was everywhere, at Sandia Labs, in Los Alamos, in the hospitals, even in the industry that came in to build microprocessors. Once created, the element was going to be around for thousands of years. The goal was to stop the creation of the poison.

Around him the pungency of junipers filled the air, the sweetness of roses, the sperm smell of the towering cottonwoods of the valley.

A spiderweb glistening with dew hung on a rosebush. The garden spider moved tentatively toward the fly that had crashed into the web. Then swiftly the spider was on the struggling fly. Arachne feeding on the juices of the fly it held tightly, leaving behind the emptied carcass.

Birds called from the nearby trees, the shrill cry of the colorful oriole, the startling song variety of the mockingbird. The clarity of their songs sharp in the clean air. In the distance a peacock called, the mournful cry that sounded like "Le-on, le-on." A neighbor raised peacocks.

The rain had settled the dust, brought relief from the dry heat of summer. The valley was refreshed; the June heat wave was broken. Now, hopefully, the rains would come on a more regular schedule, the moisture rising in giant anvil-shaped clouds over the mountains and swelling to fruition in the afternoon

The valley was becoming too populated, Sonny thought. Up on the West Mesa they were building new cities on soft sand, and when the summer rains came, the arroyos flooded, homes and streets would buckle. Water could destroy anything. As builders disturbed the old arroyos, the rains would cut new channels, the worm will turn.

Tamara's patio appropriately faced the Sandia Mountains to the east. Grandfather Sun had burst over the crest of the mountain and flooded the valley with its light. Warm, life-giving energy of the first full day of summer. Now the sun begin its journey south, to Mexico, the pyramids of the sun, to Machu Picchu, the gatepost of the sun.

In six months, on December 21, was the winter solstice, and that day was even more important, because if the sun didn't have enough energy to return, it would sink into the darkness of the southern horizon and all life would end.

Those devoted to the beneficence of the sun would offer prayer and ceremony to help the sun return north.

Rita was Catholic, but on December 21 she performed a ceremony. Songs, food for a few invited guests, poetry, the exchanging of stories. In the blood she felt the need to pray for the sun's return.

Don Eliseo would go to Sandia Pueblo to pray with the old men. To talk about Christmas, but to watch carefully the day the sun dipped to its southernmost point on the horizon. To pray for its return.

Around Sonny, the light penetrating the earth and lighting up the green plants and trees; a fuse burning within. Brilliant, living light, not the fire of Raven, but the light of the Señores y Señoras de la Luz, the ancestors of don Eliseo's world, dropping in radiant raiment to touch the Earth with light.

I could spend the rest of my life contemplating this, Sonny thought. The light that draws painters to paint, to capture the meaning of color. The same light calls the medicine man of the pueblo to awaken long before dawn to climb the hill east of the pueblo to await the morning sun. Both painter and medicine man were in search of the Señores y Señoras, the daily illuminating fulfillment.

Somewhere a boy called, and Sonny thought of baseball. Last night's game had been canceled. Que suerte! Kismet! His destino had been good to him; tonight he could go to the game. He smiled. Like his namesake, Elfego Baca, he had shot it out with the enemy and lived to tell about it. He would tell his grandchildren about the fight with Raven at the bridge on the Arroyo del Sol.

It might become as famous as the Bisabuelo's shoot-out at Frisco Plaza, or the fight at the OK Corral. Maybe someone would make a movie out of it?

He heard a door open and turned to see Tamara appear at the patio door. She hesitated when she saw him, then she boldly stepped toward him, smiling, calling, "Sonny, buenos días, I am so happy to see you. . . ."

She was dressed in a gold gown, so revealing that he could see the outline of her body. An offering. Around her thin waist was a bright belt, glittering with precious stones, the buckle also gold, a Zia sun design.

Queen Tamara, he thought as he removed the Walkman earphones. Quite a beauty. He felt a stir as she walked seductively toward him, and he stood and took her hand.

"Buenos días." He kissed her cheek lightly. Lilac cologne stirred in the air.

"What a wonderful surprise to find you in my garden," she exclaimed. "Have you changed your mind about what we can learn from each other? It is the first day after the summer solstice, a very propitious day," she said, and touched Raven's medallion on his chest.

"I'm afraid I have bad news," Sonny replied, but he knew that she knew. "Raven's dead."

A dark look crossed her face. Then she whispered, "Raven cannot die."

"He fell into a flooded arroyo last night," Sonny said. "I reached for him: I tried to grab him, and all I caught was this."

"The medallion? Then it was meant for you to wear it. It is appropriate. No other man could wear this sign of power. It fits you."

"Did you hear what I said. He fell into—"

"I heard," she snapped back. "It is you who have not heard. Raven cannot die. But for now you are the keeper of the Zia medallion. You don't know what this means, do you?"

"It's not mine." Sonny shrugged. "I came to return it to you."

"No, you must keep it," Tamara insisted, her voice softening. "It is a gift for the moment. You see, darling, Raven will return and claim it when it's time. In the meantime you have become the new Raven!"

"The new Raven?" Sonny mused.

Tamara's eyes glistened with dark fire. She was serious.

"Yes! It is a gift! You are my Raven," she whispered, her arms encircling him. She pressed her body against his, her eyes holding him with their strong, mesmerizing light. A dark jade reflecting centuries. Mystery. Her body an offering in the morning light.

"It is a perfect morning for making love," she said. "Today is the first day of the sun's journey south. Our love can guide its way," she said softly.

"I have a woman," he said, even as he felt the stirring in his loins.

"Ah, Sonny, you are trapped in your way of life, trapped by such old rules. Don't you see, I am willing to share you with your woman. Keep her, go to her when you want, eat her tacos and chile and make love to her. That has nothing to do with us. We are old souls who were destined to meet. We are not bound by those old rules."

"A tempting offer." He smiled.

The guys at the Fourth Street Cantina would kick his ass if they knew he had turned her down. Maybe he'd be kicking himself.

"You give yourself so little credit. You are golden, like the sun, you are a warrior of the sun," she said. "Some of your ancestors were the Aztecs of Mexico, the bronze people of the sun. You have never used your potential to look into your past lives, Sonny."

"Because I've never made love to you?"

She smiled. "That will come with time. There are so many ways to join in union. Our souls may unite, even as I wait for you to come to my bed. I have come to pray to the morning sun of summer. Come, join me in prayer," she said, and turned to face the rising sun.

Just like don Eliseo, Sonny thought. But the old man prayed for clarity. The old man prayed for humanity. Tamara and her Zia cult friends offered sacrifice. Offered Gloria.

She closed her eyes and raised her arms to the sun. "Feel the power of the ancient sun. Pray that the soul of Raven finds a new temple, a new body. . . ."

Sonny strained to hear her mumbled words. He looked at her and saw the powerful concentration she possessed. The ecstasy of prayer and the energy of the sun shining on her made beads of perspiration break out on her forehead. She chanted a song for Raven. He would return, she sang.

Sonny's gaze lingered on the light that surrounded Tamara. The outline of her lithe body was revealed by the penetrating light of the sun. She was absorbed in her prayer to the sun, lost in the elemental world that gathered around her. Yes, a real beauty, Sonny thought, a strong woman.

When her song was done, she let her arms down slowly and turned to face Sonny. She drew a deep breath; the communion with the sun had taken her breath.

"I have seen Raven rising into the sky. The sun's power draws his soul like it sucks water from the sea. 'Keep the Zia sign safe until my return,' he said."

She shaded her eyes. "During the day I must cover myself from the sun. It is so strong and masculine, so penetrating. But in the morning it is a gentle lover. Morning is a time for making love."

"Yes," he agreed.

"The moment when the sun rises is a special time. It brings with it the memories of time past. Ah, it was my destiny to come to this land of the sun. Land of enchantment."

"You've become a worshiper of the Zia sun?"

She smiled. "Darling, I have always been a sun worshiper. The king has different names, but he is the king. In a prior life I was an attendant to the god Osiris. I was there when the sun disc was held aloft by Osiris. I saw his transformation into Sun King. In all my prior incarnations, I have walked by the side of the Sun King!"

Her voice rose, the pink flush of exhilaration spread along her throat. "You have never opened your soul to believe in prior lives, Sonny."

"No."

"But you have had dreams, you have tasted a little of the mystery. I know you have. I sense it in you."

Sonny nodded. He had a secret. Something he hadn't told Rita, or his mother. Sometimes, in dreams, he felt he was actually the reincarnation of his Bisabuelo, Elfego Baca. But he didn't know if the visions came simply because all his life he had been inspired by the stories he heard of the famous sheriff, or if there was something more to it.

Words, stories, images, dreams, myths, sounds, and smells were stored in the brain, and the mind could create a million connections with the material. Memory stretched back to the beginning of time, and the spirits of the ancestors flitted through the air, visited in dreams, spoke, and gave guidance. Souls wandered the universe, they became the Señores y Señoras de la Luz. Their voices whispered in the wind. Why should he deny that they renewed themselves in new bodies?

"You have no faith," Tamara laughed. "That makes you vulnerable. That is why you resist me, Sonny. You know you and I are very much alike. My origins are Egyptian, but I am an old soul who has wandered the earth through many reincarnations. I was in the court of the Aztecs when their gods decided that to keep the sun moving, they had to offer him the blood of sacrifice. I have been in those places, and now I am here. I do my duty and keep the sun on its journey!"

"By offering sacrifice?" Sonny asked.

Tamara's eyes narrowed. "By honoring the sun."

"Gloria wasn't honored. She was a frightened woman who was running away, and for that she was murdered."

"Is that why you came here? To talk about Gloria? I have nothing to say about her!" Tamara nearly shouted. "Gloria was a stupid woman!"

"Why? Because you couldn't keep her under your control?"

It was his turn to feel anger. The woman standing in front of him believed in sacrificing people. That wasn't faith or belief, it was murder.

"Gloria died because she didn't believe in Raven!" Tamara retorted.

"No!" Sonny shouted, grabbing her by the arms. "She died because you needed the money!"

Tamara winced, broke loose, her face livid. "She wanted to leave our group!"

"And you were afraid she would expose you!"

"Expose what?"

"You financed Raven!"

Tamara hesitated, calmed herself, then coldly replied. "No, I helped Anthony Pájaro's group fight to save the Earth. You knew that all along!"

"You knew Raven was going to blow the truck."

"He was willing to do anything for his cause! What greater love can a man have?"

"You believe that?"

"Yes. His body was swept away, but his spirit will rise like the phoenix to be born again. He will return to us, Sonny." Her smile was enigmatic, arrogant. "Perhaps at this very moment his spirit is coming to rest in you. You are wearing his medallion, and it fits you."

"For him you murdered Gloria."

"I murdered no one," Tamara replied, her voice cold and in

control. "Raven's wives carry out his orders. I am the queen of the Zia Sun," she said haughtily. "I do no one's bidding."

She was not going to confess anything, and perhaps she was telling the truth. She didn't join in the dirty business with Raven's wives; she was too smart for that. She let Veronica execute the sacrifice. Tamara was the Sun Queen, the commanding presence who orchestrated the ceremony, but not the one who groveled in blood.

"Veronica's been charged with Gloria's murder. The DA will offer her a plea bargain. A lesser sentence if she tells who was with her."

Tamara smiled. "She can say what she wants, but you know I would not be so stupid. That I was there when the sacrifice occurred is nonsense!"

Sonny shrugged. Yeah, Tamara was not so stupid.

"The police will question you anyway—"

"Let them, darling, let them. I'll tell them the woman was my housekeeper. I found her taking some of my valuables, and I fired her. So she will try to drag my name in the mud. The police will see through her lies."

Tamara had figured it out to the last detail, Sonny thought, and just maybe she was telling the truth. She made plans in the background, but the cult did the dirty work.

"Why did Gloria join you?"

"Women," Tamara replied, "have been wounded by life. Man is a very violent animal. You know that, and you know what she suffered as a child. So we gather to protect each other. Gloria needed help. She thought she had cancer, but the 'tumor' she had was clearly the abuse she went through as a child. She came to me for spiritual counseling. She told me about her abuse as a child, and I set out to purge the memory."

"By brainwashing?"

"I helped her!" Tamara's voice rose in anger. "She was thankful. No one had ever helped her. She had been used all her life, and I helped her!"

"She was to become one of Raven's wives."

Tamara turned to look at the blue cloisonné vase that sat at the edge of the patio. "I wanted to help Gloria," she whispered. "Like her, I, too, have known real suffering. We were Gypsies, branded inferior, subhuman. My mother was homeless when I was born, on the day of the summer solstice, 1952—"

"And your father?"

"I call no man father," Tamara retorted. "It is my mother who brought me into the world! She was scorned and rejected for her ways. 'Sun worshiper,' they cursed her. She kept us alive by reading Tarot cards. . . . Yes, those hypocritical Christians came in her back door to have the cards read. The same cards they denounced as instruments of the devil in church! She was a brilliant woman, she had the gift of divination. She told me stories, told me about her past lives as a votary of the sun. Before she died she made me promise that I would escape to a land where the sun shines. There I would use the power of the sun to illuminate my past lives. I honor her vision."

Sonny sighed sadly. The mother filled the daughter with stories, and that was natural. But the child had grown to adulthood and twisted those stories to evil ends.

Tamara drew close and put her arms around his neck. "Is it so difficult for you to understand? You are the new Raven. Anything you ask for is yours. It is time for us to be together."

She pressed her lips on his, but now the sexual warmth she had aroused before was gone. The sweet smell of the lilac perfume overwhelmed him. He saw images: Gloria's dead body, the Zia sign cut around her navel, the dead cow at Escobar's ranch, the dead goat hung in the basement. This woman of the sun was really not a woman of the sun but a pale creature associated with death.

She would cover him with gold, make him the hombre dorado. He would wear Raven's gold medallion, but he would lose his soul.

"Make love to me," she whispered. "Come inside and make love to me. I will illuminate your path—"

"Sorry, I can't," Sonny said. "Afraid we have company." He gestured toward the house where Howard and the police chief were coming around the corner.

32

"Good morning, Ms. Dubronsky." The chief smiled and bowed slightly.

Sonny looked at Tamara. She'd been caught by surprise; nevertheless, she smiled and pulled herself up straight, assuming the role of the gracious hostess.

"Guests so early in the morning," she said to the chief, and held out her hand. "Although you come without announcing yourselves, may I offer you coffee?"

"No, Miss Dubronsky, I'm here on business," the chief answered. "I have a warrant for your arrest in connection with the murder of Gloria Dominic."

"A warrant? Are you playing games with me?"

"Afraid not," Garcia mumbled. "The DA will be here shortly. If you have any questions, he will be glad—"

"I understand," she interrupted, and turned to Sonny. "You

373

were right, the police would come and ruin this most important date. I didn't give you enough credit, darling. I always thought you were just a small-town detective."

"I am," Sonny said, "but I guess Grandfather Sun just watches over his small-town people."

Tamara shaded her eyes and looked up at the sun. The sun had turned against her. Perhaps Raven was dead, and at that moment the forces he commanded no longer had power. She shook her head and moaned softly.

Sonny drew close and placed his hands on her shoulders. There was one final question he had to ask.

"What did Veronica do with Gloria's blood?"

She gazed into his eyes and smiled.

"I know nothing—"

He shook her shoulders. "I am wearing the sign of the Zia sun," he said. "I must know!"

"Yes," she whispered, "you are the Sun King. . . ."

She turned slightly to let Sonny's gaze follow hers. For a moment her gaze rested on the blue-and-orange cloisonné vase that sat at the edge of the patio.

Ah, he thought, so that's why it drew my attention. That's why I sensed Gloria here. The orange design *was* the Zia sun symbol swimming in the New Mexican sky.

Tamara rose on her toes and kissed Sonny's cheek. "This is an inconvenience. I know you will call me as soon as this is cleared up." She turned to the chief. "I believe it's a waste of your time and mine, but I am ready. You will allow me to call my attorney," she said resolutely.

"Of course," the police chief answered.

She nodded and held out her arm for the police chief to take. She turned to Sonny. "Darling, I am sorry it ended this way. Remember, Raven lives."

Sonny nodded and watched as the chief led her away. When they disappeared into the house, he walked to the vase. It was filled with dark, clotted earth. They had mixed the blood with earth sometime during their perverted ceremony.

The ancient Egyptians buried the organs of the body in canopic jars, he remembered Howard saying the day Gloria was murdered. They then buried the jars with the mummy. The delicate cloisonné vase was Gloria's canopic jar.

"Gloria's blood," he said to Howard.

"In the vase?" Howard said in surprise.

"You were right, Howard," Sonny said. "Gloria was a sacrifice. They mixed her blood in with earth— Damn!"

People were apparently capable of anything. The innocence of the city had died long ago; the oasis was now attracting diablos from all directions, the hombres dorados.

"Any word on Veronica?" Sonny asked.

"She was questioned last night, but she's a tough woman. All the evidence is against her. The question is, will she testify against Tamara?" Howard replied. "The DA is going to need her testimony."

"Yeah. He has to get Veronica to testify against Tamara. Split the team." Sonny sighed. "At least Raven got what he deserved."

"And the money?"

"Raven probably used it to buy the dynamite, the Jeep, other supplies. If there's any left over, it probably wound up in the arroyo, on his body."

They stood in silence, looking at the vase that held Gloria's blood. What will it mean to Frank? Sonny thought. Probably nothing.

On the day of the solstice, while Sonny was tracking down Raven, Frank Dominic had lost the mayoral primary election to the incumbent, Marisa Martinez. The rain had kept many away from the polls, but loyal Martinez voters from the valley had braved the storm. The predicted sympathy vote had not materialized for Dominic, and the people of the city were content to let the talented woman who had led them for the past four years lead them four more, even without a commitment from Akira Morino.

What about Akira Morino, Sonny thought. He didn't have to go to the DA now, didn't need to smear his name in public. He could return home to wife and kids and leave the dream of a high-tech corridor between Los Alamos and Sandia Labs behind.

Perhaps that was best. The cities of the Southwest were still watering holes in the desert, tents put up on the sand hills on the banks of the river. That's what characterized the cities of the Southwest, the whimsy of homes built on sand. As if nothing was permanent; as if deep down the people knew they were only passing through and the time would come for them to move on.

The first settlers had built homes from adobe brick, from the clay and sand of the river valley. Some of those old homes were still around. Adobe had the permanence of earth. It was earth. Perhaps that's why the newcomers liked to build their fashionable million-dollar homes from adobe. It gave them a sense of permanence.

Sonny had been in a Santa Fe home built by a wealthy man only a few years before. The adobe walls were hand plastered, and the wood antiqued to look old. "Isn't it great!" the man boasted. "We've only been here three years, but the place looks like one of the original homes!"

Foolish dreams! They longed for permanence. They longed for roots.

Sonny looked toward the West Mesa. On the perimeter of the city the wild coyotes waited to return to their old hunting grounds. He glanced toward the river bosque and a shadow moved in his peripheral vision. Two coyotes had been surveying the scene, no telling how long, and now they disappeared into the shadows. He thought for a moment they might be the same coyotes he had seen at Lorenza's house.

Overhead, a crow cried and circled, then its dark shadow flew toward the river, interrupting the moments of revery the vase had created. Sonny shivered in the hot sun.

"What now?" Howard asked.

"Just wondering what to do with Gloria. . . ."

"She led you on quite a chase."

"Yes."

"Ashes to ashes . . ."

"Así es la vida," Sonny said. "Un puño de tierra, as the song says. I've found her soul. Now will she let me rest?"

"What are you going to do?"

"Bury her," Sonny said. He knew what he had to do.

Howard nodded. "Garcia didn't say it, so I will. Gracias."

Sonny smiled. "I should thank you, amigo," he said, and gave Howard an abrazo. He picked up the cloisonné vase and carried it to his truck.

He called his mother on his cellular, told her what he had found, heard her sob of relief, a sigh thanking God.

"It's over," she said, "this terrible thing is over. Call Delfina."

"I will," he said.

Tía Delfina sobbed. "I'm glad it's over," she said. "I knew you would find those guilty, Sonny. Gracias a Dios."

"I thought we should take the earth that holds her blood to the cemetery," Sonny said.

"Yes, you're right. Let her be united. Let the earth that holds her body hold her blood."

The third call was to Rita. She, too, cried when he told what had happened. "Que descanse en paz," she said.

When Sonny arrived at tía Delfina's she was waiting, still dressed in black, standing stiffly, trying not to give in to grief again. Sonny opened the truck door for her. She looked at the cloisonné vase on the seat, then took it gently and held it on her lap as they drove to pick up Rita.

Rita was waiting for him. She wore a dark shawl over her head, and she had cut roses to take to the cemetery. They drove in silence to the cemetery and parked. With tía Delfina between them they walked slowly to Gloria's grave site.

They stood looking at the marble grave marker, remembering

Gloria, feeling the tragedy of her death, what she had meant to them. Feeling also relief. The search was ended.

"Tía?" Sonny said.

Tía Delfina nodded, awakening from memories. "I think it would be nice if you spread the earth in the vase on her grave," she said. "Let it nourish the grass. My daughter can rest now," and then she added in a barely audible whisper, "and I can rest."

Sonny took the vase and emptied it on the grass, spreading the earth and blood over the grave. The blood was joined to the flesh again.

Tía Delfina whispered a prayer for her daughter, and among the jumbled thoughts and emotions Sonny felt, the words of a Mexican corrido kept repeating.

"La vida es un puño de tierra," he said. Life was a handful of earth, and it returned to earth. Only the light within remained.

He placed the empty vase at the head of the grave, and Rita put the roses she had cut in the vase.

"It's done," she whispered.

Part of it, he thought. He had learned that the dead had a presence that could complicate things for the living. Gloria's spirit was still in him. Rita was right. Sometime in the future he had to return to Lorenza Villa and go through the cleansing cere-mony, la limpieza, the washing away of Gloria's soul with eagle and owl feather, the lighting of candles, incense, sweet grass, and chamisa burning in a small dish, prayers, the chanting and the praying.

It was the old way, the traditional cleansing, a way he wanted to keep, for his children and grandchildren, as long as his blood was alive in the Río Grande valley. Like others of his generation, he had forgotten a lot of the old ways, but with don Eliseo's help and Rita's love, he was returning.

His parents had given him a history, a sense of the traditions of the valley, the stories of the Bisabuelo and the heritage of the antepasados, the ancestors. But somewhere along the way, he began to get separated. Getting a degree at the university meant entering a different world, and living in the vast change that swept over the land meant losing touch.

Now he was returning.

He pulled Rita and his tía Delfina close to him, held them in an embrace as they looked down at Gloria's grave.

Around them the grounds and trees of the cemetery were a throbbing green with light, the strong, dazzling light of morning that filled the valley. The Señores y Señoras de la Luz were blessing all of life, lifting the souls of the dead into their embrace.

33

A full moon glittered on the pieces of glass that littered the graveled parking lot of the Fourth Street Cantina. It glistened on car tops and the cracked windshields of old pickups. Ranchera music drifted out of the bar and mixed with the drone of the cicada song in the trees.

Inside, Sonny and Rita sat in a booth enjoying the music. Across from them sat Howard and his wife, Marie.

Tucked in a corner, a trio played Mexican rancheras and country-western. The place was considered a nice family place if you wanted to dance on Saturday nights. Dave McPherson, who owned the bar, ran a tight ship. You started one fight and you became persona non grata.

They had been to the ballgame, the kind of pitching game Sonny liked. 1–0, Dukes. And El Gallo had retired fifteen batters. Now they sat drinking beer.

"Great game, great game," Howard said, extolling the pitching. Sonny agreed as they relived the innings.

"I think we're not going to get to dance," Rita said to Marie.

"We'll dance, we'll dance," Sonny said, smiling. "What do you think, Howard, do we give our women too much freedom?"

"You don't give us freedom, darling, we take it," Rita said, imitating Tamara.

"You tell them, sister!" Marie exclaimed.

"It was a great game," Howard said, tactfully changing the subject. "But I promised Marie we were going to dance all night," he said, and grabbed his wife's hand. "Come on, honey, let's show these Chicanos that black folks can dance rancheras. Ajua!" he cried, and swept his wife toward the dance floor.

Sonny took Rita's hand and they sat in silence. He looked at her and nursed his beer; she fiddled with the plastic straw of her ginger ale.

"You okay?" he asked.

"I'm okay. How's your foot?"

"How'd you know my foot had been bothering me?"

"The rains are here."

"Yeah. It's okay." He nodded. He was wearing Raven's medallion beneath his shirt; he didn't want Rita to know. It would upset her, but since Raven's disappearance, because the cops still hadn't found the body, he for some reason felt naked if he didn't wear it. Of course he would turn it over to the DA—it was state's evidence—but not just yet.

"You've been quiet," he said.

"I'm okay." Rita sipped her drink.

"Good game."

"Yeah."

"So, qué pasa?"

"I don't know. Maybe it's because we haven't had time together."

"Yeah." He put his arm around her. "But we have tonight, changa. Time to dance, time to make love."

"Let's leave now," Rita responded.

"What about Marie and Howard?"

"They'll understand." Rita drew close and kissed him lightly. Her lips were warm, her voice beckoning. "Just the two of us. . . ."

"Am I still your vato?" Sonny asked, nibbling at her ear.

"Only you, amor," she smiled.

"Pues, vamos," he whispered, but too late. A loud clamor made him turn. He spotted don Eliseo, Concha, and don Toto marching into the bar and toward the booth, pushing the dancers aside to get to Sonny.

"Sonny, hey, Sonny!" Don Eliseo shouted.

"Don Eliseo!" Sonny called back, and motioned.

"Oh no," Rita moaned, "say it isn't true."

La Concha pushed Sonny and slipped in next to him. She was done up in her Saturday-night best, a low-cut, bright red satin blouse and hip-hugging black skirt. On Saturday nights she took off her battered tennis shoes and put on her patent leather boots, a pair she had picked up at the St. Jude clothing store and that she treasured, because, she said, she just knew they had once belonged to a swinger.

"Sonny, cómo 'stás? How about a dance?" She nudged him. "Hi, dearie," she said to Rita. "You won't mind, will you?"

"Yes," Rita replied, "tonight I *do* mind."

"Hijo," Concha said, grinning, "she really takes care of him!"

"Hello, Concha, you're looking great." Sonny welcomed her with a hug.

"You made my day, ese. This man knows how to treat women," she said to don Toto.

"Yeah, pues, everything still works for him," don Toto said with a shrug.

"We hope." La Concha grinned and patted Sonny's hand. "You feeling better, dearie?"

Sonny laughed. "I feel great!"

"Got something to tell you," don Eliseo said, and leaned over the table. It was clear they had been drinking.

"How about a beer?" don Toto asked.

"Seguro que sí! A drink for my friends. Snap, Crackle, and Pop," Sonny shouted at the waitress. "Hey, Mary Bess, bring us a round!"

"Coming right up," she answered kindly.

Mary Bess used to teach Shakespeare at the university, where Sonny had taken her class, but a love for Lone Star and the funky bar drew her to the cantina, where she occasionally helped out her friend Dave. "I always wanted to be of service," she said happily, a cigarette dangling at her lips. She loved to quote the bard to the Chicanos, lone cowboys, and Indians from Sandia Pueblo who came in to drink beer.

"I'm thirsty! Haven't had a drop all night," don Toto swore. "Come on, Concha, let's dance."

"Vamos, viejo," la Concha laughed. "We'll show these young kids a step or two!" She pinched Sonny's cheek and winked, then let don Toto lead her out ceremoniously to the dance floor. The couples on the floor parted to watch the old couple do their thing.

"Ajua!" Concha shouted. "Viejo loco!"

"Gimme, gimme, gimme, honey!" Don Toto shouted back, and they swirled to the forties jitterbug tune the band struck up for them.

"Got something to tell you," don Eliseo said, tugging at Sonny, his wine-laden breath spewing on Sonny's face.

"What?"

"The Señores have brought life. It got green."

"What got green?"

"My alamo! A branch put out leaves. Little green leaves, moist and tender. They're growing! The branch that faces south is green, Sonny. It's a miracle! The tree is alive! It's alive!"

"You're kidding me," Sonny answered.

"No! Not kidding!"

"Did you hear that, Rita!" Sonny shouted, jumped to his feet, and embraced don Eliseo. "Hey, the tree's alive!" he shouted, and danced the old man around.

"That tree is like us, we got a little bit of that juice left, eh, Sonny," don Eliseo said, gasping for air.

"You damn right we got juice left!" He turned to Rita. "Come on! Let's go see the tree!"

"I thought we were going to . . ."

"Later, morenita, right now I want to see the miracle of the leaves!"

Don Eliseo nodded happily.

"Anda, vamos," Rita agreed, smiling, and Sonny grabbed her. "Call you tomorrow, Howie!" Sonny shouted and Howard waved and shouted back, "Pleasant dreams, compadre!"

"Toto! Concha!" don Eliseo called.

Sonny and Rita hurried out of the bar, followed by the three old friends. Rita, Sonny, and Concha jumped in the cab while don Eliseo helped don Toto onto the back of the truck. Then they sped down Fourth Street to don Eliseo's home.

The full moon was hanging over the valley like a holy wafer, bathing the dirt roads and potholed streets of the valley in a sheen of silvery light. The full moon after the solstice was a moon of magic, rich with portents the old people of the valley believed. Magic strong enough to bring life back into the dry, gnarled limbs of the tree.

Sonny turned down don Eliseo's dirt road and put on the brakes. The truck slid ten feet on the graveled road and stopped. In front of them rose the dry branches of don Eliseo's tree, the huge alamo gordo. They stumbled out of the truck and looked up, looking for the leaves don Eliseo had seen, and yes, the huge southern arm of the tree was greening. The pale green leaves shimmered in the moonlight.

"See," don Eliseo whispered, pointing. "Entre verde y seco."

Between green and dry, some old trees grew like that, one side would began to dry out, but the spirit of life was too great to be denied, and they put out one green branch to show the roots were yet alive. Entre verde y seco, life on the Río Grande high plateau was like that, dry and harsh as the summer that had baked the valley, and then soft as love under a summer rain.

Dry and green, like people whose juices dry up momentarily, whose spirit withers, then they cast off the dread, and the blood flows again, renewing body and soul. A man is like a tree, and the blood of the man like the sap. Don Eliseo was like a tree, and his spirit was alive with life-giving light. He would live many more years.

"It's beautiful," Concha said softly. She put one arm around don Eliseo and one around don Toto, and together they stood looking at the mystery.

"The Señores y Señoras de la Luz have blessed it with life," don Eliseo said.

Sonny held Rita close. Yes, he thought. The Señores y Señoras. Maybe the rain had kicked life into the roots, or the solstice sun reminded the tree of its need to bear leaves quickly. It couldn't be explained; it didn't need to be explained, as many other miracles in the history of the valley didn't need explaining.

He whispered to Rita. "Time for love. . . ."

She smiled in the moonlight, and arm in arm they walked to his house, leaving the three old friends together.

"Buenas noches, Sonny," they called after him. "Buenas noches, Rita."

"Sweet dreams," la Concha added.

"Buenas noches," Sonny and Rita called back, and paused at the door to wave to the three duendes.

They watched as don Eliseo put dry pieces of wood in the embers of the fire. He blew on the coals, and the flames rose. Don Toto took out his bottle of wine, and they sat around the flames of the small fire and passed the bottle around.

Tonight they would talk about the appearance of the leaves on the old tree. It was a miracle, a new story to add to the stories of the North Valley, a blessing of the Señores y Señoras de la Luz.

Many would remember the summer as the Zia Summer, and they would tell stories about the terrible murder of Gloria Dominic. But the viejitos of the valley would remember it was the summer when don Eliseo's tree recovered miraculously and offered forth its green leaves.